FREAKS

Annette Curtis Klause

SIMON PULSE

NEW YORK   LONDON   TORONTO   SYDNEY

FOR HUMAN ODDITIES EVERYWHERE

This book is a work of fiction. Any references to historical events, real people, or real locales are used fictitiously. Other names, characters, places, and incidents are the product of the author's imagination, and any resemblance to actual events or locales or persons, living or dead, is entirely coincidental.

᭦᭦

SIMON PULSE
An imprint of Simon & Schuster Children's Publishing Division
1230 Avenue of the Americas, New York, NY 10020
Copyright © 2006 by Annette Curtis Klause
All rights reserved, including the right of reproduction
in whole or in part in any form.
SIMON PULSE and colophon are registered trademarks
of Simon & Schuster, Inc.
Also available in a Margaret K. McElderry Books hardcover edition.
Designed by Ann Zeak
The text of this book was set in Simoncini Garamond.
Manufactured in the United States of America
First Simon Pulse edition July 2007
2 4 6 8 10 9 7 5 3 1
The Library of Congress has cataloged the hardcover edition as follows:
Klause, Annette Curtis.
Freaks / Annette Curtis Klause.—1st ed.
p. cm.
Summary: After leaving home in search of adventure, romance, and riches,
seventeen-year-old Abel, the "normal" son of freak show entertainers,
is haunted by a mysterious spirit.
ISBN-13: 978-0-689-87037-8 (hc)
ISBN-10: 0-689-87037-X (hc)
[1. Freakshows—Fiction. 2. Abnormalities, Human—Fiction. 3. Supernatural—
Fiction. 4. Reincarnation—Fiction. 5. Adventure and adventurers—Fiction.] I. Title.
PZ7.K67815Fr 2006
[Fic]—dc22
2005001363
ISBN-13: 978-0-689-87038-5 (pbk)
ISBN-10: 0-689-87038-8 (pbk)

"[C]ome, Hop-Frog, lend us your assistance. Characters, my fine fellow; we stand in need of characters—all of us—ha! ha! ha!"

—Edgar Allan Poe, "Hop-Frog"

WHEN A BOY'S FIRST ROMANTIC *interlude is with Phoebe the Dog-Faced Girl, he feels a need to get out into the world and find a new life.* So I thought as I stood in the wings and watched Colonel Kingston introduce the next act. Not that I had anything against Phoebe. She was a sweet girl under all that fur. "Oh, Abel," she whispered prettily whenever I brushed her lips with mine, and perhaps she blushed—who could tell?—but I was seventeen and yearned to kiss a mouth sometimes without getting hair up my nose.

Out on the stage, Orlando the Magnificent, star illusionist of the Faeryland 1899 Review, requested a volunteer from the audience. A man of pleasant appearance in a long overcoat rose to his feet amid applause and laughter from the crowd. I smiled. He was my uncle Jack.

Orlando bowed his turbaned head to the volunteer as if he were a stranger and beckoned the man up the steps with both arms, which caused the flowing sleeves of his satin robes to shimmer in the stage lights.

I wish there were other girls my age in Faeryland, I thought as Uncle Jack lay down in a long, coffinlike box on a platform. Maybe then Phoebe wouldn't assume I was hers for the taking. There were older, unmarried ladies, of course, but none of them took my fancy enough to risk breaking my mother's heart. Although, I admit, when I was fourteen years old, Miss Makepeace, the Amazing Rubber Woman, came pretty darn close. Anyway, how could a boy take a few liberties in a home where everyone knew his business?

Uncle Jack disappeared from sight as Orlando's young "Ethiopian" assistant closed the lid. A head appeared through one end of the box and feet out the other, and Orlando reached into his starry case of tricks and pulled out a large saw. There were a few groans and titters from those who found the sawing-a-person-in-half trick a mite old hat, but I'd been looking forward to this.

The expected sawing began, accompanied by the usual banter. At one point the "victim" let out a cry, which was echoed by a few delicate and susceptible ladies in the audience, who then laughed along with their friends to cover their embarrassment. When the saw had completed its task, another dark-skinned boy ran onstage to help pull apart the box and show the halves separate—toes wiggling from one, head wagging from the other. Polite applause filled the hall. I grinned, not put off at all by the lukewarm response.

As was predictable, the box halves were rejoined, the magician waved his arms and incanted a spell, the box was opened, and the man rose from the box whole once more. Again there was polite applause and knowing laughter.

The volunteer smiled, waved at the audience, and headed for the steps, accompanied by cheers and bravos, but halfway there he stopped and frowned. He tottered to the left. He tottered to the right. The audience hushed. He cried out, toppled over—and split apart at the waist. His legs scurried off in one direction, and his body crawled off in the other, dragged by his arms.

Gasps and screams filled the air. People rose to their feet. An old man fled up the aisle toward the back doors. At least three ladies slumped, willy-nilly, sideways in their seats as friends and family fanned and patted them. I was still laughing as the torso reached me.

"That was great, Papa!" I said. "Really great!"

"Yes. Perfect," my father answered, and grinned. "But we'd better put them out of their misery quick."

He stripped off the doctored overcoat to reveal the evening clothes beneath, carefully tailored and pinned, for he had no legs whatsoever. He trotted back out onstage on his hands in time to meet his other half, a midget, now with the trouser waist rolled down to reveal his head. Someone pointed at them and nudged his neighbor. Then through the rear curtains emerged the original volunteer, my uncle Jack, whole and complete with legs, the spitting image of my father, for he was his twin.

Someone hooted as the joke dawned on him, another joined in, and soon the auditorium echoed with thunderous applause. I put my arms around the boy assistants, who stood to either side of me, and squeezed affectionately. "Magnificent, wasn't it, lads?" I said.

In the dressing room after the show Colonel Kingston clapped my father on the back and almost knocked him off the wooden stool where he perched, swaddled in his cut-down dressing gown. "Wonderful idea, Andrew! Absolutely wonderful."

"You should thank Florence," said my father. He nodded at my mother, who sat in a cozy chair crocheting with nimble toes.

"I would have played the bottom half myself," she said. "But alas, I am too tall. I'm afraid we shall have to stick to bicycling."

My parents had an act wherein they rode a bicycle together. He, with no legs, was able to steer; she, with no arms, could nevertheless pedal admirably, despite her long skirts and petticoat.

"How were receipts, Arthur?" asked my father as he massaged Macassar oil into his hair and smoothed his locks into glossy place.

Colonel Kingston shook his head and leaned on his cane with both hands. "Could be worse, my boy," he said, but his mouth was pinched and his white whiskers bristled. The crowds were smaller these days, and performers had begun to leave and join new shows. The better acts could make more money elsewhere. Colonel Kingston had hoped that the shows at Faeryland would finance him through his old age, but a stationary show needed continued variety to keep the audience coming back, and no new acts had joined us. Lately I had more than once interrupted a worried conversation between my parents.

Faeryland had formerly been a spa where the rich from Washington and Baltimore took the waters for their health. It had fallen into disfavor years ago, and Arthur Kingston, veteran of three circuses and one war, had bought the property for a song to create a resort that would offer the finest educational entertainments and display of oddities to be seen in one place since the great Barnum's second New York museum burned to ashes in 1868. I had lived in Faeryland most of my life.

The grounds of Faeryland consisted of a Colonial mansion called the Castle; the Elvin Gardens; and Pixie Village, where the midgets and dwarfs lived in miniature houses, alongside a tiny church and a fire station complete with a pint-size fire wagon pulled by Shetland ponies and manned by a troupe of "pixie" firefighters. When customers walked through Pixie Village at certain times of the day, a bonfire was almost certain to be out of control and in need of extinction for their delighted pleasure.

The rest of us, including three giants, lived in the Castle, where visitors attended matinee and evening performances in the great hall—"an extravaganza of amazing oddities, mystifying the audience with their uncanny skills, death-defying deeds, and wondrous physiognomy."

After the audience had gone and the theater had closed for the night, I made my way up a back staircase to my family's apartments, but before I reached my front door, Phoebe's little brother scampered up to me, yelping my name.

"What is it, Apollo?" I asked. I tousled the twelve-year-old's silky blond hair. Like his sister and mother, Apollo the Puppy Boy had long hair everywhere. Like his father, he was prone to excitement.

"Violet and Rose are leaving," Apollo said between gasps.

My gut sank. The Giovanni Siamese twins were stars of the show. I hurried after Apollo down to the main entrance.

In the front hall a small group of performers and staff were whispering and glancing to where Colonel Kingston talked to the Giovanni twins' father. Apollo bounded over to where the pinheads had gathered with their nurse. All three wore long, colorful shifts, even though two of them were male. Apollo pretended to lift their hems up, which made the simple creatures giggle and grab their skirts around their knees.

Violet and Rose stood by a stack of trunks and boxes, back-to-back of necessity, dressed in their best traveling gown and matching black veiled hats with cherries. Long black gloves graced their hands. Next to Violet stood her dark-eyed gentleman, quiet as always. My mother swore he was sullen—and after her money, at that—but perhaps he was shy.

Every time Violet edged toward her beau, Rose tugged the other way. Joined irrevocably to a stronger soul, Violet had no choice but to follow. Both girls appeared ready to burst into one of their famous spats. I felt a little sorry for Rose, even if she tended to bully her sister. After all, Violet was the one who had found love, and it must be hard to ignore one's sister's beau when one was joined to her at the rump. I had heard some cruel speculation about what married life would mean to the maiden twin.

"That's my final word," proclaimed Signor Giovanni, his stormy temperament finally getting the better of him. "The offer is too good to pass up."

More than once my mother had shaken her head over Colonel Kingston's informal business practices. "A contract is better than a handshake," she had warned. Lately she had often been proved right.

"Where are they going?" I asked Jolly Dolly, the fat lady.

"Europe," Dolly said, and wiped the eternally present sweat from her brow.

"They are going on tour with Fortuna's Circus," said her younger sister, Baby Betty, in a voice too hushed and tiny to come from a woman of her bulk. Together the sisters were billed as One Ton of Fun.

Dolly warbled with laughter. "And Violet thinks she and her fancy man may have a chance to be wed there," she said.

Violet and her beau had been turned down for a marriage license in at least five states. There was some question as to propriety, as well as whether Violet and Rose legally constituted one person or two.

I supposed the twins couldn't be blamed for their decision to join Fortuna's. A considerable amount of money could be made on tour by an act like theirs, but what about those left behind?

I went to say my farewells, and Violet raised her arms to welcome me. Rose elbowed Violet aside and took my hands. "Good-bye, my dear," she said. "I shall miss you most awfully."

"Not as much as I," declared Violet. She elbowed Rose back and claimed one of my hands for her own.

I blushed. Why did they always have to make a fuss of me?

"Why should you miss anyone, hussy?" spat Rose. "You have your slimy lothario to comfort you."

"Jealous."

"Deluded."

I squeezed their hands to get their attention. "Please don't go," I said. "What will we do without you?"

"Have some peace and quiet," Archie Crum said from behind me.

I ignored the hurtful words of the dwarf strong man. "Who will I talk about our books with?" The twins and I shared a passion for the novels of Mr. Kipling and Mr. Haggard.

"Oh, darling, you will find someone else to read to," said Violet, wiping a tear from her eye with a gloved finger. "Someone younger and prettier—"

"And unattached," inserted her sister.

At that moment their carriage to the train station arrived and ended the impending squabble. Trunks and cases were carried through the front door, and the twins were bundled into the coach, despite the coachman, who fell over his own feet several times, too busy looking over his shoulder at the assembled oddities to watch where he went.

"Go on, kiss 'em good-bye, Tall Dark and Handsome," Archie Crum said, and slapped me on the rear.

I glared at him before I poked my head through the window to give each young woman a peck on the cheek. They were argumentative, it was true, but they were witty and bright when not fighting, and made me feel important.

"You're a sweet boy, Abel Dandy," said Violet. "I swan, if you were older, I wouldn't be going. Wear this to remember me by." She pressed something small and hard into my hand.

I found a gold ring in my palm, fashioned in the Egyptian style with a turquoise stone carved into the likeness of a scarab beetle, the details of which were etched in a darker green.

"Not the rubbish from that half-wit professor," said Rose. "The one he said a goddess in a dream told him to give to you."

Violet knit her brow. "No, hon," she said. "I think that was my dream. She told me to give it to Abel."

"Whatever you say, you mixed-up hussy," said Rose. "I thought you were going to treasure it forever."

"I was, wasn't I?" Violet said. "But I now want to give it to him."

The ring was thrilling. It spoke of far-off places and exotic lives. I wasn't sure if it was quite my style, but I was honored to receive such an intimate gift from a grown woman. "It shall be my good-luck charm," I said, and slipped it on my finger. What were the odds? It fit perfectly.

The world shifted.

For a moment my eyes were blinded as if by bright sunlight,

hot air seared my nostrils, and I heard birds and babbling water. I swore lips brushed my cheek. Then the dim interior of the carriage came into focus again—and the worried faces of the twins.

"Are you all right, hon?" asked Violet.

"Yes," I mumbled. I felt foolish.

The coachman cracked his whip, and I half fell, half jumped off the running board. "Thank you," I called, and waved at the carriage until it reached the end of the long driveway, too stunned by my odd spell to do more.

Finally I took a deep breath and followed the others indoors on unsteady feet. Was I so unnerved by the twins' leaving that I would have a fit? Did I fear this was the end of life as I had known it? If Faeryland closed down, my parents might have to go on the road again to make a living. They hadn't done that since I was small. Now I was almost a man, I would have to pull my weight too, but was I afraid I wasn't up to it? I was so ordinary, after all. I didn't have an unusual physical difference to trade on; did I have enough talent? Was my knife-throwing good enough?

A crowd still loitered in the lobby, and worry hummed in the air. My parents had come down to find out what the fuss was about, and Phoebe had joined her ma and pa there. The people present were as firm a part of my home as the furniture: midgets, dwarfs, fat ladies, one of the giants on tottery legs, and Apollo holding on with hairy hands to two of the pinheads, who wanted to dance. They were proud of their skills and defiant about their appearance. I loved them all, but for the first time in my life I felt different—and alone.

"What's wrong, pretty boy," said Archie Crum, "you never seen freaks before?"

The laughter around me was meant to be harmless and

friendly, but this evening it placed me across the universe from them. I hung my average head, clenched my commonplace fists, and marched myself to my room.

That night I dreamed that I stood beside a garden fountain tiled with a design of lotus flowers. A dusky beauty barely dressed in white linen, the reflection of water sparkling in her eyes, slipped a scarab ring on my finger. She uttered words in a strange language that flowed and clicked; yet I knew what she said. "Wear this to remember me always." My heart held the heat of the red clay garden walls. The pungent fragrance of flowers and spices enveloped us, and our lips touched in a soft kiss that melted me with desire.

I woke short of breath and smiling, with an ache in my loins.

Where would I find a girl like that? I wondered. Not at home, I was sure.

FOLLOW THROUGH, FOLLOW through," Uncle Jack called across the barn. "You stopped short and flipped the knife. No wonder your aim is east of Bethlehem."

I tried to concentrate and wipe from my mind the delicious dream kiss that had haunted me all morning, but my next knife went awry like the last and clattered to the boards. I threw my arms in the air with a snort of disgust.

"Maybe you need a heavier knife for distance," Jack said. "Try these." He handed me the bandolier he wore over his shoulder.

I strapped it on and tested the balance of the knives, then pushed up my sleeves and walked to my mark.

Colonel Kingston insisted that everyone develop at least one skill, so I had studied with Jack for a year now. That expectation included the human oddities. "Nobody sits on their hind end here and gets by on their pretty looks," the colonel said. "A two-headed man can amaze the audience three times at the most, but a two-headed man who juggles his hats—that's a show!"

I flipped a knife from each hand, and my scarab ring caught the light, splintering it into shards of sun. Perhaps that was a charm. Each knife pierced the target. I pulled two more from their sheaths and struck in quick succession, then two more; all hit around center. I felt like crowing.

Jack held up his stopwatch. "You need to work on that speed."

I almost cried a protest, except Jack's lip twitched in amusement, and I realized he was teasing. I was good, and he knew it; maybe soon he would recommend that the colonel let me throw onstage. Perhaps then I could prove I was an asset to the show, even though I had no difference.

Jack's difference currently hid beneath the billowing front of his white shirt. When he worked onstage, he stripped to the waist to reveal the stunted legs that should have been attached to my father, his twin, if not for some strange accident in the womb. The other night I expressed surprise that the audience had not recognized Jack when he rose from the seats as a volunteer. "Do you think they ever look at my face when I'm onstage?" Jack asked.

At least they saw him. I was too much like the audience to be noticed. In my nightmares I found myself trapped in the seats, unable to find the aisle, forever forbidden the stage. I often wished I were not so ordinary.

My normality made me a useful errand boy, unfortunately. Today I had to go to the post office to collect some packages.

They were probably the usual items: special shoes for the giants, custom-made clothes for the midgets—they would rather rot in hell than wear children's apparel—and, if I was lucky, the books I'd sent for.

Phoebe met me outside the stables. The hair of her face was neatly brushed and held back with ribbons under her ears. "Your mama says to remind you to take Apollo if you go swimming today," she said, lashes lowered shyly.

I rolled my eyes. Why was I always put in charge of that boy? What if I had plans? Oh, no—dependable, boring old Abel wouldn't have plans, would he?

Phoebe glanced around the deserted yard. "And she says not to forget her wool."

I noticed a breathy quality to her voice that hinted of anticipation, and wished I hadn't. The coast was clear and she wanted me to kiss her. The memory of that dream kiss still haunted me, and I couldn't bear to erase it with a furry, real-life substitute.

She hesitated; then, "I'd advise you to talk to my father soon if you've intentions," she said all in a rush, and giggled.

Oh, heavens! What had I started with a few kisses? Did she expect me to ask her father for her hand?

I backed away. "Um, tell Apollo I'll meet him by the gate." I groped for the stable door. "Well, I'd better hurry," I muttered. The disappointment in her eyes filled me with guilt. I bolted for the shadows of the barn, where I harnessed Old Sukie to the buggy and silently begged that Phoebe wouldn't linger outside. To my relief, my prayers were answered.

All the way into town I berated myself. I should speak to her honestly. I had obviously given her false hopes. It would be cruel to let her go on thinking I had serious intentions. I had let this go on too long. What if she ran to her father with tales? Her father had a furious temper. What if he decided his daughter had been compromised? Would he make me marry her? My mouth dried, and I tried to think of other things.

Redbrick row houses lined Main Street. They'd been there for a hundred years. Down side streets were the newer houses, with wood sides and large front porches, some with turrets, as if they were gingerbread castles. I had never lived in a town, gone to a regular schoolhouse, and attended the same little church each Sunday. Before we came to Faeryland, when I was seven, my life had been spent in boardinghouses, trains, and stage-coaches.

Outside the post office two young ladies dawdled. One of them held a bicycle at her side and wore a sensible long, dark skirt and dusty boots. The other wore frills and carried a parasol. I tipped my cap as I passed them, but they cut me dead. My heart fell, although I could have predicted that would happen. It was useless to search for a sweetheart in Smithville. They all knew where I came from. I lived with the freaks and was a common charlatan, and probably degenerate into the bargain.

Dust floated in the sunlight that slanted through the post office windows, and a smell of ancient sealing wax permeated the air. The sound of my boots on the wooden floor caused the postmaster to raise his head. He grunted a neutral greeting and proceeded to stack parcels on the counter. Sadly, none was from Burke and White, Booksellers.

When I came back out with the packages, two young men had joined the girls. Although I hardly came close to them, the young men reached for the arms of the girls as if to move them out of harm's way. A worm of anger squiggled in my gut. They didn't even know me. I called out a cheery "Good afternoon." I would make them work hard to ignore me. The bicycle girl nodded, and her girlfriend elbowed her. The boys scowled. One of them spit casually in my direction, his eyes bright with anger. I wished I had left well enough alone.

My heart thumped as I tossed the packages under a tarp in the buggy and crossed the street to the dry-goods store. My back prickled with the sense of the boys behind me. I wished I had brought the mail in with me, but I didn't want them to know I was worried. I did worry, however, all the time I waited for the salesman's attention. When I emerged with my mother's wool, the young people were gone, replaced by an elderly lady in black, who then entered the butcher's shop, and a spotted dog sniffing in the gutter. My packages lay undisturbed.

On my way out of town a colorful poster on the fence outside the blacksmith's shop caught my eye. I pulled over to look at it. MARVEL BROTHERS CIRCUS, the large yellow and red type proclaimed. The performers depicted were strong and beautiful men and women, not a freak among them. The acts listed included acrobats, tightrope walkers, and equestrians—all acts that depended on talent rather than unusual looks. Was that where I belonged? Yearning welled up within me. The circus's advance men were ambitious in their advertising, for the show was to set up in a town more than fifteen miles north of my home. It was too far to drop by casually for a look. I stifled my disappointment and snapped the reins.

On the ride home I pondered love. There was someone for everyone, I knew. Whether you were short, tall, wide, or thin, someone somewhere would appreciate your qualities and inspire your love in return. I hadn't met a fat lady yet who didn't have a string of admirers, and my parents had found each other, hadn't they? Who was the girl for me and where would I find her? *Perhaps the girl who gave me this ring in my dream,* I thought, and smiled fondly at it. I laughed. I would have to go pretty far to find her. Beyond this world, I should think. I wouldn't mind trying, however, I decided.

"I rather like the term *prodigies*," whispered Jolly Dolly, mopping her brow with a voluminous handkerchief. "Much more dignified than *freaks,* don't you think, Abel?" She was referring to the text of the new advertisement Colonel Kingston had sent to the newspapers.

Onstage Albert Sunderland, the four-legged man, kicked a soccer ball around. I'd heard a rumor that limbs were not all Albert had extra of. Once, when I was younger, Archie Crum had called to a heckler who mocked Albert's skills, "Come up here and say that. He's twice the man you are." It took me a year to figure out why Albert had laughed.

Albert wove and dodged as the ball spun an intricate pattern from foot to foot, and his arms executed circles in the air to maintain his balance. It was an odd sight no matter how often one saw it, for no two legs were of exactly the same length; indeed, one of the central pair hung nine inches above the ground, and it took considerable skill to give that foot its fair share of kicks. He looked like a dancing spider.

"The giants prefer the term *anomaly*—'something that deviates from the general rule or the usual type,'" I said.

"My, the child swallowed a dictionary at birth," exclaimed Baby Betty in her little voice. The droopy flesh of her arm swayed as she fanned herself.

Dolly sniffed, and her ample bosom jiggled. "There is no talent implied in that term. *Anomaly*'s just a fancy way to say *freak*. We are much more than that. Did you know that *prodigy* also means 'a marvelous thing'?"

Her sister, Betty, grunted. "I am not a thing."

"But quite marvelous," I said, not wanting them to fight.

Betty favored me with a brilliant smile. "Always the gentleman," she said, and giggled, an earthquake that resulted in a tidal wave of flesh.

"With the face of an angel," said Dolly.

"And the body of a devil," Betty crooned, and poked me gently in the chest with a sausagelike finger.

Albert Sunderland exited stage left to thunderous applause, and the sisters quieted. They never failed to enjoy their introduction.

"And now, for your delight and amusement," proclaimed Colonel Kingston, "those wonders of pulchritudinous plumpness, those beauties of remarkable adiposity, those portly pretties and roly-poly riot of laughs—the sisters known as Jolly Dolly and Baby Betty. Ladies and gentlemen, One Ton of Fun!"

"I hope the boards hold up," Betty muttered in her baby voice. She said this every performance, almost like a prayer. No matter how many times she'd been reassured, she remained deathly afraid of falling through.

The sisters launched themselves, wheezing, onto the stage, and I couldn't help but smile. From behind, in their bathing suits made of bloomers and frilly short skirts, they looked like two hippos at a fancy dress party, but I would never tell them. In their minds the humor was to be found in their clever repartee, not in their vast size, even though most of their act concerned jokes about their weight. Even if they had been thin, they would be funny—but in show business you have to grab the attention of the audience first. I didn't need to move scenery until the next curtain, so I stayed to watch even though I knew their jokes by heart.

After the show the performers gathered around the perimeter of the grand ballroom next door to the theater. The public was invited to walk a lap and converse briefly with the entertainers. I circulated among our guests and sold photographic souvenirs and a charming memoir written by Gladys Dibble, the Pixie Queen.

My father took advantage of these occasions to spin dreadful tall tales. Hopping from one hand to the other, he told gullible folk, "If you think I am remarkable, you should have seen my father—he didn't have a head. It was quite amazing how he got about, and how he became enamored of my mother I shall never know—perhaps it was the glossy feel of her scales. . . ." He lied, of course. My grandparents were perfectly normal. As I moved through the crowd, I listened for his cheerful tenor so I might eavesdrop.

I also liked to watch the young ladies.

"She will break your heart, Abel," Mama warned if she saw me glance at an ankle, "and her daddy will break your nose."

"Not good form to mix business with pleasure, Abel," my father said.

I ignored them, of course, and smiled at as many pretty girls as I could.

I did a brisk business this day, with a portrait of Phoebe's family entitled *Mrs. Papandreou the Dog Lady and Her Human Puppies,* as well as a photographic tableau of Dolly and Betty posed in the unlikely historic meeting of Helen of Troy and Cleopatra, an event that could truly be called monumental. When a handsome lady in a fashionable little hat and veil approached me, I held out my wares, but she ignored the photographs and eyed me like a dog eyes a bone. "Do you have any *unusual* qualities to show me privately?" she drawled in a husky voice.

"No . . . no, ma'am," I stammered.

"What a shame," she said, and chuckled.

Albert Sunderland hobbled by on three of his four legs and caught her attention. As the woman left me in pursuit of him, I remembered the gossip about what lay between those legs, and understood her desire. I blushed to the tips of my normal extremities. I wanted a sweetheart who thought me an interesting fellow, not a novelty act.

After work I grabbed my towel and walked down the driveway to meet Apollo. I knew that he'd be mad enough to bite fleas at having to wait for me to take him swimming, but no madder than I was at always being assigned as nursemaid to the boy. The swimming hole lay outside Faeryland, and Colonel Kingston wanted none of his special people to go there unaccompanied. Perhaps he feared they'd be kidnapped by a rival show.

As soon as I reached the wrought-iron gates, Apollo ran through the trees yipping, as happy as a dog on a summer day, and any ire I felt, dissolved. He danced a little over the hot gravel of the road in his bare feet, but he didn't slow down. I swear he looked like he was wagging a tail as he finally panted before me. He'd been called a puppy for so long he believed he was one.

"Come on, Abel," he said. "I'm about to bake like apple pie."

"You're the hairiest apple pie I've ever seen," I answered. "Someone must have dropped you on the rug." I took a playful swipe at him, and he growled at me but then ruined the effect by laughing.

Down at the hole we stripped to our birthday suits and hung our clothes on the bushes.

"Race you in," said Apollo, but I won.

What a shame we had no time to enjoy the water.

"Well, lookit here," a voice whined as I surfaced from a

clumsy dive. "I've heard of a catfish, but I ain't never heard of a dog fish."

Two boys stood at the edge of the pond—the two I'd seen in town that noon. They had big boots and mean faces and meant to have business with us whether we wanted it or not.

THE HOT DAY SUDDENLY FELT much cooler as I stood waist deep in glass green water, facing a pair of bullyboys.

This was my fault. Had I not stepped over the invisible boundary in town, all would be well. Now I had put Apollo, a mere twelve-year-old boy, in danger. Perhaps all opponents appear much larger when one faces them stark naked; these boys were bigger than I remembered. My mind raced to think of a way out of this awkward situation. Would a witty quip, perhaps, win them over? Could I bluff my way out without a fight?

"We thought we'd have to throw rocks at you over the wall," said the dark-haired one. "We didn't think we'd discover you out here."

"And with a bonus freak too," said the one with crooked teeth.

Apollo growled.

"Stop that," I whispered from the side of my mouth. "How may I help you gentlemen?" I asked.

Crooked Teeth laughed and caricatured a bow to his companion. He put on a hoity-toity voice. "We gentlemen wanted to inform you of our displeasure at your addressing the ladies of the town—with your not being a gentleman, and all. We was hoping to put the point forcefully so you'd remember it."

I glanced over to the bushes and wondered about my chances of retrieving our clothes, not that one could dress while being pummeled.

"Want these?" the dark-haired one asked, and pulled Apollo's knickers from behind his back, along with my canvas trousers. "Guess you'll have to come out and get them, lest something happen to them."

I was getting cold and feeling foolish. I didn't care to be trapped in the water like a stag at bay, and I couldn't allow Apollo to be hurt. As much as I didn't want to fight, I had to settle this. "Stay where you are," I told Apollo. I summoned as much dignity as I could muster and waded to the bank.

The young thugs roared with laughter and slapped their knees.

"Lookit him," said the dark-haired boy. "In nothing but his cheap Gypsy jewelry. Stole it from a girl, did you?"

I put my ring hand behind my back before I could think twice.

"There's his doggy, paddling after," gasped the crooked-toothed boy. Apollo had ignored my wishes. Drat the boy.

"You've had your fun," I said as I stood before them. "Now hand over those clothes." I tried to smile. Papa said that joining in the joke sometimes helped in dealing with bad situations.

"What? You care to dress before you flee?" asked the dark-haired one.

"Yes sir," said his companion. "He wouldn't want to run away like a yellow coward while in the altogether, would he?"

"Naw, he'd rather run away like a yellow coward fully dressed," said Dark Hair, "but that don't matter to the little fellow. He carries his suit with him."

Crooked Teeth grinned. "Yeah, a monkey suit."

Well, you could call Apollo a dog all you wanted and he'd simply wag his imaginary tale, but call him a monkey . . .

Apollo shot by me and landed on Crooked Teeth, sinking his fangs into the culprit's shoulder. The youth proceeded to howl and flail, for the dog boy wouldn't be budged.

The dark-haired boy yelled and picked up a sturdy branch. He raised it, ready to strike my young friend. I had to hit him. My blow to his shoulder made him drop the stick, all right, but only so he could commence beating on me with his fists. I was sure my opponent's pugilistic moves were not in the rule book, especially when he laid a mighty kick on my shins that left me hopping. I landed one blow to his three and, rules aside, was pleased to note that my "cheap Gypsy jewelry" did some noticeable damage. But as I reeled from an uppercut to the jaw, Apollo's opponent recovered sufficiently to punch the dog boy in the gut. Apollo fell gasping to the ground, and his bitten foe swung a boot back for a kick I couldn't allow.

I ducked under a sockdolager aimed at my head and ran for my fallen friend. I grabbed his arm and dragged him aside, and the boot caught air, throwing its owner off balance. The crooked-toothed boy toppled into his charging partner. They tangled and fell.

"Run!" I cried as I yanked Apollo to his feet.

We crashed through the undergrowth back to the path. If we reached the gate, we would be safe. I heaved a gasp of relief when I saw the road, then it dawned on me. The evening audience would be arriving. We couldn't make a scene. "We have to go in the back way," I cried. I jerked Apollo to a halt by his scruff and plunged back into the woods, pushing him ahead of me. I prayed the way would be clear, because the jeers behind us told me we were not safe yet.

We thrust through vines, jumped bushes, and wove in and out of the trees. I tried to ignore the stabs to my feet and the branches that whipped my flanks. My calves stung with bramble scratches. Finally we came panting to the wall.

"Quick," I said, and bent over as the enemy burst through the bushes behind us, favoring them with a seldom-seen view of my rear.

Apollo leaped on my back. He scrambled to my shoulders as I straightened, then hoisted himself to the top of the wall. I clambered up after him, using the rough stones as handholds and toeholds. Apollo helped me straddle the peak.

The townies stood below shaking their fists, but they dared not follow.

"You wait, freaks," yelled the dark-haired boy. "We'll catch you."

His taunt set a fire of anger alight in me. "I'm not a freak," I almost yelled, then choked the words back. How would that make Apollo feel? It would sound as though I thought I was better than he.

"Come on," I said to Apollo. "We've got to get out of sight."

Apollo waved a rude gesture in the direction of the town boys before he leaped into the kitchen garden. I followed him down into the neat rows of squash.

"You were marvelous," Apollo cried, jumping up and down with excitement. "The way you tackled both of them together."

"I might not have had to if you hadn't bitten that lad," I complained in hushed tones. "Keep your voice down. Do you want to be discovered like this?"

Apollo gazed at me blankly. Embarrassment was not in his vocabulary.

"Let me put it this way, then," I said. "Would you like to scare a lady and be beaten by your papa for it?"

"Oh!" he said, light dawning.

I caught the glitter of fear in his eyes. My words had more than a shadow of truth to them, I guessed. "Just be cautious," I told Apollo. "If we can get back to our quarters without being spotted, all will be well."

A giggle from behind the pea trellis crushed my hopes. Apollo yelped and grabbed my arm.

Out from the vines swaggered Archie Crum. Behind him a kitchen maid rose to her feet. She stood taller than the dwarf by a foot and a half, as tall as the trellis, in fact. Although I was surprised to see Archie in the kitchen garden, I was not surprised to see him with a woman. Archie had a knack with the ladies. She peeked through her fingers at us, then covered her eyes again, which I thought hypocritical, considering what she had recently been up to.

Apollo let go my arm. "Archie! We've had an adventure."

"My, my, my," said Archie Crum. "Working on a new act, are you? Let me guess—the Flying Birthday Suit Boys?"

The girl giggled again, and I felt myself grow red.

"Go find something to cover the Acrobats au naturel, why don't you, my dear," said Archie.

The girl ran for the kitchen door.

"You should have seen Abel trounce a pair of bullies," Apollo said.

"Thieves, were they?" Archie asked, looking me up and down.

"I didn't trounce them," I objected. "We had to run away."

"Townies caught us while we were swimming!" Apollo said.

"Swimming in thorns, apparently," Archie answered.

What a sight I must be. Apollo's fur had protected him, but I was a mass of welts and scratches. Before I could think of an adequate retort, the kitchen maid came back with sheets fresh from the airing cupboard. I flung the one she offered me around myself. I didn't ask Archie to be quiet about his discovery because I knew it would be useless. "Come on, Apollo," I said. I was tired of being mocked.

Apollo struggled with his sheet. "But you *were* heroic," he insisted in his sweet voice as he followed me around to a little-used side door, dragging a train behind him. "You came to my rescue when I was done for."

"You've been reading too many penny dreadfuls," I told him.

Fortunately, I ran into no one, and when I arrived at our apartments, my parents had already gone down to the dining room. I dressed for dinner and joined them and Uncle Jack at our family table before they had finished the soup. To my dismay, Archie Crum sat at the next table with Orlando the Magnificent. He was table-hopping. He winked at me and grinned. I knew that by the end of dinner half the hall would know of my predicament this afternoon. I might as well tell my parents before they heard a lurid version from someone else. I took a deep breath that didn't escape the notice of my mother.

"What is it Abel, my love?" she asked. The foot holding her spoon paused halfway to her mouth.

"I'm afraid I had a misadventure this afternoon," I admitted, then told them all that had passed, including our discovery by Archie Crum.

"Well done!" Papa exclaimed. He pushed down with his hands and flipped himself around on his chair to face me. "We can always trust you to protect young Apollo."

I couldn't look at him. "I didn't do much," I grumbled. "I ran away." Those boys had been there because of me, but I couldn't say that and let him down.

"It's no shame to run in the face of superior forces," Papa said. "It's the wise thing to do, and don't let anyone tell you otherwise."

Uncle Jack slapped me on the back. "However, in case you don't get away so swiftly next time, I'll show you a trick or two tomorrow at practice."

I tried to control my temper. They were being kind. "I'm sorry about the clothes, Mama," I said.

"Pish!" she answered. "If they are not in the mud by the pond tomorrow, I'm sure I can sew up more. They were not your good clothes, after all."

"I suspect that Mr. Papandreou is not of the same mind," said Papa.

At the Papandreou table the normally dour head of the family appeared thunderous. Mrs. P., Phoebe, and Apollo sat with their heads bowed and ate silently. Apollo's hand crept to his face as if he was brushing away a tear. Had his father beaten him after all?

What would Mr. P. do to me if he thought I had been toying with his daughter? Would he beat me also, or would he just insist that I make her an honest woman? My appetite left me and I put down my fork.

"Are you not hungry, dear?" my ever vigilant mother asked.

"I'm full," I lied.

I sat and fiddled with my ring as I waited for my family to finish their meal, examining them from under lowered eyelids. I loved my parents, but now I saw them as the boys in town did, strange and distorted. Perhaps it frightened the townies even more that they couldn't see what my difference was, although they were sure I had one. If I went out into the world, would young ladies think me handsome when they didn't have the image of my mother and father in their eyes? The surge of yearning I felt for this made me uncomfortable—hot and prickly with betrayal.

"Stop kicking the table leg, Abel," my father said.

"Sorry," I mumbled. I stared at my ring so I wouldn't have to look at him. I felt ashamed that I could so easily abandon my parents, if only in my mind.

The bezel setting, which held the turquoise stone in place, had the form of a gold snake with its tail in its mouth. As I turned the ring back and forth, the gold caught the light and dazzled my eyes with sparks. Pleasure caught in my throat as I mesmerized myself with the tiny fireworks show. I narrowed my eyes and the room faded—all I saw were sparkles. My anger drained away, I relaxed, and the annoyance of the world grew distant.

A Gypsy ring, the townie had called it. My eyes were fully closed now.

Colors swirled behind my eyelids. They began to take form. A dancer in white gauze trimmed with azure and crimson emerged, her breasts bare. Pleasure cupped my loins with a firm, hot paw.

She held a string of beads in one hand and a rattle in the other, twirling its two-pronged frame to make metal disks hiss and shush in harmony with the clicking of her beads. She danced to the rhythm of the chants sung by swaying girls and of the *chock-chock* sound of their ivory wands knocking. She rolled her hips and embraced the music with her arms. Pipes soared in melody, harps chimed, the rhythm grew faster and faster, until she twirled in a blur of whites, reds, blues, and golds. People clapped, they clicked their fingers. I shook with internal thunder and felt I might spiral into the maelstrom of the dance. She spun closer and closer, her dark eyes flashing promises, until she stopped, breathless, in front of me, so near I could smell the spices she wore, heated by her sweat, and my blood surged sweet and effervescent.

Come to me, a voice whispered in my ear like the rustling of leaves.

My eyes shot open and I looked frantically to either side. Surely that had been a real voice.

"Flea bit you, son?" my father asked.

"Um, I think I fell asleep," I said. My heart thumped as I tried to work out what my mind had turned into a voice. The rattling of cutlery? A sneeze? "Perhaps I should get to bed early."

"You are excused," said my mother.

I was too deep in thought to pay much mind to the chuckles I heard on the way out, but as I passed the table of Gladys Dibble, the Pixie Queen, and her fairy court, a raucous voice burst into song.

"He flies through the air with the greatest of ease. The naked young man on the flying trapeze . . ."

Archie sat between Betty and Dolly like a fly in a bun, singing at the top of his lungs. Archie, all the time ready to take a poke at me because I was so ordinary. The other diners clapped time as they laughed, and Baby Betty blew me a kiss.

Did they all think me a joke? Underneath their affection was there pity for the normal boy who would never quite belong? Or was there a streak of resentment under their teasing?

I strode from the room, gazing straight ahead. I wanted to keep on going, to march right out of the house.

I CAME EARLY TO THE PRACTICE barn the next morning and found Apollo in the hayloft, sobbing into a bale of last summer's sweetgrass. Through his rumpled fur I could see a bruise on the cheek turned my way—his father's work, no doubt. Damn the man. Apollo was only a child. I sat at the boy's side and pulled him to me. He clasped me and wept into my shoulder. Although my neck felt damp and itchy with his tears, I held him until he'd finished crying.

"Cheer up," I told him. "You'll soon be all grown up and your own man."

"Wish it was now," he said, and hiccupped.

The barn door creaked. "Jack's here," I said. "I'm to have self-defense lessons. Want to watch?"

Apollo perked right up. "Yeah!" he said, and wiped his nose on his sleeve.

Uncle Jack's lesson turned out to be no more than the boxing pointers he had given me in the past. I dutifully sparred with him and listened to his advice, but my heart wasn't in it.

I heard laughter. "Why, it's the water baby at his practice. Very gentlemanly, I must say." Archie Crum swaggered though the barn door.

"What do you want, Crum?" Jack asked.

Archie ignored his question. "It's not Marquis of Queensbury rules you need when the odds are against you. What you need are barroom moves. Come on, Jack, let's show the boys some real fighting."

Jack was a fine, muscular man and more than a match for a four-foot dwarf, no matter how burly or how experienced a stage strong man.

Archie saw my doubt. "I shouldn't worry if I were you, young frog. I've toppled bigger giants than our Jacko here." With that, he kicked Jack in the left shin. Jack howled and lifted the injured leg. Archie hooked the remaining leg with one of his, and Jack fell to the ground.

Apollo whooped, and my mouth fell open.

"At this point you jump on him or run," Archie said to me. "If it's you that falls, tuck, roll, and bolt. Don't lie there like this idiot and let your foe kick you."

"That's dirty fighting," Jack said, scrambling to his feet.

Archie rolled his eyes. "Of course it's dirty. When a man's in danger, he does what he can to survive. Always take your opponent by surprise when you can, Abel. Especially when he's bigger than you. Hit him where it hurts the most—stamp on his instep; kick him in the shin, or in the privates if you can do that without him grabbing your leg. Of course, if you do hit him in the privates, be prepared to run like hell. If you're fighting in close, poke him in the eyes."

"Hold on there," said Jack. "That can inflict permanent damage."

"Who do you want permanently damaged?" Archie asked me. "You or the bastard who's knocking your block off? If you don't want to hurt him, turn tail. If you stay, be prepared to maim."

Jack shook his head. "I don't know where you picked that up, Archie."

"You've led a sheltered life, Mr. Loose Shirt and Pretend I'm Normal," Archie answered. "Remember, boys, anything sharp and pointy is useful. Hit 'em with that ring, Abel, and don't be afraid to pull hair and bite if you have to." He hitched up his pants and left.

"Coward's tactics," Jack grumbled.

I nodded, a tight, worried knot clenched in my stomach. Was this another joke at my expense? But I had to admit, I was impressed.

To my surprise, all week long I received similar advice from the most unlikely sources.

"Stick him with a hatpin, sweetie," said tiny Gladys Dibble. "I always keep one at hand."

"A handful of dirt or sand in the eyes is helpful," said Albert Sunderland.

"Step on his foot," said Jolly Dolly. "That always works for me."

I wouldn't have believed so many of my friends had been in need of self-defense.

✳

A few days later, Uncle Jack surprised me at practice with a new set of throwing knives in a leather bandolier. "These are weighted for distance," he told me, and grinned.

I accepted the bandolier with delight and pulled out a knife to feel the balance. It had a pleasant heft to it and sat in my palm like an old friend. These were just the knives I needed. "Will I get a chance to show them off in front of an audience soon?" I asked, made hopeful by his gift.

"I'm sure we can round up some of the fellows," he answered.

"No, I mean a real audience," I said. "When are you going to let me join your act?"

"My act?" He cocked his head, and my heart sank as I realized it had never crossed his mind.

"So why did you bother to teach me? Where am I supposed to use these skills?" I demanded as anger flamed through me.

Uncle Jack looked taken aback. "Another show, I suppose."

I glared at him. "You mean I'm not good enough for this show?"

"No. I mean, yes, I . . ." Jack reached for me, but I stormed out of the barn.

It was true, then. I didn't belong. I was useless here. I was handicapped by my normality. Why would an audience care about me? Who would come to see a normal boy throw knives, with all these exciting oddities around? I wanted to be seen, but if I wanted a chance to stand out, I would have to find a place with people like me.

Ha! People like me. I felt sad at setting myself apart by those words. I had always thought we were alike, all of us who lived in Faeryland—we laughed and cried and loved and hurt—but I was ordinary, and they were stars. I needed to be in a place where skill alone could set me apart. I remembered the poster I'd seen. A place like that circus.

As I entered the front hall, Phoebe came down the stairs.

"Abel!" she called, and ran lightly to meet me, her silky facial hair a nimbus about her. "Would you like to join my family for dinner tonight?"

"Why?" I asked, annoyed at the interception.

The smile on Phoebe's face dimmed a little. She hesitated. "You waited too long and my father has something to say to you."

"About what?" I was being deliberately obtuse.

Her smile disappeared completely. "I thought . . ."

"You think too much," I snapped. "And use your imagination in excess when you do."

Her face crumpled into a ball of anguished fur, and I brushed by her, my anger fueled even hotter by my guilt.

"Wait until I tell my father," she called after me, but I stormed on.

Up in my room I stewed. What control did I have over my life? None. I didn't have a career, and if I didn't watch out, I would find myself married to Phoebe, the son-in-law of a brutal man. All they thought me good for around here was being an errand boy and a nursemaid. It was time to take charge. I would join the circus and make a career of my own. I grabbed a battered suitcase from beneath my bed, and as I packed my good suit, my new knives, and assorted necessaries, I made my plans.

I would have a long walk ahead of me. If I left around midnight, when everyone was safe in their quarters, I should be at the circus grounds by dawn. I consulted the almanac in my father's study. Most of the way would be dirt roads far from any streetlights, but the moon was full and not due to set until the early hours, so I should be able to make my way.

I forced myself to eat dinner—I would need my strength—but I didn't join the conversation. From the corner of my eye I saw Phoebe staring, and my food tasted like sawdust. I turned away, but my neck prickled and I could imagine the heavy hand of Mr. P. landing on my shoulder, and his loud demands.

"Are you well, Abel?" my mother asked.

"I'm fine," I mumbled. I tried not to think of the tears she would shed on the morrow.

I fled the dining room as soon as I was able.

I worked through the show like a mechanical man, fetching and carrying and shifting scenery as always. When Phoebe passed me in the wings, she paused as if to speak, but I hurried away. *I am a rotten scoundrel,* I told myself, but that didn't influence me to go back and find her.

I went to my chamber early and stared at my packed suitcase, my mouth dry. I half expected to talk myself out of leaving before the time came, but exhilaration overcame doubt, and I penned a brief letter to my folks.

> *Dearest Mama and Papa,*
> *I have gone to seek my fortune, since it is not to be found here. Do not try to find me, or worry about me. I will return rich. Never doubt my esteem and love for you.*
>
> *Your son,*
> *Abel*

At midnight I left my room, suitcase in hand, and crept down the corridor. When would I see these walls again? I wondered. This filled me with a sweet mélange of nostalgia and excitement. I walked carefully so as not to creak a floorboard. If someone stopped me now that I had committed myself to leaving, my heart would surely break and these walls become a prison. When I reached the back stairs, I thought I heard a floorboard groan behind me. I swiftly took the turn and hurried downstairs, throwing caution to the wind, my heart thumping. At the bottom I paused and listened, my breath ragged, but I heard no more sounds. No one followed.

The kitchen door was ajar. The large, brick-walled room was lit dimly by the remains of a fire in the old cooking hearth. Perhaps I should raid the larder for some bread and cheese for my breakfast. As I made my way carefully past the big oak table, a hand gripped my arm, and my innards leaped into my throat.

"Since you are going, I shall tell you your fortune," peeped Gladys Dibble, the Pixie Queen.

I gaped at her. "How did you know?"

"You're carrying a suitcase, my darling." She stood nimbly on her stool and stepped onto the table in front of me, beside her cup and saucer. She held out her minuscule hands, and automatically I gave her my left hand to study. "You will go on a long journey," Miss Dibble began in her gossamer voice.

"As you said, I *am* carrying a suitcase," I answered; now I was able to be angry at my scare.

Miss Dibble silenced me with a withering glance. I have never known a woman who could command that much authority despite her size.

"You will face great danger," she said. I hadn't expected that.

"I see . . ." Miss Dibble paused and frowned. "A skeleton," she finally said.

A skeleton? I scoffed silently. Was this some child's Halloween skit?

"You will fail where you set your sights and succeed where you least expect," continued Miss Dibble. Her fingers skimmed my ring. "And when all seems lost, you will fall in love with an older foreign lady." She shook her head, as if this last seemed unlikely even to her.

It was nonsense from a midget lady with insomnia, I thought. But my lips gently curled at the thought of this older foreign lady—there was an adventure I would like to have.

Miss Dibble removed a chain from her neck. "I suggest you wear that ring on this," she said. "You don't want to call the attention of thieves." She pooled the chain into my still-outstretched palm and then took both my hands in hers. Her grip tightened on me like little mouse paws.

"When you set off to find your fortune," she said intently, unnerving me with a fierce and disturbing fire in her eyes, "be sure to be kind to ugly strangers, for there may be a princess among them."

I thanked her politely, stuffed the chain in my pocket, and left as fast as I could, without the bread and cheese.

I walked all night, down dusty country roads, under a fat, abetting moon. Near morning, or so I judged, when the moon sank low over the horizon, I saw the shadows of large tents in a field. This must be the circus.

I would have to wait until a decent hour before I found the manager and asked for a job. So I climbed over a pale wooden fence and—before I stumbled too far and broke my leg in a rabbit hole—I found myself a comfortable seat next to a bush. It wasn't long before my head began to nod.

"My love! At last!" whispered a sweet, trembling voice.

I froze in mid nod. I had never stayed up all night before. I had never walked so far. I took a deep breath. My mind was playing tricks on me.

"You are at the threshold of dream, and my spirit can reach you through the ring, I think," said the eager voice. "Open your eyes, but slowly, and perhaps you may see me."

I did as the voice asked, expecting the dream to dissolve, but beside me sat a shadowy woman veiled in gauzy cloth. I shuddered.

"Did you like my dance?" she asked.

"Dance?" I frowned.

"I danced for you to the music of harps and pipes." The shadow leaped to her feet and rolled her hips, then flung herself down beside me again, breathless laughter on her lips.

"That was another dream," I said.

She laughed again. "You were always stubborn, Ankhtifi." She leaned forward and seemed to peer at my face. "How strange, my heart knows you but my eyes do not. You have changed in looks." I couldn't place her accent.

"Madam," I said, sure I was speaking to a ghost and thankful I was only dreaming, "I do not believe we have met."

"Do you not remember me?" she asked, oh so sadly.

"I can barely see you," I answered. The moon was low in the sky, and the oval that must be her face was a blur.

Her outline appeared to waver as she sighed. "I shouldn't expect you to remember," she said. "You went to your spirit and left your worldly body behind. But your heart spoke for you at the great judgment when it was weighed on the scales of justice, and the lord of the underworld sent you back to search for me, at the request of his lady wife, she who is life, she who pities me. I felt it the moment you walked beyond the gates of death and reentered the world. I am but a shade," she whispered, "but I have traveled years and miles to find you."

"Why?" I asked. I couldn't fathom any of her words, let alone what a ghost would want with me.

She laughed as if surprised by my ignorance. "So our love might live again." Then her tone grew desperate. "I am in danger. A man of bones has kidnapped me. Each day takes me farther toward the setting sun. I am among brigands who would think nothing of disposing of my body if it suited them. If they destroy what is left of me, we may never be together again."

"Can't you tell anyone?" I asked, wondering what on earth I could do.

"I am a prisoner," she explained. "No one who can help can hear me speak—no one but you. We are connected because of the ring. It is my heart—your heart. Find me, help me, and I will explain our bond."

I glanced nervously at the ring I wore.

"Where is it you go this night?" she asked.

She was a very inquisitive dream ghost. "I thought to join that traveling show, if they have a job for me," I answered, gesturing toward the tent, "and find my fortune."

"Which way does this caravan travel?" she asked.

I tried to visualize the poster I had seen. "West, I think."

She sat up straight and threw her arms open with joy. "You are coming."

"Um, no," I said, leaning back a touch.

"Yes, your heart knows it even if you do not," she insisted. "And what employment do you seek? What is your skill?"

"I'm a knife thrower," I admitted.

She chuckled huskily. "Ah, that makes much sense, my love. Still a warrior after all."

A bird warbled close by, and I looked up, surprised. The sky in the distance had lightened to a smoky pearl.

"I must go," said my strange companion. "There's not much time left to meddle with dreams."

I turned back to ask her what she meant, only to see a wisp of fog disappear to nothing.

"Find me before the serpent of the night devours me," her voice echoed.

I closed my eyes against the unsettling mystery, and when I opened them, the sun was up.

I STRETCHED, AND SUNLIGHT GLINTED off my ring, reminding me of my dream. *How curious,* I thought. *What strange fancies fatigue brings.* Exhaustion had tumbled Miss Dibble's odd words of a skeleton and a foreign lady into a delirium that seemed very real.

I felt a little peculiar about the ring now, and maybe it was a mite garish, with the gold snake setting and the turquoise stone carved to look like a beetle. I wanted people to think me an upstanding fellow suitable for employment, not a bohemian. Perhaps I should follow Miss Dibble's advice. I fished the chain she had given me from my jacket pocket and hung the scarab ring safe but out of sight around my neck.

I stood up and brushed myself down. It was time for me to find a job.

Across the field was a huge red-and-yellow-striped tent—the big top. A multitude of smaller canvas tents scattered the meadow to the left of it, like a village at the foot of a castle. That must be the circus backyard. Beyond those tents the circus train rested along tracks that ran parallel to the road I had left. Perhaps one of the train cars contained the manager's office. As I wound through the village of tents, shabby, plump women hung wash on improvised lines, and barefoot children chased dogs over tent pegs and under ropes. A delicious aroma of bacon wafted through the air. My stomach yearned for breakfast. I hoped I could join the circus in time to get some.

I walked along the train, a string of multicolored passenger carriages, flatbeds, and livestock cars, and searched for any sort of sign amid the decorations and emblems on the carriages. A door opened ahead of me, and six young men with white tights evident beneath flowing blue capes tumbled out and hurried by, laughing and jostling. They disappeared into a tent before I thought to ask them directions. Music came from a passenger car I passed—a tuba, I guessed—and from somewhere an elephant trumpeted as if in answer. Excitement buzzed in my throat.

I had stopped to look at an amazing desert scene that meandered the length of an entire sleeper car, when two clean-shaven gentlemen approached. They were dressed in robes and Arabian headdresses, as if they had dismounted from the camels in the picture.

"Excuse me," I said, and they stopped to eye me with amused curiosity. "Could you please direct me to the manager's office?" I inquired.

"Are you selling something?" one of them asked. He sounded English rather than Arabian, I fancied.

"I'm looking for a job," I answered.

His companion, who appeared to be his younger brother, nudged him with an elbow. "Standards are rising, Eddie. The dung shovelers wear suits to interview these days."

"I'm . . . I'm a knife thrower," I stammered.

Eddie laughed, and his younger brother winced. "I'm afraid we've got one of those," the younger brother said.

"It's a knife thrower's assistant we're missing," said Eddie, raising his eyebrows.

"So we are," agreed the younger brother. "They just had a bang-out fight in the cookhouse. Mr. Rose had a dream last night that he stuck her full of blades. He was telling everyone in detail. He thought it very funny, but she didn't, because she'd had the same dream, so she quit."

I remembered that the ghostly woman had spoken of meddling in dreams, and I came over funny for a moment. I shrugged the feeling off. This was coincidence, that's all.

"So if you want to work for a man not known for his sensitive nature, the way is clear," said Eddie.

"It's a start," I said.

Eddie nodded approvingly. "You'll find the manager five cars down."

"Hide Mr. Rose's bottle before the show," said the younger brother.

"And don't get him mad," said Eddie.

They entered their desert-painted carriage laughing.

They're teasing me, I decided as I found the manager's car. This man couldn't be all that bad, else the circus wouldn't hire him. What a stroke of luck there was a place with a knife thrower open. Perhaps he could tutor me and even give me my first chance in the ring.

A smart young man with a middle part in his hair and a small mustache looked up as I entered the business office. The plaque on his desk identified him as A. Marvel. My lips twitched, but one look at his face convinced me he wouldn't enjoy the joke. I presented myself as an apprentice knife thrower, happy to serve as an assistant to the incumbent.

"Well, aren't you a godsend?" Mr. A. Marvel said. "But this is only until we find him a pretty girl to help, you understand."

I nodded; I would cross that bridge when I came to it.

Mr. A. Marvel had me sign papers for my wages and gave me a book of vouchers for my meals. I would be issued a new one each week. "You've missed breakfast," he said, to my dismay. "Lunch is at noon. You can present your voucher book to get into the show later. That way they'll know you're not a rube. Watch how professionals do it."

I am a professional, I thought, but decided I would likely cut my employment short if I argued. "Where should I sleep, sir?" I asked.

The young man shook his head and flipped through a logbook.

"There's room in one of the men's dormitory cars," he told me. "It's bright green and gold, next to the elephants. Leave your bag there and then go report to Mr. Rose."

I found the sleeper car, and a motley assortment of young men who didn't seem annoyed to see me.

"Oh, we get all sorts through here," said one fellow. "What's one more?" He pointed me to a place I could stow my luggage and to an upper berth where I could sleep, halfway down the bunk-lined carriage.

"It's not bad diggings if you don't mind the occasional stench of elephant," said another fellow. He waved a hand under his nose.

Down the far end was a washroom with a tank of water. The other facility consisted of a seat over a hole in the floor—a drafty perch above a honey bucket hung below. I suspected it wouldn't be just elephants I'd be smelling.

"Parade's starting!" called an acrobat from the door, and the young men scrambled to leave.

"Where do I find Mr. Rose?" I asked.

"Oh, he's in Happy Times," said one of the boys.

"Constantly," said another, causing gales of laughter.

"Three cars that way," said a fellow, pointing, before he left.

Down the train I mounted a crate to knock on a dark green door. The words HAPPY TIMES embellished the center panel in silver paint.

"Who's that?" came a gruff voice.

"Abel Dandy, sir," I replied. "Your new assistant."

"Is that so? Well, come in, then, damn you."

I opened the door and climbed into a tiny salon with heavy curtains pulled back from the windows by gilt ties. The near wall, free of seats, allowed passage to wood-paneled sleeping compartments beyond. On the far wall a pair of embroidered settees, affixed to the floor like regular train seats, faced each other to either side of a dark wood table. A middle-aged gentleman sat there in dressing gown and slippers, his waxed mustache askew, a stack of playing cards on the table beside a bottle of whiskey.

"My new assistant, are you, now?" Mr. Rose sneered.

"Mr. A. Marvel hired me this morning," I said.

Mr. Rose narrowed his eyes. "You don't look like a girl."

I gritted my teeth. "No, sir, but Mr. Marvel said I would have to do until he found one for you."

My anger seemed to amuse Mr. Rose. He relaxed into his seat and paid full attention to his cards. "Clean shoes, can you?"

"Yes, sir."

"Know how to press a gentleman's jacket?"

"Well, yes."

"Can you stand still with a knife coming at you?"

"I've done it before."

"Then, until I can find a pretty girl with a short skirt, you'll stand target."

I should have been happy to be in the act; instead I eyed the bottle of whiskey on the table and felt a cold slug of apprehension.

"Will you also give me an opportunity to throw?" I asked, surprising myself with my forwardness. "I have my own knives."

"Throw?" he asked. "In the act? I don't need a young upstart tripping over his own feet and skewering the audience."

"I don't trip, and I hit the target," I snapped. "I would ask you to see me throw before you make judgments."

Mr. Rose shrugged. "All right, maybe we'll talk about me watching you throw sometime, boy," he said. "Right now I'm busy."

"Isn't there a show this afternoon?" I asked.

"I've given myself a holiday," he answered. "I'll be in the evening show, however. You may as well watch then, so you'll be prepared when we rehearse tomorrow. Now, go gawk or something."

"Thank you, sir," I said to his dubious offer, but he didn't reply; he just sat at the table and shuffled his cards.

I found my way to the cookhouse and was first in line when lunch was announced. I could barely keep my eyes open to watch the performers returning from the parade. Since I didn't have an obligation until the evening show, I decided to try out my new bunk. Seconds after removing my jacket and shoes I was fast asleep.

I was in a huge stone room, the ceiling held up by bulbous painted columns. One side was open to water, palms, and sky. I was amid a crowd of dark-skinned people wrapped in slight linens who surrounded a circle of girls in the middle of the room. The girls displayed more jewelry than clothes. Some played harps and double-horned pipes, others sang a melodious and repetitive refrain and beat wands in time. My gaze would have lingered upon them if it had not been stolen away by the dancer I recognized in their center, a voluptuous, undulating, dark-haired beauty.

She swayed her hips, her face ecstatic. She turned, she writhed, she twirled; she stomped out the rhythm with her feet; she cried a victory to the skies. Faster and faster she whirled. The music rose to a crescendo, then ended with a crash.

Silence.

The dancer stood, arms raised above her head, her chest heaving, her eyes on me. The crowd disappeared. The distance between us telescoped impossibly, and she was right in front of me.

"You are coming," she said joyously.

I woke up, and a trace of responding joy still clung to me.

I shook my head. *I fell asleep thinking of attending a show, and I got a show,* I thought with amusement. I climbed from my bunk and set off to watch the circus.

I took my seat, facing the center ring. The air was close and warm under the big top and thick with the smell of sawdust. I removed my jacket and laid it across my lap. While I ate the frankfurter I had purchased outside for an exorbitant price, I examined the scaffolding, the wires made ready for the aerialists, and the electric lights strung between quarter poles high underneath the canvas. The excited audience hummed like the generator that no doubt powered the lights. There had to be thousands more here than could have fit in our theater at home, but the three rings, and the oval track of the hippodrome that ran around them, guaranteed everyone a good view.

Home. I had avoided thoughts of home up until now. Were they looking for me there? I wondered. Or did they assume I would show up when good and ready?

A brassy fanfare sounded.

Through the curtains came the band, playing a rousing overture to lead the grand entry. A squadron of performers on horseback followed, welcomed by thunderous applause. Behind the equestrians acrobats tumbled and leaped; next came a pair of camels ridden by the brothers I had met earlier, then men in tights, aerialists perhaps, shadowed by a fleet of bicyclists. On and on marched the performers around the hippodrome track, grouped by the color of their clothes or the items they juggled or the banners they carried, while a motley array of clowns in striped stockings dashed here and there, throwing confetti and hitting one another with oversize pillows.

This was a very different show from the one I had left. How perfect in form all the participants were. Nothing less beautiful than a tubby clown graced the arena. All limbs were present, all flesh firm, and the costumes were cut to display this pulchritude. A man could become dizzy with the display of legs. No wonder the audience teemed with awestruck men. Ah, but those men hadn't been graced with dreams like mine. I smiled.

As the elephants came into the tent, the front of the parade completed the circuit, and the whole show met in a glittering circle of wonder. At the last moment the band peeled off and took seats on the bandstand to play the rest of the parade out, then the equestrian director, a strapping man in top hat and red coat, strode into the center ring, and the band hit their final chord and fell silent.

The equestrian director blew a blast on his silver whistle. "Ladies and gentlemen," he began to the hushed crowd. "Welcome to our scintillating cavalcade of marvels, acrobats, and wild beasts." The broadsheet I had been given as I entered identified the master of the ring as Mr. Geoffrey Marvel, one of the three brothers who owned the circus. He was a more mature version of the young man in the business office and had a walrus mustache.

"Derring-doers from every corner of the globe are gathered here to thrill you," he boomed. "Children, may you laugh with the antics of our beloved animals and clowns. Ladies, let your hearts flutter for the handsome strong men who will risk their lives to entertain you. And gentlemen, we bring you pretty and accomplished girls aplenty." This last was received with laughter and applause. "Now, to begin our program, I present to you, straight from the court of the emperor of Japan, where their family has entertained for five hundred years, those amazing Asian artistes, those Nippon nimbles, the Rising Sun Jugglers!"

The audience burst into applause as the band played an Oriental tune.

Such an astounding array of animals, aerial acts, ground acts, and thrillers followed that even I, a seasoned hand, sat amazed. Sometimes the performers used one ring while the others were set up for the next acts; sometimes all rings were in use at the same time. The knife thrower, Mr. Rose, dapper now in a suit with his waxed mustache symmetrical, competed for attention with a team of jugglers and some acrobats. I judged his throwing not as accomplished as that of my uncle Jack, but perhaps his act was more exciting when he had an assistant.

As they had ended the parade, the elephants also ended the show. I clapped as hard as anybody as all twenty pachyderms exited on their hind legs, each, except the leader, with its huge feet on the back of the elephant in front.

I hurried out the back door as soon as the show ended, eager to meet and congratulate my new compatriots. I would have introduced myself to Mr. Geoffrey Marvel first, but he was conversing with a gesticulating man.

"It's not one of my monkeys," the man bellowed. "Mine are all accounted for. Blame this on someone else."

I was pleased to see one of the trick riders, a handsome brunette woman who had bewitched me with her exquisite figure as much as her skill. She held a horse's bridle while a blacksmith inspected a horseshoe. This was no dream but a real beauty. I decided to make my first conquest and grinned as I walked toward her.

"Madam," I said. "I hope you don't mind if I say you are quite the most accomplished horsewoman I have ever seen."

"Why, thank you, young man," she said, hardly looking at me. "Do you have a picture for me to sign?" I had intended to introduce myself, but my words died on my lips and my cheeks flamed. She didn't wait long for me to answer, but thrust the reins of her horse into the hands of a waiting groom and left without a word.

The groom and the blacksmith laughed.

I could feel my lower lip tremble, and I turned hastily away. She thought I was a townie, and not worth a glance at that. The ladies at home had always called me a good-looking fellow, but perhaps the ladies at home were not qualified to tell. I kicked a clod of dirt, shamed by my quick dismissal of those who loved me. Still, what if I wasn't beans compared with the sturdy young men of the circus? Was I a fool to think that romantic adventures awaited me? Was I optimistic to think I could fit in here at all?

The roustabouts were already dismantling the tent, and five of the elephants had been stripped of their fancy blankets and harnessed to chains, ready to bring down the poles. Performers packed up props left near the exit, and the clowns folded up Clown Alley. The tents in the backyard were gone.

Slowly I made my way back to my new sleeping quarters.

I felt lost and useless, with nothing to do in the midst of this hustle and bustle. For the first time in my life I was a stranger, and I hated that.

THE MEN IN THE DORMITORY WERE young, and all were performers. Some were clown apprentices, some were older sons who wanted independence from the family quarters, and others were part of an acrobatic act that didn't earn enough yet to afford a compartment in the fancier cars. There wasn't much room in the crowded carriage, but they put up with the situation with good cheer, and everyone tried to do his best to keep his belongings stowed and his elbows in. There existed a comfortable camaraderie between them that made me ache for the old friendships I had left behind.

That night, when we had all climbed into our bunks and the train rumbled under way, I discovered an evening ritual.

"It's your turn, Georgie," said the fellow who had settled me in. "What have you got? A story? A song?"

"Anything to drown those elephants out," said another fellow. "They've been all-fired noisy lately."

Georgie did not have a good singing voice, but he made up for that with enthusiasm as he launched into a popular song. The others drowned out his wavering voice when they joined in for the chorus:

"My Jeanne, my Jeanne, she's my little circus queen.
She's just seventeen, fairer you've never seen.
All dressed up in spangles and gold,
She's a beautiful sight to behold.
Sweet as a dream; bright as any sunbeam,
And she's my little circus queen."

I sighed. I'd like to find my own little queen someday, someone like that beauty who had been popping up in my dreams lately. "Find me," she had said in that vision in the field. I would have loved to think she was out there waiting for me, but that was foolish. There were fortune-tellers, however, who said that the objects in one's dreams often stood for something else. What was it I was looking for when I left home? Adventure and fortune, that was what. Perhaps this dream girl was the personification of my search for adventure, luring me on to find her.

I didn't pay much attention to the story that came next, for I lingered deep in my own thoughts, where a dark-haired woman with luminous eyes undulated in a dance full of promises. *I will find you, Lady Adventure,* I silently vowed. Before I knew it, I woke up to daylight and jolly roughhousing all around me. My life with the circus had begun.

The vibrations I felt through my bunk, and the gentle *tickity-tack* I heard, told me the train was still in motion. The other train, which carried the cookhouse, the canvas, and the poles, probably sat at its destination already, and the cooks and roustabouts would be scurrying about their duties. My stomach rumbled. By the time we arrived, breakfast would be prepared, the tent pegs hammered in, the canvas laid out, and the poles ready to be raised.

I felt fuzzy headed. Perhaps the excitement had disturbed me, or the strange bed, but many times throughout the night I had come awake in a haze where the purrs of lions turned into the rumble of metal wheels. Sometimes my unexpected surroundings blended so quickly back into dreams that I barely knew I was conscious. Once I even thought I saw a blurry face peer in at me through the window—impossible, since the train was moving. All through my dreams wafted the smell of pungent spices and a voice that called my name, only it wasn't my name.

While I put on my shirt, I wondered if I should wear my ring on my finger now, but something told me it would get me nothing but jokes from these boys, so I left it hanging from the chain around my neck. As I buttoned the last button, the train squealed to a stop in a new town.

On my way to the cookhouse I stopped to watch the teams of elephants and men haul cables and raise the canvas of the big top. Crews of roustabouts hurried around the perimeter of the tent, tightening guy ropes and lashing them into place. Local people had come to watch. Their children ran after the elephants with handfuls of hay for them to eat. I smiled. Apollo would love to do that. I hoped he'd forgive me for leaving him behind.

In the cookhouse I lined up and received a breakfast of ham, eggs, fried potatoes, and fresh-baked bread. The cooks were squabbling with one another because the monkey on the loose had raided their stores of fruit and vegetables. I was surprised to see linen on the tables and real silverware, although the long trestles decked in checkered cotton that I glimpsed on the other side of the dividing curtain showed me the laborers had simpler accommodations.

I spotted the Arabian brothers, now dressed in jackets and trousers, and asked if I might join them. They welcomed me jovially.

"I'm Frank Bridgeport," said the younger.

"I'm Eddie Bridgeport," said the elder.

The brothers were lively, talkative fellows, which saved me from having to think of conversation. I enjoyed their banter and was content to listen. I must admit, I also was proud to be seen in their company—they were well built and handsome, and I hoped this reflected upon me. *Here I am, girls,* I announced silently. *I'm just like them. There's nothing up my sleeve but a regular arm.*

After we'd eaten, the brothers said they would show me where the parade would start, before they went off to change. As we rounded the big top, I noted that small tents and cages again formed a midway in front of the large tent.

"What kind of sideshows have you?" I asked Frank.

"Sideshows!" he exclaimed. "Oh, no—Marvel Brothers doesn't approve of sideshows. Much too common. Gives the place a bad name."

"All those dancing girls doing the hootchy-kootchy," Eddie joined in. "Terrible, terrible. Morally corrupt."

"Dash, I'd like a few dancing girls," said Frank.

Eddie laughed. "Dash, me too. All we've got is a menagerie. Much more wholesome."

"What about games?" I asked.

"Even if the games are honest, every time someone loses, it perpetuates the idea that we're all thieves and criminals," said Eddie.

"Anyway, it's gambling—Marvel Brothers doesn't approve of gambling," said Frank.

The Marvel brothers didn't approve of much. I wondered why they went into this line of business. "So, there are no human oddities?" I asked.

"The proprietors of the Marvel Brothers Circus do not approve of people with physical differences who exhibit themselves," said Frank.

Eddie put on a pompous voice. "God's creatures should not be gawked at for their imperfections."

"That's kind of them," I answered. "I'm sure that many people with differences would prefer a regular job instead."

"Oh, that's not in the Marvel Brothers philosophy either," Eddie said.

"I hear some poor woman once tried to sell her baby to Geoffrey Marvel," said Frank. "It had webbed feet, didn't it?" he asked his brother, who shrugged. "Mr. G. Marvel had her arrested for white slavery."

"What about the baby?" I asked. I almost agreed with Mr. Marvel about the mother.

"Had it put in an asylum, I think," Frank answered, shattering any sympathy I might have had for the Marvel point of view.

"But that's for mad people," I protested.

"Well, those with deformities like that don't usually have their wits about them, do they?" said Eddie. "It was the kindest thing to do."

My heart ached to think of that poor child—as smart as any, probably—brought up as an imbecile, if someone in the madhouse didn't kill it first. I opened my mouth to contradict and then shut it again. Would it do any good to disagree? Perhaps in time, when they knew me better, I could set them straight.

I supposed that the Marvel brothers wouldn't approve of human oddities having children, either. They wouldn't approve of me. *How dare they?* I thought, and then it hit me. If I were to keep my job, I would have to be quiet about my family. That didn't sit well. I had left my family, yes, but I wasn't ashamed of them. Or was I? I had just been basking in the reflected normality of the Arabian brothers because it gave me a chance with the girls. I flushed uncomfortably.

Eddie pointed out where a crowd had formed to watch the workers run here and there between wagons, harnessing the horses, camels, and elephants for the parade. Frank waved cheerfully as the brothers headed back to their car. I joined the knot of observers and marveled at the wonderful, ornate tableau wagons, bursting with primary colors and etched in gold. Scenes from mythology and the Bible enhanced the flat panels; creatures of story grew out of the carved adornments. A few of the wagons had plate glass sides—dens, I heard someone call them. One contained the largest lion I had ever seen, another offered a nest of live serpents, according to its painted sky board. I could make out something mottled and thicker than my thigh, twined around a tree limb propped within.

Riders on every sort of mount joined the assemblage, including Frank and Eddie on their camels. They waved me over to join them. Mr. Geoffrey Marvel stalked up and ordered the procession. Another big man acted as his lieutenant and looked so much like him that I could only assume him another Marvel brother. I no longer wanted to introduce myself. I had an uncomfortable feeling that they would divine my flaws and condemn me on the spot.

The band arrived and took its place on the lead wagon, creating a jumbled cacophony as they tuned their instruments. When the trumpeters raised a fanfare, the loose ribbon of gaudy participants took on a tighter discipline, then the Grand Street Pageant of Glorious, Gorgeous Cavalcade moved off. I trotted along beside the camels, as excited as the town boys who whooped and cheered and turned cartwheels in the street. I loosened my collar. Darn this being a grown-up. I missed the baggy shirts and bare feet of childhood. Clowns ran in and out of the crowd that lined the street, pinching the boys, pretending to kiss the girls, and throwing buckets of confetti at one another. I laughed with the townies and nodded to all who caught my eye, including a few blushing local girls. If I stopped to think, however, I amounted to neither fish nor fowl, with no clear place in the parade or out. How I wished I could be on a camel beside the Arabian brothers.

I imagined myself high above the street on a leggy beast. Behind me sat a dusky beauty, her arms around my waist. I waved to the crowd, and they cheered. The girl whispered in my ear that I was wonderful and what rewards she would give me.

Then I tripped over a curb and almost fell.

I must get that phantom girl out of my head, I thought, *else I'll do myself some damage.* I grinned. I should know better than to let a fortune-teller's tale of love and foreign ladies turn my head and give me dreams, but now that dancing girl was even haunting my waking hours. Ah, well, the feelings that accompanied her were delicious and worth indulging.

In a little over an hour we were back at the circus lot, and I hurried to the Happy Times carriage to meet Mr. Rose for our first rehearsal. I felt the sweat on my brow as I stood in front of the target. I swore not to let Mr. Rose see me flinch, no matter what, but as it happened, the practice session went well. Although a few hits were a little snug for my taste, none actually touched me.

"Perhaps you could give me some tips on my technique now, sir," I said, which was a little deceitful on my part, for I really wanted to show off. But you catch more flies with honey, so they say.

The smooth practice must have mellowed Mr. Rose. "Oh, go ahead," he said.

"Wait, I'll get my knives," I said, almost bouncing like a child.

"Well, make it snappy," said Mr. Rose. "I want some luncheon."

Uncle Jack's gifts were splendid. They flew from my fingers like cupid's arrows headed straight for love, and I hit the target from much farther away than I had ever done before. I bowed to Mr. Rose with a flourish and couldn't keep a grin from my face.

"Quite good," said Mr. Rose. The words were delivered like an offhand slap and drove my smile away. "You have a rather plain style, though."

"But I got excellent distance, did I not?" I asked, dismayed to hear a quaver in my voice.

"Distance isn't what they want; they want thrills. Thrills and not kills. You can't get the accuracy you need to trace a live target from that far away."

"Perhaps I can," I answered, my dander up.

"You'd best learn how not to hit your subject at a sensible range before you try that sort of grandstanding," Mr. Rose said. "Now, find yourself a good evening suit so you can look presentable with your back to the target."

"I have one, thank you," I snapped, and I walked off before I said something I'd regret.

By the time I was waiting for my cue in the small tent near the back door of the big top, I had regained my composure. I wore my good suit and thought I made a dashing figure. Mr. Rose hadn't made an appearance yet, and I hoped fervently that he wasn't keeping company with a bottle.

Performers bustled this way and that through the open staging area, in and out from behind screens. They fiddled with ribbons and bootlaces, conferred about last-minute changes, or sat for the application of stage makeup. I thought I might be the only one apart from all this purposeful chaos, until I saw an apparition. The sweetest young lady I could imagine stood like a still and silent mirage amid all the activity. She wore an innocent pink confection—a cap-sleeved peasant blouse and short bloomers combined into one with smocking at her tiny waist. Red tights clothed her legs, and on her feet were pink ballet slippers with ribbons that tied halfway up her most attractive calves. Around her upper arms and her throat were ribbon bows to match. Her long, dark hair was secured in a knot at the nape of her neck.

Her compatriots, three men and a boy, wore yellow shorts and red waistcoats over their leotards, and fancy matching calf shields above soft leather boots. By these costumes I recognized them as the trapeze artists. Her partners bantered with one another in a guttural language I didn't recognize. They laughed, clapped one another's backs, and ignored the girl beside them, who looked to be their little sister. She gazed about her with huge, dark eyes in a solemn face, and she seemed lonely.

Ah, this is the foreign girl I'm fated to love, I thought half seriously. She didn't look the sort to be scornful and cruel, like the equestrienne, so I drew up the courage to approach her. Surely no one would mind with her brothers standing right there, and she looked like she needed a friend.

"Hello, my name's Abel Dandy," I prepared to say. "I'm new to the show. Would you take pity on a stranger and offer me conversation?"

Her eyes grew even larger as I walked up, and her lovely lips parted in surprise. I gulped down the tremor that her lips invoked in me, and squeaked, "Hello," like a fool.

"Marika?" One of those brothers turned our way. He glared at me and nudged the man next to him.

"Are you annoying my sister?" asked the first.

"No, sir, truly," I answered.

"How dare you," said another brother, and moved toward me. I stepped back involuntarily. "Sorry, sir. I was being friendly."

"We decide who is friendly to our sister," said the first brother.

"Do we have to teach you manners?" asked a third.

"No, sir." I backed away another step. Marika gave me a little, hesitant smile and glanced anxiously at her brothers in case they had seen. Well, all the girls weren't stuck up, then, I decided, but how did one talk to them? I beat a retreat right into Mr. Rose.

Mr. Rose bent double with laughter and slapped his thigh. "Leave the virgins alone, young Dandy," he wheezed. "Find yourself a married lady with a busy husband."

Catching me in an uncomfortable predicament put Mr. Rose in a good mood. He acted quite chummy with me before we went on to perform, and I was relieved to note he didn't smell of whiskey. "Always enter the ring with your right foot," he told me. "It's good luck." He managed to put a reasonable distance between his knives and me during the act, and after the show he invited me along to sup with him. I was glad of the company, even though I didn't much like him. Supper proved quite bearable, except we had to listen to the elephant trainer complain endlessly that someone had taken one of his beasts out for a walk again without his permission and given all of the elephants treats. More than once Mr. Rose rolled his eyes.

I fell asleep that night to thoughts of the pretty trapeze artist, but the dancing girl strode up to me with a face like a petulant flower and placed her hands on her hips.

"Stay away from that girl," she demanded. "You are mine."

THE SHOW TRAVELED UP THROUGH Cumberland, into Pennsylvania, and on through part of West Virginia into Ohio. We didn't travel the hundred miles a night we could have, but took shorter hops to reach as many towns as we could play in that richly populated area. We went through the midsize towns, the ones that wouldn't get the biggest shows—like Ringling Brothers, and Forepaugh-Sells, although the backdoor talk said Marvel Brothers planned to carve a larger niche for themselves, with Barnum and Bailey out of the country for so long on their extended world tour. The advance crews placed ads in the paper, slapped bright, bold posters on fences and walls, and swapped tickets for space in merchants' shop windows. The neighboring towns were papered also, and the barn sides in between, until everyone in the surrounding communities and farms knew where to come for a day of excitement and amusement.

I continued to serve as Mr. Rose's target; that was the only way I could enter the ring. Never again did he condescend to watch me throw, and not once did he offer to coach me. How was I going to further my career, I wondered, if I wasn't helped with my craft? Instead I found the time to practice alone.

If I couldn't have a mentor, at least I could make friends, I decided. Friends in the business could do me good in the future. However, while the fellows in the show were polite and helpful, they already had their pals. When we spent the Fourth of July— my first holiday away from home—in Muncie, Indiana, the circus was packed. After the show the Marvels put on a fireworks party, but not one of the boys thought to ask me along for a beer.

I always kept an eye out for Marika, the trapeze girl. I was sure she'd be friendly if I could catch her away from her brothers, but this only seemed to happen when I was in conversation with Eddie and Frank, and I couldn't sneak away to talk to her.

"I think she's smiling at me," I confided one day.

"Oh, I don't think so," said Frank. "She just has a cheery nature."

"And very large brothers," added Eddie.

"Not thinking of girls already are you, young Abel?" asked Frank.

The Arabian brothers must have thought me a child, and maybe I was. The most success I'd had with women was in my dreams.

Someone must have had regard for me, however, because sometimes I came back from breakfast to find my bed made, or I'd come home at night to discover a piece of fruit on my pillow.

This made me feel all-overish because it had to be one of the boys. I hoped that it constituted a sign of friendship and not an intimate interest, because I didn't want to be put in the awkward position of disappointing a fellow traveler. I searched the faces around me but found none that beamed on me with particular fellowship.

The closest I felt to belonging was during those entertainments before bed.

"What about you, Abel?" said one of the junior acrobats one night. "You say you're from the theater. You must have a song or two to share."

A chorus of agreement followed, and I must admit I liked the attention. I rolled from my upper berth, where I found it impossible to sit up and get a deep breath, and took a seat offered me on a lower bunk. The song I had heard on my first night in the dormitory car had put me in mind of another song about a circus queen, one of Jolly Dolly's favorites.

"'She kept her secret well, oh yes, her hideous secret well,'" I began in my passable tenor, and fellows nudged one another and exchanged winks.

"We were wedded fast, I knew naught of her past;
for how was I to tell?
I married her, guileless lamb I was, I'd have died for
her sweet sake.
How could I have known that my Angeline had been
a 'human snake'?"

Some fellows howled with laughter, which I found a little premature, since the funny part came later in the song, but I continued anyway.

66

"We'd only been wed a week or two, when I found
her quite a wreck,
Her limbs were tied in a true lover's knot at the back
of her swanlike neck.
No curse there sprang to my pallid lips, nor did I
reproach her then;
I calmly untied my lovely bride and straightened
her out again."

I thought the lewd catcalls that the clowns made were uncalled for, but I understood their point. One of the young acrobats blushed.

"My Angeline! My Angeline! Oh why didst disturb
my mind serene?
My well beloved circus queen!
My human snake! My Angeline!"

It didn't take my audience long to catch on to the refrain, and all but a couple of the older fellows joined in heartily, then hushed for the verse.

"At night I'd wake at midnight's hour with a creepy,
crawly feeling,
And there she would be in her white robe de nuit
a walking on the ceiling.
She said that she was the 'human fly' and she lifted me
from beneath,
By a section slight of my garb of night, which she held
in her pearly teeth."

This last line, which at home elicited sympathetic chuckles, here provoked rude laughter, but it pleased me that the fellows liked the song.

"Oh, for the sweet sake of the 'human snake' I'd have
stood this conduct shady,
But she skipped at last with a gentleman friend who
had starred as the bearded lady.
But oh, at night when my slumber's light, regret
cometh o'er me stealing.
Oh, where are those limbs that tied four-in-hand
scarf? How I miss those steps on the ceiling."

I ended to enthusiastic applause.

"Hwaurr! I know what I'd do with a human snake," said one of the clowns, to gales of laughter. "Introduce her to another snake."

"Ugh! I'd as soon touch a woman like that as touch a . . . well, a . . . I don't know, something foul," said a young acrobat.

"I think she's a contortionist," I said gently. "Not a real snake woman." I was sorry I had upset the lad.

"That's still not a lady, is it?" he said. "Taking on those . . . those positions."

I would have explained that many folk wouldn't consider the women who worked in the circus ladies either, even though, by all evidence, they were pure young women, but salacious laughter drowned me out, and suggestions of which positions a snake woman could take.

"I don't think you're a good influence on these gentlemen, Abel Dandy," proclaimed the senior acrobat, who hadn't joined the singing. "You've aroused unhealthy thoughts. Nothing good can come of such thoughts. They destroy a man's health. They sap his strength."

"I'd like my strength sapped," groaned the vulgar clown. "Even a freak would do me."

"If the roustabouts don't beat it to death first," said someone else.

My jaw dropped at their words.

"Get to bed, the lot of you," the acrobat said, "or I'll report you to Geoffrey Marvel." That shut everyone up. "If this happens again, I will. The Marvel brothers don't employ those with unclean habits, and they don't tolerate those who advocate unnatural acts." Those last words were aimed straight at me, and they stung. "You, sir"—he pointed at the vulgar clown—"what would your mother think of your debased suggestion?"

The young men slid embarrassed glances at one another, and the clown lowered his eyes.

We all climbed into our bunks. Some of the fellows gave me dirty looks. "Freak lover," the clown hissed.

I had simply wanted to sing a funny song, and now they considered me a scoundrel. I hadn't thought the song rude, and what was wrong with a little amorous adventure, anyway? I tossed and turned. Were the dreams I'd had recently merely unhealthy thoughts? Did that make me a bad person? I hated the smell of close-packed, sweaty boys and the harsh sheets. I missed my own bed and my friends. I wanted to quit; I couldn't, though. I would look a fool if I ran home with my tail between my legs. When I returned home, it should be with money in my pocket and a career well on the way. I clutched the ring at my neck. *Be my good-luck charm,* I begged.

❋

I stood in a garden of exotic blooms and clambering vines. The air hummed, and in the distance tiny cymbals chinged. A rustle behind me sent shivers down my back, and I caught the scent of flowers and spices I couldn't name. I was drenched with the awareness of the one I knew and didn't know. Every mote of me recognized that presence and cried out to it.

I turned to see a shadowy figure just beyond the moon-light—a curvaceous form with flowing hair. "Come to me," whispered a voice that sounded as cracked as old parchment yet hot as the desert sun, and an unbearable arrow of pleasure and pain shot through me from groin to heart.

I awoke in the night, rigid with desire, and too afraid to relieve myself lest someone hear.

The nighttime stories and songs didn't stop, but I was never asked to participate again, and I didn't try. Perhaps they were right about me. Perhaps I was dissolute and I hadn't known it. *Who cares?* I decided. I didn't want to give up those dreams. In fact, I spent considerable time imagining the end of the last one. *I am reaping my reward from years of diligent novel reading,* I told myself.

The senior acrobat redirected the young men's taste for the sensational from womanly charms to the safer thrills of ghost stories and tales of train wrecks and, best of all, circus-train wrecks that resulted in haunted tracks. Everyone had a "friend of a friend told me" story on that topic. If you believed them all, there wasn't a stretch of rail from New York to California that didn't have phantom elephants trumpeting late at night.

One night the tales featured "wereanimals"—men possessed by the souls of circus beasts. I shivered as I imagined the panther man with icy eyes stalking the fellow who had caused his family's death by fire.

"I reckon that's what that escaped monkey is," said a juggler. "No one's seen it right good. It's a demon monkey."

At that moment the train chose to shudder and grind to a halt.

A split second of pregnant fear froze us, and then one of the clowns laughed—the one I always thought of as the vulgar clown since the night of my controversial song. "Look at Abel's face." He had never lost a chance to taunt me since that night.

I joined in with the others' laughter, refusing to let them see me embarrassed, but I was irked. They'd all been scared for a moment, why should I be singled out?

"Must be something on the tracks," said an acrobat.

"Probably a cow," said another.

Time passed and the train stayed put.

"Someone go look," said the senior acrobat, to a chorus of groans.

Everyone glanced at one another and out to the pitch-dark night between towns. Something mysterious blocked the tracks, a thing perhaps a mortal should not see. Had a disaster befallen the engine crew? Was the cabin empty even now and blood smeared down the tracks?

"Abel can go," said the vulgar clown.

"What?" I protested.

There was no use complaining. Others took up the call, and they dragged me from my bunk. "Wait!" I cried, and struggled into my pants before they pushed me out in only my nightshirt.

The fellows hustled me to the door. "Run up the tracks and see what's up," called the juggler who had talked of weremonkeys, and he threw my boots after me.

"But what if the train starts?" I asked as the door slammed.

There I was, out in the middle of cricket-chirping nowhere, with nothing but the full moon to guide my way, and the occasional lit window down the length of the train. A rattle in the undergrowth made my heart lurch—a beast coming? No, just a breeze. Did I see someone on the roof? *Don't be silly,* I told myself as I pulled on my boots.

From where I stood, I could find no reason for our stop. No one else had come out. They were sensibly tucked up in bed. I took a deep breath and walked down toward the engine. I hoped the boys would appreciate me after this.

A whistle split the night and I sucked in a breath. The engine chugged, chugged again, and again. Metal squealed and wheels ground. I ran for a door, jumped, and missed the handle. The train moved a little faster. I aimed for the next door. This time I achieved a toehold and grabbed the handle, but it wouldn't turn. My foot slipped. I dropped to the ground before my arm tore from its socket.

The train picked up more speed. I ran back toward my own door. There were rungs below the threshold. The fellows would let me in. Somehow the door passed me quicker than I expected. *Oh, help.*

That's when I saw the open cargo door of the elephant house approaching fast. I had to jump in or be stranded.

I flung myself through the gaping, dark hole. The momentum of the train skidded me sideways on my belly across boards and straw. I hit the doorjamb. It knocked the wind from me. My legs slid out of the door again. I grabbed for a hold and couldn't find one. I'd be out of the door and under the wheels in a trice.

Then a hairy arm grabbed me, and I didn't know which fate was worse.

"Hold on, Abel," cried a familiar voice.

APOLLO!" **I GASPED, AND CLUTCHED** the offered arm. "Lord in heaven!"

The wiry dog boy, surprisingly strong, dragged me back into the car.

I scrambled to a sitting position in the straw, my breath harsh in my throat, and looked around me nervously. When I had ascertained that the elephants were in stalls and I was not in imminent danger of being stepped on, I gave in to outrage. "What in Sam Hill are you doing here?"

"Someone woke me up," Apollo said. He squatted on his heels in canvas pants and a cotton shirt that hadn't seen wash day in a month of Sundays. His golden pelt was knotted and snarled.

"I meant here in the circus," I said, making no sense of his answer.

"I saw you leave," he said. "I was sneaking up with a note from Phoebe, and there you were, sneaking too, with a suitcase! A suitcase, Abel! You were running away—without me! I had to follow."

I had really heard someone in the corridor behind me after all.

"I kept quiet because you'd have sent me back, wouldn't you? I heard you talking to that dotty Miss Dibble in the kitchen, so I went out the side door and waited for you."

"Why on earth would you do that? You didn't know where I was going."

"Why should you get all the fun?" he answered. He knit his furry brow. "Abel, how could you leave me behind with *him*?"

"Where's this note from Phoebe?" I asked gruffly. It wasn't my fault that his father beat him.

He rummaged inside his shirt and shoved a fist at me. I retrieved a crumpled, sticky envelope from his grasp. It was too dark to read, so I put the letter in my hip pocket for the morning.

"You know, Phoebe won't be happy you're making eyes at that trapeze girl," Apollo said.

"But you're happy to be here meddling in my business," I complained.

"Yes, I'm glad I came," said Apollo, sticking out his chest. "I wouldn't have met Rosie if I hadn't. Isn't she grand?" He waved a hairy arm toward the nearest stall, where an interested eye surrounded by gray wrinkles peered out from between the slats. My eyebrows shot up. "You're the one who takes the elephants for walks?"

"Aren't they lovely?" Apollo said, and sighed.

"How could you not get caught?" I asked.

"Oh, it's surprising what you can do when everyone is busy," he said.

I thought of asylums and beatings, and that made me so scared I yelled, "Do you know what they'll do if they catch you?" The elephant snorted.

"I don't want to be sent home," wailed Apollo. He didn't understand. "It's wonderful here! I love the animals—they're so friendly! I had no idea."

I tried to calm down. "How have you fed yourself?"

Apollo's eyes lit up with excitement. "Oh, that's easy. There's hampers of fruit and vegetables all over the place—for the animals—and I raid the cookhouse when no one's looking."

"You're the escaped monkey!" I didn't know whether to scold him or laugh.

Apollo frowned. "I am not a monkey!"

I didn't argue the point. "Have you been making my bed and leaving me fruit?"

He nodded and grinned. "I wanted to look after you."

I groaned. "What am I to do with you?"

"You can't let them send me home," Apollo insisted. "You need me. What if I hadn't been here to grab you?"

We settled down in the pungent hay beside the food bin at the far end of the car. "There's supposed to be men here," Apollo said, "but they socialize a lot. They must be jolly sorts. They always talk about smiling with their friends."

I hadn't the heart to tell him that *smile* was another word for *drink*.

Apollo produced a torn and stained rag of a blanket from behind the bin and offered it to me, but I eyed the unknown hairs on it and shook my head. "Too warm," I said.

What am I to do? I wondered as I fidgeted in the prickly straw. I couldn't take him home; how would I explain my absence to the Marvels? I'd lose my job, and why should I have to give up my quest for Lady Adventure?

Apollo had to leave this place—who could tell what might happen if he was discovered?—but if I wired the colonel, he would probably make me come home too. Could I put Apollo on a train and hope he stayed on it until he got home? Could I even afford the fare? I would be furious if I had to take him back myself. If I took Apollo back, could I deposit him at the door and leave again without being caught? Damn the dog boy's father. If he weren't such a scoundrel, Apollo would have stayed at home and I wouldn't have this problem.

"How am I supposed to keep you hidden?" I grumbled. "They don't take kindly to deadheads around here." How could I tell him they would consider him less than human? Despite his father's temper, he had been brought up to believe himself one of God's children, with a rightful place in the world. I prayed that I could get him away from here before he learned anything different.

Apollo laughed. "I've done a good job of it this far, haven't I? There's lots of places to hide, like the storage boxes under some of the cars. They call them *possum bellies*. Isn't that a caution? And there's a crawl space over the ceiling of this very car, with a trapdoor I use to get on the roof. It's fun to ride up there."

I sat up. "The train roof! Are you plumb crazy?" I remembered the hint of a face I'd seen at my window that first night. I had thought it was a dream.

Apollo inflated with outrage. "I practiced with the acrobats back home; I've got great balance. Maybe that will be my act."

"Your act?" What was he blithering about?

Enthusiasm replaced his indignation. "Yes. I've been staying out of sight until I figure out what my act is. As soon as I show them all how clever I am, they're bound to let me stay."

"You shouldn't have followed me," I said. "You really shouldn't have."

Apollo sounded surprised. "Why not, Abel? You're my friend. I love you."

How could I argue after that?

The fellows were mighty surprised to see me when I came through the door that morning.

"We thought we'd lost you," said one of the acrobats, shamefaced.

"Oh, I knew he was all right," said the vulgar clown, although I didn't see how he could be so sure.

I edited the truth and told them I had spent the night with the elephants.

"Whew! And you smell like you did," said one of the lads.

Right after I freshened up, I followed the tracks to the train depot and enquired what the train fare to Maryland was. I was shocked. One ticket was a week's salary, and I hadn't even had my first pay envelope yet. If I took Apollo home, we would have to wait twice as long for me to have the fare for both of us. That left more time for Apollo to be discovered. *I'll have to think about this some more,* I decided.

Brightly colored posters covered every available flat surface I passed on my walk back. Sometimes several layers were stacked up—posters of past shows covered over, or maybe those of rival shows still on their way. I knew that the advance men made a war of this; each show tried to obliterate all evidence of the competition. Someone had been sloppy, however. On a wooden fence the edge of a black-and-white notice still peered over the top of a luminous lithograph. DR. MINK'S TRAVELING MONSTER MENAGERIE, the gothic letters proclaimed. All the way up the path to the circus I wondered what those monsters might be. I took a professional interest in such things, and I liked animals, even those that nature had chosen to play tricks on. We had a dear five-legged goat at Faeryland who behaved sweetly with children. I hoped I might have the opportunity to see Dr. Mink's show.

As I passed the office, I noted with curiosity a well-dressed gentleman of color hustled out the door by Mr. Geoffrey Marvel himself.

"We don't hire freaks," said the circus owner. He slammed the door.

The man scrambled backward down the steps and almost fell. He lost his hat in the process. I hurried to pick it up. Did the Marvel brothers consider Negroes freaks? I was not so naive as to be blind to the common scorn heaped upon the Negro race, but this didn't usually go as far as to term them sports of nature. We had people of color on our staff at home and in the troupe, and I had yet to remark upon any particular handicap. When there were those among us who were set off from the common man in such exceptional ways, skin color seemed the least of considerations.

"Your hat, sir," I said, and handed him his bowler. He appeared to be no older than my uncle Jack, if that. I smiled and met his eyes, for I most honestly hoped that he wouldn't judge all show folk based on Mr. G. Marvel.

He brushed his hat off with the sleeve of his coat and placed it on his head. "My thanks," he said. "That is most gracious of you." He returned my smile, but it didn't wipe the sadness from his eyes.

He sounds like an educated man, I thought with surprise as I watched him go. While intelligence was common to his race, the opportunity for education was not. I wondered what act he had to offer.

I peeked into the elephant car on my way to change for the performance but found two men in blue jeans and whiskers there cleaning out the stalls. I hoped Apollo would stay out of sight until I could get him out of this predicament.

When I took off my trousers, paper crinkled in my pocket, and I remembered the letter from Phoebe. I hesitated. Did I care to read words that berated me for my cruelty? Curiosity got the better of me, however, and I opened the dirty, smudged envelope.

Dear Abel, I read, *I wanted my father to present you with this news, as it seemed appropriate and polite, given your interest in me, but perhaps someone has already alerted you to my situation, because your treatment of me of late has been so cold.*

News? Situation? Fear clutched my chest. I had only kissed her. I was prepared to swear to that. Maybe my fingers had strayed once or twice, but she had nipped that in the bud.

I read on breathlessly:

I admit, then, the news is true. My father has affianced me to Mr. Thomas Robinson, known in the business as the Monkey Man of Baltimore. If only you had spoken for me, but I am afraid that our love is not to be and all tenderness between us must cease. My father considers this a most promising personal and business engagement. Mr. Robinson will join our act, and if there is any issue of our union (I blush), the chances are the family business will continue into the next generation. I beg your forgiveness. . . .

"Well, damn you and your furry little children," I snapped as I crumpled the letter. I had thought that I was the apple of her eye, and now she was consorting with monkey men. There I was, running off into the night, and she had no designs on me after all. It stung.

All through the act I either stewed about Phoebe or chewed at my problem with Apollo. I didn't notice if Mr. Rose came close to sticking me or not. Worn out with thinking, I stayed by the back door after my turn to watch the rest of the show and take my mind off my cares.

A spiral track had been raised in the center ring while Mr. Rose and I performed in the front-end ring and the jugglers entertained at the back. Now a cart drawn by Shetland ponies, driven by a pretty girl in riding skirts, brought in a large, colorful wooden ball. Two of the biggest clowns lifted the heavy sphere and laid it at the foot of the track. The crowd hushed in expectation, and people craned their heads looking for the performers, but none arrived. Instead, as if by magic, the ball moved, and the audience inhaled audibly.

The ball edged up the track. I knew the man inside was on his hands and knees and must move the center of gravity forward but not side-to-side, else he would lose control. This acrobat was clumsy. The ball wobbled ferociously at times; once it even rolled backward, and I didn't think it would stop. I had never seen the act performed so awkwardly.

The bicyclist next to me mumbled an oath. "LaPierre had one too many glasses of wine with dinner tonight," he said to no one in particular.

That's when a horrible idea hit me. I could barely draw breath as the ball made its hesitant ascent around the track. Perhaps they wouldn't guess. Perhaps he'd roll it up and down again safely. Perhaps he wouldn't emerge at the end to take his bow. But Apollo wanted to impress the Marvels. He would take his bow, and all tarnation would break loose.

All tarnation didn't wait until Apollo's bow, however; it came in the form of Monsieur LaPierre through the back-door flaps, his leotard legs smeared with mud. He shook his fists in the air and babbled in French. The elephant trainer followed close behind him.

LaPierre skidded to a halt when he saw the ball near the apex of the ramp, and his arms fell to his sides. Those around him backed away, for he smelled to blue blazes.

"Who ees in there?" he demanded in a voice on the edge of hysteria.

Mr. G. Marvel stalked up. "Keep your voice down," he growled. "I'm glad to know it isn't you I am about to kill. How could you allow this?" His aristocratic nostrils pinched in disgust, although he made no comment on the smell.

"I was trapped," Monsieur LaPierre exclaimed. "There was an elephant in front of the outhouse door. I tried to climb over the transom, but I slipped. . . ." Here he lapsed into colorful French and gestured wildly once more, and I tried not to look at the stains on his legs.

"Rosie wandered off," said the confused elephant trainer. "She usually stands in line with the others, quiet as you please. She don't need no watching."

The crowd burst into applause. The ball had reached the platform. It trembled there like an egg before it hatched. *Pop!* Two hairy arms emerged from holes in the sides and waved flags.

The audience, who knew no better, cheered.

"Haw! Haw! A monkey can do your act, Frenchie," mocked the vulgar clown.

"Get it. Get it," Monsieur LaPierre demanded.

Mr. Marvel gestured a boy over and sent him outside with a

message. Within seconds roustabouts closed in toward the ring. My heart raced with fear. How could I bear to see Apollo beaten? I would have to run to his aid. I would die right there beside him—and I didn't want to die.

The ball inched down the ramp, slowly, slowly, but then something went wrong. The ball lurched forward. Apollo must have turned head over heels inside. He lost his balance. The ball careened around the curve. It flew off the track. The men ran forward, but the ball hurtled over their heads. The audience screamed; some fled their seats.

The ball crashed into a tent pole and shattered. Apollo splayed upon the ground. He sat up, rubbing his head and blinking. The first thing he must have seen was a wall of thugs headed his way.

"Run!" I cried. I prayed that he wasn't hurt.

He staggered to his feet, shimmied up the tent pole, grabbed a rope, and swung over their heads to land in the front ring, then raced for the exit.

"Send in the clowns! Send in the clowns!" screamed Mr. Marvel above the panic. His face bloomed purple with rage as he followed his bullies.

I chased after Apollo, the roustabouts, and the ringmaster and heard a shriek from outside.

I arrived just in time to see Marika pointing at a nearby painted wagon. "It was a giant monkey. It went under there." She flung herself into the arms of one of her brothers.

A burly roustabout dived under the wagon. The others surrounded it so there was no escape; behind them some of the audience who had followed us outside gaped and gawked.

"The little bastard bit me," roared an uncouth voice from under the wagon, and a lady near me gasped. The roustabout emerged from between the crimson wagon wheels. He dragged a thrashing, crying Apollo by his shirt collar. Apollo's nose was bloody.

"Let him go!" I pushed through the onlookers, but before I reached Apollo, rough hands clutched my arms.

"Abel, Abel," my little friend called. "He hit me!"

"What is it?" a man exclaimed.

"It's a freak," cried someone else. "A dirty freak!"

A woman squealed.

"He's not a freak," I yelled. "He's a boy." I struggled to free myself and ran to defend my friend.

"Get them to my carriage," ordered Geoffrey Marvel in a voice as cold as doom.

FOR THE FIRST TIME I SAW ALL THREE Marvel brothers together. The two older ones were strapping, big fellows with large mustaches, interchangeable; the fellow from the office was also big but probably a decade younger than the other two. They towered over Apollo and me like outraged Olympic gods in suits. A roustabout guarded the door of Mr. Geoffrey Marvel's magnificent Wagner Palace car; another two were posted outside.

"What are we to think of this, Jacob?" asked Mr. G. Marvel.

"I do not know, Geoffrey, I do not know at all," answered Mr. J. Marvel.

Mr. G. Marvel scowled at me. "What is the meaning of these shenanigans? Have you been harboring this creature?" he demanded.

"He's not a creature!" I cried.

"He didn't know I was here," said Apollo simultaneously.

"Quiet!" roared the equestrian director. He came much too close to me for comfort and stuck his face in mine. "We hired one person, sir, not two, did we not?"

I tottered back and didn't hazard an answer.

The equestrian director rose to his full height once more. "Yet you bring along this stowaway, this deadhead, to steal our hospitality."

"He didn't know," said Apollo. "I followed him from home. He just found out yesterday, and he was very angry with me."

"Why did you not inform us when you discovered him?" Mr. G. Marvel asked.

"I don't know, sir," I mumbled. What was I to say—that I didn't trust them?

"Meanwhile, he steals our food," said J. Marvel.

"And frightens our ladies," said young Mr. A. Marvel.

"Imprisons a respected performer and ruins his act," said Mr. G. Marvel.

"Endangers the audience," added the middle brother.

"Destroys property," said the youngest.

"What kind of home do you come from where beings such as this are raised?" asked Mr. G. Marvel.

"A very fine home indeed," I proclaimed, drawing myself up.

"A place that instills no moral character," said the equestrian director, ignoring me. "A place that teaches stealing and lying."

"What are we to do with them?" asked J. Marvel. "Call the law?"

"But this boy needs help," said the youngest brother, gesturing at Apollo. "How can a degenerate creature be held responsible for his actions? He hasn't the wits or moral sensibilities of normal men. He needs guidance and care."

The noises that Apollo made at that statement didn't do much to correct anyone's assessment of his wits. "Be quiet," I whispered, and put my arm around him. Apollo shut his mouth, but his face remained crumpled and sulky.

"I doubt if Mr. Rose will have you back," said Mr. G. Marvel to me. "There's no room for plug-uglies and street Arabs around here, but you owe us money for the magic ball and stolen food and must work it off."

"The advance men could use another poster boy," said A. Marvel. "We could send him on the express from the next stop to join them in Illinois."

"Excellent," said Mr. G. Marvel. "He can work off his debt with them."

I couldn't believe it. They bartered my future away as if I were an indentured servant of days gone by, and it was likely I wouldn't see a cent of what I had already earned. "We'll see about that," I said.

"It's that or the sheriff," answered Mr. G. Marvel.

That shut me up. I couldn't reason with these people. When they were through with us, I would gather as many of my belongings as I could and hightail it with Apollo. I had no money to take him home, so he would just have to come with me after all. We'd search for Lady Adventure together.

I didn't expect what happened next.

"Lock that unfortunate in the caboose with a bucket and a keg of water," said Mr. G. Marvel. "I understand there is a good asylum in the town after next. Just the place for an unruly imbecile."

"No, send him back to his family," I cried as the thug

who guarded the door yanked Apollo from my grasp.

"His family is obviously not doing their duty, else he would not be here," said the equestrian director. "They have abdicated responsibility."

Heaven knows, I didn't stand a chance, but I swung at the man who seized Apollo—and landed on my back, with stars dancing around my head. I wasn't sure who had hit me.

When I pulled myself to my feet, Apollo was gone.

"Make sure you're on board this evening," said Mr. G. Marvel. "If you want us to keep you apprised of the whereabouts of your companion, that is."

I took my leave of them without a word because I could think of nothing civil to say. I would have to set Apollo free, or what could I tell his dear mama? How could I ever face his sister again? What would my parents think of me? Was there no one here who would take my side?

I sought out the Arabian brothers. Surely they would help me. This wasn't some stranger baby with webbed feet, but someone a friend cared for. They were fine young men; they wouldn't tolerate injustice.

But I had thought too highly of them.

"Sorry, old fellow," said Frank, his tone distant despite the friendly words. "Nothing we can do. Can't rile the boss, you know."

"I suggest you find more-suitable friends," Eddie said, and put an arm on his brother's shoulder to steer him away. "That lad has lost you an excellent position."

"He's a better friend than you'll ever be," I called at their backs as they walked away. My outburst mortified me.

I retreated to my quarters and changed to my older suit of clothing. I packed my knives and my good clothes in my suitcase.

I would never use them with this circus now. I had no act and no friends. I was a pariah. There was no place for me here. With no reason to show up for the evening show, I walked to the end of the train and inspected the caboose.

The door was sealed up tight with a padlock. "Are you all right?" I whispered through a crack in the door.

"Abel? Is that you?" came Apollo's muffled voice.

"Of course it is," I answered. "They haven't hurt you, have they?"

"I'm hungry," he said a little louder, and I imagined him pressed up against the door. His breathing sounded loud and stuffy, and I knew he'd been crying.

"I'll ask them to send you something to eat," I promised. I hoped someone would.

"They won't really put me in a madhouse, will they?" he asked. His voice trembled.

My heart sank. "Of course not," I said. I would do anything to stop that.

A solid roustabout with a shock of ginger hair came around the back of the train. "Hey, you!" he growled, and I left in a hurry—but not before I saw he carried a covered dish. At least my friend wouldn't starve while I planned a way to rescue him.

As I walked back to my quarters, one of the equestrian director's messenger boys intercepted me.

"I've looked for you everywhere," he grumbled. "You're to report to the back door of the big top." To my dismay, he insisted on escorting me there.

That's when I found out my servitude had already started—in the menagerie and around the big top back door with a pan and broom, cleaning up animal dung and urine-soaked sawdust. *I'm doing this for Apollo,* I told myself as I forked pungent elephant droppings into a wheelbarrow, *else I'd shove one of these nuggets up* . . .

Marika walked by and cleared her throat. She peeked at me, deliberately dropped a piece of paper, and moved on. I swept it to me with my broom before anyone noticed.

I am sorry, her note said. *You friend was a surprise for me he frightened me. When he was drag from the wagn I saw yr friend was only little boy. If I can help I surely will. Yrs truly, M.*

Despite all my troubles, I smiled. There was nothing she could do to help, but I didn't feel quite so alone anymore.

I made plans while I swept. I'd head back to the caboose after the show. Perhaps I could waylay the man who would bring Apollo supper. When he opened the door, I'd hit him over the head. The blow might not knock him out, but it might slow him down long enough for Apollo to run by, then we'd be off.

My plans were ruined by my fellows from the dormitory car. They were ordered to escort me to our carriage. They took their duties seriously and were not above a little shoving. Their eyes were bright, and they wore fierce grins, which made me think of the menacing high spirits of a wolf pack.

As the train pulled out for the next town, the younger fellows surrounded me.

"Are you a lunatic?"

"Where did you hide that monkey boy?"

"Can it talk?"

The taunting continued as the train left town.

"What's the matter, freakmonger? Ashamed to talk to your betters?" said the vulgar clown, glad of another opportunity to pay me back for the night he was dressed down in front of the others by the senior acrobat.

"Maybe he's a freak too," said an acrobat.

They gathered around my bunk, and I steeled myself for a fight.

"Maybe we should strip him and see," said one of the boys.

The vulgar clown grabbed me by my shirtfront and pulled. The ring I hid was bunched amid the cloth in his fist, and the chain bit into my neck. Another kid took my leg. They had me halfway off the bunk.

"I'd rather not see," cried the youngest acrobat—the one who had been upset by my song.

The others hooted and cackled.

"He's not good enough to be in here with us," said the vulgar clown, who almost choked me with his grip. The chain around my neck flared red hot, and I yelped. The vulgar clown's eyes glazed over, and he jerked like a faulty clockwork mouse. I feared he was having a fit or going crazy, and I cringed from him. "Let's red light him," the clown yelled, then let go of me and looked surprised at his words.

"Yeah! Red light him. Like they do to uppity roustabouts," cried someone.

"Red light, red light," others took up the call.

More hands landed on me, while I struggled and protested my unknown fate between gasps and coughs. The senior acrobat, the one supposedly in charge, leaned against a bunk at the end of the car with an evil grin on his face.

They dragged me fighting down the carriage. I banged my knee against a bunk, hit my head on an oil lamp.

"Mr. Marvel wants me whole enough to work," I cried, and managed to get the heel of my hand under a fellow's chin and push.

"He'll thank us in the morning," the fellow countered, and smacked me in the face.

I found myself at the carriage door. One of the jugglers

pushed it open. The night skimmed by in a gray blur of bushes and trees. Horror consumed me as I realized what they were about to do.

"No!" I screamed as hands let go and someone kicked me in the back, sending me flying into the night.

For a moment I thought I would never land, but gravity won. I skidded through gravel, which peppered my palms with grit and stung like acid, then crashed into a bush.

Something large hurtled by me, almost hitting me in the head.

The red lights disappeared down the track, and I understood what those scoundrels had meant.

And with those red lights went Apollo. How would I ever catch up?

AS I SCRAMBLED OUT OF THE BUSHES, groaning, my foot thudded into an object that gave under the blow. I felt about with my stinging hands and discovered smooth, worn leather. In the dim moonlight I made out what appeared to be my suitcase. I sighed with relief. I had something to call my own, so I would not appear a beggar. I didn't know if one of my former companions had taken pity on me or just wanted to be rid of anything to do with me. I was destitute except for a little pocket change, but at least I would have an extra suit of clothes and my knives to earn my keep.

I was almost sure I was somewhere in Indiana. Should I turn back or continue? I had no idea how far the next town was ahead or the last behind, and whichever way I chose, I would have to earn my fare before I could board a train again. I needed a good-luck charm now more than ever. I clutched the ring I wore and then winced. My neck was abraded from the way that clown had twisted the chain. I snorted. Some good-luck charm. I glanced behind me. When I thought of going back, my heart turned to lead, but when I looked ahead, despite my sorry plight, my heart leaped. I had wanted adventure, and there it was. Apollo was traveling that way on a fast track to disaster, and I had no time to waste if I must rescue him.

I limped through the rock debris along the side of the tracks and listened for a whistle that would warn me to back away from the sucking airstream that could sweep me under the wheels of a train. The damp odors of summer night were made all the more incomprehensible by the intermingled smell of cinders left by the trains. My head throbbed where it had hit the oil lamp, and my back ached where I'd been kicked. The moon set, and I stumbled repeatedly in the dark. To guide myself, I felt with my foot for the wooden cross slats that supported the rails, stubbing my toes often. My left hip throbbed from my fall, my right knee hurt from its collision with a bunk, and the handle of my bag chafed the scrapes on my hands. *So, this is misery,* I thought. I wondered if the sun would ever rise again, and if it did, if I would ever see a town, or whether there would be nothing ahead all the sweltering day but steel rails, undergrowth, and the occasional cast-off trash in the rubble of the embankment. That was if the tracks didn't cross a bridge before daylight and I fell to my death from a trestle.

Self-pity will get you nowhere, I chided. Apollo was in much more serious peril than I. Where was this vaunted asylum in which the Marvel brothers wished to deposit my friend—in the next town ahead or farther on? Could I find Apollo before he was locked away? If I had money, I could send the name of this asylum in a wire to Colonel Kingston and get on with *my* adventure, but here I was, looking after the dog boy again.

Then I wasn't alone. I sensed a presence to my right, even though I heard no footsteps, even though no one took a breath. Somehow I felt the weight, the volume, the aura, of another human beside me displacing the air. I dared not look. I quickened my speed, and the person beside me quickened too. Did a robber pace me? He would be disappointed. I hoped he wasn't a murderer as well as a thief. I shuffled and bumbled as fast as I dared, my breath shallow. The stranger stayed with me.

"I apologize," a woman's voice said. "Do not run from me."

It was the shadow woman from the field. Surely not? Had I hit my head in the fall from the train? Was I addled? I decided to ignore the voice.

"I did not want to throw you from the carriage, but you were traveling too far."

That settled it. No doubt, in reality I was curled up asleep by the tracks. I stopped and faced the shadow beside me. A faint glow outlined the dark shape of a woman. "You were not on the train, dream," I said. "A gang of plug-uglies threw me off the train."

"I'm afraid I did suggest it," she said, and hung her head.

"That was a man."

"Who held your ring in his fist. I can touch others via the ring. His mind was weak with fear, and I was able to speak through him."

My hand rose automatically to the ring. I remembered the glazed eyes of the clown and shivered, then snatched my hand away. I set off walking briskly again, looking straight ahead, and hoped to leave this dream behind.

"There is a house by a barn," she called after me. "A skeleton man will come and take you to me."

Several minutes passed and she did not speak again. The air felt thinner, and the world expanded around me. With surprise I noted the night sky had taken on the silvery gray of predawn and dispelled the walking dreams of dark. Up ahead the track divided, and along the right-hand spur a large building loomed. I was alone.

I struggled up the embankment at the back of a barn with a peeling and faded livery sign painted on the wall. *It isn't unlikely that there would be a barn near railroad tracks—or houses, for that matter,* I told myself. That had been no prophecy, and there was no strange woman speaking through other people's mouths because of my ring. That lady was a ridiculous hallucination brought on by stress and fatigue. And pain. My body screamed a protest all the way up the incline, and I yearned bone-deep for a pile of hay to curl up in. I had to rest before I could go on. I met great disappointment around the side, however, for there sat a modest, high-sided cart under a stand of trees, and a figure was astir in the shadows of the canopy. How could I slip into a barn to sleep while the owner guarded the door, and how would I explain myself to a stern, hardworking farmer, alone as I was, and coming out of nowhere at dawn?

I crept by in the shadow of the barn wall. Oh, how I ached for the soft straw bedding inside. Then, down the dirt road out front, I noticed a house with windows lit, and I cheered up. If I had to explain myself, I would rather it be to a sympathetic farmwife in her cozy kitchen, with prospects of a real bed in return for chores. I hurried through the dewy grass to the road, accompanied by the scuttles of awakening wildlife. Somewhere behind me a rooster crowed.

As I drew close to the house, unexpected piano music met me, and not a serious paean to the dawn by a long-dead composer, or a lilting Broadway air, but a raucous, jangling, rollicking, tinkling tapestry that made even my own weary legs want to dance. I recognized the music as ragtime—the new style played by Negro bands. *What is this place?* I wondered as I walked up the hedge-lined path and knocked on the bright red front door.

Laughter signaled a woman's approach. I smoothed my hair and wiped grit from the corners of my eyes and noticed, too late, a tear in my trousers. The door opened not on the simple farmwife I had anticipated, but on a lady still clad in the fancy garb of a night on the town, her face painted in a way I would not expect a country face to be.

"What is it, darlin'?" she asked.

I lost track of my words when I glimpsed a giggling lady in her chemise flash by an open parlor door at the end of the hallway. A man in shirttails and black socks, with his bowler still on his head, chased her. With a combination of excitement, anxiety, and awe, I realized this must be a house of ill repute.

"Please, ma'am . . . if I do you some chores . . . would you provide me with a bed?" I managed to stammer out.

"Well, darlin', we usually provide you the bed, and then you do the chores," she replied with a wicked grin, and I blushed.

"Truly," I said. "I could chop wood or do kitchen work. Or perhaps I could entertain your guests." I was too tired to debate morals with myself. "I have some skill as a knife thrower."

The woman cocked her head with interest. "I thought you might be circus folk," she said, much to my puzzlement. "Well, you can come in, but your monkey has to stay outside."

"What?" I turned in haste to look where her eyes were fixed. A familiar face poked out through the bushes. "I am not a monkey!" exclaimed Apollo, and he struggled the rest of the way into the light.

The woman screamed, her eyes rolled up, and her knees buckled.

I grabbed Apollo's arm and dragged him down the path. In moments, angry and frightened patrons and ladies of easy virtue would run to the door; maybe they wouldn't wait for explanations. I didn't stop until a stand of trees hid us from the house.

"Where did you come from? How did you get here? How did you get out?" I gasped between rasping breaths.

"A man let me out and gave me a ride here," Apollo said, as if that were the most natural thing in the world. "Come on, I'll introduce you." This time he took my arm, and he tugged me back toward the barn.

"Is he from the circus?" I asked as we walked.

"No," answered Apollo. "He was looking for someone and found me instead. He said, 'Is that you, Willie?' and I said, 'No,' and he said, 'Damn.'"

How curious. "Did he break the door down?"

"He didn't have to," Apollo answered. "That girl you're sweet on showed up. She had the key. She stole it, I think."

Marika. She did try to help. "Did she know him?" I asked.

"I reckon not. I heard a girl squeal like she was startled. Then there was a deal of whispering. Then I heard a key in the lock, and I shot out of there, and there they both were. He looked angry."

"Maybe because you weren't whom he wanted to find," I said.

Apollo shrugged. "He was going to leave, but the girl begged him to hide me. She said she'd tell you what happened at the next stop and you could come back for me. The man said he couldn't hang around, but he'd drop me off at some dry-goods store where he knew a man, but I don't recollect what town."

"But you found me instead." It seemed miraculous.

"We stopped to rest by that barn, but I couldn't sleep," Apollo explained. "Then I saw you go by. I couldn't believe my eyes at first, but I'd know you anywhere. I wanted to yell, but I didn't want to wake the nice man, so I followed."

I remembered the sounds I had assumed were animals in the grass and chuckled.

"You look a mess, Abel, and you've a bruise on your cheek. Why do you have a bruise? What's wrong with your leg?"

We approached the cart by the barn. The horse grazed nearby, but perhaps the man still slept.

"Did you ever ask who he was searching for?" I whispered.

"I was just happy to get out of there," Apollo answered. "What happened, Abel? Why aren't you on the train?"

I rubbed my arm. "The fellows threw me off, Apollo. They didn't want my company."

His eyes widened. "Threw you off!" he exclaimed.

A head with a serious, coffee-colored face and crisp, dark hair poked out from the front of the cart.

"You didn't say he was a colored gentleman," I whispered.

"Was I supposed to?" Apollo answered.

"Why, you're the lad who picked up my hat for me," the man said in a rich, deep voice, and I recognized him as the gentleman Mr. G. Marvel had evicted from his Wagner Palace car. He climbed down from the cart.

"This is my friend Abel, Mr. Northstar," said Apollo. "Abel Dandy. He's the most best friend in all the world. He'll steal you an apple in a minute and knock down your enemies in a trice."

"A fine friend indeed," Mr. Northstar said, and broke his

solemn demeanor with a smile as he held out his hand to me. The smile merely served to make the sadness in his eyes plainer. "William Northstar, at your service."

I shook his hand.

"They threw him off the train!" Apollo said.

Mr. Northstar sucked his teeth in disapproval. "I've some witch hazel," he said. "You look like you have need of it. I found some eggs while you were gone, young man," Mr. Northstar told Apollo gently. "Why don't you gather some fuel for a fire?"

"Yes, sir." Apollo scampered off into the trees.

"You have a way with puppy boys," I noted with amusement when Mr. Northstar reemerged from his cart with a dark green bottle. "He's not so easily bidden, as a rule."

"He's still chastened by his experience," said Mr. Northstar as he dabbed at my face with a cloth soaked in cooling potion, "but if he's like most boys, he won't remember long. I shall, however." His fist tightened and his eyes narrowed. Witch hazel dripped from the rag. "No child should be locked up like an animal."

I nodded in agreement. "I don't mean to be ungrateful," I said, "but what were you looking for in that caboose? It wasn't Apollo."

He sighed and sank against the cart. "I was looking for a boy," he said. "My child, Willie. He is only six years old, and someone has stolen him."

My mouth fell open. "Why would anyone steal him?"

"He was born with skin as spotted as an Indian pony's," answered Mr. Northstar. "I believe someone decided to take him for a show."

"Who? What happened?" I asked.

"I left my boy in Ohio with my old granny, who had helped

me raise him since his mother died in childbirth," he explained. "A colored man with a law degree has a hard search for a job ahead of him."

My head cocked in surprised interest. I didn't know there were colored lawyers. The grim line of his lips and his knowing eyes showed me he had expected this reaction. How uncouth I felt.

"When I came home," he continued, "I found the door wide open, my grandmother dying of a blow to the head, and Willie gone." His eyes flashed anger, and his words came from between clenched teeth. "I don't know how long that old woman had been lying there hurt. 'The show—the show took him' were her dying words."

"What show?" I gasped. Surely no show would steal a child.

"I don't know," he answered. "I asked everywhere." He scanned the woods around us as if he still searched. "The circus had been through days before—Marvel Brothers—and a mud show the previous week, also two small medicine shows. After my grandmother's funeral I left. I had no time to waste. The circus would be the easiest to find, but it also moved the fastest. That's where I decided to begin my search."

That explained Mr. Northstar's harsh exchange with Mr. Marvel. "And that's why you were looking around the train."

"A man brought food to the caboose and locked the door. I thought my boy was there," said Mr. Northstar. He sighed. "Have you seen such a child?" I could tell by the hopeless look in his eyes that he knew I would have spoken up before now if I had.

I shook my head.

"I've found lots of dry wood," cried Apollo. He tripped and tottered, with his arms full of branches and a trail of twigs behind him. "Isn't the morning glorious? I saw a fox! Honestly!

A real fox." He tumbled the wood onto the ground. "I told the bunnies, 'Beware.' Then I laughed because I was talking to bunnies. That's a caution, isn't it, Abel? But us furry folk gotta stick together, right?" His laughter pealed like Christmas bells in the clear morning air.

I resolved not to mention the piebald child. He didn't need to learn that people kidnapped boys who were different.

"You *will* take this child home, will you not?" asked Mr. Northstar as he built a fire.

"No, Abel!" cried the puppy boy with a short memory.

I felt a lump in my throat. "Yes, sir," I said, glancing down. "As soon as I can." *Well, I'll send him home, at least,* I thought. "I'm afraid I shall have to earn some money first, however," I added. That was true enough.

"If there are colored folks in town, I may find news of where there are jobs to be had," he said. "Get that basket by the rear wheels," he told Apollo. "Bring the pan that hangs on a hook inside the back of the cart," he told me. "There are plates and forks in the red storage box." He rummaged in a pack and pulled out a loaf of bread. Soon we were gobbling down mouthfuls of scrambled eggs and bread toasted over the fire. Breakfast had never tasted so good.

After I ate, I could barely keep my eyes open.

"You need sleep," I told Apollo, watching him yawn cracks in the dried egg around his mouth. He refused to look at me.

"There's a mattress in back. Use it," said Mr. Northstar, with tenderness in his voice despite his stern words.

"Abel hasn't slept either," protested Apollo.

"Both of you," said Mr. Northstar. "Boys need their sleep."

"Go wash your face in the stream," I told Apollo. "You'll give me nightmares if you sleep next to me like that."

"That's an unusual last name you have," I said while we waited for Apollo.

"Indeed," said Mr. Northstar. "I have my grandfather to thank for that. He named us after the star that led him and granny to freedom, rather than bring a name with him from slavery. I'm glad the man had more dignity than humor, else I would find myself named Dipper, not Northstar."

My heart warmed at his attempt to be funny, knowing how unhappy he must be. "How did you become a lawyer?" I asked.

"I had a sponsor," he told me. "A Quaker woman whose parents helped my grandparents on their journey north. She came to visit us in Ohio once and took a liking to me. She said she'd pay my way to Howard University, in Washington, D.C., if I did well in school."

"We were almost neighbors," I exclaimed. "We're from Maryland."

This time his smile reached his eyes. "Neighbors, but far apart," he said.

At that moment Apollo ran back from the stream. "There's a lady coming."

FOR A SECOND MY BREATH LEFT ME as I imagined a dancing girl coming down the path, but it was a handsome, dark-haired woman of middle years, wearing a checkered morning dress, who bustled up to us and brought me back to my senses. Was she about to throw us off her land?

"Are you the boy who knocked on my door this morning?" she asked me, ignoring Mr. Northstar.

"If it is a red door, yes, ma'am," I answered. I wondered if I should change that to "madam." Why was a businesswoman out on her own errands?

She coolly inspected Apollo. "I thought as much. I am Mrs. Delaney. I had a dream I should find luck on my doorstep this day."

I wasn't the only one having odd dreams. I introduced my companions and myself. "How may I help you?" I asked.

"It seems I am in need of a boy after all," she said. "Mine has left, and it's hard to get help from town when you're in my line of business." She glanced at Apollo again. "I'm sure I could find enough work for two—if you mean to stay."

This amounted to a generous offer, and yet I was apprehensive.

"What kind of work would you be offering these fine young men, Mrs. Delaney?" Mr. Northstar asked. He kept his eyes lowered and his tone even. He didn't have to worry about two boys not his own, but I was glad he did.

I don't know whom she believed him to be—not our father, obviously. She sized him up and must have decided that a civil answer might be expedient. "Nothing a lad would be ashamed of," she replied. "Kitchen chores, gathering up glasses, fetching and carrying for my gentlemen."

"Is this a boardinghouse you run?" he asked.

"We ply the oldest trade at my establishment," she said.

Her honesty surprised me. I peeked at Apollo but saw no glimmer of understanding there.

"But my girls are clean," Mrs. Delaney continued, "and I teach them manners if they have none. This includes leaving the staff to their business."

"Well, you speak fair and plain," Mr. Northstar admitted. "For the sake of their mothers I would beg you to honor their youth, however."

A spark of irritation lit her eyes.

"How much does it pay?" I asked. I appreciated Mr. Northstar's concern, but I hoped my youth would not be respected too much.

"Eight dollars a week for both of you," she replied as if this were a fortune.

I almost protested. I had made ten dollars a week with the circus all by myself, but where else in this unknown place would I find employ? "Does the job include room and board?"

"Certainly," she answered, and bestowed a glowing smile upon me. "As well as clean bed linens, and a bath on Sunday. We lodge the boys down by the kitchen, away from the business, before you ask," she told Mr. Northstar. Her lips tweaked with amusement.

Mr. Northstar accompanied us back to the house, leading his horse and cart. He declined to come inside, however.

"I'll check on you boys before I leave town today," he said, "in case you find the work doesn't suit you after all. Mind you keep Apollo out of the parlor and away from upstairs," he said to me.

"I'm housebroke," complained Apollo.

Mr. Northstar shook his head and smiled.

"My dear child," said Mrs. Delaney, stroking Apollo's furry cheek with her fingertips. "No one doubts it, but we wouldn't want to cause a stir among the guests, would we? You know how ungenerous some people can be."

Indeed, Apollo did now, if he didn't before. He beamed at Mrs. Delaney. "I'll keep out of sight," he promised.

"I'll bid you good day, then," said Mr. Northstar. He mounted his cart and cracked the reins. I hoped he would find good news in town.

"Here are the boys, Elsie," called Mrs. Delaney as we walked through the door. The girl we'd seen earlier ran downstairs, now clad in an Oriental wrapper.

"Try to be sensible and not swoon this time," said Mrs.

Delaney. "This is simply a very unusual boy. Now, off with you to bed."

That seemed an odd thing to say in the morning, but of course, the lady in question must have been up all night.

Mrs. Delaney rang a bell, and the frazzled maid who appeared showed us to our quarters—mine a small room off the kitchen, Apollo's a box room under the back stairs, just big enough for a cot. The maid pulled a worn but serviceable canvas shirt and a pair of pants from a nearby airing cupboard and handed them to Apollo gingerly. They appeared to be almost the right size for him. She offered me a pair of dungarees. I hesitated but took them. I didn't know when I might clean and mend the garments I wore. She then directed us to the outside pump, in case we wished to rinse off, and scurried away, with one last wide-eyed look behind her. I stowed my suitcase under the bed and insisted Apollo join me outside.

"I washed in the stream," he protested.

"Not with soap," I said.

The rough lye soap made my scrapes sting, but I felt the better for the wash.

After he'd scrubbed and I'd combed the tangles from his fur, Apollo brought water in for the cooking and cleaning, while I refilled the kerosene lamps. There was no indoor plumbing and the gas lines didn't come out this far, although the houses down the road by the train station had their water and gas piped in, even if they weren't rich folk, the cook told me with envy and pride.

I chopped wood for the cookstove and groaned with pain every time I raised the ax. Then I was sent to clean the grate and lay a fire in the parlor in case the night turned chilly in the wee hours, and my bad knee played up rotten when I knelt. As I set down a layer of kindling, the door opened and a pair of girls in summer frocks entered. The redhead, who appeared to be the younger of the pair, whispered in her blond companion's ear and giggled.

"My name's Lillie," she said to me. "What's yours?"

Surely this was not a woman of easy virtue—she couldn't be older than me—but she was bold, I'd concede to that. "Abel Dandy, miss," I said, and rose awkwardly to my feet. A twinge in my hip made me grimace.

"Oh, and he is dandy, isn't he?" said the blond girl.

"Hush," said Lillie, but she burst into laughter nevertheless.

"Are you a little stiff?" asked Lillie.

The blonde choked back a snort.

"Do you need to be . . . rubbed with liniment?" asked Lillie in a breathy way that suggested slippery caresses of the one muscle that hadn't throbbed until now.

I wasn't used to girls that forward. I didn't know how I should act. I would have liked to be saucy in return, but words abandoned me. I stood there like a codfish out of water.

"Cat's got his tongue," said the blonde.

"Has it?" said Lillie huskily, drawing closer. "Let's see." She reached out a finger and grazed my lips, and my knees went weak.

"Lillie! Agatha! Leave that boy alone, you trollops," said Mrs. Delaney, entering the room. "Save that for the paying guests. Off with you, Abel."

I left on unsteady legs, and I don't think I took a breath again until I reached the kitchen, where I was brought down to earth with a jolt right beside Apollo, cleaning chamber pots with carbolic soap.

"I don't like working," complained Apollo.

I had to agree with him in this instance.

Right before supper, when I was in the middle of filling the bedroom pitchers with fresh water, a maid called me to the kitchen door.

"I came to check on you, as I said I would," said Mr. Northstar. "Do you think this situation will suit you?"

"Yes, sir," I replied. "The staff are pleasant, and the work is tolerable." I didn't mention that cheeky red-haired girl I wished to see again.

"Well, keep in mind what your dear mother would want for you," he said.

I hoped I didn't blush. "Did you find any news of your boy in town?" I asked as I walked him down to his cart.

"I read an advertisement in the paper for a show of oddities in a town north of here, so that's where I'm headed. Damn these unnatural exhibitions."

Mr. Northstar had been nothing but generous, but his words bothered me. In the everyday world my parents would have been confined to the home at best, living on the charity of their parents, having none of the rewards of a normal life, never meeting each other, and seeing only those who either pitied or scorned them. "Even oddities deserve to make a living," I said.

"And to live a normal life," he agreed. "But more than one person has offered to buy my son, as if he were chattel. My family had to struggle for their freedom; I'm not about to sell my son back into slavery."

"No, sir," I said. His point was clear.

"I'll come back to see how you fare," he said. "I'll be on my way home if I find my son, and retracing my steps to pick up another trail if I don't. Say good-bye to young Apollo for me, and be sure to cherish and protect him. Don't let him fall into evil hands."

"Yes, sir," I answered, and held out my hand. "I wish you luck."

He took my offered hand and shook it solemnly. "And luck to you also."

At dusk I lit the kerosene lamps. As I worked my way down the corridor from the entry hall and through the parlor, women rustled downstairs in cheap finery that, like stage costumes, owed its elegance to the concealing magic of artful lighting. They talked in hushed, excited tones like ingenues before the performance. In the parlor the dark, flocked wallpaper and the heavy, ornate furniture took on richer tones in the lamplight, and the aspidistras formed an impenetrable jungle between the overstuffed sofas. As the women took pains to arrange themselves around the room, someone tugged on the doorbell pull.

"Showtime," Lillie trilled, and giggled as she left to answer the ring.

This was a different show than I knew. Part of me wanted to see it, but the stronger part hastened me away. I felt dead on my feet, and I knew Apollo must be too, but I needn't have worried about putting him to bed; he lay curled up on his cot, fast asleep already, in his clothes. I undressed him, covered him up, and then retired myself to a strange bed in a room more larder than bedchamber, where the ghost of bacon lingered in the air. The sheets were rough and reeked of disinfectant, and the straw mattress crunched as I tossed and turned my aching bones despite fatigue, while unfamiliar voices burbled in the distance.

What if someone tried to kidnap Apollo like someone had stolen Mr. Northstar's son? I had to earn him train fare home. This should be simple, but nothing had gone right lately, and I had already led him to employment in a house of ill repute. What else could happen?

I was creeping from a stone room, a roll of paper under my arm, when around the corner she came, and my heart nearly leaped from my mouth in panic. She was supposed to be at the market.

I tried to act as if all was perfectly normal and greeted her courteously. "I came for a scroll your husband kindly offered to lend me," I said.

There was not a shred of belief on her face, but plenty of interest.

"He must trust you, indeed, to loan you a scroll that bears the royal seal of secrets," she said. I think she enjoyed the panic in my eyes. She peered into her husband's study. "And how kind of you to seal the jar the scroll came from as if it had never been opened. How tidy and considerate."

"I can see you are not a fool," I answered. I sank to my knees and offered up a hand of supplication. "Chantress of Hathor, be my ally," I begged. "I know you care not for your husband. Please don't betray me to him."

"Why should I not?" she asked. I think she was furious that I had seen the misery of her marriage.

"Because you of all people would want to see the gods restored to their rightful order, a true king on the throne, and the two kingdoms united once more," I replied.

"Pick that up and follow me," she told me, and led me to a secluded bower in the garden. "Explain yourself," she said.

That was where I told her who I really was. "If you are a true daughter of Kemet, you will protect me," I said.

For a second I thought I was lost, but then I saw the change on her face. Disdain fled and her features softened, her eyes sparkled and her breath quickened. I was distracted by the rise and fall of her breast.

"I will return the scrolls once you have copied them," she said, and opened her arms as if to embrace me.

I edged away; she moved forward.

She slid her arms around my neck and gently touched my lips with hers, and I trembled.

She released me abruptly and hurriedly stepped back, a blush on her cheeks, shame and fear in her eyes. But I had waited too long for her lips, and I pulled her roughly to me, wrapped her in my arms, and took her mouth completely and thoroughly with mine. She surrendered to my exploring, urgent caresses, and I think we both stopped breathing and our flesh became one fire as we sank to the ground.

"You remember," she said, and her eyes glowed with the fire within.

I AWOKE TO THE GRAY OF DAWN piss-proud and stared wryly at the tent in my sheets. Was this the influence of my new lodgings? I groped under the bed for the chamber pot.

Why was Lady Adventure haunting my dreams? I wondered as I pulled on my trousers. I was already having my adventure, wasn't I? She was still in the guise of an exotic foreign lady, too, but who was I supposed to be? I couldn't recall what I had said in the dream. *At least there was no skeleton man, like Miss Dibble predicted,* I thought, and laughed.

My knee had stiffened overnight, and I hobbled to the bowl and pitcher. I rinsed my face in chilly water and went to shake Apollo awake. It was time to earn his train fare home. Apollo had already abandoned his bed, however. He sat in the kitchen, mopping up the remains of an egg with a thick crust of bread. "I found the eggs," he announced proudly. "Cook showed me where to look."

Cook glanced over from the big iron cooking range, a broad smile on her face. "He's a clever boy," she said. "Reminds me of a Skye terrier I once had."

Cook was in charge of the household staff—two kitchen girls and three upstairs maids who did the housework and looked after the ladies. She gave me my marching orders after she had filled me with a hot breakfast.

I left Apollo cleaning the silver at the kitchen table and went to split logs before the sun grew hot. I was pleased to note that my back and elbow gave me less trouble this day. Next I trimmed the wicks in the downstairs lamps and ran a brush around the insides of the glass chimneys to clean them of smoke, then I scrubbed out the tobacco spit from the cuspidors in the parlor, a chore I had never had to do at home, thank the Lord.

When I went back to the kitchen for my midday meal, Apollo was grinding coffee beans. "All I seem to do is crank handles," he grumbled. "Today I have turned the washing machine paddles to swirl the laundry, turned the clothes wringer wheel to squeeze out the wash water, ground peppercorns until I sneezed my brains out, and turned the handle on the coffee bean roaster on the stovetop. Now this. I shall have arms the size of a dockworker's by the time I leave here."

"Ah, he's a dear boy," said Cook, patting his head. "Put the ice card in the window, would you, Abel? Twenty-five up. I don't want the iceman to miss us."

After I ate, I went out to throw the slops over the wall to the pig, before I fed the chickens. Apollo's tasks kept him indoors. I suppose the mistress of the house didn't want to risk the attention of the occasional passerby. I couldn't blame her. Her domicile wouldn't pass close inspection.

The next few days were full of chores, but with hot meals and a warm bed at their end, and my aches and pains quickly vanished. The kitchen girls gave Apollo a wide berth, and the upstairs maids giggled behind their hands at both of us, but Cook always had kind words and even mended my trousers for me. Overall it wasn't a bad life.

Apollo behaved amazingly well. Maybe he'd had some sense knocked into him after all. Mrs. Delaney would visit with him when she came to give Cook orders, and treat him to penny candy, which surprised me because she seemed a distant and strict woman. He became quite her pet. She found him a novelty, I supposed.

Apollo should be home with his parents, not acting as pet to some stranger lady, I thought, but I couldn't do anything until I had some money, not pay for a ticket or even send a telegram.

I didn't think Apollo had given a second thought to the composition of the household, until one day when he asked, "Is this a girls' school?"

More like a school for young men, I said to myself. "No, it's a type of boardinghouse for ladies," I answered.

"Perhaps you'll find a sweetheart," he said, and then pretended to gag. "I'll tell Phoebe if you do," he warned.

"Phoebe has given me the mitten," I told Apollo, "so I doubt if she'll care. That letter you gave me says she's to marry some monkey man from Baltimore."

"A monkey man!" Apollo howled with laughter. "What a caution! I reckon you're a free man, then."

I should have known better than to expect sympathy from Apollo.

Finding a sweetheart didn't seem likely, however. The girls at Mrs. Delaney's weren't shy little things like Marika, the circus girl, and I wasn't sure how to converse with them. I avoided them mostly, except in the evenings, when I collected dirty glasses from the parlor and emptied ashtrays.

Mrs. Delaney ruled the parlor from a wing chair as if she were a duchess, whispering assignations and discreetly taking offered envelopes. The gentlemen smoked cigars, of course, and to my astonishment, some of the ladies smoked cigarettes, languorous wafts of smoke escaping from pouting painted lips. The music and laughter were loud, but the women kept their clothes on and there was a minimum of fondling. The conversation could be ripe, however, and gave me an education while I gathered up abandoned glasses as couples took to the stairs. I supposed Mrs. Delaney preferred a boy for this job so as not to expose her female household help to any indignities. One didn't like to lose good maids.

Lillie sometimes blew me a kiss, and I felt a thrill of desire. However, when I thought of how she earned her living, my ardor dimmed. This world did not offer many opportunities to a woman without a man's support, I told myself. I did not know what choices she'd had in life, if any, and if people of my acquaintance could make their living by exhibiting their bodies, why should I condemn her for making a living with hers. Nevertheless, it made me sad to think of beautiful intimacies cheapened by money.

Perhaps it saddened her, too. Some mornings she strolled in the backyard, wrapped in lace, watching the sunrise with a distant and pensive look. I never approached her at these times; I guessed they were sacred. As it happened, another wasn't as considerate.

One morning the dairyman delivered the milk early, and I took the bottles down to the springhouse to keep cold in the stream. As I approached the low stone building, I heard voices and I slowed down. I didn't want to intrude.

Then a male voice rose in anger. "You little whore. I know what goes on in that house. If you don't give me a taste, I'm going to see the sheriff."

"That'll make a change," said a voice I recognized as Lillie's. "He usually comes to see you." She yelped, and I knew he'd hit her.

I shoved the milk into a clump of weeds and pushed open the rickety door. In a ray of light I saw Lillie with a hand to her red cheek and a gangly young man, squinting and angry.

"I think you'd better leave," I said through gritted teeth.

"Who the hell are you?" he asked, and strode toward me, fists raised.

"Archie Crum," I answered, and kicked him in the knee. As he bent over, I punched him in the face. He went over backward into the stone trough and landed amid the cheese and butter. Archie would have been proud of me. His lesson in dirty fighting had taken hold.

"I don't want to see you in this yard again," I told him, trying to ignore the pain in my knuckles and the thumping in my chest. I offered my arm to Lillie. She took it, and I escorted her to the door.

"Who was that?" I asked when we were outside. I prayed she didn't hear the tremble in my voice.

"Just a local boy who makes a nuisance of himself," answered Lillie, her voice breathy and excited.

"I hope you won't be in trouble with the sheriff," I said.

"Not to worry," Lillie reassured me. "If that boy had come

any earlier, he would have met the sheriff going." She tugged me close and kissed me on the cheek. "Thank you, darling. You are my knight."

I'm sure I blushed for the remainder of the day.

Life wasn't all work at Mrs. Delaney's establishment, I discovered. The day before payday I followed the sound of laughter to the front of the house and found a croquet game in progress on the front lawn.

"Here, Abel, take my turn," said Lillie, holding out her mallet.

I glanced at Mrs. Delaney, who presided from a wicker chair by the front path. She presented an impressive sight in a crisp summer dress of cream and black stripes and matching cream shoes with black buttons. I expected her to wave me away, but she smiled and nodded.

The rules were not strictly followed and the language not what one expected from female companions, but good cheer ruled the day, and I laughed heartily as I, too, bumbled through the game. If I half closed my eyes, the sunlight and the filmy dresses of my companions made this look like any other croquet game on any other front lawn across the country. When Cook and the kitchen girls carried out bowls of fresh-made ice cream, the afternoon was complete.

"Run and get Apollo," said Mrs. Delaney. "He shouldn't miss this treat." When the puppy boy arrived, however, she positioned him under a large parasol so he would be hidden from the road.

"You know how ice cream is made, don't you?" he told me, rolling his eyes. "You have to crank a handle." This didn't stop him from digging into a big bowl of strawberry and chocolate.

The sight of all those wantons licking their spoons with little pink tongues had me so distracted that I didn't notice wagons approaching.

"Look!" cried a dark-haired girl called Mabel. "Isn't that Lazarus Mink? What's he doing back?"

Two canvas-covered wagons, with a wood-paneled wagon in the lead, rumbled down the road and came to a halt in front of the house. Two of the drivers were of standard build; the last, however, was a bearded dwarf. Each wagon canvas was emblazoned with the same proclamation: DR. MINK'S TRAVELING MONSTER MENAGERIE.

Well, I never, I thought, remembering the poster I had seen after I inquired about train fares home.

A man in a suit and tall hat climbed down from the lead wagon and came to the front gate. His clothes flapped oddly about him, as if he were a scarecrow made of twigs. Mrs. Delaney swept to meet him.

"Lazarus, my dear. How delightful," she cried.

No wonder Mrs. Delaney was undisturbed by Apollo. She had friends in the business.

After a brief conversation Dr. Mink remounted, and the wagons pulled onto the field across the street.

"Shoo, everyone," called Mrs. Delaney. "Get some rest and freshen up. We shall have a show tonight for our gentlemen."

"A show!" cried Apollo, as if he'd not performed in them all his life. "Abel, there's to be a show!"

"Well, stay out of their way, Apollo," I said. "They don't want you underfoot while they set up." And after Mr. Northstar's tale I wasn't sure I trusted any itinerant showman. On the other hand, maybe they had need of a knife thrower. Here was my chance to get away, I realized. I could leave Apollo here and mail a letter home with his whereabouts. By the time someone came to collect him, I would be long gone. I almost laughed out loud.

In between my chores I checked on the progress across the road and noted where Apollo was. The wagon drivers raised a tent. In front of the tent a wall of brightly colored banners advertised the attractions within. A small bally platform was erected beside the banners. Apollo made no pretense of work, but sat under the bushes at the side of the house and watched the whole time, so I had no chance of visiting Dr. Mink unseen. Apollo was reluctant even to come in for supper, and afterward he ran outdoors to the bushes again. I might have to wait until he was in bed before I sought employment.

Finally it was time for the show. The ladies of the house were joined by men from town—upstanding gentlemen, by the cut of their clothes, pillars of the community, no doubt. Not one brought a wife or daughter. They all gathered in front of the bally platform in the evening sunlight, while the ladies giggled and nudged and pointed at the pictures on the banner. I knew from experience that these were exaggerations, but I was curious nevertheless. I was delighted to see no knife thrower depicted.

I looked around for Apollo and realized he was absent. After all the attention he had paid the setup, he was nowhere to be seen. Panic got the better of me. Should I search Dr. Mink's wagons? But then Mrs. Delaney arrived with a small figure beside her, bundled in a cape and a floppy hat. I breathed a sigh of relief and felt quite foolish. I needed no clairvoyant powers to guess who the swathed figure might be, but why was he got up in that fashion? He must be stifling inside those wrappings. Perhaps Mrs. Delaney didn't want Apollo to upstage the performers, or perhaps she was smarter than I and had disguised her pet from the eyes of a greedy showman.

The girls giggled behind their hands, and the gentlemen stared, but before anyone had a chance to inquire who the mystery guest was, a trumpet sounded from behind the banner and out walked Lazarus Mink in tails and top hat.

He was possibly the thinnest individual I had ever seen, almost as thin as the ebony cane he carried. He wore formfitting tights instead of trousers, which only served to emphasize his knees, which were like giant knots in his twiggy legs, and I noted that under his suit jacket he wore no shirt. He was a curious sight as he climbed the steps to the bally platform. His knobby wrists protruded from his coat sleeves like mere bones. His head appeared too large for his emaciated body and bobbed precariously on an unclad neck that was near as thin as his wrists. His caved-in cheeks, and eyes deep in their sockets, gave his pale face the appearance of a skull wearing a mustache and goatee.

I didn't know whether to laugh or shiver. Here was the skeleton.

WELCOME, LAAAADIES AND gentlemen!" Dr. Mink wheezed and squeaked. "Welcome to the most amazing show you will ever have the privilege to observe."

Would there be a dancing girl? I wondered. "A man of bones has kidnapped me," the shadowy dancer had said in my strange waking dream before I joined the circus. "A skeleton man will come and take you to me," she had told me as we walked down the railroad tracks. For a moment fear and excitement snatched my breath away. What would I do if it was true?

"Yiss," Mink continued. "Today you have the opportunity to observe some of the most unusual human beings in existence. Only step inside and I will introduce you to the tallest man in the United States—eight feet tall and still growing. He has confounded the doctors in Philadelphia and stunned the experts in New York City. Here, too, you may shake the hand of the smallest woman you will ever meet and the most unusual bearded lady to be found."

A squat bearded lady appeared on one of the banners, but no midget woman. Were there others inside not depicted on canvas—if not a dancing girl, maybe Mr. Northstar's stolen son? I glanced at Apollo, glad he was disguised. Could I protect them both from burly roustabouts? Or even myself?

"See the alligator girl, cursed by the ancient Indian gods of the bayou, forever trapped as half human, half beast," invited Dr. Mink. He pointed with his cane to a picture of a well-formed woman in evening dress with diamond-patterned green skin and the snout of a reptile. "Wonder at the living caterpillar man." He gestured with a skeletal hand toward a picture of what appeared to be a large striped sock with a human head, smoking a cigarette. "'How does a creature without limbs survive?' you will ask yourselves. And finally, the most astounding person of all—no words can adequately describe this lusus naturae, this hideous freak of nature—the man with two heads."

Curiosity got the better of my apprehension. I was eager to see what this two-headed man could really be.

Dr. Mink leaned toward the audience and lowered his creaky voice as if imparting a confidence. "Now, some people revile me for exploiting the unfortunate, they curse me for my lack of compassion, but I'll let you be the judge. Am I heartless to show these wretches? Am I?" He swept his coat aside to reveal his chest, each rib as clear as if it had been carved in marble, and behind them, on his left side, a dark shadow throbbed beneath the almost transparent skin—his heart, beating in his chest.

The audience inhaled as one.

He let the subsequent silence hang in the air a moment, and then he dropped his jacket and walked down the steps and into the crowd. Some moved back, but Mrs. Delaney and her shrouded companion stayed put.

"No, I'm not heartless, as you see. I give them sustenance and shelter, and a job to do. All these medical curiosities are here today for your education and edification. Yiss. All these marvels are waiting for you to step inside so they may show you the wonders of the world. Look around you." As he said the word "around," he turned his head until it faced completely in the opposite direction. The audience muttered, and one of the girls squeaked. He didn't turn his head in a complete circle, of course, he brought it back the same way, but I would bet there were those there who would later swear he did.

"Yiss, there are wonders in your very midst," he continued, and he swooped the cloak from Apollo's shoulders. My hairy friend stood there clad in nothing but his underdrawers and personal hirsute glory.

Men cried out, and women screamed, even though they knew the boy.

"Arf, arf, arf," barked Apollo, in obvious delight at performing once more.

I choked back a curse. What was that stupid boy playing at? Was he asking to be carried off? Then it hit me. He was. He wanted to join this show. I couldn't let that happen.

As I tried to work my way through the crowd to get to Apollo, Dr. Mink ran up the wooden stairs to the bally platform again. He silenced his babbling audience with an upheld bony hand. "Tonight, and tonight only, this is a free show for the ladies. Step up, step up, my dears." The girls came forward in a rustle of summer petticoats, further hindering my progress.

"But, ladies," warned Dr. Mink, "do not venture inside without your smelling salts. I would not wish you to swoon and hurt yourselves."

"Excuse me, excuse me," I repeated as I maneuvered by two of the upstairs maids, enjoying a holiday.

Dr. Mink turned his attention to the men. "The admission for gentlemen will be a mere two bits if you wish to lend the ladies an arm to lean on."

A big man came out with a starry cash box, and Dr. Mink entered the tent. The gentlemen pressed forward, money in hand, pulling me with them. Apollo ran behind the banners and followed Mink into the tent. I fumbled in my pockets. I couldn't let Apollo go in by himself, but I had no money. As I reached the entrance, Apollo ran out to me and tugged my arm. "It's all right, Abel," he said proudly. "You're with me." I took Apollo's arm, ready to pull him away, but the man with the cash box moved in behind me, and the only way to go without a fuss was in.

I was irked. Apollo had made a target of himself, and already he claimed privileges with a show that I had wanted to join.

"Let me go," squeaked Apollo, and I released my grip on his arm with a snort of irritation.

The audience entered one end of the tent and traveled the length, while a wiry roustabout watched for improprieties. The exhibits were lined up on the other side of a velvet cord. I didn't see a dark-haired dancing girl. So much for Lady Adventure kidnapped by a man of bones. I was actually disappointed. What a fool I was. At least there were no children on display. That was one less thing to worry about.

The first of the human exhibits was the alligator girl—more of a woman, actually. She hadn't the face of that beast, but indeed, as attested by her low-cut gown and shortened skirt, her body was covered by a rough, corrugated growth that mimicked the scales of an alligator. Some of the girls stroked their own fair skin nervously, and more than one of the gentlemen appeared a little ill. The alligator girl herself smiled and nodded at all, though no one spoke to her.

They have no acts, I realized. *They just sit there like museum pieces or*—I swallowed hard—*animals at a zoo.* My heart went out to them.

"Good evening, ma'am," I said as we filed by. "I hope it finds you well."

"Why, honey pie," she answered in a pleasing voice. "How kind of you to ask, and indeed it does." She tilted her head as she noticed Apollo at my side. "Are you here to join us, sugar-plum?"

"I hope so," said Apollo.

"No," I said, and put my hand firmly on his shoulder. *She didn't ask if I was here to join them,* I thought glumly, but why should she? I wasn't covered in fur.

"Well, lookit that," said a gruff alto voice. "I ain't seen one a them before." The speaker was the next exhibit, a lady dwarf with a large head, a protruding forehead, a broad, saddle-shaped nose—and a beard. The joke took me by surprise, and I laughed. I hadn't listened closely to Dr. Mink—the smallest woman and the most unusual bearded lady were one and the same. Not only that, she was the driver I had mistaken for a man. Trust a show-man to make it sound like you were getting twice as much for your money, and still make you feel like you'd received a bonus when you found out the truth.

"What you laughing at?" growled the bearded lady, and she tugged at the sleeve of her flounced satin gown. Her arms were short and brawny and looked odd emerging from that confection. I couldn't help but notice the dirt under her fingernails.

"My apologies, ma'am," I said. "I merely laughed with delight at the economy of your design."

"Well, don't he talk like a book?" she said, rolling her eyes. "You could take lessons," she called over to her left.

There lay the caterpillar man in his striped tube of a shirt, the difference from the banner being the lumps on the sides of his trunk where his arms should have been. He was bald and swarthy, with a scowling face that belonged on a man in his thirties. His lips were pressed closed as if he rarely spoke at all, so perhaps she joked.

"Well, doesn't that beat the devil?" Lillie said. She slid in beside me. "He makes me feel all-overish." She shivered.

"Hello, gorgeous," the caterpillar man rasped, and gave me a start. "I'd feel you all over for sure." He undulated in a most disgusting parody.

"Ewwww!" Lillie stepped back.

"What's he doing, Abel?" Apollo asked.

"Scratching an itch, I believe," I answered. I was beginning to have second thoughts about my joining this show, let alone Apollo.

"Stop that!" The bearded lady smacked the culprit on the head.

I tugged Apollo along. Perhaps the poor man didn't have all his wits.

We found ourselves in front of the giant next. He certainly wasn't eight feet tall, but he could have been seven and a half feet or more. Even if he'd been eight feet tall, he wouldn't have been the tallest man in the country, for I'd met the winner of that title. He appeared sickly and lethargic, as giants often do, with swollen facial features and an oversize head. His hands were puffy and hamlike, and I would bet anything that he limped. I couldn't tell how old he might be, as giants tend to age fast. He wasn't much interested in what went on, but stared at the tent wall. He seemed sad.

Apollo must have sensed that too. "Hello!" he called, and waved up at the man. "You're a very fine giant indeed." The giant's eyes didn't even flicker, but I smiled at Apollo's sweet attempt to cheer him up. I would hate to see the puppy boy exhibited like this, unkempt and uncared for.

We gathered at the far end of the tent in front of a curtained display that promised a finale.

"Man alive! Did you ever see such an all-fired sight?" said a gentleman.

"I will allow I have never," said another. "Oddments, the whole boodle."

"Land sakes!" said a woman, hand at her heart. "When I saw that caterpillar feller, I thought I'd have a conniption fit."

The crowd hushed as Dr. Mink stepped in front of the curtains.

"And now the most amazing sight you will ever see in your life. A person you will tell your grandchildren about. A creature that defies the laws of nature. For a mere one dime more."

There were some grumbles, but the gentlemen coughed up.

Dr. Mink took hold of the curtain. "May I present to you Mr. Eustace Ginger—the two-headed man!" He pulled the curtain aside.

We all gasped.

A man sat in a straight-backed chair, his hands folded in his lap. He appeared normal in every way, from his modest suit to his neatly trimmed beard, but out of his forehead grew a second head, a third of the size of the original.

A girl exclaimed and, by the sounds, someone fainted, but I couldn't tear my eyes away to look.

He was no humbug. The second head was a miniature parody of the first, complete with beard. The eyes blinked and appeared to be able to see, but they were dull, with no sign of intelligence. The mouth opened and closed constantly, although no sounds came forth. I suspected that it was moronic.

Before I could ask Mr. Ginger some questions—like could his second head swallow, and did it catch cold?—Dr. Mink stepped forward and dropped the curtain.

"Thank you, ladies and gentlemen, for your patronage," he said. "Souvenirs are on sale outside."

"Well, that's a swindle," I muttered to Apollo.

"What did you think?" asked Mrs. Delaney as we left the tent. Dr. Mink walked at her side. He carried his hat under his arm, revealing spiky white hair.

"Impressive," I said. I didn't want to be impolite and tell Dr. Mink that it bothered me that none of them did anything.

"Would you and the young fellow here care to join my troupe for a late supper?" asked Dr. Mink.

And have Mink fill Apollo's head with ideas? I didn't think so. "Oh, it's much too late for a boy his age." I didn't like the way Mink looked at me when I said that. "Run in the house, Apollo. It's time for bed."

"Abel!" my dog-faced friend complained.

"I've a bedtime story to tell you about a dancing girl and a thief, if you behave," I said, meaning an edited version, of course.

Apollo couldn't resist a story. "It better be a good one," he muttered before he ran off.

"Dr. Mink," I said to the showman. "It strikes me that you

may be in need of a performing act. Could you use a knife thrower? I have excellent skills and would be glad to demonstrate."

"A knife thrower, eh?" the skeleton man said, and grinned. "And a dog boy."

"No," I said. "Apollo is going home, back to his parents, who miss him."

"What a shame. What a shame." Dr. Mink stroked his goatee and thought for a moment. "Well, I may have need of a knife thrower. Why don't you show me what you've got in the morning, when the light is better?"

I took my leave of Mrs. Delaney and Dr. Mink, my heart buoyant. I might have a career after all.

I had almost drifted off to sleep when someone tapped on my door. *I shall thrash that puppy boy if he's come to bother me for another story,* I promised. To my surprise, I found Lillie there clad in her chemise and wrapper. I gaped at her like a ninny.

"Will you invite me in?" she asked.

I stood back to allow her to enter, still unable to find words.

She pulled a pin from her hair, and her red curls tumbled about her shoulders. "I thought you might like some company," she whispered.

I realized that I was standing there in just my shirt. My mouth dried.

She wriggled and shrugged, and her wrapper slid to the floor. My luck was really changing, I thought, as she undid my top buttons and slid her hand beneath my shirt.

"You have a fine build," she purred, and my knees went weak.

"What's this?" she asked, and pulled the scarab ring from

under my shirt by its chain. "A token from a lover?" She chuckled.

"A good-luck charm from a friend," I said, gently taking the ring from her. Why did I feel peculiar? I had no one to be faithful to.

Lillie leaned close and her musky perfume enveloped me. She ran her tongue up the side of my neck, and I tossed my foolish reservations aside, pulled her to me, and pressed my mouth to hers.

Her teeth nibbled my lower lip, and my mouth parted in surprise. Before it could close, her little pink tongue slipped within and tangled with mine. I squeaked before I could help it. Her muffled laughter hummed through me, and I grasped her tighter and tried to follow her lead. I was tentative, clumsy, and afraid to prove myself a fool, but she sighed and I took encouragement.

She pushed me and I pulled her, and we stumbled backward to the bed. The heat of her flesh beneath her flimsy nightdress seared me, and the smell of her dizzied my senses. My hands molded the curves of her hips and glided to the mounds of her wondrous breasts. *Is this really happening?* I wondered as she sank beneath me onto the humble straw mattress.

She took my hand and drew it up her leg to guide it where the fire burned hottest, dragging her chemise along with it. I trembled. "Lillie," I whispered. "You are the most beautiful creature."

Her lips tickled up my chest to my throat. "Ouch!" she cried, and her hand flew to her head. Her hair was snagged in the chain about my neck. She lifted the ring to untangle herself. She yelped and dropped it.

"What's wrong?" I asked.

"I heard my conscience, loud as life, say, 'Leave him alone,'" she replied, her eyes wide. She began to tear her hair free.

"Shhhhh!" I said, trying to still her fingers. I felt an undertow of disquiet. She had touched the ring before she said those odd words. Was it only coincidence? "Why on earth would your conscience speak to you?"

"Oh, you are such an innocent!" Lillie blurted out.

"Not in five minutes," I said, squashing flat my apprehension. I pulled her to me.

She wriggled out of my embrace. "No, it's not fair on you. I can't do this when you were so good and helped me with that bully."

"Not fair? Leaving me in this state is unfair," I protested, to my immediate embarrassment.

"You don't understand," she said. "Mrs. Delaney sent me to distract you."

She was right. I didn't understand. "You're succeeding," I said, too aware of the ache of my desire to question Mrs. Delaney's interest.

"I don't want to fool you, you're too sweet," Lillie said.

"Fool me?"

Lillie placed a hand on my shoulder. "Dr. Mink is stealing away with your friend. Please don't hate me."

The scoundrel! He had no intention of watching me perform in the morning. He was making off with Apollo instead! It crossed my mind that Apollo couldn't get too far in ten or fifteen minutes, but I dismissed that idea as dishonorable. Mr. Northstar had warned me not to let Apollo fall into evil hands, and I had done it nevertheless. I leaped to my feet, buttoning my shirt. "I don't hate you, Lillie," I said. Which was true. I hated fate, which gave me a present with one hand and took it away with the other.

As I pulled on my trousers, Lillie explained. "Dr. Mink is

Mrs. Delaney's half brother. He visited recently. When she saw Apollo, she knew he would pay well for knowledge of him. She sent her boy after Mink on the pony."

I raced out the door and headed for the field.

The wagons were loaded and the horses hitched, but they were still lined up in the lane. I hammered upon the rear door of the wood-paneled wagon. The door opened a crack. "It's a little late to come a-calling, ain't it?" said Dr. Mink, a knowing smirk on his face.

I set aside my manners and pushed the door open farther. As I guessed, Apollo was inside, seated on a bunk. "I thought you were asleep," he said. I hoped he had the decency to blush under that fur.

Dr. Mink sat on a stool. "Apollo has accepted my offer of a job."

"It'll be wonderful, Abel. I shall have star billing and my very own banner."

Two seductions had been taking place, it seemed. "What about your family?" I asked. "And your friends at home?" *And what about* my *job?* I thought. I wondered if I could pick him up and remove him by force. Dr. Mink, the little stick man, would be no hindrance.

"I can't go back home. You know that," he answered. "Things were bad enough before I defied my father."

The door behind me slammed, and I turned to see the largest driver blocking my way out. So much for grab and run.

"Colonel Kingston will watch out for you," I said. "I promise you, all will be well."

"You can't promise him anything," said Dr. Mink, "and you have no authority over him either. You are no relation."

"Perhaps the sheriff will see it differently," I answered.

"Yiss, go get the sheriff," he said, grinning like death, and I knew he was thinking the law would care nothing for a freak boy, and by the time I returned, they would be gone.

"You won't have fun with all those grown-ups," I told Apollo. "They'll always be bossing you around."

"Oh, we have children," said Dr. Mink. "They're waiting for us farther west. Don't worry, Apollo. You'll have fine playmates to cut shines with."

"Are those stolen children too?" I almost asked, before the terrible truth of those words stopped me. Could that be where Mr. Northstar's child was? I had to find out. How could I abandon a child in need? I almost choked on my next words. "Well, if you've made up your mind, so be it," I said to Apollo. There went all my plans, flying out the carriage window. I could have cussed a blue streak. "But I can't let you go off with strangers," I told the boy. "Perhaps you have room for a knife thrower after all?" I asked Dr. Mink.

Dr. Mink paused a moment to look me up and down. He flicked his tongue across his lips. Perhaps he was deciding how much trouble I would be. Finally he spoke. "Not a knife thrower," he said, "but I need a driver."

I ran back to the house to grab my suitcase. Lillie was still in my room, curled in a ball on my bed.

"Apollo and I are leaving," I explained. "Could you give a message to Mr. Northstar, should he return? Tell him I think I know where his son may be. Tell him to follow Lazarus Mink."

"Will you forgive me, Abel?" she said, and wiped a tear from her eye.

"There's nothing to forgive, Lillie," I said. "Take care."

We were a mile down the road when I realized that once again I had left a job without my pay. I was still broke.

MINK ASSIGNED ME TO THE WAGON formerly driven by the bearded dwarf woman, who now rode discreetly inside with the alligator girl. A skinny fellow drove the giant, the human caterpillar, and the two-headed man. The muscular brute who had collected admission money drove Mink's wagon. I had expected Apollo to ride with me, so I bristled when he chose to ride up front with his newfound friend, Dr. Mink. But I figured if I were him, I'd rather see the country ahead than the back of another wagon.

Two hours along the road, we stopped so the drivers could sleep, curled up under the wagons. The skinny fellow shook me awake at dawn and tossed me a packet of cheese and bread wrapped in brown paper for my breakfast. I hitched my team, climbed groggily into my seat, and followed the other wagons out, grateful that the horses seemed healthy and cooperative.

We traveled down dirt roads between windswept cornfields, and across stretches of green and purple prairie. The women in my wagon kept to themselves. The alligator girl seemed shy, and the dwarf was gruff, so I didn't want to intrude. But I didn't mind being left with my own thoughts. I thrilled with the excitement of a journey to unknown parts. The freedom that suffused me as I basked in the glorious smells on the warm July breeze made it easy to push aside worries. I felt sure that I would find Mr. Northstar's missing child up ahead, but what I would do about that boy and Apollo would have to wait until I saw what circumstance offered me.

We traveled all day, with only a few comfort stops. On these occasions the women went first and then the men, spreading out into the bushes and trees. The human caterpillar rode under the arm of the giant—I tried not to dwell on that predicament—and the short, skinny driver led the two-headed man, who seemed to have problems navigating. Apollo trotted along behind Dr. Mink and babbled nonstop at the man. It stung me that he didn't bother to see how I fared.

That evening we pulled into a stand of trees by a stream. I struggled from my perch and hobbled to the bank for a drink. The bumps and jars of the road had invaded my every bone. No one else seemed to suffer as much as I. They were used to traveling all day in a bouncing wagon, I supposed. I helped unhitch the horses, then the skinny fellow gathered sticks, and the tall, muscular man disappeared into the trees with a rifle over his shoulder. Apollo came out of Dr. Mink's wagon, still chattering, and Mink smiled at him indulgently and covered a yawn. Mink noticed me, and his smile twisted into a sneer. He clapped Apollo on the back and sent him toward me. Apollo hesitated, then watched the showman return to his wagon before he ran to me. I wanted to spit.

"Abel," the puppy boy cried. "Dr. Mink has a lady in a box!" Apollo didn't give me a chance to ask what on earth he meant by that. "Dr. Mink said I should be in charge of the children's acts. He says I'm as smart as a steel trap."

"Is that so?" I said. What a devilish judge of character Dr. Mink had proved to be. He knew how to capture Apollo's devotion. I kicked at a clod of dirt. "And did he tell you anything about these children?" I asked. "How many are there? Are they girls or boys? What do they look like?"

"There's the alligator lady," Apollo cried, totally ignoring my questions, and ran to her as if she were a long-lost auntie. I followed, hissing with frustration.

The alligator girl beamed a smile at him. "How lovely that you could join us, my dear," she exclaimed. She glanced shyly at me. "And your friend is an excellent driver."

I nodded my head in acknowledgment. "How generous of you, Miss . . ."

"Ruby Lightfoot," she informed me, now favoring me with a warm smile.

"I'm Apollo," said my eager little friend. "This is Abel."

"Abel Dandy," I said. She seemed kind. Would she help me protect Apollo from harm if need be?

The skinny driver toppled a pile of twigs and branches before us and skittered off again to rummage in the back of a wagon. I helped Miss Lightfoot build a fire. The skinny fellow came back with a sack and a pot. "Thank you, Mr. Sweet," she said, taking the pot. "Abel Dandy, this is Billy Sweet."

"Pleased to meetcha," the mousy man said with a grin, and pulled a big potato from his sack. "Who wants to help?"

"Apollo and I will," I said. "We've had extensive training in such tasks."

Apollo groaned, and I patted his back. He was a child, after all. I shouldn't be vexed with him for enjoying a new friend. "I'll peel, you chop," I said.

"I'll be off for the water, then," said Mr. Sweet, winking at me. I didn't trust people who winked for no discernible reason.

"There you are, Bess," cried Miss Lightfoot.

The bearded lady fought with her long skirt and struggled from the back of the men's wagon with a large, lumpy bundle in her brawny arms. Was it laundry? A sack of turnips? She leaned over and placed the bundle on the ground, where it commenced to wriggle through the grass toward the cook fire, and I recognized the caterpillar man.

"The giant's still sick," said Bess when she joined us. "Poor bastard's getting worse." She was much rougher than Miss Lightfoot, but she seemed concerned for the giant. Maybe she'd care about what happened to a boy like Apollo.

The caterpillar man banged her on the side of her leg with his bald head. "You pay 'im too much mind," he complained gruffly.

Bess bent and tweaked his ear. "You're dear when you're jealous, Gunther," she said. Her beard bristled with her efforts to repress laughter, and I decided that maybe I liked her despite her roughness.

"Mr. Dandy, I'd like to present Miss Tuggle and Mr. Bopp," Ruby Lightfoot said.

"Bess will do," the bearded lady replied.

"I likes Mr. Bopp just fine," said the caterpillar man. Bess rolled her eyes.

In the distance I heard a shot fired and then another. We'd have fresh rabbit stew tonight, I guessed.

We sat around the fire to eat on what seats we could muster—a barrel half, a log, a folded blanket, and the like. I wasn't surprised when Dr. Mink ate in his wagon with the big man I suspected to be his bodyguard, but where was the two-headed man?

"Why doesn't Mr. Ginger join us?" I asked.

"Oh, he's worried that Mr. Ginger number two will put us off our grub," said Bess.

"He would," said Mr. Bopp as he raised his dripping chin from his bowl.

"He doesn't feed it, does he?" asked Apollo.

"No, my honey bun," said Miss Lightfoot, "but it does drool dreadfully at the smell of the food."

Apollo made a face. I wanted to also, but I stopped myself.

"Do you have a game?" asked Billy Sweet, changing the subject.

I must have looked blank, for Miss Lightfoot chimed in, "He means bunco, lovey pie. A swindle."

I shook my head in quick denial.

"Come on," Billy Sweet said. "A boy on the road like yerself? We all got a game to bilk the marks. Some of 'em uses their looks." He tipped his head at Miss Lightfoot. "Some of 'em uses their skills."

"He's a knife thrower," said Apollo, sounding prouder of me than I would have expected.

"There you go," Billy Sweet said happily. "I run a mouse game, meself. The folks bet on which hole the mouse will go down."

I had a hunch that the hole the mouse chose was not a random one.

"And if the pickings ain't good there, I can fan a mark and

weed a wallet in the blink of an eye. Yeah, they calls me Billy Sweet 'cause I always got the sugar." He rubbed two fingers and a thumb together as if he were caressing money.

A pickpocket! I should have been appalled, but instead I was fascinated. I decided to keep my ring well hidden under my shirt nevertheless. I didn't want it to disappear. And I didn't want anyone to touch it, I realized. It might be coincidence, but situations became very odd when people touched that ring, and I didn't want to risk it. I set aside that foolish fancy because it made me too uncomfortable. "What about that big fellow with Dr. Mink who took the gate at the performance?" I asked.

"That's what he does, all right," said Billy, "and he takes his privileges, too." He winked. "But don't *you* be accusing Al Bonfiglio of shortchanging the customers, else you'll land in the middle of next Tuesday with a bloody nose."

As if I would voluntarily challenge that bruiser.

Bess snorted. "At least you both see some money."

"I see riches," said Mr. Bopp, startling me by pushing his face under the hem of her skirt.

Apollo roared with mirth. I hoped he wouldn't pick up any bad habits from these men.

"Stop that, you miscreant," said Bess. She grabbed Mr. Bopp by the scruff and wrestled him into her arms. "Time for bed."

"Aw, no," complained Mr. Bopp, although he didn't struggle.

"Ow!" Bess exclaimed as she staggered out of the firelight. "Don't bite. You are such a heathen." She sounded amused, however.

I heard muffled laughter from Mr. Bopp as they took off into the night.

"Love, ain't it wonderful?" said Billy Sweet.

Well, yes, I thought. But I'd never seen it take quite that shape before.

Apollo and I slept on blankets under the wagon. Apollo must have been worn out, for he soon emitted gentle puppy snores. I followed his lead, lulled to sleep by insect chirps and the warm, sweet smell of grasses. My dreams thrummed with happiness, although I couldn't put them into words when I awoke.

We ate our oatmeal in the silver light of morning. Dr. Mink took it upon himself to join us. He strutted up like a matchstick man in a black suit taken in as much as a seamstress could bear. He wore his usual stovepipe hat even while he ate. He put me in mind of an undertaker. "We'll turn northwest today," he said, and flicked a crumb from his wispy goatee. "We've a river to cross, and I know of a decent bridge. Make sure you follow." He knocked invisible dust from his knees with a glove as he rose. "Come along, boy," he said to Apollo. "I believe I've some gumdrops saved for a good little fellow." He never looked at me.

"See you later, Abel," Apollo cried, leaping to his feet.

I smacked my wooden bowl down in the dirt. I thought Apollo had left home to follow *me*.

That day commenced much the same as the last: more pancake-flat country, more grass, more corn, and more endless blue sky. I hoped that Apollo was royally bored. I hoped he drove Dr. Mink mad with nonstop questions. Still, the songs of chickadees and blackbirds filled the air above, sunlight gilded the tassel-topped grass, and I saw a fox slink after a quail through the purple-shot prairie. We traveled through two small towns, and eager boys ran beside the wagons, begging us to stop. I pitied their disappointment. We crossed the Spoon River near Galesburg.

That night the giant joined us for dinner. He perched, all

knees and elbows, on a chest Billy Sweet pulled from a wagon for him. Dr. Mink and Bonfiglio, the bodyguard, stayed away once more.

Perhaps I should have felt at home with people more like those I had grown up with, but these were strangers, nevertheless, and I wasn't sure of them.

Apollo shoveled down his plate of beans and sausage and excused himself. "Dr. Mink said I could read his notices," he said by way of excuse.

"Mink's playing his games again, isn't he?" said the giant in a voice so deep and muffled it might have come up from a well. "Divide and conquer."

So it wasn't just my jealousy that saw manipulation in Mink's ways.

"Doesn't always work," Bess said, and patted Mr. Bopp on his shiny head.

"Don't you bad-mouth Dr. Mink," said Billy Sweet to the giant, with a mean squint to his eyes.

"Don't you threaten our giant," said Bess, raising a beefy fist. My mouth fell open at the idea of a fistfight between the pair.

Miss Lightfoot agitated a napkin in front of her face like a fan. "I'll take a plate to Mr. Ginger," she said overloudly. She slopped spoon after spoon of beans from the pot in quick succession.

"Now you've gone and upset Ruby," complained Bess, wiping her beard with her fingers.

"Please, let me," I said, rising to my feet. I tried to take the plate from Miss Lightfoot before food overflowed the sides. I didn't think of her comfort entirely; I was eager to talk to the two-headed man and find out more about him.

"I don't know, sugar cake," she said. "He's a reserved gentleman."

"Oh, let him, Ruby," said Bess. "Abel's a well-bred lad. Mr. Ginger may take to him."

Miss Lightfoot sighed and let go the plate.

A blanket hung across the back of the wagon. I tapped on the wood of the frame. "Excuse me, Mr. Ginger. I have your supper."

"Who's that?" came a timid query. "I don't know that voice."

"I'm new," I answered, "and an admirer of yours."

"Admirer?" he whispered. "You admire me?"

"My parents raised me to respect the unusual," I said.

"Then, they are unusual in themselves," he answered.

I chuckled. "You have no idea."

Rustling sounds came from inside. "Perhaps you could give me an idea," he said. "Do come in."

As I entered, he slid some sheets of paper into a portfolio on top of a small folding table. The draft from my entrance caused one sheet to fly. I caught it as it floated to the floor. It held a fine watercolor likeness of Miss Lightfoot, if she had no scales on her face.

Mr. Ginger stared at me aghast, in stark contrast to the second face attached to his forehead, which appeared to be fast asleep. "Please, don't tell her," begged Mr. Ginger. "I should be embarrassed."

"But it's excellent," I told him. "I'm sure she would be flattered."

He lowered his eyes. "The others would laugh," he whispered. "I don't care to be mocked."

"Of course not," I said. "No one does." I knew then that if Miss Lightfoot became my ally, Mr. Ginger would follow. I found surprising comfort in this.

As Mr. Ginger reached for a tumbler of murky water and

paintbrushes, the eyes of his second head opened. Mr. Ginger overshot the glass, and his sleeve almost knocked it over. "Drat," he said. "Edward is awake."

I tilted my head in question.

"We seem to have mixed-up vision," he explained. "When Edward opens his eyes, my sight becomes confused. I don't know what Edward sees, for he is incapable of telling me."

"Why don't you cover his eyes with your hand?" I asked.

"He nips," said Mr. Ginger. "I do wear a hat sometimes, but that's dreadfully hot in the summer."

The second nose must have smelled food, for the little mouth below it dribbled. Mr. Ginger knew somehow and reached up to dab it with a handkerchief. The fluffy tuft of hair on the second forehead moved like a cockscomb in response to the wrinkling of the tiny face.

"If you will excuse me," said Mr. Ginger. "I am more comfortable dining alone."

I hated to see him so timid of me. "You know, I grew up with show folk like yourself," I said. Maybe that would put him at ease with me. "May I come back to tell you about it?"

Mr. Ginger's primary countenance brightened with a smile. "I should enjoy that," he said.

"Honey pie," said Miss Lightfoot when I returned to our campfire. She appeared quite recovered. "Would you do me a favor and come put cream on my back? I would ask dear Bess, but she has retired, and I'm itching out of my skin."

"Um . . . ," I said. What kind of invitation was that?

"Aw, I'd do it," said Billy.

"I'm sure you would," said Miss Lightfoot, "but I feel Mr. Dandy is more likely to stick to the task at hand."

I followed her nervously. She comported herself like a lady, not a temptress, but what if she expected more than I was willing to give?

Inside her wagon Miss Lightfoot handed me a bottle of Hawley's Corn Salve and turned her back on me. As I fumbled with the bottle, she slid her bodice from her shoulders. My mouth dried.

"Don't put too much on, sugar; I want to get rid of the itch, not ruin my act."

I poured a dollop into my palm and smoothed it on her back, which was as cracked as a mudflat in summer.

"Oooh," she sighed. "That's much better. You have no idea."

I tried not to venture too far around her sides. "Does this work?" I asked, for conversation's sake.

"Well, I do prefer Wrinkleine," she said. "It soaks in faster, but it's much more expensive, and if I were an ordinary lady, I would be annoyed at them. I think I have proved without a doubt that they cannot live up to their guarantee to permanently remove all forms of wrinkles and blemishes."

I had covered her back with lotion, and planned to take my leave, when she raised her hand to her shoulder and laid it over mine. I almost dropped the bottle. I took a deep breath while I searched for gentle words to let her down.

"Honey pie," she said in a hushed voice before I could speak. "You and Apollo are gentlefolk. Are you sure you want that little friend of yours on the road with the characters Mink employs?"

I took her lead and answered quietly. "I haven't had much choice." I hadn't expected this to be the topic of conversation. "He ran away from home to follow me, and I don't know what to do with him."

"You have no money, have you?" she said, removing her hand from mine.

"No, ma'am."

"I believe I have the price of postage, if you'd care to send a letter," she offered.

My fingers more certain now, I screwed the bottle cap on tight. I felt ashamed that I had considered her anything but virtuous—and felt truly relieved. "That's very kind of you," I said. "If I can find a place to leave Apollo so he won't be able to follow me, I might send that letter."

"Oh, precious biscuit. You don't want them to take you home too, do you?"

"No, ma'am."

She was silent for a moment, as if she pondered this. Finally she spoke all in a rush. "Be careful of Billy Sweet. He seems friendly enough, but his loyalty is to Mink. Mink's show is his bread and butter, and it is in his interests to keep the show well stocked with acts, no matter what the method employed." She turned to me, her bodice clutched to her chest, tears in her eyes. "Mink is a villain, Abel. Do not trust him or any of his minions." She stopped suddenly, as if stunned at her own statement, then spoke in her regular voice. "Now, get out of here before my reputation is as blemished as my skin."

"Thank you, ma'am," I said, and left.

Hot, sticky night drew in close, but her gentle warning chilled me. If I understood her correctly, I was right in thinking Dr. Mink was the sort of villain who would steal a child for personal gain, and if he had taken Mr. Northstar's son, then he or someone in his employ had killed Mr. Northstar's grandmother. Yes, I would be careful of him. He was cultivating Apollo's friendship and binding the boy to him. Who knew what he would do if he found I had plans to take Apollo away.

I HELD THE MOST BEAUTIFUL WOMAN in the world in my arms, her vibrant, lithe body pressed to mine. Slowly I lowered my lips to hers. The evening air was perfumed by the flowers on the vines that concealed us. The throaty songs of frogs serenaded our love.

Then came the thrash and hiss of ripping vines behind me and a man's incoherent shout.

She stared over my shoulder, eyes wide and stricken. "We have been discovered!"

I tried to shield her with my body, but brawny field servants tore us from each other, and a man with a shaved head, in the linen robes of a priest, struck my face—her husband. His lips pulled back in a snarl that revealed blackened teeth. I struggled for a weapon I could not reach and cursed his name, Sethnakhte.

He towered above us like the god of destruction he prayed to. "How dare you betray me?" he roared at his wife. "Observe what happens to adulterers, for you are next."

Servants stripped me despite my thrashing, while others flourished their whips. They pulled off a tube bound to my waist, and the hide split when it hit the ground. Out unfurled a map.

"Stop!" cried her husband, and the world stood as still as pictures in a tomb except for the man who reached for the stolen document. His face grew thunderous as he examined it.

"So," he said to me, "you are a traitor to your king, as well as to your friend."

"Not *my* king," I said, knowing I sealed my doom.

"I should never have begged you to come back for me," my love cried.

"If you bear witness against him as a spy and say he forced himself upon you, I will protect you," said her husband. "If not . . ."

"Yes," I cried. "It was I. She tried to fight me off, but I was too strong."

There was not a second of debate in her eyes. She raised her chin and defied her husband, her face a mask of despair. "I gave myself willingly," she declared. "I love him and will never betray him." She condemned herself because of me. Oh, my love. My heart broke. I could not save her.

The servants forced me to my knees. I saw the biggest man raise a sharp sickle. My love screamed and screamed. My perception shriveled to a burning hole of fear and pain and flashing lights and falling, falling, falling. . . .

A voice whispered in my ear, "Don't let anyone take me from you again."

*

I woke in a sweat, my blanket a knot around my knees, and reached in panic for my darling.

"Abel, watch your elbow." Apollo kicked and scuffled his way out from under the wagon.

I crawled after him, suffused with sorrow, and sat in the early sunlight, confused and muzzy. I truly felt as if those events had really happened, and those last words—it was almost as if someone was sending me a message. *Oh yes,* I thought. I removed a pebble from beneath my rear and laughed at myself. *Lady Adventure is a real person luring me to her with exciting stories of romance.* What kind of a woman was able to do that? Yet I thought of the buxom curves and inviting lips of the dream dancer, and I thrilled at the notion of finding her.

The day was already hot, and I couldn't eat. Miss Lightfoot pressed an apple on me and insisted I should save it for later. The sight of tears in her eyes distracted me from thoughts of my dream.

"Are you crying, ma'am?" I asked.

"Bless you, sweetie toes," she said. "I am not. I am unable to perspire because of my skin. This is what happens instead. I am afraid it does not keep me cool, however." She sighed. "It will be a difficult day."

When I climbed into my driver's seat, the lingering melancholy of the dream evaporated with the rising sun, until at last I could see the woman's face no longer, nor feel the pain of being parted from her.

Perhaps my passengers had their own dreams to consider, for the ladies were quiet, and I was left with my thoughts until we paused for our luncheon. Nobody appeared to have much appetite, and it was not long before Dr. Mink spurred us on again. I made a quick trip to the bushes, and when I returned, I saw the others gathered around my wagon.

"We don't have time for your vapors," Mink snapped at Miss Lightfoot, who sat crumpled over on the tailgate.

"Oh, let the girl have her bath," growled Bess. Her beard bristled.

"Miss Lightfoot needs a bath 'cause it's hot and she might die," said Apollo to me, all the while glancing from Miss Lightfoot to Dr. Mink and back. The fine hair on his face floated like gossamer in his nervous breath. He moved as if to tug Dr. Mink's sleeve but jumped back as the skeleton man flung up his arm for attention.

"Move out," Mink ordered. "Anyone not aboard gets left behind."

Billy Sweet ran for his wagon. The giant shambled after him, shaking his head. Apollo ran off too.

"Well, I'm not shifting," said Bess, brawny arms akimbo.

"Please, sugar," said Miss Lightfoot to her faintly. "I'll be all right."

"You'll shift," said Dr. Mink, and he nodded at Bonfiglio.

The big man flexed his arm muscles, enjoying his moment, and then he scooped Bess from the ground as if she were a doll.

"Hey," I cried. He had her arm bent up her back.

Bonfiglio tossed Bess past Miss Lightfoot into the wagon and turned on me, fist raised. "I guarantee Dr. Mink will not mind if I knock you down," he said, eyes narrowed.

"Don't, Abel," said Bess as she struggled to her knees and rubbed her arm. "Don't give him the pleasure."

I hesitated, not sure what to do, but then Apollo returned with a bucket of water and a sponge. He strained to lift it up to Miss Lightfoot, but it was too unwieldy, and he slopped water everywhere. I was proud of him. "Good lad," I said.

Mink wheezed with laughter. "Look at that. A doggie with a heart of gold."

I glared at Mink and Bonfiglio, then fished out the dripping sponge and handed it to Miss Lightfoot.

"Oh, you sweethearts," Miss Lightfoot declared. "I thank you." She dabbed her arms and face with the welcome water.

Mink grabbed Apollo by his scruff. "A valiant act, my lad," he said, and dragged him away. I couldn't believe Apollo looked pleased despite his pulled hair.

That afternoon a thunderstorm took us by surprise. The wind whipped up, the air grew chill, and dark clouds descended like the four horsemen of the apocalypse. I tried to lean back under the canvas bonnet, but the wind drove the rain in on me, and it soaked me like a drowned rat in the blink of an eye. The track we followed churned into a river of mire, and we plodded along with frequent stalls and jolts when the wheels stuck in the mud, then spat dirt as the persevering horses pulled them out again.

At least Miss Lightfoot will be more comfortable now, I thought, and I glanced over my shoulder to see her sitting at the rear of the wagon, with the canvas curtain raised to catch the spray.

As the lightning flashed and forked overhead, I wondered whether it was good or bad that there were few trees. Were you supposed to stay away from them or hide under them? I had a terrible feeling that it wasn't good to be the tallest thing around in a prairie storm. I prayed I wouldn't see a funnel cloud.

The storm ended as quickly as it had begun, and the only sign that it had ever been was the line of boiling dark that retreated across the sky, leaving a vaporous white that deepened to blue once more. The grasses sparkled with jewels, and the air tasted of fragile fairy-tale oceans.

We built a fire that evening from dry twigs and sticks Bess had been smart enough to stow away in a box. All of us gathered around the flames—except Mr. Ginger and the giant, who felt poorly once more. Mink had a cane propped beside him. It had a silver skull handle.

"You need to take the giant to a doctor," said Bess to Mink.

"All giants are complainers," said Mink. He made me think of a skeleton I'd seen in a medieval picture—Death bringing the plague.

"Giants get sick easy," replied Bess. "You want a giant to show, don't you? How's he gonna sit there if he's sick?"

Mink glared at her. "I've a bottle of stomach bitters in my wagon I'll give up for him. That'll set his digestion right."

Bess didn't look convinced, but she let the matter drop.

We were all damp and uncomfortable, and no one talked much as we ate tiresome beans again, not even Apollo. "Well, you could have had your bath after all, Ruby," Mink said, meshing and cracking his bony fingers. He had a satisfied sneer on his thin, cruel mouth. "You could have stripped naked and dangled out the back of the wagon. I guarantee you, my dear, no one would have cared to look."

Miss Lightfoot lowered her eyes.

"Aw, Doc. You shouldn't talk to a lady like that," said Billy, surprising me.

"Sweet on Ruby are you, Billy Sweet?" wheezed Dr. Mink. "Billy Sweet on Ruby." He chuckled at his own crude joke. "A weasel and an alligator, well, well, well—that would be miscegenation indeed. Keep me informed. I'll have a job for the offspring." As he left, he swiped a nasty blow at Billy's knees with his cane.

Billy yelped and grabbed his legs.

"Don't talk back to me," Mink hissed, and his brawny body-guard laughed.

"Why do you stay with him?" I asked after they had gone. "There are other shows."

"Why, he's going to make us rich, of course," said Billy Sweet. "He's taking us to Cally-forn-eye-ay, where the streets are paved with gold. Venice, young feller, named after the city in Europe."

"They have canals with real live imported gondoliers from Italy," said Miss Lightfoot. "And there's shops, hotels, theaters, fancy Roman statues, and a pier out into the Pacific with a Spanish galleon restaurant."

"That sounds marvelous," I said. "I'd really like to see that."

Billy Sweet nodded knowingly. "All they needs is some ten-in-ones. It's a prime spot for a freak show."

"And I'll train the children," said Apollo, his eyes wide with excitement. My enthusiasm waned. I didn't want Apollo to go there; I wanted him to go home.

"Mink says it could be the new Coney Island," continued Billy Sweet. "Ain't much competition in California, Mink says. We can make big money. They got money comin' down from the Klondike goldfields. Mink's gonna be the new Barnum, and we're gonna grow rich with him."

"No one's gonna get rich with that old miser," grumbled Bess. "The only one who'll end up with money will be him, unless you all get wise and ask for your dues after each show. If we stood together, he'd have no choice."

This had the feel of an old argument. So old no one bothered to argue back. In the silence that followed, I offered to take a plate to Mr. Ginger.

The two-headed man glanced beyond me, and for a second he appeared disappointed, but then he greeted me with shy affection and offered me a stool. The little face in the center of his forehead slept as I told Mr. Ginger of the cruel behavior of Dr. Mink.

"That fiend Mink," said Mr. Ginger. I hadn't expected such strong emotion from him. The eyes of his twin flickered, as if he sensed his brother's anger. "He betrayed Miss Lightfoot, you know. Lured her from her home with promises he never meant to keep, and now she is compromised and can never return."

His words shocked me into silence.

"I can't bear to see a gentle soul mistreated in that way," said Mr. Ginger.

I nodded in agreement. "But what's your story?" I asked. "A man of your unusual appearance could find work in much bigger shows. You could earn a fortune. You could draw huge audiences."

Mr. Ginger sighed. "I have no need of a fortune, merely a living, and to be honest, I have no love of large audiences. This suits me fine."

I was rudely persistent. "Why this show if you despise Mink so?"

"I have hopes," he said, and left it there.

On the fourth day we crossed the Mississippi and entered Iowa. We must have traveled almost one hundred miles.

At midday we pulled onto a waste lot at the edge of a small town to join a wood-paneled caravan painted with Gypsy patterns and Mink's name. As the troupe climbed to the ground, a figure rose from the caravan's back steps and approached us. I wasn't sure what this person could be, for it wore a flowered wrap and a turban but walked like a man in a man's boots. Billy

Sweet greeted the new person with a sibilant name that sounded like "see-see."

"Who's that?" I asked Bess.

"Oh, he calls himself Cecil-Cecilia, like he's a girl and a boy," growled Bess, "but we call him Ceecee for short. He says he's a hermaphrodite, but his real name is Theodore Spittle, from Hoboken, New Jersey, and he's as male as you . . . or do you have a secret?" She stared at me head-on, which meant crotch level.

I caught myself moving my hands to cover my privates, and Bess laughed.

"Where are the puppies?" Mink called.

Ceecee spoke in a high voice with a mean edge. "They were a nuisance, so I locked them up." The creature inspected its nails.

"And Earle?"

"I sent him out to drum up business."

"Taking your chances, aren't you?" Dr. Mink snapped.

"Little Beauty said you'd be here."

"Christ Almighty, Ceecee," Dr. Mink exclaimed. "And you believed her? That clairvoyant bull crap's for the marks."

Ceecee shrugged. "She's been right before."

Mink turned his back on Ceecee in disgust and barked out orders. The usual bustle of setting up camp commenced.

As I unhitched and hobbled the horses, I couldn't take my eyes from the painted wagon. That Ceecee talked like he'd locked up a litter of dogs, but was Mr. Northstar's missing child inside? Finally I couldn't stand to wonder any longer. I glanced around to make sure no one was watching, walked up the caravan steps, pulled the outside bolt, and opened the carved back door.

I reeled at the stench and almost fell down the stairs.

A pot lay spilled on the floor, and soaked newspapers were covered in odorous piles. *There are dogs in here after all,* I thought. Then over the edges of the built-in bunks and around from the back of a trunk peered solemn little faces of all shades. Human faces.

I **REACHED IN TO DRY THE TEARS** of the nearest child, and she flinched away. The weight of her distended head toppled her backward, and when her delicate hands hit the boards to save herself, feces oozed from between her fingers. She had water on the brain. The poor little mite would probably never become a woman, and this was her childhood.

I clenched my fists. I didn't want to deal with this, I wanted to grab Apollo and run, but my parents had taught me better than that. Having to take charge made me angrier than ever. I looked around for Mink and found Bess behind me. Words stuck in my throat.

She nodded at me, and her eyes matched my fury. "Mink!" she yelled.

The showman walked over, twirling his death's-head cane, and my heart pounded. Apollo trotted behind him.

"Go on," said Bess, giving me the lead.

"How can you treat children this way?" I demanded. My voice cracked.

Mink's knuckles went white as he tightened his grip on his cane. "I expect they were making a nuisance of themselves," he said through his teeth. He cared more about my insolence than their condition.

"See?" said Bess. "It's not just a troublemaking dwarf who notices. A complete stranger knows the tune."

"They're filthy," I said, taking strength from her support. "They could get sick and die from those conditions." I jabbed a finger at the wagon.

Mink appraised me with a cold look and then examined the scene in the wagon. His tongue flicked out to lick his lips, and I thought of a snake. "Ceecee!" he shrieked.

"Dr. Mink?" Ceecee sauntered through the other performers, who had gathered to see what the commotion was about. He had the remnants of colored powder over his left eye and the start of a beard on his right cheek. A cigarette in his hand sent a thin line of smoke skyward.

"What are you?" Apollo asked, and I winced.

Ceecee's laughter sounded like a whinny. "Who is this boy?" he asked, and he looked Apollo up and down in a greedy way I didn't like at all. "I am the star of the show. Cecil-Cecilia—half man, half woman, wholly unique." He bowed, then curtsied, showing a leg of trouser under his flowered wrap.

"Stow that star-of-the-show bull. This feller tells me you're diseasing my investment," Mink said.

"Disease?" Ceecee's eyes widened, and he yanked his wrapper close around him.

"From the shit, you imbecile!" Mink roared.

"You should put Abel in charge of them," said Bess. "They'll last longer."

Ceecee snarled, "You hairy little bitch."

"She's right, you're done with them," said Mink. "You can drive the gentlemen performers. Billy will drive the brats, and . . . this fine lad is now in charge of them." He tugged Apollo over by his whiskers.

Apollo yelped and rubbed his cheek, but he managed to grin.

Ceecee swiveled his mannequin head between Bess and me, his eyes slits. He couldn't seem to decide whom to hate more. He flicked his cigarette into the observers, who ducked and scattered. "Who are you to interfere?" he hissed at me. He reached inside his robes with a spidery hand and stepped closer. I didn't know his intent, but I moved back as a chill ran through me.

"You won't touch him unless I say, if you want a job," Mink said.

Ceecee whirled and left.

"Well, clean them," Mink ordered Apollo. "We've got a show to set up," he snapped at the others. "Get cracking."

Billy Sweet shook his head as he walked off, and Miss Lightfoot's scaled face was drawn with worry, but Bess gave me a wink. That heartened me.

"Come on, Apollo," I said. "I'll help you clean up this mess."

"Do I have to?" Apollo pinched his nose with his fingers.

I felt much the same way, but, "He put you in charge, didn't he?" I said. "And my guess is you'll live here with the children."

Apollo gulped. "I'll get the bucket."

While the puppy boy ran for a pail, I evacuated the wagon. "What's your name, darling?" I asked the lantern-headed girl as I lifted her out.

"Minnie," she whispered.

"Well, sit right here, Minnie," I said, and placed her on top of a large wooden crate I had removed before her.

"I'm the frog boy," claimed a hoarse voice, and a skinny young man of about eight or nine clambered out of the wagon under his own steam. "You sure told the doc what's what. I never seed someone sass him before. No one 'cept Bess, that is. You're gonna be sorry for that."

No doubt, I thought. "What's that?" I asked, pointing at a trunk under the wagon.

"That's Ceecee's goods," said the frog boy.

I climbed into the wagon and found another girl huddled in a lower bunk. She stared at me with huge, dark eyes that peered over a dirty sheet. She wouldn't come out no matter how sweetly I entreated her, but I didn't want to reach in and lift her and frighten her to death.

From the corner of my eye I noticed a figure in the shadow of a crate at the back of the wagon. I felt a surge of excitement and took a chance. "Is that you, Willie Northstar?" I asked.

The figure in the shadows gasped. "How'd you know that? Told nobody here my last name."

"I know your daddy," I replied triumphantly. "I came to find you."

The boy edged out into the shaft of daylight from the back door. He wore ragged short pants and a matching ragged shirt. I could see that his skin was marked in white and brown patches like an Indian pony.

"Where's my daddy?" he asked, urgency in his voice.

"I don't know," I answered. "He's out searching for you." It pained me to see the hope die from his eyes. "But I'm sure I could find him again."

"Now?" he asked.

Silently I prayed that Lillie would give Mr. Northstar my message to follow Lazarus Mink. "Dr. Mink won't let me walk out of here with you, you know," I said. "He's going to make money from showing you to people, and he's not the sort of man who'll give up money without a fight."

Willie nodded solemnly. "He tells his bad men to hurt people."

This poor child had seen his grandmother struck down in front of him, no doubt. "Yes, and we don't want to be hurt, therefore we need to keep it a secret that we plan to leave here and take you back to your daddy. You know what a secret is, don't you?"

His eyes grew big, and to my surprise, he backed into the shadows again. "That's when you don't tell," he whispered with a catch in his voice.

"Right," I said, and wished he didn't know. "I have to figure out how we can leave without being hurt. Okay?"

"Can I come too?" I could have kicked myself. The girl had been so quiet I had forgotten she was there. How could I tell her no? "All the children can come," I said, "but don't tell the grown-ups." Oh, Lord. What had I promised? I couldn't be responsible for *all* the children.

"This is Bertha the Bear," said Willie.

She tossed the sheet off and rolled out of the bunk. She wore a thin brown shift, ragged at the hem, and as she lumbered to the door, I noted how the stocky girl had gotten her nickname— for she had no wrists or ankles, but had hands and feet right at her elbows and knees, and she could walk only on all fours.

In the sunlight specked scabs showed on Bertha's arms. "Are you injured?"

"Insect bites," she said, avoiding my gaze. "I scratched 'em."

I couldn't help think they resembled burns, but I didn't pry. "What's your real name, Frog Boy?" I asked.

"Moses, sir," the leggy boy said. "Moses Quick."

"I'm not a sir," I told him. "I'm Abel Dandy. I hope I'll be a friend."

He exchanged wary glances with Bertha.

Apollo came back with two buckets banging his thighs. "I tried to boil the water," he said, "but it's barely warm." He surveyed the brood. "I reckon we should start with you fellows. You seem to have missed your Sunday bath."

"This is Apollo," I told them. "Dr. Mink says he's to be in charge of you, but if he gets too bossy, you come to me."

The four children stared silently at Apollo. I prepared myself for the protests. Why would any one of them welcome the authority of a strange, hairy boy not much older than themselves?

"Does that mean Apollo will sleep in our wagon?" asked Bertha.

Before I could answer, Ceecee swept by me, followed by Billy Sweet. "I've come for my personal effects. Get that, Billy." He gestured extravagantly with a black cigarette holder, and smoke wreathed in the air. Minnie seemed to shrink into herself. The children on the ground edged away. I eyed the cigarette with suspicion.

"Get out where I can see you, you little monster," Ceecee shrilled at Willie, who was sliding behind the crate.

Apollo started, then growled at the star of the show.

Ceecee took a quick step back, and the children burst into giggles.

"You're not in charge of us anymore," said Moses with obvious delight. "Apollo's our boss. He's going to stay with us."

Minnie laughed, and the other two children cheered.

Ceecee turned away in a swirl of flowered wrapper. "We'll see how long he stays." Billy followed with the trunk. He didn't smile.

Moses poked out his tongue at the departing figure. It was a long tongue indeed, but a typical rude-boy gesture, until he popped his eyes out of their sockets so they bulged, showing how he had earned the name Frog Boy.

"Why did he lock you up?" I asked when I returned with a washtub owned by Miss Lightfoot that would serve as a bath.

"Oh, he don't need no excuse," said Moses as he frowned at the tub and backed away.

"He just didn't want to bother with us," said Bertha.

"I found extra clothes," said Apollo, dragging an open box from the wagon. He wrinkled his nose. "They don't look much cleaner."

They would have to do until we did laundry. "A frog boy shouldn't be afraid of water," I told Moses as I filled the tub.

Moses stuck out his scrawny chest. "I ain't afraid of nothin'." He glared at Bertha.

"I won't look," said Bertha the Bear, and she turned her back.

Moses stripped off his shabby clothing and climbed into the water.

Apollo scrubbed Moses with a rag. The water became filthy in seconds.

We were on our fourth tub of water when a large, open cart pulled by two horses rumbled onto the field. An enormous fat man, red faced and out of breath, held the reins. A sign hung on the back of the cart—COME SEE DR. MINK'S MONSTER MENAGERIE. The location of the show had been painted over repeatedly. Today's show would take place "behind Ringgold's Livery."

"What took you so long?" scolded Dr. Mink.

"I had to stop for lunch once or twice, didn't I?" the fat man answered.

That was my introduction to Earle Johnson, the man who never left his cart.

"Get over here. We need to set up," said Mink.

I helped the two other drivers unhitch the horses and raise the show tent around the fat man and the giant. Extra sections were added on to each end, and a small section on the back for the performers' convenience. The gaudily painted canvas banners were set up along the front of the tent to create an aisle behind. The audience would enter the aisle through a gap in the center of the banners after they paid for a ticket outside. This time a second set of smaller banners hung above the first. They portrayed the children, even Willie Northstar, now known as the Piebald Boy. I wondered how Dr. Mink had managed to have one painted while he traveled, and then I glimpsed the initials in the lower right-hand corner, E. G. Eustace Ginger.

"Where are their parents?" I asked Billy Sweet, who helped me raise the bally platform from which Dr. Mink would entice his audience.

He glanced up at the banners. "Sold 'em," he said. "Took the money and signed legal papers that give Mink custody."

Well, one paper had to be a forgery—how many others were as well, and where were they kept?

As I glanced over at Dr. Mink's wagon, the door opened and a man shook Mink's hand before he left.

"I see the boss is 'fixing' things for us," remarked Billy. He noted my blank look. "Greasing the palm," he said. "Paying the law to look the other way."

A dark, queer lump settled in my gut. Forged papers must be one of the things sheriffs could be paid to overlook.

I helped Billy set up a canvas shelter. Underneath it he pieced together two halves of a large wooden wheel.

"I use ammonia," said Billy, obviously pleased to have someone to boast to. "I keep a bottle under the wheel in a dish. I wait till the dupes place their bets, then dabs ammonia under a hole with few or no bets on it. The mouse thinks there's one of its own at home and runs down that hole."

This must be another activity the sheriff had been paid to ignore.

By now local children were watching from the perimeter of the lot. Apollo had the sense to usher our children into the show tent as soon as the others showed up. No sense in giving a free look or becoming a target. As I checked the guy ropes, two figures swathed in cloaks made their way to the raised flap in the back of the tent. By their sizes and the shrouded load they struggled with, I took them to be Miss Lightfoot and Bess Tuggle carrying Mr. Bopp between them.

Al Bonfiglio stalked past with a crate, from which came the *ching* of glass against glass. The next time I saw him, he maneuvered a long wooden box from the back of Mink's wagon with the help of Billy Sweet. That must be the lady in the box. What kind of trick could it be?

Dr. Mink sent me inside the tent to set up the fancy ropes that divided audience from display. In a larger show there would be a platform for the acts to sit upon. I was grateful, however, not to have another structure to set up.

"Good afternoon, Abel," Mr. Ginger greeted me. I don't know when he had slipped inside.

"That's fine work you did on those banners," I told him.

He waved my compliment aside. "Oh, slapdash," he said, "I could do that with four eyes open." But he smiled with pleasure. I noticed he had trimmed both his beard and that of his twin in preparation for the show.

The air clung hot, thick, and sweet under the canvas. I had to work in my undershirt or else I'd be sick. I apologized to the ladies.

"Oh, please, honey pie," said Miss Lightfoot, "don't think of it at all." She dabbed at her neck with the sponge, which had become her constant companion.

"I shall think of it constantly," Bess said, and leered at me.

Mr. Bopp bit her ankle, and Earle Johnson laughed so hard the springs of his wagon creaked, and I worried that it would collapse with his weight. "They're a caution, ain't they?" he said to the giant, who stood beside him.

The giant nodded, but he didn't look amused. His face was pale, and he wiped his mouth with a handkerchief that seemed tiny in his gnarled hand.

Apollo had the children lined up on stools at the far end of the tent. I couldn't hear what he said to them, but they listened intently. I hoped he was telling a story and not planning one of his schemes. They were dressed in clean costumes that had been in Miss Lightfoot's care. Moses the Frog Boy sported green tights, and his knees stuck up so high he did look like he had frog legs. Little Minnie had on a Chinese jacket and short black trousers. Her thin, dark hair was pulled back in a slender braid. Embroidered slippers graced her feet, and a matching skullcap made her head look all the bigger. Bertha wore a brown outfit with puffed sleeves and pantaloons, which showed off her short-ened limbs. Willie was garbed in short pants only; consequently the audience could experience the full impact of his distinct and unusual skin patterns.

Ceecee swept into the tent. The turban was gone—on one side of his head the hair hung down past his shoulder, on the other side it stopped at the ear. He had painted the half of his face on the long-haired side, and he wore an earring on that ear. The children became quiet and moved in closer to Apollo.

"Does Ceecee beat the children?" I asked Miss Lightfoot.

"I cannot say," she answered, "but Bess saw him cut a man across the face once, cheek to cheek. He always carries a straight razor folded in his pocket."

I remembered how Ceecee had reached inside his robe as he advanced on me, and I shuddered anew.

The he-she glowered at the huddle of children and then swept toward them. He wore a white shirt with voluminous sleeves and an odd pair of trousers—one leg stovepipe thin, and the other flared as if to emulate a skirt. On the trouser side he wore a sturdy boot, on the skirt side a buttoned shoe. How he could appear ominous in that getup, I don't know, but he managed. He halted in front of the children and stood in silence.

"Boo!" he cried.

Willie shrieked. The others cringed. Ceecee whinnied with laughter.

Apollo pushed the children behind him. "I'll bite you," he proclaimed.

"I'll bite you first, you hairy little monster," promised Ceecee.

I thought of that razor and hurried over. "Apollo, you have prepared everyone for the show but yourself."

"He called me a monster," Apollo complained.

"You are," I answered, and put myself between them, my

back to Ceecee, although that made the flesh between my shoulders flinch. "A beast who is really a prince, like in *Beauty and the Beast.*"

"That's my name!" chimed in Minnie. "Little Beauty."

That caught Apollo's attention. "Is it?" he asked.

I was surprised too. "There," I said. "You must be Little Beauty's beast."

"I think grooming is in order, sweetie toes," said Miss Lightfoot, joining us, accompanied by Bess. With scaly fingers she handed me her own ivory comb.

I gave Miss Lightfoot a thankful smile.

"Hey, the brats aren't yours to bully now, remember?" Bess told Ceecee. "Better not let Mink see you taunting the real freaks, or you'll be biting, all right—biting the heads off chickens like the geek you are."

"You'll get your just deserts one day, you harridan," Ceecee promised.

Minnie wrapped her arms around Bess and buried her face in the folds of the dwarf woman's bodice.

"Don't cling so hard, chick," said Bess. "I'm going nowhere."

The so-called half man–half woman spat and stalked away.

"Is that the Little Beauty who predicted our arrival?" I whispered to Miss Lightfoot. "Can Minnie actually see the future?"

"That's hard to say, since she doesn't talk much," Miss Lightfoot answered softly. "However, some of the words that come out of her mouth, well, honey dumpling, it does give one pause."

I grabbed Apollo before he slipped off. He submitted reluctantly as I combed his face where he had two to six inches of silky fair locks.

"You should tie it back from your eyes or you'll bump into stuff, like Mr. Ginger," said Bertha.

"You know, I could manage a topknot," I said, to gales of laughter from the children.

Mink entered, clapping his hands, and the laughter halted abruptly. "Take your places, we've got an audience outside." He had dressed in his tights and evening coat once more, his top hat on his head. "Stop primping that boy," he snapped at me. "He's supposed to look like a wild animal."

"I should go change," I said. I wasn't ready for the show myself.

"Don't bother," said Mink. "Your job doesn't require fancy clothes."

"What is my job?" I asked. I had hoped Dr. Mink would take advantage of my knife-throwing after all.

"In there," Mink said, and gestured toward the first section of tent. "Since you're keen to look after things, you can keep the yokels' hands off my exhibits. And don't move from your post until we pack 'em up again."

I stifled my disappointment and pushed through the curtain.

On a table made of planks sat three big jars; something floated in the murky liquid within each. Next to the table was the crate the jars had been packed in, and on the other side of that the long box from Mink's wagon had been set up on trestles like a coffin in a parlor, the lid propped upright against it. There appeared to be faded designs on the lid in blue and red and yellow. *Well, let's have a look at the lady in the box,* I said to myself.

I expected to find a doll, or a gaff made of papier-mâché, but inside the box lay a figure wrapped in crumbling bandages, its wrists crossed at the groin. A clawlike hand with yellow nails poked through the linens. Someone had partially removed the wrappings to reveal a brown leather face with slits for eyes and a sunken nose. The tips of a few dark teeth protruded from under tight, shrunken lips.

An Egyptian mummy?

It had to be a fake.

But the cloth was old and yellow, and a smell rose from the object like the sands of time. I felt hot sun beat down on my back, and I reeled. The music of pipes played in the distance.

IT MUST BE THE HEAT, **I THOUGHT** as I sat down carefully on the crate and wiped my brow with the back of my hand. What a fool I was. "My apologies, madam," I said to the mummy. "The sight of your beauty quite overcame me."

I strained my eyes to read the faded copperplate writing on a yellowed card pasted inside the box near the feet of the mummy: UNKNOWN FEMALE, SECOND INTERMEDIATE PERIOD, EGYPT. I examined her face and tried to imagine what she had looked like when alive. "You do have lovely, high cheekbones, but I'm sure you were not so tanned." I smiled at my own joke.

How odd to see an Egyptian mummy in a tent in Iowa. A peculiar little shiver danced up my throat like fluttering wings, and my hand went to the ring, which formed a lump beneath my undershirt. No odder than to be given an Egyptian ring by a Siamese twin in Maryland. I frowned. I had the strange sensation of almost understanding something. I shrugged it off. The universe held many a fantastic and meaningless coincidence. I untied my shirtsleeves from around my waist and shook the garment out. Heat or not, if an audience was on the way, I could at least not greet them in my undershirt.

The hubbub of the crowd outside quieted as Mink launched into his pitch, inviting all to the "attractive, instructive, and elevating exhibition" inside the tent. This time he extolled the marvels of the children as well as the adults—all of them "alive, on the inside."

"Frightened by a bear while carrying her child, a mother gave birth to a baby more ursine than human," Mink said to describe Bertha. Willie, according to Mink, descended from natives who had mated with leopards to celebrate their god. I didn't think Mr. Northstar would be amused. Mink called Little Beauty an amazing Oriental creature. He assured the audience that as she grew, she would develop incredible mind-reading skills because of the exceedingly large size of her brain. I chuckled. What balderdash.

I examined the jars set up on planks across trestles to my right. They were of the type used by doctors to preserve specimens, and when I saw the contents, I understood why. Within each floated a baby—waxy, pale, and distorted like a nightmare doll.

In the first jar was something labeled a mermaid—the lower two limbs were melded into one and had a single foot that faced backward like a flipper. The second jar contained what one could argue were two babies, except they had nothing from the waist down but each other. They were joined at one pelvis, with a head on either end instead of legs. The label called this a playing-card freak. I found the final baby the most disturbing, however. It had merely a dent between the shoulders where the head should have been; instead one could see the beginnings of a face peer out from its chest.

They were fine examples of lusus naturae, nature's mistakes, and I understood why people would be fascinated, but they made me feel squeamish nevertheless. I know many would argue otherwise, but it seemed sad and disrespectful to display dead children, even if those children had never had one breath of life in them.

Outside Mink introduced Cecil-Cecilia, "the single true half man–half woman on the northern American continent at this time." The gentlemen who doubted his words could come back for a special viewing this evening. The ladies were not invited, of course.

Soon I heard the rattle and *ching* of money in the box, and the first of the townies chattered as they came into the tent, the men in white shirtsleeves with suspenders holding up their canvas pants, the women in summer calicoes. Every kind of straw hat imaginable graced their heads. They milled and exclaimed and pointed and laughed. Some ladies averted their eyes from the babies, and who could blame them? The tent filled up and still more entered, so I urged them on. "Step through, ladies and gentlemen," I said, gesturing to the next section. "There are wonders, alive, on the inside."

Finally, Dr. Mink ushered the last of this audience in. Outside, the burly Al Bonfiglio would put a silk rope across the entrance and post a time for the next show as a new audience gathered. Ceecee would mince about and give them something to wonder at while they waited, and Billy Sweet would run his mouse game to amuse and beggar those who played.

Mink led his audience through to the main tent, leaving a few curious stragglers behind with me.

"What is it?" asked a potato-nosed girl, peering in at the mummy.

I couldn't resist. "An Egyptian princess who died three thousand years ago," I said. "She was bound in bandages and placed in a desert tomb. She lay there for centuries until discovered by explorers last year."

"So, what's she doing here?" asked the astute Miss Potato Nose.

A scream saved me from having to answer.

The stragglers hurried through the curtain. I followed in time to see a couple of gentlemen help a lady with closed eyes to her feet while another lady fanned her with a hat. Moses Quick, the Frog Boy, squatted on his stool above her and watched. As soon as she opened her eyes, he popped his. She screamed and went down again. The audience roared with laughter.

I could see by Mink's face that this hadn't happened before, and I could see from Apollo's face that he had engineered the incident. *Good showmanship,* I thought, and grinned. Mink wasn't about to let the audience think he had lost control. He came to assist the lady and offered her a ticket to the next show for being a good sport. Once he saw her return with a few more paying guests, Apollo would be out of trouble.

Mink noticed me and waved me back to my post, so I took my seat by the mummy once more.

Was it real? I wondered again, looking at the leather-brown face and clawlike hand. And how had Mink come to possess such a thing if it was? *By thievery,* a voice inside of me suggested. My heart skipped a beat, for that didn't quite feel like my voice.

I laughed at myself. I suffered from the heat still, that was all. "If you were stolen," I told the mummy, "you aren't alone. There are children here who were taken from their parents. The adult performers can't help—they depend upon Dr. Mink for their livelihood—and Mink has his roughs and his crooked lawmen. What am I supposed to do?"

Why did I talk to this thing as if it were alive? The petite form lay rigid, but even so, the delicately crossed arms and the curve of the tightly bound hips exuded an innate feminine presence.

"Perhaps you *were* a princess," I said. "Fed on honey and figs. Dressed in the finest linen. Cooled by peacock fans. How rude of someone to peel back your bandages and expose you to the world."

Barks and growls came from the tent next door, then titters from the audience. Apollo's mother would be mortified. She would much prefer he use his beautiful voice for singing.

I half dozed in the stuffy tent as I listened to the questions from the audience, answered by Miss Lightfoot's gentle explanations of her alligator skin or the gruff replies of Bess about the care of her beard. Earle Johnson, the fat man, revealed his weight and listed the items in his daily menu—I'm sure he exaggerated—and our giant gave his height at various ages and told his shoe size. He sounded quite disinterested, but giants were never known for their showmanship. I didn't hear Mr. Bopp speak, which I deemed wise, considering the blunt nature of the caterpillar man.

It was very hot. A bee buzzed close by on the other side of the canvas, the smell of warm hay wrapped me in a delicious cocoon, my eyes closed.

I faced a stone wall built to the scale of giants. The sun beat on my back, and the pale rock reflected shimmering light into my face, almost blinding me. The dry air scorched my lungs.

Water splashed somewhere far behind me, and large birds cried. Something lay beyond the wall that I had to reach, something I yearned for with all my being, something lost I would never have again. I stood, near tears and in misery.

I raised my hand to caress the stone with longing and felt a shock from palm to shoulder. The bones within my hand lit up and faded again, and a thunderous crack came at once from the wall and from inside me. The stone crumbled to dust at my feet and left a cavernous hole. Foul smells drenched me but were gone in moments, as if evil, banished, fled past on carrion wings.

I detected movement in the depths within, and my heart beat in my throat.

Slowly a figure walked from the shadows into a pool of light. Sunshine traveled up the form like dawn ascending an obelisk. First small bare feet were revealed, exquisitely shaped, then robed limbs. Finally only the face remained hidden by shadow, and I saw she was a woman wrapped in filmy gauze that accentuated voluptuous curves—no, *the* woman, for all others were as nothing compared with her. The white of her attire set off the tawny color of her rounded arms and delicate hands. The scent of sandalwood drifted on the newly arisen breeze. My breath was held hostage in my chest; I dared not exhale.

She took another step, and the veil of darkness lifted entirely. She tossed back a glistening torrent of inky hair and raised a languid hand to shield her eyes from the sun, but the sun should have shielded itself from *her* glory, for her face was a hymn of praise.

Joy shot from my breast like a homing bird. It was my love, who had been torn from me. It was my love returned.

"I have waited for you," she said in a voice made of hot, liquid honey, "and now you are here."

I jolted awake. Someone tugged my arm.

"You won't be bored for the next show," Apollo said, "I'm improving the act. Come help."

I blinked stupidly until foolish disappointment set in. I had half expected to see a beautiful foreign lady happy to see me.

The audience had left, and Dr. Mink strutted once more outside, drumming up another. I accompanied Apollo into the next tent, rubbing sleep from my eyes. Why did I always wake up at the good part? I was doomed to stay innocent even in my sleep. Apollo's improvements soon dispelled my dream, however.

First Willie the Piebald Boy demonstrated some very wobbly tumbles and somersaults, then Bertha the Bear did a little dance on all fours as she hummed "The Battle Hymn of the Republic." It appeared rather ungainly but had a certain charm.

"What do you think?" Apollo asked.

"Very entertaining," I said. "Much better than sitting like a lump. But I'm not sure you have found the perfect talent for Willie as yet."

"Minnie neither," Bertha said.

"Can you think of what Minnie could do?" asked Apollo.

Minnie gazed at me expectantly. A little smile blessed her rosebud lips, and her large head wobbled on her neck. I saw no reason why she couldn't trade on what Mink had already set up. "Tell people's fortunes, Minnie," I said. "Do you think you can do that?"

She stared at me, her smile unchanged; perhaps she was too young to understand.

"Say nice things to people, like 'You will have much love in your life' and 'You will come into money.'"

"Why?" she asked.

"Because that makes people happy," I said. "It gives them something to look forward to."

"I'll help you think of nice things," said Willie.

Minnie closed her eyes and toppled sideways. Willie caught her before she fell. When she opened her eyes again, they seemed distant even though she stared right at me. "A dark-haired lady loves you," she said.

I laughed. "That's the ticket." She understood after all. I was a little startled, however. It was uncanny—almost like she knew my dreams.

"Hey!" Earle Johnson gestured me over. "I think I've got an act too." The fat man leaned over and whispered.

"Well," I said. "I hear it's been done on the French stage."

"Really?" Earle wheezed with the effort it had taken him to bend.

"But I would suggest you build your repertoire," I said.

I peered through the curtain to watch the second show. The audience loved the dancing, they squealed in delight at Apollo's growls, and Minnie informed several young ladies that they would have pretty children or handsome beaus. Dr. Mink appeared puzzled by the increased activity of his performers but did not show displeasure—that is, until Earle Johnson tilted his bulk forward and tooted two verses of "Pop Goes the Weasel" by means of his own flatulence.

"I have tolerated your shenanigans today because you entertained the audience," Mink said after the show, "but I draw the line at farting songs. You're not the only fat man in the world, Earle Johnson. You can be replaced."

"But he got applause," Apollo pointed out.

"And eight people departed," said Dr. Mink. "Yiss. Eight people who will complain to others. I want no more surprises like that. Hear me."

The children gathered around Earle after Mink had stormed off.

"Now, don't that cap the climax? How did you learn that?" asked Moses.

"There's not much to do when a feller can't get around," answered Earle, looking pleased at the attention.

"It was powerful funny," said Willie.

"It was an aeronautical ballad, a fancy in flatulence," aped Apollo.

"It stunk up the place," called Mr. Bopp, but his mouth gaped open in a silent laugh.

"Good show, fat man," Bess said, and strained up to pat his hand.

Dr. Mink needn't have worried about bad publicity; enough people arrived for several more shows, and I actually saw Mink beam at Apollo and tousle his hair.

"Dr. Mink says I'm a smart manager for thinking up those acts," said Apollo between shows. "He says to keep it up."

I groaned inwardly. Here was another reason for Mink to hang on to the dog boy.

When the audiences dwindled, Mink ordered us to pack up everything except the end tent. The children trouped past on their way out. Minnie waved and left the tail end to come over.

The tiny girl stood on her tiptoes to look in at the mummy. A smile lit her face. "Lady T. is pleased you're here," she said. "She looks so pretty when she's happy." I would have to find Minnie a doll more her size.

The giant hunched through the curtain door from the center tent. "Good-bye," Minnie said to the giant, her expression solemn, and he spared her a small smile. I found it odd she should bid him farewell, for she followed right after him. Still, she was a small child, with a small child's logic.

It grew dark, and we had packed up all except for one small

tent lit eerily from within, when men from the town appeared again on the lot. Mink, lamp in hand, welcomed them through the canvas door. He left his lamp outside, where Al Bonfiglio loomed, arms akimbo—a warning that there should be no trouble. My curiosity got the better of me. Bonfiglio leered at me as I approached, and I almost turned back, but he motioned me in.

The dimly lit interior smelled of sweat, tobacco, and whiskey. Men pressed around a small platform in front of dark curtains. A sinuous piping began, an oboe perhaps, but I couldn't see the musician. Ceecee slid through the curtains, now clothed in diaphanous veils that hinted of curves.

Ceecee commenced a snaky foreign dance of insinuation, and there were murmurs and embarrassed coughs. As Ceecee undulated, the veils swirled to suggest but never reveal the truth of what lay beneath. The dance disturbed my senses, for I knew him to be a man, but my eyes kept on forgetting. His gyrations were a distorted reflection of the dancer in my dreams—a lie wrapped in silks and candlelight. I looked nervously at those around me. This was dangerous fare. Someone could take strong offense if disgust overwhelmed desire. But the audience was swept up in the illusion. Men whistled and called encouragement. Lust hung in the air like a mist.

Ceecee slowly peeled away veils and dropped them to the floor. Finally no more than a filmy skirt surrounded his hips and two scarves crisscrossed his chest. He ran his hands up and down his body, taunting the audience with their unvoiced question. I squirmed, aware of the breathing around me. He slid the gauzy sliver from his left shoulder—and revealed a man's smooth chest. Someone laughed, and the man in front of me groaned, but before discontent could turn to anger, Ceecee stepped back into shadow and drew the other scarf aside.

Perhaps it lay in the way he hunched his shoulder, or maybe it was a trick of light, but beneath the scarf I could make out the beginnings of a snowy mound. Ceecee narrowed his eyes and smiled spitefully as he let the scarf slip into place again. He made a moue at the audience, twirled, and bowed.

"Is that all?" a man cried harshly, and I feared for the worst, but Ceecee smirked, then slowly drew his skirt past his knees and swayed his hips, revealing one shaved leg and one hairy. I realized I had leaned forward with the others—repulsed yet unable to look away.

The skirt rose past his thighs, and I clenched my fists, fearing a fight, but the audience gasped.

The lantern went out.

"Thank you for coming," announced Mink. "Please follow the outside light to the door."

I stumbled after the rubes, as stunned by the ambiguity I had seen as they.

"How does he do that?" I asked Bess when we pulled over to sleep miles away. Everyone else had gone to bed, and we were alone by the fire. "It was a trick, right?"

"Oh, there's tricks of the trade, all right," she said as she combed out her beard. "I wager you didn't know that half of all cooch dancers you see are men."

That was a shock. I lowered my voice. "Is he a homosexual?" I couldn't believe I had asked a lady that question, but Bess wasn't an ordinary lady.

"I wouldn't care if he was a nancy-boy," she said. "They love other men, that's all. Pain is what he loves. Pain and laudanum."

"Laudanum!"

"Laudanum was why he was a geek when I first met him," she said.

"It's true?" I asked. "He earned a living biting the heads off live chickens and rodents?"

"Yes, being a he-she is a step up for Theodore Spittle," Bess answered. "Back in New Jersey, when it was just Mink, a mediocre sword swallower, and me, we joined a cheap tent show for a spell. There we met Theodore Spittle, enslaved to laudanum so bad that he sat in a pit, drooling, and killed chickens with his bare hands for dope money. He hates it that I saw him like that. He fancies himself a slick and dangerous creature, and he prides himself on terrifying others, but every time he starts to scare me, I remind him of those days and how pathetic he really is."

"How did he end up a he-she with Mink's outfit, then?" I asked.

"Theodore Spittle cut a man's face up for taunting him," Bess said, "and Mink liked that. A little man like Mink needs minions to do his dirty work. In the confusion before the law arrived, Mink spirited him away. He weaned Spittle off the dope and had someone teach him tricks, and Spittle became Ceecee, the Star of the Show. In his spare time he performs nasty little duties for Mink. But if Ceecee is back on the dope, he's not reliable. If I find a bottle of syrup or some such in Ceecee's care, I'm going to enjoy handing it to Mink. Ceecee won't be star of the show for long. Mink won't trust him to wipe his own ass." Bess flung her comb into her bag like game into a sack.

I rubbed my chin thoughtfully. Bess was right. It helped to think of Ceecee as a pathetic geek rather than a dope fiend with a razor. "I guess Billy Sweet should watch his mice," I said.

Bess laughed. "You're a huckleberry above a persimmon, you are, boy."

We were interrupted by Miss Lightfoot, all of a fluster. "Come quick," she said to Bess. "The giant is vomiting something fierce."

Bess took off at a run and I followed, but it wasn't to the giant she ran.

"Send for a doctor, you damn fool," she yelled at Mink. "What kind of businessman are you, who doesn't protect his investments?"

"Wasn't that bottle of stomach bitters enough?" he complained.

Bess snorted. "That's probably what made him puke."

"Puking is good. It gets the disease out." Mink strode gawkily to the giant's wagon, where the others had gathered. Through the wheels I could make out the hands and knees of the giant as he knelt retching. Perhaps this amounted to more puke than even Mink thought tolerable, however. He smacked Billy Sweet on the shoulder. "Ride back to that settlement and see if they have some sort of medical man. This better not cost a fortune," he growled at Bess.

I left Miss Lightfoot and Bess to help the giant in what little ways they could and retired to my blanket on the stony ground.

I awoke to sunlight and yells, and crawled from under my wagon.

"You quack," Mink accused. I followed the voices up to the giant's wagon. Bonfiglio and Ceecee were positioned behind Mink like bodyguards. Miss Lightfoot bowed her head into a handkerchief, and Bess had her arm around Miss Lightfoot's hips, which was as high as she could reach.

"I dosed him with bismuth," said a dark-suited man I assumed to be the doctor, "but his heart couldn't stand the stress of the vomiting."

Coldness gripped my gut. "What's happened?"

Billy Sweet shook his head. "The giant's dead."

YOU'RE CHARGING ME NINETY-FIVE cents a mile to come out here and kill my giant?"

"If you'd prefer I come back with the sheriff, that suits me, *Dr.* Mink." The medical doctor emphasized Mink's honorific sarcastically. "And I'll charge you for those miles too."

Mink and the doctor matched glares in a silent duel, and Miss Lightfoot wrung her handkerchief between her scaly hands, but Mink pulled out his purse and smacked some coins into the doctor's palm, and I remembered to breathe. "Get that shovel out of the back wagon," Mink said to Billy Sweet. "You've got an all-fired large grave to dig."

"Hold your horses," said the doctor. "You can't plant him on someone's property uninvited."

"What do you suggest I do with him?" asked Mink. "Stuff him?"

Was it my imagination, or did the glint of an idea flash through Mink's eyes at the sound of his own words. I swallowed. He wouldn't, would he?

"I suggest you bring him into town for a decent burial," said the doctor, "else the sheriff will be out to find you after all. I'll write you up a death certificate at my surgery when you come in." With that, he boarded his buggy and clicked the horse into motion.

"You know, we *could* boil him down for his bones. That would make a good display," Mink said to no one in particular.

Miss Lightfoot let out a distraught squeak, and I gulped for words.

"You bastard!" Bess cried, and stuck out her jaw, beard bristling.

The children ducked back behind wagon wheels and bushes.

"Now, now!" Mr. Ginger, heretofore silent, spoke up. "He will do no such thing." The second face on his forehead twitched rapidly, revealing the stress Mr. Ginger tried to conceal. "I suspect the good physician will be true to his word and send the law if we are not in town soon."

"Not to mention, we don't have a pot big enough," muttered Billy.

Town consisted of Main Street and not much else. A sign at the first wooden building announced its name as Horizontal. What that referred to was anyone's guess. We traveled the length of the single thoroughfare as people stood in their doors to watch—they were silent and clutched the collars of boys who would follow. We stopped at the far end of town behind a graveyard attached to a clapboard Lutheran church. Two men were digging a grave. A wave of melancholy swept over me. Did the giant have kin who would never know where he lay buried?

The performers kept to their wagons while Mink went in search of the doctor. He came back fifteen minutes later with the undertaker in tow. The undertaker peered in the back of the wagon, then had a few words with Mink, and they proceeded to argue. "At that price we'll knock together our own box, thank'e," concluded Mink, and Billy Sweet was set the task.

Since we dared not carry the giant far in a homemade coffin, we laid the giant out directly in his grave, rather than in the church. We drivers wrestled the coffin there with the help of the two gravediggers, plus the undertaker, the doctor, and a sheriff with a walrus mustache, all of whom had arrived for the formalities along with their wives.

The children stayed in their caravan with Apollo and Mr. Bopp on Mink's orders. Of course, Minnie had already said good-bye to the giant, hadn't she? The idea gave me gooseflesh.

Miss Lightfoot and Bess disguised their looks with dark veils so they could attend, and Mr. Ginger wore an oversize soft cap pulled low over his eyebrows. It bulged in front in a quite peculiar way. I changed into my best suit of clothes, and Mink donned his top hat for the occasion and added a shirt under the tailcoat he wore for shows. Ceecee had on an elegant evening suit and makeup. The town women glanced sideways at him and at one another.

Earle sat in his cart by the graveyard fence. No disguise could hide him. Townsfolk gathered there too, reluctant to come close for the service, yet unwilling to give up the spectacle, either.

As Miss Lightfoot spoke quietly to the pastor, Dr. Mink surveyed the crowd. "A pity I can't charge," he said.

My mouth dropped open, and he had the nerve to laugh.

Prayers were spoken, and the representatives from the community led the hymn singing with dour determination, as if they had to make up for our sins. The pastor said a few words about our giant: "He was a big man, in heart as well as body, but even a big heart fails in the end. He will surely join his dear wife and child in heaven and find comfort there." I hadn't even known he had a family.

The sheriff dispersed the townsfolk after the funeral and left the gravediggers to finish their work. We all gathered by the wagons.

"Well, I never gave him credit for his timing before," drawled Ceecee, "but he went out horizontal in Horizontal." He giggled, and I glared at him.

"I'm not thrilled to lose one of my acts, Ceecee," said Dr. Mink. "So shut your trap. Set up the tent, boys."

I gasped, and even the stoic Al Bonfiglio appeared surprised.

Miss Lightfoot struggled for words, her gloved hands waving in frustration. "We can't," she managed with a gulp.

"And lose out on this publicity?" said Dr. Mink. "The town may be a pimple on an elephant's ass, but we've got their attention."

"Right by the graveyard? Have you no decency?" wailed Miss Lightfoot.

"He was a trouper. He'd understand," argued Mink. His color deepened.

"No, no, no, no," said Miss Lightfoot. Her voice rose. "I refuse. I absolutely refuse. This is the last straw. No, no, no—"

Mink slapped her. He raised his hand to hit her again.

Mr. Ginger and I raced forward. Bonfiglio blocked my way. Mr. Ginger stumbled and fell. Bess arrived before either of us and kicked Mink in the shin.

"You pig!" the stocky dwarf roared up at him as he hopped on one foot, swearing.

Canvas smacked and a striped torso rolled out of the back of the nearest wagon. Mr. Bopp humped toward Bess as fast as a caterpillar man could.

"You weren't above ruining her, and now you dare hit her," cried Bess. She tossed back her veil, the better to aim her bile.

Mr. Bopp reared up like an angry snake at his beloved's side.

"Please!" Miss Lightfoot begged, but I wasn't sure if it was Mink or Bess she pleaded with.

"You ruin everyone," Bess continued. "You enslave the unprotected, take advantage of the needy, steal from the innocent, and harbor fugitives from the law. The only reason I stick with you is so's I can get to California and find my sister. As soon as I get there, I'm gonna pull foot and leave your sorry show."

"What do you mean 'fugitives,' you crazed dwarf?" Mink rubbed his leg with both hands.

"You know damn well they'd lock him up in New Jersey for slicing that man." Bess pointed at Ceecee. "If you set another hand on Ruby, I'll go tell that sheriff, and you'll be bagged too, for aiding a criminal."

Ceecee advanced on her, his eyes narrowed, but Mink waved him back.

"Do you think that yokel will believe you, let alone care?" snarled Mink. "And if he does, how do you explain waiting until now to turn me in?"

"Boss, boss," hissed Billy. "That yokel's on his way here."

The sheriff rounded the church. Maybe he'd heard the uproar. He certainly regarded us with distaste. His eyes widened and his lip curled at the sight of the limbless Gunther Bopp. "You forgot this," the sheriff said, and shoved what I guessed was the death certificate at Mink.

"Sheriff?" said Bess. Would she denounce Mink and Ceecee? Eyes flicked here and there. Glances met. Apprehension. Hope. Fear. "You coming to the show tonight, Sheriff?" asked Bess, her eyes narrowed with guile.

I almost laughed in appreciation.

"Show?" The sheriff looked as aghast as we no doubt had a few minutes before, but he pulled in his belly and stuck out his chest. "There's no show. We don't need your kind here parading deformities and stealing washing off the line. You'll leave town right now while I watch you go."

I was surprised that Mink didn't try to charge him for watching us leave.

"You need me," Mink sneered at Bess as she climbed into the wagon.

For a state that didn't have a lot of people, Iowa sure had a lot of railroads. We were forever crossing either a track or a river, and every time I had to put my shoulder to a wheel mired in bog, I remembered why a wagon show was sometimes called a mud show. Between the tracks and streams were cornfields everywhere, and on one of our rest stops I gathered some of last year's corn shucks from a ditch, for I'd had an idea to please Minnie.

We arrived at the next town, rattled and damp, early enough to set up the tents on a patch of common land between a wheelwright shop and a lumberyard, but too late to round up an audience for a show.

The next day was Sunday, and there would be no show, for the law said we were to rest whether we wanted to or not. I decided that throwing a knife for my own pleasure did not count as work, and I went off into the trees that bordered the river beyond our campsite to practice. It felt good to have my knives back in my hands. I took joy in the thunk of the blades hitting the stump I chose as my target.

Rustles and giggles from the nearby bushes alerted me that I wasn't alone. The children must have thought they were fine fellows to spy on me. It didn't take me long to find where they lurked, although I couldn't see their faces. I pivoted and sent two knives smack into the tree above their heads.

They screamed, and instead of our children, two boys I didn't know ran hell for leather.

"Oops!" I said. Then I couldn't stop laughing.

When I came back, I found our children and Apollo gathered around Miss Lightfoot while she bleached a white patch into Willie's hair with peroxide.

"This completes the Piebald Boy's look, does it not?" she said to me.

I said I would allow that it gave a dash to his appearance.

I went to stow my knives and fetch the corn shucks I had put aside, after which I begged some thread from Miss Lightfoot and some stage makeup, if she pleased. As I twisted and tied the corn, I told the children about the incident in the woods, exaggerating the dismay on the faces of the locals and the screams they made. Much to my pleasure, the children found my tale riotously funny. I daubed little dark eyes and a tiny cherry mouth on the bundle in my hands and, at the end of my tale, handed Minnie her very own corn doll.

Minnie squealed with delight.

"Now you have a doll the right size to talk to instead of the mummy lady," I explained.

Minnie blinked. "But she won't stop talking to me. I should talk to her if she talks to me. That's manners. She's sorry the bad men hurt you, Abel." Minnie stared off into space and hummed, then she sang the end of a nursery rhyme. "'Here comes a candle to light you to bed, and here come a chopper to chop . . . off . . . your . . . head.'"

For a moment I saw an exotic garden, felt the grip of strong hands on my arms, and saw a glittering sickle blade swing toward me. I shuddered. How could she know my dreams?

"Are you all right, Abel?" asked Miss Lightfoot.

"Someone walked on my grave," I said, repeating one of my mother's expressions, and tried to laugh off the fear that surged through me. "I'll make something for you next time," I told Bertha, trying to push Minnie's words from my mind. "And maybe the boys."

"Not a doll!" exclaimed Moses.

"Not a doll," I agreed.

Ceecee languished on the grass in the shade of Mink's paneled wagon, once more in his flowered wrapper and turban. The smirk he wore on his face made my skin crawl. When Bess emerged from her wagon with a basket full of towels, he writhed to his feet and approached.

"Nice coiffure," Bess said to Willie.

"Ceecee had the peroxide," said Willie, pouting.

"Miss Tuggle, dearest," Ceecee interjected. "I purchased a gift for you as well." When she turned from him and wouldn't take the bottle he offered, he dropped it into her basket.

She glanced at the bottle, then grabbed it and flung it at his head. He shrieked with laughter and ducked. The bottle landed at my feet. I tried to read the label, but it had landed facedown.

"And what else did you pick up at the drugstore, Theodore Spittle, you geek?" she asked. "Was it perhaps in a green bottle?" The smile died on his lips. Did laudanum come in a green bottle? I wondered.

"I'm headed to the river for my weekly whether-I-need-it-or-not," Bess told Miss Lightfoot, and took her leave.

I didn't think it wise to tip her hand like that. What had annoyed her enough to be so rash?

I picked up the bottle Bess had thrown. KOSMEO DEPILATORY, the label announced. NO BLEMISH SO TERRIBLE TO A PRETTY WOMAN AS SUPERFLUOUS HAIR UPON THE FACE.

Ceecee snatched it from my hand. "My dear," he said. "You are the last person to need this."

His comments stung. I stomped off, too busy stewing to see Apollo approach. He grabbed me by the arm as I reached my wagon. "What do you mean by telling the children you'll take them away?" he demanded. He looked as stern as anyone could with tufts of hair quivering in his ears.

"Keep your voice down," I said, looking around for Dr. Mink or one of the drivers. None was in sight.

"Bertha told me," he said in a harsh mockery of a whisper. When I had asked Bertha not to say anything to the grown-ups, I hadn't considered Apollo.

"Land sakes, boy. You saw what condition they were in when we arrived."

"I'm here to watch over them now."

"Great heaven!" I exclaimed. "Can't you get it through your skull that Mink is not a nice man? He's mean and neglectful and only out for himself. The giant might not have died if he'd been given help sooner, and I honestly believe Mink would have boiled the man for his bones if that sheriff hadn't been on hand. How can I leave the children with Mink and his men? Do you think he'd care if any of them died, Apollo? It would just be an inconvenience to him. What if Minnie died? Would he put her in a jar like the babies?"

"But Dr. Mink put me in charge of the children," Apollo argued. "I can help them now."

"And so you shall," I answered, trying to be patient. "Remember that good Mr. Northstar who rescued you from the train?"

Apollo nodded, looking confused by my change in subject.

"You know who he was looking for when he let you out? He was looking for his son, Willie, who had been stolen by a show. That's our Willie, Apollo. Mink stole him away and left his grandmother for dead, and the best way you can help Willie is to get him back to his father."

Apollo's mouth opened and closed for a moment like that of a fish. "Why didn't you tell me this before? Are you making this up?"

I sighed. "I didn't tell you before because I didn't want to scare you, but it's time you were scared, Apollo, so you'll be careful."

Apollo's confusion would soon lead to a sulk. I should take another tack. "You're doing a magnificent job of caring for those children," I said. "All I'm saying is you could care for them else-where."

He cocked his head.

"Imagine," I said. "Apollo Papandreou and His Band of Incredible Children. What an act, huh? *And* you'd be the only boss. Consider my suggestion, but keep mum. We don't want Mink to get wind of our plan."

"Well, I'll think on it," he said, knitting his furry brow.

I took a deep breath. That would have to do for now.

The afternoon was quiet and hot. Most everyone napped under the wagons, except Billy Sweet, who headed for the woods with a whiskey bottle. Earle, stuck inside the tent built around him, fanned himself lethargically with a copy of the *Police Gazette* in between reading the scandals. Dr. Mink hid in his wagon as usual. Who knew what occupied him there? He wasn't one to share his secrets.

After I checked to see if the horses were hobbled comfortably, I too rolled under my wagon, taking a straw hat with me to fend off the flies.

Screams roused me from a sticky stupor. I scrambled from my nest and joined Miss Lightfoot and Mr. Ginger, who were headed for the ruckus.

BESS, BESS, BESS!" MINNIE screamed, banging her heels on the ground beside the children's wagon and flinging her arms this way and that. She beat aside Apollo's hands as he tried to calm her. Tears streamed down her face.

The other children stood around her, helpless.

"She won't stop," said Apollo, his face distraught.

"What's the ruckus?" called Earle from inside the tent.

"Minnie's having a tantrum," answered Miss Lightfoot over Minnie's cries. "She's got a hankering for Bess, and Bess isn't here."

It was late afternoon. "Bess not back?" I asked Mr. Bopp.

"Nah," he replied. "She likes her times alone."

Ceecee crawled from the back of a nearby wagon, his face pinched. "Shut that ugly urchin up!" he demanded. "I'm trying to sleep." He wiped an arm across his mouth. His turban was gone and his hair hung in oily, uneven locks. Mud-covered boots stuck out from beneath his wrapper.

"The water's full of angry!" screamed Minnie. Then she saw Ceecee. "Him, him, him!" she cried.

Ceecee stalked over, rage in his eyes. He leaned over the child, his fist raised.

"Hey," Apollo protested, and tried to grab Ceecee's arm.

I ran and swept Minnie off the ground.

Ceecee changed his aim. Apollo yelped and was knocked to the ground.

I thrust Minnie into Miss Lightfoot's embrace and rounded on Ceecee, ready to strike, fear clawing my throat.

Ceecee pulled out his razor and flicked it open.

"Abel, stop!" cried Mr. Ginger.

I froze.

Everyone around me stared at Ceecee as if he were Medusa and had turned them to stone. Even Minnie was silent.

Ceecee yanked Apollo to his feet by his hair. The boy's eyes were wide with terror, his hands curved into rigid claws as if he were clutching at far-flung safety.

I had to do something. Apollo was about to be scalped. Or worse. Just then Al Bonfiglio came out of the woods with his shotgun over his meaty shoulder. He took in the scene with a glance and immediately lowered the gun at Ceecee. "Let the boy go, you pervert." I relaxed. I could see the pleasure in his eyes at the thought of shooting Ceecee.

Ceecee spat out a curse. He slashed at Apollo, and I choked on a cry. The blade sliced through Apollo's locks, and the boy fell back to the ground. Ceecee kicked the lad once and retreated, a clump of hair in his fist.

"I give shaves, too, Bonfiglio," he snarled over his shoulder. "Nice close shaves."

Bonfiglio sneered, shouldered his weapon again, and walked off with no mind to Apollo whatsoever.

I rushed to the dog boy. He moaned, clutching his side where Ceecee had kicked him.

"Ceecee killed him, too!" shrieked Minnie. What terrible things she must have seen. Miss Lightfoot hushed and rocked her.

"It's okay now," I reassured Apollo. "Ceecee's gone." Inside I fumed.

Bertha took one of Apollo's hands, and Willie patted the dog boy's shoulder. Moses helped me pull Apollo to his feet and dust him down. Apollo shrugged us all off and ran to the safety of the children's wagon, shutting himself in, but not before I saw the tears in his eyes.

I was surprised that Dr. Mink hadn't emerged with all the noise, but hours later, as dusk fell, he walked in from the road to town swinging his death's-head stick, and I realized he hadn't been home at all. I wondered if I should tell Mink what Ceecee had done, but would he even care?

Apollo eventually emerged from the wagon, but he was silent and sullen for the rest of the day. He had run away from a father who beat him, and now he was beaten anyway. I guessed he was angry and probably frightened, too. The children were quiet and careful about him. Perhaps they believed he'd be mean to them in turn. I figured I'd better keep a closer eye on them this day if Apollo was too upset to do it himself.

"How about a story?" I offered when I rounded them up for the night and shooed them toward the caravan. I had always liked a story at bedtime when I was a child. "Come on, Apollo. You curl up too."

A prairie wind had arisen. It cooled the air and swept the nearby trees into a rustling orchestra. Apollo obediently joined the children inside and snuggled silently into his top bunk. When I settled onto the floor, Minnie climbed into my lap with her doll. "What sort of story would you like?" I asked them.

"A ghost story," said Moses with relish, and all except Apollo clamored agreement.

I would have thought they would want a more comforting tale, but since it was their request, "You know that last railroad crossing we passed?" I said, remembering a story I'd heard on the circus train.

The children nodded. They were all my willing accomplices in the telling of the tale.

"Well, fifteen years ago there occurred a terrible accident at that place." No one asked how I would know. "A circus train was coming down the tracks. The night was dark and an early frost iced the rails. A farmer was riding home late from market, and his wagon wheel became stuck in a rut between the tracks. The engineer tried to stop, but the engine couldn't grip the rails. The impact made the tender leap the tracks, and the rest of the train followed in an accordion of doom."

Most of the children stared at me wide-eyed, but Minnie had a skeptical little smile on her face.

"The train went up in flames," I said. "People and animals died in agony. But the elephants were heroes."

Apollo leaned over the side of his bunk. "Rosie would be a hero," he said, referring to his favorite circus elephant and partner in crime.

My heart lightened at this sign of interest. I told how the elephants had pulled away burning wreckage to free the trapped performers. "Even after their keeper was crushed by an iron wheel, they knew their duty and carried on. They worked all night and one after another succumbed to poisonous smoke and terrible burns. In the morning the heroic pachyderms had saved many who would have perished, but most of the elephants lay dead by the side of the tracks."

"Ahhhhhh," sighed Bertha.

"All except the biggest, smartest female elephant," I added hastily for Apollo's sake.

"What happened then?" asked Moses.

"The circus folk had to bury the elephants right there, they were too big to move." I thought of the giant. "Perhaps you saw the mound we drove by."

Willie nodded, although there had been no such thing.

I leaned forward and lowered my voice to a hush. "Now, they say, on lonely nights, when the prairie winds blow, you can hear ghostly elephants trumpet in the distance."

There was silence inside, but outside the wind hissed, and I swear I almost heard elephants myself, even though I'd made most of the story up.

"Do you think the giant will make ghostly noises?" asked Willie.

"Probably puking sounds," said Moses.

"Moses!" Bertha chastised.

But the frog boy wouldn't be quelled. "I expect when Earle dies, we'll hear ghostly farts."

There went the mood entirely. Even Apollo cracked a smile. Bertha took the chance to comfort him. "You know, your fur will grow back," she told him.

Apollo's smile faded. "I hate him," he snarled. It pained my heart to see him so angry.

"We all do," Bertha said, and held out her stumpy right arm

to show the dotted scars. "He burns me, all the time, just to laugh at the way I jump." I swallowed a groan. I had made myself believe they were bug bites like she'd told me. Nobody had to ask who Bertha meant by "he."

"That's horrible," said Apollo, distracted from his own plight.

"He knocks me around something fierce, but he can't hurt me," said Moses. "I'm gonna smack *him* the next time he hits me." He threw punches at the air.

I knew how he felt. I wanted to punch Ceecee too. Willie stared at the ceiling. His voice was small. "He twisted my arm and made me lick his boots. I cried."

"Not me!" snapped Moses. "I don't cry." He pushed by me and out the door.

"Don't pay him no mind," said Bertha. "He gets like that."

My heart went out to Moses and all the children. There was so little kindness in their lives. I was more determined than ever to get them all to safety. "Let him have a few moments," I said when Apollo moved to fetch Moses back. "I'll check on him soon."

"That's the way of the world, though," said Bertha. "You gotta put up with the grown-ups if you want to eat."

How tired and ancient she sounded with her jaded wisdom. "No, it's not, Bertha," I said through clenched teeth. "It doesn't have to be."

She shook her head as if I were a fool.

"What about you, Minnie?" I asked, and cuddled her close. "Does Ceecee hurt you?" I swore if she said yes, I would drag him out of wherever he lurked and beat him myself, even if he cut me with a razor.

"No," Minnie said, and her head wobbled with the effort of talking.

"He's afraid of her," said Bertha. "One day she said to him, bold as brass, 'You're dead in a barn, soon.' You should've seen the colors he turned."

I snorted with laughter, taken by surprise. "Good for you, Minnie," I whispered, but the weight of the little girl against me, and her even breathing, told me she was asleep. "I'll go see if Moses is all right," I said, and laid Minnie on a bottom bunk.

Before I found Moses, however, I was intercepted by Gunther Bopp.

"You seen Bess?" he asked.

"Not since this afternoon," I answered.

"I'm worryin'," he said.

"What have you to worry about, Worm Man?" Dr. Mink walked out of the shadows.

"Bess hasn't come back from her bath," I said, starting to worry myself. That was hours ago.

"Run off and left you, has she?" Mink said to Mr. Bopp.

Mr. Bopp trembled, on the brink of violence. "She ain't."

Mink smiled smugly. "Sure she has. Gone off to join that sister of hers without you."

"She wouldn't. She wouldn't go without me."

"You want me to go and look?" I offered. "I was looking for Moses anyway."

Mr. Bopp considered this. "Naw," he said. "She's a brawny lass. She can take care of herself, and she does like to get off on her own sometimes when the world gets her down. She'd smack us in the head fer our trouble."

He was almost certainly right, but I liked the forthright woman, and her absence now troubled me. "In the morning, then?" I offered.

"If she's not back, which she will be," he said as he crawled away.

"Aren't you at all worried that one of your acts is missing?" I asked Mink.

He gave me his death's-head grin. "Like Bopp said, she's a brawny lass. And if you're so all-fired keen on being nursemaid, why are you letting the kids run wild?" Mink accused. "I just sent that frog boy back to the wagon where he belongs."

Well, there's one less worry, at least, I thought.

Mink sneered with pleasure, like he'd caught me out. "Go help Bonfiglio set up the mummy and the babies, and we can have an earlier start in the morning. You'll sleep in the exhibit tent tonight," Mink told me. "Yiss. So the local rats don't creep in."

After Bonfiglio had left me in the tent for the night, I looked around at the exhibits. *My nighttime companions aren't exactly the stuff of my dreams,* I thought wryly. Poor Mr. Bopp. The girl of his dreams was absent too. I wondered if Bess would be back before morning. Gunther Bopp was more sentimental than he let on, I decided as I laid my blanket on the floor. I wondered how much Bess did for him. Did he need her or miss her or both? *I'd like to have someone to need and miss,* I thought, and as if in answer, the ghost of a feeling came over me, and I longed for someone I could almost name. The mood fled, but it left my knees weak, and I sat on the crate next to the coffin.

"Well, here we are again," I said to the mummy. "You're still stretched out there, and I'm still fainting like a girl."

"Of course, anyone would faint with what goes on here," I added after a pause. "The giant died, you know, and the bearded lady's missing, but there's worse. The children are burned and beaten, and they accept that as part of their lot in life. I'm sickened to think they can be hurt and believe they deserve nothing better."

What a relief to talk, even to someone who couldn't talk back.

"I had a good home, you know, except I wanted some adventure and freedom. Only look at me now. I feel responsible all the same. Responsible for Apollo, who followed me and ended up among ruffians, and responsible for those children because no one else will be."

A sigh bubbled up from within me. I missed home—my uncle's lessons, Archie Crum's rude jokes, and the warm support of everyone around me. My hand went to my neck and the ring Violet Giovanni had given me.

How shameful. I had hidden a gift given in affection more likely because I was embarrassed by it than because I worried it might be stolen, yet how would this ring make me stand out more than the exotic creatures around me? All those fancies about the ring making people say and do odd things were just that—fancies, excuses to hide it away. It seemed to me there was a lot less affection out in the world than at home, and gifts of love should not be taken lightly. I slipped the chain over my head and undid the catch to allow the ring to slide down the links and tumble into my palm. The ornate gold band fit perfectly on the ring finger of my right hand.

What had seemed bulky when hung from my neck took up a new elegance on my finger. Were those pincers or mere ornamental fancy that sprang from the scarab beetle's shoulders and met above its head? I was neither entomologist nor archaeologist to say. The ring appeared exotic and mysterious and quite beautiful. How kind of Violet to have given it to me.

"Did you wear jewels like this?" I asked the mummy. I laid

my hand on her chest so I might imagine the ring as an ornament at her throat. "I would love to look across time and see you as you were."

The mummy opened her eyes.

I SAW, WITH HORROR, MY HAND AT her breast, but no amount of willpower could make me move it. I was frozen. A chill licked my fingers and crackled up my arm to the vault of my chest, where it grabbed my heart in a viselike grip.

The mummy's dry lips parted, and air sucked past me to fill a void within her; then she exhaled in a rattle, as if she were filled with pebbles and crushed paper. She spoke in a voice like dry autumn leaves and smoke.

"I have waited forever for you."

I snatched my hand back and stood.

"Don't go!" Her voice broke with so much loneliness and fear that I sat again.

"Who are you?" I whispered, aghast.

The only sound was her labored breathing. Lungs, unpracticed for centuries, would find it hard to do their work once more, I supposed. Except she couldn't be a real mummy. I had heard of ossified men. Did she have an illness like that, which had hardened her to leather and bone?

She coughed, and dark spittle frothed on her lips. She struggled weakly, but her arms were bound. I pulled out a handkerchief and dabbed her mouth. The cloth came away stained. Her ailment must affect her lungs.

"You are always kind, Ankhtifi," she whispered.

That name! I had heard it before. Fear tightened its hold once more. "Who are you?" I asked again.

This time she answered, in a voice thin and strained. "Know me not? I have talked to you in that world between waking and dream. I have danced for you."

"No, no, no." I shook my head. This couldn't be the beautiful dancer, Lady Adventure. Not this. It was a cruel joke.

"I am Tauseret, Servant Priestess and dancer in the *khener* of Hathor; daughter of Tetien, scribe of the court at Avaris, and Nenufer, mistress of his house; reluctant wife of Sethnakhte, high priest of Set; lover of Ankhtifi; cursed by Set, blessed by Hathor, saved by Isis." She paused, then, "I am not a princess," she said. Her last words were weak, but her green-flecked brown eyes were luminous with the laughter within.

She fell to gasping again, no doubt exhausted by this recitation.

"I think you are a clever girl," I said. "You may even have some mind-reading powers, since you are trapped in an infirm body." Hadn't I dreamed of the dancer as I sat beside her only the other day? "But an ancient Egyptian? I doubt it. Mink has taught you well," I said. I wondered what plans he had for her.

She waited so long to speak that I thought I had imagined that she had said anything at all, but at last she answered. "The bone man has taught me nothing." Was that a sneer on her lips? "My home is Kemet—land of the rich, black mud of the Nile. They are fishing there, cats hunt, children play, and I cannot return."

She had a guttural accent I couldn't place, and she tripped over words, her vowels wrong and her rhythm off; but she could be from anywhere foreign. "And how did an ancient Egyptian lady come to speak English?"

She continued in the same hushed voice, oddly halting and fluid in turns. "I stood for many years in the study of a scholar in one of your cities. My mouth was sealed, yet by the mercy of the great Isis I needed no eyes to see, my ears could hear beyond walls. I listened to his words with visitors, his commands to servants, and the disputes with his wife. He spoke with scribes and priests. They pointed to the writing of my people and said their own words. This unlocked the mystery."

Her answer was logical and well thought out but could still be the clever words of a performer.

"Ah, Ankhtifi, do you not remember me?" she said. "My heart, my *ka,* lives in you. You are my life. You are my other. The one cannot know itself without the other; the other cannot exist without the one."

"What connection could I have with you? I don't know you," I said, yet part of me thrummed and sang in response to her words.

"It is no wonder you don't know me," she said. "You are transformed. Your *ba,* the eternal spirit that your priests call the soul, has taken a new form, and your *ka,* the life in your heart, is reborn and forgets all except the tastes, the thoughts, the desires, of this existence. I know you, however, despite your skin is pale, your features sharper. I still covet those lips." Her gaze told me she yearned to touch me, and I drew back a little. She coughed again, and more dirt befouled her lips. I felt shame for cringing from her. I reached for the pitcher. "Would you like some water?"

"I would," she rasped, "but I am afraid. My organs may be . . . incomplete."

I swallowed hard. "How about if I dab your lips and forehead instead?" I said hastily, and I dipped my handkerchief in the water with nervous little jabs. Half of me believed her, half of me thought her a clever and ill young actress. As I bathed her face, I noticed her lips were plumper.

"I will tell you of us," she said, her voice a little stronger. "Lean over me that I may see your cherished eyes."

I did as she instructed, still wary, but eager to hear the tale she would concoct. "Wouldn't you like me to free your arms?" I asked.

Her eyes flashed fear. "It is not time," she said. "Only listen."

Mummy or ossified woman, she must need the bandages for support.

"In that life," she said, "Kemet was ruled by invaders from the land my scholar called 'Palestine.' They took our ways as well as our land, but they mocked us by naming their pharaoh Apophis, after the snake of the netherworld. Worse," she said, "they raised the worship of Set over the other gods. Set, who killed Osiris, the husband of Isis, cut him to pieces and cast him into the Nile.

"My father worked as a scribe of the court," she continued. "He supervised the records of the royal stores. His house was prosperous, and my mother had many servants to guide."

She moaned.

"Do you hurt?" I asked, not sure what I could do if she did.

"Yes," she answered. "I hurt with all time lost. That life is all gone. Except for you." The smile she attempted unsettled me, but her lips now covered more of her teeth. How could that be?

I tried not to dwell on that. It was too strange. "And you were a dancer?" I prompted.

"I was," she agreed. "When I became a woman, I entered the temple of Hathor as a priestess." Her eyes glowed and her voice took on a breathy youth. "When I danced, I became the goddess on earth." Her odor sweetened, as if capturing the memory of that goddess.

I tried to imagine this wizened, leathery body that lay rigid in yellowed, crumbling linen as a beautiful dancer, and I could not. She was spinning a tale to please me, like any sideshow fakir.

Tauseret was unaware of my doubt. "But when I danced at the feast of Min during the time of inundation, I caught the eye of a man whom one should not be noticed by," she said. Her voice cracked. "Sethnakhte."

I don't know why, but I shivered.

"He was of mixed foreign and Kemet blood and had traveled," she told me. "He knew languages, and the court valued him in talks with foreign kings. He had studied in the temple of Set at Tanis. He knew the ways of *khemi*—magic, you would call it, or maybe science. The pharaoh, impressed by his knowledge, made him priest of Set in Avaris, servant of the despised god of deserts, storms, and war.

"The servants of Sethnakhte followed me all feast day. They gave me flowers. They laid sweet fruits before me. They entreated me to come to him, until I finally agreed, if only to put an end to his attentions.

"I met him in a palm arbor. He stood too close to me, and his breath stank of the pellets of natron that he chewed to cleanse himself, the same natron used to preserve the bodies of the dead. I saw the lust on his face as he asked me to be his mate. I feared the anger of a powerful man, but he was much too old. I should marry a beautiful youth, not a man twice my age. I tried to refuse.

"He trapped me against a tree and threatened me with the unwelcome length of his body as well as his words. With the same lips he pressed against my neck he said he could prove that my father wrote false records for his own gain. His accusations were not true, but Sethnakhte had the ear of the pharaoh. What chance did a lesser man have? For love of my father I submitted.

"As soon as I moved my possessions to his house, he demanded that I forsake my service to her of music, dance, and happiness, as that did not become the wife of Set's priest. What husband is shamed to have a dancer of Hathor under his roof?" Her voice strengthened with her wrath.

"I threatened to take him in front of the judges. Again he promised to ruin my father. I had no choice. I took off my *menat* and laid my *sistrum* down. More fool he, for the *menat* stands for joy and fertility. He would have neither of me. I shuddered in repulsion at his touch, and my body rejected his seed. In turn he treated me with disdain for my barrenness. He called me less than a woman, yet he forced me repeatedly to his bed."

I found Tauseret's honesty brutal.

"I lived in misery," Tauseret told me. "I relished my freedom in the hours he worked on the documents he brought home to translate."

She fell silent, perhaps to gather strength. I let her be and listened to the gentle, chirping night as I watched over her. Far away a train whistle blew. Her head jerked and her eyes widened.

"It's just a train," I said. "A steam carriage."

She nodded solemnly. Her lower lip trembled. "Yes, my scholar spoke of trains, but I didn't know they screamed. I thought I'd heard the Eater of Souls."

As if in response to the lonely train whistle, a child cried inconsolably.

"Ah," said Tauseret, "the little seer frets."

"You do talk to Minnie!" I exclaimed with relief. "You're just a real girl after all."

Tauseret's lips twitched into a smile. "I do not speak to her with my mouth. She can see my *ka*—my double that speaks for me. You saw it too."

"Lady T.," Minnie had called the mummy, and said she was pretty. I stared at the creature that lay before me and tried to see what Minnie did, what I had seen in my dreams. I found that impossible. "Maybe Minnie does have a gift," I muttered.

"Indeed," answered Tauseret, "but she is too young to understand much of what she sees."

"I wonder why she's crying," I said, unsure if I should go and help, but reluctant to leave this newfound mystery. "Perhaps she's had a nightmare."

"It's death," said Tauseret. "She sees death."

DEATH?" I ASKED, AND LOOKED over my shoulder before I could help it.

"She may have seen an animal die on a farm down the road," Tauseret answered. "Or a man meet his end a thousand miles away. The death could be this night or next year. Her visions keep her awake. She whispers what she sees to me, but I have had no arms to comfort her."

Even now Tauseret's arms were immobile, crossed down her front, tied at the wrists at hip level, individually bound with ancient cloth. "How did you end this way?" I asked to change the subject. My heart would break if I dwelled too long on a tiny child who could foresee death. There were others to comfort Minnie; Tauseret was here alone.

"Since you cannot remember, I will tell you," she said, and her little yellow teeth looked ready to bite. I felt aggrieved. How would I remember?

"On one of my cherished visits home, my father brought a student from the school of court to the evening meal," Tauseret told me. "I was married. I should have looked at the food and not at him, but he had the body of an acrobat and the eyes of a poet, and I could not look away. I wanted to know the limits of that body. I wanted poetry from those lips." She turned her head to me, as far as her bindings would allow. "That man was you, Ankhtifi."

My cheeks burned. She lay there in tatters, yet now I heard the voice of a voluptuous woman. And I knew that voice. Excitement and fear knotted together in my throat. It was the voice of the woman who had haunted my dreams. How could this be? "How old are you?" I asked. These had to be the daydreams of a girl. She couldn't really be an ancient dancer from the past.

She smiled, and the skin of her cheeks folded like oiled leather and no longer threatened to crack. "How old am I? I have lost count," she said. "But then . . . I had celebrated eighteen inundations. I was a woman grown." Did I detect a hint of self-mockery?

"I changed my opinion of you when you asked about my husband," she said. "You proclaimed you admired him. How I seethed when you said you wished to discuss theology with him, but a disciple would distract my husband from me, therefore I arranged a meeting. I underestimated my husband's thirst for praise; he sucked up your attentions like a parched man drinks water. You asked his opinion on the Book of the Dead. You gasped at his collection of rare scrolls, the ones I knew he had bought to impress the pharaoh and never read. You remarked on his taste. I wanted to vomit. You offered to order his library for him, and soon you were a constant visitor and had the run of the house, like a pet.

"Yet you didn't confine your attentions to my husband. You watched me constantly, and I was infuriated." She must have stared at this Ankhtifi quite a bit herself, to notice how often he looked at her.

"You don't remember this?" she rasped. "Nothing?"

I shook my head.

"Where are you, Ankhtifi?" she muttered. She took a rattling breath. "One day everything changed. I came home from the market and found you creeping from my husband's study with a papyrus roll in your arms."

I felt the blood drain from my face as I remembered the dream I'd had on my first night in Mrs. Delaney's house. "I was stealing," I said in a small voice.

"And I discovered you," Tauseret answered with delight. "'Chantress of Hathor, be my ally,' you begged, and, safe in the garden, you told me who you really were."

"But I don't *know* who I was supposed to be," I said. This was crazy. "It was just a dream."

"You were a soldier in the army of Kamose of Thebes," Tauseret told me. "Sworn to drive the foreign rulers from our land. You gathered information for the rebel army to use. The documents my husband had might save the kingdoms of the sun. I already thought you were beautiful, but now I admired you," she said, caressing me with her gaze. "Your bravery thrilled me. You were no puppy of my husband's, but his nemesis. 'I will return the scrolls once you have copied them,' I promised. I brazenly slid my arms around your neck and gently touched your lips with mine. You trembled, and I believed it was for fear of discovery or, worse yet, fear of me. Shamed, I released you, but desire ignited in your eyes. You pulled me to your chest, and you kissed me in return as if you would devour me. I lost my breath as your hands turned my flesh to fire and your mouth made hot, sweet honey of me." She sighed with the memory. "I seduced you in that bower, and you became mine."

For a moment her voice carried me away, but when I looked at her wizened form, I couldn't begin to think what she told me was possible. She couldn't be that girl in the dream, and the dream couldn't be real. Parts of me shriveled at the idea. Tauseret laughed at her memories of happiness, unaware of my silent rejection, and I felt sorry.

"We met often," she said. "You brought me poems—sad and yearning for what you could not have all for yourself—then you tried to wipe away that sorrow with desperate pleasure. You were my cat that drove away the snakes." Her voice still sounded throaty, but richer now, with the hint of a purr.

"I ached that I could not shed my husband like a useless skin, but I was yours alone, despite him, and I gave you a token of that—a scarab ring. The scarab beetle is Khepri the sun, which rises like the scorching heat that rose in my loins for you; the scarab protects the heart and means rebirth. I had it blessed at the temple of Hathor, she who is love, so our love would never die."

I rubbed the band of the ring on my hand with my thumb, but I dared not look. A peculiar dizziness overtook me.

"I remember clearly," Tauseret said. "We were by the fountain, and the dance of the water was reflected in your eyes."

A shiver ran down my spine. I had seen that in another dream the first night I owned the ring. I remembered the clay tile walls of the garden, the abundant flowers, and a beautiful woman who couldn't possibly be this corpse.

"I loved that fountain," Tauseret said. "The sound of the water calmed my spirit, and the lotus flowers that grew there delighted me."

"The lotuses grew in the still pool at the center of the garden," I blurted out. "The fountain had lotus-patterned tiles on the rim." I choked on my last word. I had scared myself.

"Yes, you are right," she exclaimed. "And you remember!" She slowly closed and opened her eyes in satisfaction. "I asked you to keep the ring always in remembrance of me." Her voice trembled with excitement. "The centuries have passed, but you were true to your word, you wear my ring still."

"No," I said, my fist clenching. "How could this be that ring? It was given to me less than two months ago."

"Do not deny me," she pleaded, her voice full of hurt. "Look on the back of the stone."

I removed the ring and searched within the band, using my left hand to shield it from her view, but I already knew she would tell me what lay there.

"I had an inscription carved on the back of the scarab," she said. "First is the half circle that represents the 'tuh' sound that begins my name. It looks like the rising sun of rebirth. Second the ankh—a looped-top stick with a crossbar; it is the symbol for life and the sound that begins your name. Thus, we were joined in heart, in life, and in rebirth."

I swallowed hard. Indeed, the symbols on the back of the scarab were a half circle and a sort of cross. There was no way she could have known they were there unless her story was true.

"It is a spell that plays with words," she said. "For the symbol 'tuh,' which looks like the rising sun of rebirth, is really a rounded loaf of bread. The loaf of bread might make someone think of another symbol, 'dee,' which is also shown as bread of a different type, and together with the ankh means 'given life,' which is the spell written in tombs to ensure a person might live forever. Remember, the scarab beetle means 'rebirth' also, so I gave you a symbol of rebirth three times over—a magic number. I believe that ring has sustained our love over the centuries."

How could I deny what she said? For when I had put the ring on my finger and laid that hand on her breast, that's when her eyes had opened. I had given her life. "What happened to you and Ankhtifi?" I whispered, afraid to know.

She looked upon me with a gaze that was oh so sad. "You discovered plans for the deployment of mercenaries," she answered. "Excitement made you rash. You caught me in the empty corridor outside the kitchens and told me you must return to Thebes with the information. I pleaded with you to take me along. I would forgo my dowry to be free and divorce my husband in Thebes. You were afraid for my safety but finally agreed. You met me that night in the gardens. If only I hadn't begged you to come back for me, you would have been safe." Eons-old torment sobbed in her voice.

I knew what was coming. Someone in the kitchens had overheard our plans. We would be caught. We? When had I accepted that? "Your husband," I murmured. "He said if you condemned me as a spy, said I had forced myself upon you, he would protect you."

"He wanted to protect his name, that is all," she answered.

Her fingers twitched in the rags that bound them and startled me. I laid my hand over hers to calm them and give them warmth.

Tauseret gazed at me, eyes luminous with love. "I could not

betray you. You had taught my heart to soar with Horus in a few short weeks. Because of me, you would die. I could not let the last words you heard be my denial of you."

I glanced away, humbled. I hoped the Ankhtifi I used to be understood she had condemned herself for him.

Tauseret's plaintive voice drew my eyes back. "They cut off your head in front of my eyes. As my husband's servants dragged me off, all I could see was your blood splattered over the garden where we'd loved."

She fell silent. Her eyes were haunted.

I realized I was clutching a hand to my neck. I lowered it, hoping she hadn't noticed, but Tauseret stared past me as if she saw that blood even now, and I stroked her ravaged cheek even though I felt sick. "Here I am, safe and sound," I said, as much to reassure me as her, but she had gone beyond my touch, deep inside the terror of her past.

"They took me into the bowels of the temple of Set," she told me. "To a chamber that stank of *khemi.* 'Where is my trial?' I cried. 'Where is the judge?'

"'I am your judge,' my husband growled. 'You have shamed a priest of Set.'

"'My parents will demand to know where I am.'

"'They will think you eloped with that adulterer,' he told me.

"'Will you kill me?' I wailed. 'That is more than the law allows. I should be banished.'

"'I will not kill you,' he said. 'I will deny you death.' Madness lit his eyes. His servants held me tight while he pinched my nose and poured a noxious fluid down my throat that sapped the strength from my limbs. He then stuffed my mouth with foul powders."

I grimaced and wondered if that was the tar I'd wiped from her lips.

"He wrapped me in the linens of the dead, my body whole and sound and alive, and I thought I'd go mad before he finished—nay, I prayed I would. No protective amulets were bound inside my wrappings, no spells to open the door of my mouth. No food or drink was left for my *ka*. None of the proper words were said, although he did indeed speak words of power over me—words to give me life eternal. He lifted me like meat and put me in a rough sarcophagus. He left my eyes uncovered so I could see a spell text on the inside of the coffin lid as he lowered it upon my living face—a spell written to bar me from the afterlife. If I could have screamed, the walls would have shook with the sound."

I could almost smell and taste her horror.

"He left me deep in the underground passages of the temple of Set where no one would ever find me. I was buried alive."

I gasped for breath, as if I, too, lay in the stifling dark.

Her voice hardened with bitter anger. "I hope Ammit ate his heart when it revealed his sacrilege at the judgment."

"It's all right," I whispered. "You are safe now. It's over." Such senseless words, for I didn't know if she was saved at all. I lifted a shred of fabric at her neck and began to peel it back. It made me itch to see her in those filthy rags.

"No. Do not do that," she said. "Not yet. I do not know what is under these wrappings." My stomach lurched and I dropped the cloth. I wanted to comfort her, yet I didn't truly know what she was.

"How did you survive all those centuries and not go mad?" I asked.

"I lay in darkness so long that I saw colors where none existed, so long that the shadows whispered lies to me," she said. "I thought I had been assigned to hell and removed from the memory of mankind. After immeasurable time a blinding light flared. I steeled myself for pain, but instead a powerful sweetness came over me. I beheld the great ladies, Hathor and Isis, as if through a curtain of water and sunlight. Their voices burbled like liquid. 'You are here for love, faithful servant,' said Hathor. 'I, too, had my lover torn from me,' said Isis. 'We will ensure that you will be reunited,' said Hathor. 'Till that time let your *ka* see and hear for you,' said Isis as she gave my double the gift to travel outside my tomb and view the sky. 'Let your *ka* be your messenger in dreams.' Her gifts saved me."

Those dreams—they had truly been her, then? "How did you end up here?" I asked.

"When my scholar died, his wife, always jealous of his love of study, sold his belongings and arranged for my return to the university that employed him. She put my humble sarcophagus outside on a public highway to await transportation. That skeleton thief noticed me there and took me when I lay unattended."

Her flesh had filled out and her cheekbones no longer threatened to cut through her skin. When had her nose regrown? There were echoes of beauty on her face, and I caught my breath.

I knew her.

"But how did we come together again?" I asked, tears prickling my eyes. "It defies logic."

"Didn't you feel me calling you?" she asked. "And who told those boys to throw you from the train, lest you would leave me behind? Who took hold of the courtesan's hair to rip the truth from her?"

The night we walked side by side down the railroad tracks, she had told me she could reach out to people through the ring. I remembered the change in Lillie's heart when her hair tangled with the chain that held the scarab ring, and the blank look on the young clown's face before he suggested they throw me off the train—he'd seized the ring in the folds of my shirt when he grabbed me. Then there were the dreams and the way I'd yearned to leave home—after I wore the ring.

The tattoo of approaching feet on packed dirt stole the denial from my lips. Fear spiked my chest as I turned, my arms wide to protect the girl. The canvas slapped as if caught in a wind, and Apollo came panting into the tent.

"Abel, Abel. Come quick!"

IN THE EARLY LIGHT OF DAWN I stared into a ditch stuffed with vines, rotten wood, and last fall's leaves. A stocky, pale arm with a sturdy hand stuck out of the debris. Crumbs of earth skittered down the bank to the place where Apollo had dug away the leaves. The sting of bile rose in my throat, and I took a step back. I choked the bile down and it burned a hole in my gut.

On the way Apollo had told me how Minnie had woken up crying and insisted he come with her to this place. The distraught Minnie had been left in the care of Bertha and Willie. Moses had accompanied Apollo and me. "It's bad," Apollo had told me as we crashed through the riverbank woods. "Awful bad. You've got to tell me I'm wrong."

"Bess," I whispered now. I could barely hear myself over the rushing river.

"I thought so," said Apollo, equally quiet.

Moses whimpered like a dog in distress.

"Do you think she drowned?" asked Apollo.

"Then picked herself up out of the water and buried herself in a ditch?" I answered. "I think not."

For once, Moses had no opinion. He stared, white faced, at the rigid hand.

I forced back my nausea and climbed down the bank to dig her out. She wasn't buried deep; simply a pile of dead leaves and moss had been scraped over her, and a branch from the cotton-wood trees above laid down to keep everything in place. She lay naked, her clothes and necessary articles tossed on top. I managed to wrap her shift around her while I shielded her from the boys and tried, out of respect, not to look at her myself. When I pulled her out of the ditch, her head lolled back to reveal a black, clotted gash under her beard. It was a clean slice; the sort produced by a sharp butcher's knife—or a razor.

"Someone done cut her throat," said Moses, finding his voice.

Ceecee. Had he killed on Mink's orders? I couldn't prove that. Could a trained lawman? "Maybe we should go to the sheriff," I said.

"The law don't like us," said Moses.

"But Dr. Mink will give him money, and the law will help us," said Apollo.

Not good. Mink had been in town. Was the sheriff in his pocket? I rocked Bess. "What do I do? What do I do? What do I do?"

"Ask Mr. Ginger," said Moses. "He knows everything."

Yes, I wasn't alone. A burden fell from me.

I carried Bess back to our camp. Apollo and Moses followed. We made a solemn parade. I didn't know whether to cry or rage, so I kept my silence clutched to me, but it burned like a pyre. Bess seemed smaller and lighter than when she had been full of wiry, rude life. Beneath her whiskers her face appeared younger than I remembered. Behind the course exterior that had protected her from the world, she had been a young woman with dreams of the future and an honest desire to collect what she deserved. She had been vilely cut down for that, I was sure.

The children ran from the wagons to meet us, and Mr. Bopp wriggled behind. My breast filled with dread.

"The kids say you found Bess," Mr. Bopp said eagerly, and then he focused on what I cradled in my arms.

"Is she hurt?" he asked, panic rising in his eyes.

I shook my head, and he must have seen the truth on my face, for the words I could not find were not needed.

"My girl! My sweet puss!" he cried.

Another time this description of Bess would have made me laugh, but now it broke my heart. I knelt and placed her on the ground so he might touch her the best he could.

His cries alerted the others, and Miss Lightfoot came running. I stood to meet her. "Oh, Lord! Oh, Lord! My poor little pudding!" she cried. "Oh, the sad little dear!" She yelped when she saw the wound, and pressed her palms to her scaly face.

Bertha gripped Minnie's hand until the smaller girl winced and struggled, and Willie tried to hug Moses, but the frog boy pushed Willie away. Angry tears tracked his dusty cheeks.

Mr. Ginger wove through the tussocks of prairie grass with arms outstretched for balance, like a bad actor's rendition of a blind man, and I knew his submerged idiot twin was wide awake. "What is it? What is it?" he asked, no doubt unable to untangle the view from two sets of eyes, but Miss Lightfoot clutched her bodice, too busy wailing to pay him mind; the children were clustered around Apollo, speechless; and Gunther Bopp hunched, incoherent, in his sorrow.

Into this scene walked Lazarus Mink, and all fell silent.

"What in blazes is all this?" Mink cried. He noticed Bess, and his mouth dropped open briefly before he composed himself. Dark anger amassed in his deep-set eyes like a storm. "Where did you find her?" he demanded.

"In a ditch," I answered. "Slaughtered like an animal."

Billy Sweet and Bonfiglio, like flies drawn to offal, closed in behind him. "It's Bess," Billy said. "She's made a die of it." To his credit, he at least looked shocked. Bonfiglio was stone faced.

"The local sheriff should be found," said Mr. Ginger, who had draped a handkerchief over his forehead and set his vision straight. He still had faith in the law?

"And what do you suppose will happen then, Ginger?" said Mink. A tic flickered at the corner of his eye. "Those townies think we're capable of anything. We're all thieves, ruffians, and whores, as far as they're concerned, and they love to be proved right. We are all likely to end up at the end of a rope."

I remembered how the sheriff in Horizontal had treated us, and I believed him.

Ceecee lurked in the doorway of the tent, across the campground. His eyes and mouth were slits of anger. "What if we all testify that he carries a razor?" I said, gesturing at the accused. Miss Lightfoot squeaked. Ceecee faded back into the shadows.

Mink didn't even look. His lip curled in a snarl. "Weren't you seen throwing knives in the woods by local brats?" he asked. How had he found that out? "Don't think the sheriff won't weigh their words heavier than yours. You'll be in the jail before you can say 'habeas corpus.' And you"—he pointed at the others with a skeletal finger—"will be charged with aiding and abetting a murderer."

Miss Lightfoot cringed from him.

Mr. Bopp had stayed out of the discussion until now, too intent on rolling his forehead across that of his beloved, washing her face with his tears, but now he raised his ravaged face. "It was you gave the order, you murderous varmint. You was always afraid of the fine, strong lass."

Mink actually laughed. "Me, afraid of your hairy strumpet?"

Mr. Bopp launched himself from the stump of his frame with a powerful jackknife. He crashed into Mink's legs and lunged with his face. His teeth sank into Mink's calf, and Mink howled. "Get him off!"

Bonfiglio pulled the human torso away and ripped Mink's trousers in the bargain, revealing the knot of Mink's knee bone.

"Get a crate," Mink yelled, and Billy Sweet ran, while Mr. Bopp writhed in Bonfiglio's hands like a demon worm, bellowing curses.

I moved to intervene, but I felt a hand on my arm. "Choose your fights," whispered Mr. Ginger fiercely, and I realized Mink had pulled out a gun.

Bonfiglio and Billy Sweet wrestled Mr. Bopp into the crate and nailed it shut. Mink watched with a smirk on his face. "Stow him in his wagon," said the skeletal showman as he tucked his pistol beneath his jacket. "He'll soon come to his senses without a meal or a pot to piss in." Mink strode off, a purposeful look on his face, his suit legs flapping.

"He's gone to find Ceecee," said Mr. Ginger. "He's furious."

"He didn't order Bess dead," Miss Lightfoot said to me.

"We're his meal ticket." How could she defend Lazarus Mink?

"Neither does he want to give up Ceecee," said Mr. Ginger. "He's too greedy."

"But he murdered Bess!" I exclaimed. "None of us are safe." I had already been murdered in one lifetime; I didn't want to end this life the same way.

Billy Sweet hustled back with a shovel. "I'm right sorry, miss," he said to Ruby Lightfoot. "Honest I am. Can I dig you a hole?"

"I reckon you must, Mr. Sweet," she said. She raised her chin. "Mr. Ginger, I doubt if we will be calling on the services of a preacher; may I trouble you to speak some words? Mr. Dandy," she said to me, "would you please bring Miss Tuggle to her carriage, that I might dress her for the occasion?" Poor Miss Lightfoot. She had nothing to hide her fear behind but decorum.

"Apollo," I said. "Dress the young ones appropriately. See if they know a hymn to sing." That would give them something to do.

After I left Miss Lightfoot to her duties, I realized there existed one who had been left ignorant of today's events.

Earle Johnson, the fat man, sat on his cart in the tent that had been built around him. He glanced up from his newspaper when I entered.

"Hey, new boy," he said. "Was you entertaining last night?" He winked. "Coulda sworn I heard a lady's voice next door when I woke up once."

"You were dreaming," I said. I told him the news about Bess while he shook his head.

"Man alive, don't that cap the climax?" he wheezed when I'd finished, and his chins jiggled as if they agreed. "That puts a new coat of paint on what I saw." Excitement glinted in Earle's buried eyes. "Dr. Mink and that he-she came through here not a minute ago, and the doctor was cussin' Ceecee up one side and down the other. 'She was a troublemaker,' says Ceecee. 'That bitch would turn us in sooner or later.' 'Not so,' says Mink. 'You was just out of sorts 'cause she was a real freak, not a made-up one. You always had a problem with that. If you needed to test your razor, you shoulda done it on Dandy. He's a troublemaker, and he ain't got a freak act.'"

My mouth dried.

"It's strange," said Earle. He shifted his bulk and the cart groaned. "You'd think someone as big as me would be hard to miss, but for some reason it makes people even more likely to ignore me—like I'm too big to see. That a new ring you got? I don't recollect that."

"Mink was mad at Ceecee, was he?" I said, turning the conversation back to business.

"Oh, he was wrathy," said Earle. "He was cussin' hard enough to raise Sam Hill. 'If you ruin one of my acts again, I'll ruin you,' he says. 'I'll have Bonfiglio turn you all girl, and the only work you'll find for the rest of your life will be in second-rate cooch shows.'"

He paused. "You ever notice how fine spoken the hoodlums are in these *Police Gazette* reports?" He rattled the pink newsprint in his pudgy hand. "You think that's because they live in the big city?"

I thought it more probable that the writers were novelists who needed to pay the rent. "Could be, Earle," I said, my mind still on Ceecee.

"I been reading stories like this for years," Earle said. "But it beats the Dutch to be in one. A fat feller like me, he gets to sit a lot, and read a fine yarn if he's lucky. Travelin' with this show is the closest I usually get to adventuring. I still won't get to be a hero, nor win the girl, but I can be a chum and tell you that you'd better hightail it out of here while you can. Thems as runs away gets to fight another day."

I agreed with him completely. Unfortunately, I had others to think of too. I should devise a plan. The idea left me in a panic sweat.

As I turned to leave, Earle called me back. "Um, could you do me a favor?" he said. "Could you empty my convenience?" He pointed down under the cart. For a moment my spirits lightened. At least I wasn't trapped in a cart, able only to shit through a hole into a pot below. I could do something about my troubles. I would.

Mink didn't come to the funeral, and he refused to pull up the tent to let Earle out or let Mr. Bopp attend. Bonfiglio still sat smoking his pipe on top of the crate that imprisoned Mr. Bopp.

Ceecee appeared, however, dressed once more in his dark evening attire. He glided to the grave's edge like a wraith, his dark eyes burning. His smile was as thin and glittering as a razor blade. He bowed his head and put his hands together in mock prayer. Miss Lightfoot flushed in anger, but Mr. Ginger held tight to her arm so she didn't speak. The children huddled with Apollo as far away as possible, at the other end of the open grave amid the prairie grass. Their eyes remained riveted on Ceecee as if he were a rattlesnake. How dare he come here? I wanted to raise my fist and strike him to the ground, but Mr. Ginger shook his head at me, and I decided that this event would be hard enough for the children without their seeing me murdered in front of them, which would no doubt be the outcome of my protest. "We are here to honor and bid good-bye to our dear friend," I began through clenched teeth.

Minnie held her corn dolly up in both hands, as if to let it see Bess Tuggle dressed in her Sunday best and wrapped in a fine cotton sheet that should have been for her trousseau. Bess reminded me of Tauseret, who lay in her own grave wrappings, but I didn't think Bess would ever open her eyes again. This was the second burial I had attended in a matter of days, and I had never been to one before this summer. I had to get Apollo and the children out of here before there was another.

Mr. Ginger recited some lines of Milton, and the children sang a disorderly but touching rendition of "All Things Bright and Beautiful" in trembling voices. From that day on, I would see a giant and a dwarf when I sang the words "all creatures great and small."

We all tossed in a handful of soil, then Billy Sweet began to fill up the hole. Ceecee bowed to no one in particular and left. He was humming.

"Revenant! Ghoul!" Miss Lightfoot cried, and burst into tears. Mr. Ginger held her and let her cry it out on his shoulder.

Apollo and I led the unnaturally quiet children away. Each shovelful of cold clay earth thudded an echo within me.

Late afternoon, the shows began as usual, and I sat in the tent protecting the jars once more. A gloom hung over me like a wet fog, and despair curled in the pit of my stomach. Tauseret lay motionless, and I wondered if last night was a fantasy, but her lips appeared fuller than they had been yesterday, and I detected the slight curl of a smile upon them. I yearned to wake her and prove everything true, but thought it prudent to let sleeping mummies lie while Mink and his henchmen were out and about.

Outside, Mink cajoled the dupes. Next door, the children's shrill voices were fragile with tension and fear as they joked too hard and squabbled among themselves. Apollo lost his temper and yelled at them, and Minnie cried. I heard Miss Lightfoot comfort her.

Soon the customers trooped through, wide-eyed rubes who pointed and laughed at what they didn't understand. "What makes you so smug?" I wanted to yell at them. "Do you think that those with different bodies have different emotions, too? They should be wondered at and treated with respect." But I didn't say a word because it wouldn't make a difference.

Ceecee followed Mink through the tent and leered at me as he passed. My skin crawled. What gave him the right to pose as an anomaly of nature and exploit its gutter potential, when others had no choice and bore their difference with so much dignity? What made that self-made freak and murderer believe he was above God's laws?

Between shows, while the locals enjoyed the mouse game, I slipped into the larger tent. The children ran from where they sat around Miss Lightfoot's skirts to gather around me and complain about Apollo.

"He's a brute," said Moses. "He punched my arm when I said that he looked like the moths had got him. I was only joshing."

Apollo stood in the background. His frown, combined with the damage done by Ceecee's razor, made his expression quite fearsome.

"He's unhappy about Bess," I whispered to the young ones. "Don't you get grumpy when you're sad?"

"Frog Boy does," Bertha said, and nudged Moses with her bowed arm.

Moses glowered fit to match Apollo, and one eye popped slightly.

"I expect Apollo's quite sorry, really, but too angry with himself to say so," I told them. "Why don't you give him a hug and a kiss, Minnie?"

Minnie didn't have to be told twice. She toddled off and, before Apollo knew what had happened, flung her arms around his legs. Apollo's eyes widened with panic, and he tried to pry her off. The children squealed with laughter, and Willie, still young enough to hug another fellow shamelessly, grabbed Apollo's waist. "Hey!" Apollo cried. Bertha lumbered up on all fours. She pushed herself up on her stubby legs to throw her stunted arms around the dog boy's neck and kiss his cheek with gusto, while he tried to squirm away from her lips.

Miss Lightfoot giggled, and Earle's laughter bellowed so loud Mr. Ginger peered out from behind his curtain to see what we were about.

Apollo's lips twitched and the light returned to his eyes. There was nothing that boy loved more than affection—except for food, maybe.

Moses rolled his eyes, sauntered toward the dog boy, and patted him on the back as if there were spines there. The frog boy's reluctant gesture undid Apollo, and he roared with laughter along with the rest of them.

Mr. Ginger shook his top-heavy head and dropped the curtain.

"Could you look in on Mr. Bopp, honey bun?" Miss Lightfoot asked me. "I do fret for his comfort."

I didn't know what I might do for him, but I nodded and slipped away.

Bonfiglio had left the crate unguarded while he showed off his muscles to the country girls. I heard crunching as I pulled myself into the back of the wagon.

"You all right, Mr. Bopp?" I asked, kneeling in front of the crate.

He spat. "Ain't shat myself yet, if that's what you want to know."

I examined the wooden box. "Something flat could slide through these slats. I'll suggest skillet cakes for supper, Mr. Bopp, if that suits you?"

"Bonfiglio will be back soon to fart over me head," said the human torso. "I'd as soon have me one of them knives of yours to goose him good."

I smiled. "If I leave with the children," I said, "are you with us?"

He snorted. "Got nothing left here," he said, "but I wants to kill the fake he-she first."

I understood, but I couldn't promise him that. "Just be ready," I said.

"I'll cancel me dancing lesson," he answered.

I hurried back to my post before Mink missed me. Tauseret hadn't moved an iota. Perhaps she only came alive at night.

In the lull between the last full performance and Ceecee's late-night show Apollo came to see me. I was packing up the jars, ready for our move.

"I want to leave," he said. "Now."

He'd finally come to his senses. "It's not that easy," I told him. "We have to take the others."

"I'll load the children on the wagon," he answered. "We can go tonight."

"What about Mr. Bopp?" I asked. "We can't leave him. I'd like to ask Miss Lightfoot and Mr. Ginger to come too."

"You're crazy, Abel!" the dog boy exclaimed. "It'll be hard enough to sneak us and the kids out."

"And there's someone else," I said.

Apollo groaned. "Earle? He's huge! We wouldn't get far at all."

"Not Earle. He doesn't want to come," I answered. I paused to consider how to go on. He might think me truly crazy when I told him. Perhaps I was. I took a deep breath and guided him over to where Tauseret lay. Apollo had not spared the mummy a glance when he came for me that morning; consequently he hadn't seen her eyes wide open and intelligent, but I knew once he did, he would understand.

"This is Tauseret," I said.

"You want to take a body? You've given it a name?"

"She's not a body," I told him. "She's alive."

Apollo stared at me slack jawed, as if I'd announced I was the king of England. "Don't be mean, Abel," he said. He headed for the door.

"Devil take it, Apollo. You know I don't lie to you." My strong language shocked the boy motionless. "Wait with me awhile. If she doesn't open her eyes and talk before Ceecee's show, we'll leave tonight, I promise."

Apollo rejoined me cautiously. "You better be telling the truth," he said. "'Cause if not, I'll leave anyway, whether you or anyone else comes with me."

Tauseret lay in tatters, her face dun and cracked with the centuries. No wonder Apollo thought I'd lost my senses.

Time ticked by and slowly made a liar of me.

Wake up, I begged Tauseret silently. *Save yourself.* I knew she needed me to become alive, else why would she have waited for me? If I had to run after Apollo, I might not be able to come back for her. How could I leave her behind, trapped in a living death?

At any moment Billy Sweet would be back to see why the exhibits hadn't been loaded, and Tauseret's chance of freedom would be gone. I wiped the sweat from my brow with the back of my hand, and the scarab ring scraped my face. The ring. It was not until I had placed my ring-clad hand on the mummy that Tauseret had opened her eyes the previous night. I hardly dared breathe as I lowered my hand to her face. My fingers brushed her parched brown lips. Did I imagine they twitched?

Apollo didn't even pay attention. He stared at the exit flap, his bushy brow knit, as if he longed to be gone. "Hsst," I said, and he glared at me. "Look." I stroked Tauseret's cheek.

The change happened faster than the night before. Lips plumped, cheeks filled in, flesh gained a bloom, and her chest rose and fell with breath. Apollo gasped and bent over her. Silence held sway like the silver moment before the first birdcall of dawn, and in that moment Tauseret's lashes flickered. She opened her eyes a sultry slit, then they shot wide.

"Anubis?" Her thin voice trembled with panic.

Apollo growled and jumped back.

"He's my friend Apollo," I said.

Her eyes slid from side to side as she looked around as much as she could, then she chuckled, a sound like pebbles shaken in an earthen jar. "I thought I was finally in the underworld and jackal-headed Anubis had come to lead me to judgment."

I motioned to Apollo, and he edged forward. "I'm a dog boy, not a jackal," he said, a touch sharply.

Tauseret's lips curved. "I can see my mistake, dear heart," she said in that cracked, whispery voice. "You are much more handsome than a jackal."

How astute. Barely awake and she knew how to manage the petulant boy.

"Are you hurt?" Apollo asked, pointing at her bandages.

"I mend with each moment," she replied.

"We can't stay long," I said. "Mink's man will be back soon, and you'll need to pretend you are lifeless again. We don't want them to find out you are a better exhibit than they know. They'll guard you too closely."

"You will take me from these thieves, will you not?" she asked.

"Yes, soon. Won't we, Apollo?"

"Yes," the boy said without hesitation, and I could have cheered.

Footsteps approached.

"The show moves on tonight," I told her. "Have patience while I figure out how to get us all away from Mink. It may take a day or two."

"Why you lollygagging, Dandy?" asked Billy Sweet as he came in. "Finish packing those pickled punks." He carelessly lowered the lid on the sarcophagus, and I saw what he did not—helpless fear flash through the eyes of a girl who'd been buried alive.

WE PULLED OUT AFTER THE LATE SHOW and rumbled down a dirt road by what little remained of moonlight. Mink still fancied Apollo as a pet, and Apollo was too frightened to refuse to ride with him. We traveled into the early hours of the first of August, then slept until daylight between the wagon wheels on scratchy blankets. That day we set up camp outside another town. How fast one becomes jaded; I wasn't at all interested in this new place.

Mr. Bopp stayed locked away, and Miss Lightfoot sent Moses with his breakfast. "He's still madder than a bobcat," said the frog boy. "Why, he's been chewin' wood, he's that mad. He spit splinters at me."

As we raised the main tent around the fat man, I noticed that the work felt lighter. My hands were coarsened with calluses and rope burns, and the muscles of my arms had thickened with use. My sweat smelled pungent, a man's sweat, and when I removed my shirt, I took sinful delight in my robust chest. I would have been proud that my whiskers grew in tougher every day, but when one was a friend of the dog boy, one couldn't boast on that account.

Billy Sweet and Bonfiglio left the final pounding of the tent pegs to me and departed for other tasks.

"You look pleased with yourself, Dandy," Ceecee uttered. My swing went wild and I dropped my mallet. I straightened carefully to face my enemy. Despite the heat I shivered.

He wore smeared makeup and a sneer above his male attire. His razor was in his hand, and he waved it as if conducting music only he could hear. "You think you can join this show and take over, don't you? You think you're better than the rest of us."

There was no way to protest this accusation.

He came close, too close, and stuck his face in mine. I tried not to pull away and give him the satisfaction, but he reeked of stale pancake makeup and something sweet I couldn't name, and it took all I had to stay still. The razor burned like a hot coal just beyond my sight.

"What gave you and her the right to turn Mink against me and take my little boys away?" he demanded. "Not good enough to be in charge of children, am I?" His breath was rank, and several of his teeth were gray and dead. "She didn't interfere with the brats and me before you came. Do you think it was good for her to do that? Are you happy you encouraged her?"

I was stunned. He was actually placing the blame for Bess's death on me.

"You force me to do things I don't want to, Dandy," he whined. "That pains me. Dr. Mink never raised his voice to me before you arrived. I was like a son to him. What sort of person comes between a father and son?" His eyes were wet, but it could have been sickness, not tears. This sentiment had not prevented him from stealing Willie from his father, I noted.

"Don't sleep, Dandy," he whispered. "Don't dare sleep. Or I might give you a good-night kiss." He waved the razor in front of my terror-stricken eyes, then poked out his tongue and wiggled it like a pale slug. I cringed, and he pulled back, laughing.

He left, and the heat of the day came crashing back as if into a vacuum.

I bent over, feeling sick to my stomach. I was on the verge of vomiting when Apollo marched up to me. "That ugly lady won't speak," he said. "Bertha and Moses are laughing at me. If you want my troupe to help, you'd better show the brats I'm not a liar."

"You shouldn't have told them," I snapped.

"They have to know she's a person, else they'll believe you a thief, running off with Dr. Mink's exhibit."

"Minnie knows she's a person," I said. The way Apollo frowned told me she hadn't informed him of that fact.

I took a deep breath and slowly straightened, and the nausea subsided. Apollo allowed the children much higher moral indignation than was realistic. I considered letting him stew, but a shared secret like this might give the children a reason to keep quiet and pull together as a team. We had to get out of here. I glanced around to make sure Ceecee had truly gone. "All right," I said. "But quickly."

As soon as I touched Tauseret's face, a blush like sunrise rose up her cheeks and her eyes fluttered open. I almost gasped with the children.

"It's alive," squeaked Willie with delight.

"Knew that," said Minnie, earning me a shocked glance from Apollo.

Tauseret didn't waste time in finding her voice. "You neglect me," she accused in tones more smoky now than raspy.

Moses bugged his froggy eyes and uttered an oath I didn't think one so young should know, let alone speak in front of girls. Bertha must have agreed, because she smacked his head.

"Ah, the frog boy," said Tauseret. "I saw you with my *ka* and it was a good omen. The frog is a sign of rebirth."

"Lady T.," piped Minnie. "You're speaking with your outside mouth."

"Yes, indeed, little priestess," said Tauseret. I could sense her affection for the lone soul who knew she had a voice, before I came.

Willie tilted his mottled face up at me. "Is it a trick?"

"A trick of the universe, perhaps," I answered, and then pitied his puzzled look. "Not a trick," I said. "A miracle."

"Will you take them bandages off now?" asked Moses.

"Soon," said Tauseret, and an unexpected thrill ran through me.

"Show Earle," said Willie, tugging at my waistband. "She's better than a newspaper story."

"Earle can't come in here," chided Bertha. "He's too big."

"Take her in there," suggested Moses.

All joined in a round of excited agreement.

Lord Almighty, this had to be the worst-kept secret in the universe. I began to explain why that was impossible, when a husky voice interrupted.

"I have seen the fat man's heart," Tauseret said. "He will keep faith. Carry me."

Willie cheered, and Minnie joined in, jumping up and down until her large head wobbled and I feared she'd fall over.

"Are you sure?" I asked. "I mean, is it safe to carry you?"

"I'm stronger," Tauseret said, "and I would like to be in your arms again."

Her words brought a disconcerting pang of desire to my gut, but that died at the sight of her gray, tattered rags and clawlike hands. I bent and gingerly slid my hands under her, on either side of her torso. Something crumbled under my fingers and I froze.

"Fear not," said Tauseret as if she had read my thoughts. "The cloth erodes, but not the woman beneath."

I swallowed hard and hoisted her to my chest. I expected her to be stiff, but she gave in my arms and tumbled against me like a loose sack of laundry. For a moment a cloud of dust enveloped me. When I'd finished sneezing, I noticed she had a smile of satisfaction on her face—a face that now had the bloom of health on high, tawny cheeks, and full provocative lips.

"What you staring at, Abel?" asked Apollo, still waving away the dust. "Hey, the ugly lady isn't ugly."

I carried Tauseret into the next tent. The children clustered around me, except for Willie, who ran ahead. Her body grew warmer as we walked, and took on a voluptuous weight. I was dismayed to find respect and my baser nature at odds in my drawers. I prayed that all eyes were on Tauseret and not on me. I felt ashamed, puzzled, and nauseated by my reaction.

"Hey, Earle," cried Willie.

Earle put down his ever present newspaper and peered down at us from his cart with little eyes buried in his doughy face like currants in a bun.

"The mummy lady is a real lady," said Apollo.

"She was under a spell," said Minnie.

"I was cursed," corrected Tauseret.

"Don't ask me to explain," I said to Earle. "There's more mystery to the universe than we ever thought."

"I knew it!" exclaimed Earle. "I knew it. Goldang! A live

mummy. Don't that cap the climax." He chuckled with glee. "And don't she like you, Abel?"

I realized that Tauseret had her head on my shoulder in a most affectionate pose.

Earle lowered his voice a mite. "You're gonna rescue her, right?"

"Yes, and the children will help, won't you, children? You'll keep her a secret, and we'll all escape together."

They nodded eagerly and their eyes gleamed.

"We will be pursued," said Tauseret. "It is likely we will be caught."

"It is," I answered. I wished she hadn't said that in front of the children.

"Then, we will need reinforcements. The soldier from your home."

"How would the colonel know where to find us," I said to her, "even if I could send him a wire? I don't even know where we are or where we'll be tomorrow."

"Minnie, my flower," Tauseret said. "Close your eyes."

The little girl complied without hesitation.

"Think of us fleeing from the bone man. We are bouncing in a carriage. We are traveling down the road. We are leaving him behind. Make pictures in your head, pictures of all of us here."

Minnie nodded.

"Follow our journey into the future. Hold on to the bright thread of our lives. Where does the cold and dark try to swallow them, Minnie? What do you see of the place of our greatest peril?"

Minnie stood motionless, a frown on her face, and the absurdity of it all made me want to scream. How would this little child be able to tell us anything useful? She would burst into tears soon, and we would be none the wiser. Meanwhile the mummy girl grew heavy in my arms.

Just when I was ready to call a halt to the proceedings, Minnie opened her eyes. "Big train," she said. "Lots of men. A little red house."

We all looked at her blankly.

She waved her hand impatiently. "Stick," she said. Moses handed her a twig.

Minnie drew a lopsided house in the dirt—a peaked roof, two windows, and a door. "This is the sweet little house," she said in a singsong voice.

I groaned. It was a child's fantasy.

"Hush! She draws a picture of what she saw," said Tauseret.

Minnie added a jumble of scratches above the door.

"What are you writing, Minnie?" Apollo asked.

"She don't know how to write," said Bertha.

I moved behind her. The scratches were shaky but were letters indeed. They spilled off the side of the house because she couldn't fit them all in. If I ignored the strange spacing, I saw they spelled out TOMS JUNCTION. I spoke it out loud. "It might be a train station name," I said, amazed.

"I have touched and seen people through you while we were apart," Tauseret said. "Some may still be open to me. I will send a message for them to meet us at this tomsjunction, I will send it to everyone I can reach. I will send it and pray."

"Well, mention the state of Iowa while you're at it," I said. "That should narrow down the search a few hundred thousand miles."

"Dang," said Earle. "Trust the lady, why don't you. A lady that can turn from a buffalo chip to pretty can do anything."

I left the children babbling excitedly to Earle and carried

Tauseret back to her sarcophagus, where she closed her eyes, and moved her lips as if uttering silent prayers.

"What are you doing?" I asked.

"Saving you, as I should always have done," she answered, then spoke no more.

On a break between shows I asked to see Miss Lightfoot in Mr. Ginger's tent. She followed me with a fan in one hand and a handkerchief in the other.

"I'm taking the children away from Mink," I said to them both. "Tonight if possible, and I want you to come too."

"Abel!" Miss Lightfoot exclaimed. "Dr. Mink won't let you steal them."

"It's not stealing," I said. "They're people."

"How do you plan to go?" asked Mr. Ginger.

"We could all fit into the children's wagon," I answered.

"Now, that *is* stealing," said Mr. Ginger.

"When was the last time you were paid?" I asked. "How much money does he owe you all?"

"He's keeping it safe for us," objected Miss Lightfoot. She peppered her neck with quick little dabs of her handkerchief. Mr. Ginger stared down at his brightly shined shoes.

"I think he owes you all a wagon and horses at least—that's not stealing."

"I can't, honey bun," said Miss Lightfoot. Her voice trembled. "What if he catches us? What then? He's a cruel man, Abel." Her fan twitched in her other hand as if with a butterfly mind of its own.

"I'm taking the children, whatever you say," I told them.

Miss Lightfoot sighed. "And so you must, the poor, dear mites."

"Where?" asked Mr. Ginger.

"We'll make our way back to Maryland somehow," I said.

"My family lives in a resort where there's lots of room for children and plenty of people who will care for them—love them, even. We're all show folk. We take care of one another." I hoped that didn't sound like a criticism.

"Why on earth did you leave?" asked Miss Lightfoot.

I couldn't answer that without sounding like a selfish child. "Will you come, Mr. Ginger?" I asked.

He cleared his throat and wouldn't look at me. "Oh, I don't think I could stand the strain," he said. "I'm in delicate health."

Ruby Lightfoot paid considerable attention to fanning herself.

"There's room for you both if you change your minds," I said. Part of me was relieved. I worried that the more people we took, the harder it would be to get away.

"You are most kind," Miss Lightfoot said, and honored me with a gentle smile. I thought her done, but she took a deep breath and continued urgently. "Sugar, you'd best retrieve those papers from Dr. Mink's wagon," she said. "The ones that give him guardianship of those children, else he'll have the law on his side when he comes after you."

The curtain parted and fear of discovery jolted my guts, but there stood wide-eyed Minnie. She took her corn dolly out of her mouth long enough to speak. "I've got a story," she said in her wispy little voice.

"Well, come tell us, sugarplum," the alligator woman invited, and reached out her scaled arms.

"Thank you for the advice, ma'am," I said to Miss Lightfoot. "Have you a hairpin I might borrow?" Without questioning, she fumbled in her chestnut curls as I shook Mr. Ginger's hand. I left Minnie with them and went back to my duties in the exhibit tent.

After the shows were over, the center tent packed, and the horses hitched up, I gave Apollo his orders. "Get the children into the wagon and tell them to settle down and be quiet. I'll meet you there."

Daylight had almost gone by the time I wrestled my suitcase from behind my driver's bench in the other wagon. I strapped the bandolier that held my throwing knives over my shoulder— I couldn't lose them, whatever happened—and I threw my jacket over the top, despite the heat. I hadn't gone far in the summer dusk when Billy Sweet called my name. I tossed my suitcase into the shadows under a wagon and waited, heart thumping.

"Hey, Dandy," he said. "I'm goin' to town to visit the ladies. Want to come and make yerself a man?"

I stammered my refusal, and he brayed like a donkey.

"Well, stay and read yer Bible, then," he said. "I'll be back before the late show ends to help you pack up the babies and the beef jerky lady." As soon as he left, I breathed a sigh of relief and retrieved my bag.

"Listen," I told the children as I stowed my suitcase under a bunk. "We'll travel to where we sleep between towns, like always, but once the others are asleep, we'll move on by ourselves."

The children exchanged excited looks. Bertha pressed her wide hands over her mouth as if she was suppressing an explosion of glee.

"Moses," I said, "you're in charge." The frog boy pushed out his chest.

"Hey!" Apollo yelped.

"Come on, Dog Boy," I said. "We've got a job to do."

Apollo's protests died in his throat.

The summer night was sprinkled with distant, careless stars. Flickering torches cast uneven light and caused the shadows to constantly mutate. The crooked shades of men jerked into the late-night show, and I knew that Apollo and I were out there alone.

"You've been inside his wagon, where does he keep his papers?" I asked, and Apollo told me what he knew. I appointed him watchdog and climbed the creaky steps to Mink's front door.

One learns many skills when one lives with show folk, and it didn't take me long to trick the lock with Miss Lightfoot's hairpin and a technique I'd learned from a world-renowned escape artist. Once I'd lit an oil lamp and turned it down as low as I could, the hairpin gained me entrance to the lockbox I found chained to the frame of the wagon.

Inside were papers aplenty, rolls of coins, and a fat wad of bills. I squinted to read the documents in the sooty light, and I finally spotted a familiar name—Moses Quick. I sucked in a breath. The guardian named was not Lazarus Mink, as I had expected, but Ruby Lightfoot. I dropped the papers as if they had burst into flame, and glanced over my shoulder. Had she duped me? Could this be a trap? All I heard was the distant sound of sinuous pipe music. I picked up the spilled papers again with trembling hands and examined them. There, at the bottom, was scrawled Miss Lightfoot's signature, shaky and childlike, and Dr. Mink's name as witness. Why had she said these papers gave Mink guardianship?

I didn't waste time wondering. I tucked every paper with a child's name on it into my jacket—and, after hesitation, some of the cash, too. A quick survey of the wagon found me a sheaf of writing paper. I padded the documents left in the box so the theft wouldn't be evident right away. I hoped that Mink wouldn't notice when he stowed the night's receipts.

I extinguished the lamp and groped my way to the door. I peeked out, and when I got the nod from Apollo, I slid through and fiddled the lock closed. As we crept by Mr. Bopp's wagon, elation surged through me. We were on our way home.

"I reckon it's lucky that I stepped outside for a piss," said a voice from the shadows. "Yiss indeedy."

Mink! My stomach shriveled to a knot. Had Miss Lightfoot betrayed us?

"What were you sneak thieves up to in my wagon?" he snapped.

"Nothing," squeaked Apollo.

"I'm not afraid of you," I said, which was a lie, although he weighed less than half of me.

"Are you not?" he said. "This lad is." Mink stepped out of the dark, and Willie shuffled before him, his eyes stricken with terror. Mink held a derringer pistol to his head.

Apollo ducked behind me.

"You may be fool enough to risk your own life," said Mink, "but I'd bet my last gold dollar you're too noble to risk this pickaninny's life. Empty your pockets or I'll snuff him like a candle."

Moses ran around the wagon with Miss Lightfoot in tow. They skidded to a halt when they saw us. Miss Lightfoot looked too shocked for me to believe her a conspirator with Mink.

"Me and Willie followed, and the bone man grabbed Willie," said Moses to me.

I shot him a look, and he lowered his eyes in shame.

"Lazarus," pleaded Miss Lightfoot. "Let the little boy go."

"Why should you care, Ruby? Your family kept slaves, did they not? But then, they tried to sell you off like a slave too, didn't they?"

Miss Lightfoot cried out, "They did not. I went willingly like a lamb to slaughter. You seduced me away."

Mink laughed. "Only because your bankrupt father asked

me for money for you. That's why I had to romance you and lead you off in the middle of the night."

She tottered backward and covered her face with her hands. Something ripped. I fancied it Ruby Lightfoot's heart, but a shape like a sack of potatoes flew though the air and hit Mink in the head. It was Mr. Bopp. He'd somehow escaped his crate prison and torn through the wagon cover. Mink stumbled. His hat went flying. The gun fired skyward, jerked from Mink's hand, and thumped to the ground. Mink landed on his rump with a scream of rage. Mr. Bopp jackknifed on the turf and tried to reach Mink with his teeth, spitting between each curse.

Customers boiled out of the performance tent like ants, pulling their collars up to hide their faces and looking around for the law. Bonfiglio followed them, craning his neck to see what mischief was afoot.

"It's Dandy, you fool!" Mink screamed at Bonfiglio. "Stop him!"

"Grab Mr. Bopp and get to the wagon," I yelled to Apollo.

It took all three boys to wrestle the human torso up and away.

I took off toward the exhibit tent. The bulky form of Bonfiglio pounded my way. I hoped I could toss Tauseret over my shoulder and still outrun him.

I reached the tent. I dug my arms under the mummy and hefted her to my chest. She was stiff again and unwieldy as a log. I staggered and tried to keep my purchase. I'd never get out of the door with her placed this way. I swung her under my arm and almost toppled the jars. Bonfiglio burst through the tent flap, with Mink behind him.

"Give me my money," Mink cried. Bonfiglio advanced, his fists like hams. I felt Tauseret begin to warm and relax in my arms. I had to get out of there before Mink guessed her secret, but Mink had found his gun. All was lost.

Mr. Ginger came through the other door and found himself face-to-face with Mink. He clutched an oboe in white-knuckled fingers as he edged forward, Ruby Lightfoot timidly shuffling behind him.

"Get back," I cried, not knowing what Mink would do.

"Pay him mind," snarled Mink, waving his pistol, and Mr. Ginger froze at the table with the jars.

It may have been deliberate. Miss Lightfoot dodged out from behind Mr. Ginger, lifted the nearest pickled baby, and heaved it at Bonfiglio. Who would have known a lady would have such strength and aim? She hit him in the head. The jar shattered and he fell into Mink, shaking the glass from his bleeding brow and sending the waxy stillborn twins into the face of the showman. Mink howled and covered his eyes. Two with one blow! The air stank of formaldehyde.

"Give me her feet," cried Mr. Ginger, tucking his oboe under his arm. Did he notice the mummy sagged in the middle and had the weight of a living girl? Together we ran with the mummy as fast as we could, Miss Lightfoot in the rear. I prayed that the second Mr. Ginger wouldn't open his eyes.

We reached the paneled wagon. I passed Tauseret into the children's hands. Miss Lightfoot and Mr. Ginger followed her up. I wrestled the creaky doors closed behind them and joined Apollo on the driver's bench.

As we picked up speed, the children laughed and jeered. I leaned out to see two figures running after us: Mink, waving his arms like a crane fly, and Ceecee, clutching a flimsy wrap and tripping on his ladies' slippers. Bonfiglio was nowhere to be seen. I thanked the carnal lusts of the absent Billy Sweet. We just might get away.

HYAH! HYAH!" I SMACKED THE reins and urged the horses on. Apollo jounced beside me on the driver's bench. "How far behind do you think they are?" I yelled above the rumbling of the wheels.

"We unhitched the other horses," cried Willie gleefully from the back. "They'd have to hitch 'em back up."

"And he wouldn't leave those tents," added Bertha. "He's much too cheap."

"He'd wait for Sweet, too," called Mr. Ginger. "He's a braver man with thugs to back him up."

Perhaps we had a better lead than I'd thought. I eased up some on the horses.

"I'm glad I sent the boys to grab some of their bags while

you played tag with Mink," said Apollo, gesturing back at Miss Lightfoot and Mr. Ginger. "That was smart of me, wasn't it, huh, Abel?"

"You took a chance," I said. "What if they hadn't come?"

"Aw, I knew they were coming," he said with all the assurance of hindsight.

I handed the reins to him and let him drive for a while. He stuck his tongue between his teeth with the effort, which kept him mercifully quiet.

"How is the mummy?" I called behind me. Did Tauseret even know we were on our way?

"That's a damn funny question," said Mr. Bopp, peering through the slats behind the driver's bench.

I guessed she had lapsed into dormancy once more. "How did you get out of the crate?" I asked Mr. Bopp.

"Chewed me way out," said the human caterpillar.

I took him at his word, since he still had a splinter stuck to his lip.

"Won't we be conspicuous on this road once the sun rises?" asked Mr. Ginger from behind Mr. Bopp.

"Like a wart on a snake's belly," I heard Moses say.

They were right. I wondered where amid these cornfields we could hide.

"Might we trade this wagon for another?" asked Miss Lightfoot. "It's a sound conveyance."

"Except for 'Dr. Mink's Traveling Monster Menagerie' being painted along the side," said Mr. Ginger.

"All the more reason to get rid of it," I said.

"You'll have to make the deal, sugar pie," said Miss Lightfoot. "None of us will suit."

I wished to ask her about the papers on the children, but I

didn't want to yell the question over my shoulder; I wanted to see her face so I could judge her answer. I couldn't believe she had acted maliciously; was she merely embarrassed to be party to Mink's infamy?

In the gray light of dawn Mr. Ginger took a turn at the reins, his cap pulled down over his twin in case we met strangers. Apollo joined the children sleeping in the back. "I have an idea," Mr. Ginger said, waking me from a doze.

At the first crossroad I unloaded the passengers and we created wheel tracks east with the help of water from a nearby stream.

"He won't be fooled by that, will he?" I asked.

"Could it hurt?" asked Mr. Ginger. "And it raises the spirits."

He was right. The children had great sport running backward behind the wagon with branches to sweep away their footprints and our real tracks in the dust of the northbound road. Even Bertha lumbered along like a bear at play on her short, bowed arms and legs.

They were exhausted by the time Apollo ordered them back into the wagon.

"The lady's still sleeping," said Bertha, peeking in a lower bunk.

"When's she gonna wake up?" asked Willie.

"What you been telling these kids?" growled Mr. Bopp.

"How did you know I'd go to get the mummy?" I asked Miss Lightfoot as I handed Minnie up to her.

"Minnie told me a story about it," Miss Lightfoot said, and gave the child a kiss on the head. "She said you wanted to save it." She paused and examined me. "You don't believe it's real, do you?"

"I'm not mad," I said. "You'll have to wait and decide for yourself."

I took the reins again. The sun beat down. I removed my jacket and knife bandolier, and Mr. Ginger held them. More than once I jerked awake, the reins slipping from my fingers. The road widened, and farms and villages multiplied. We passed by several apple orchards. I should have pity on those trapped inside the wagon and find a shady place to stop and eat. My stomach rumbled in agreement. The cornfields made way for pastures where cows grazed. We came to a wide dirt road with a fancy white sign at the gate painted with the words WEBSTER'S DAIRY.

"This would make a fine wagon for delivering eggs and milk," I told Mr. Ginger, who concurred. I hoped the farmer would at least allow us a place to rest, even if he didn't want to trade. Mr. Ginger closed the gate behind us before he hid inside the wagon.

I caught Mr. Webster in the yard of his pretty wood-frame house as he was leaving from his midday meal. A plump Mrs. Webster stood at the door. Several small children peered from behind her skirts.

"No, can't say as I need a wagon," said Mr. Webster as he walked around our conveyance. "Why would you be selling, young man? Won't that leave you on foot?" He narrowed his eyes. "It is yours to sell, isn't it?"

"Yes, sir. Certainly, sir," I answered. "However, I had in mind a trade for another wagon, not a sale. As you said, selling would leave us on foot." I could have kicked myself for saying "us."

The dairy farmer examined the legend painted on the side. "Would any of these 'monsters' be aboard this day?" he asked.

It seemed needless to lie. "Yes, sir, but they are shy. One suffers much cruelty in the world when one looks as they do."

"Why would you trade your show cart?" Mr. Webster's eyes narrowed again. "Is there something wrong with it?"

"No, sir. Not at all," I said. "Except we are leaving this undignified business and going home, and we would not like to draw attention to ourselves."

Mr. Webster stroked his chin and considered a moment. "Tell you what," he said. "If you could bring yourself to do one more show, I'll give you some paint. That'll solve your problem, won't it?"

What an idea. Paint. That would change our appearance. "Who would be our audience?" I asked. "A small group?" We couldn't announce our presence far and wide if we desired to hide from Mink.

"My family and the neighbors," Mr. Webster said. "A show like yours sure would make Jim Tompson's harvest hoedown look pale."

Mr. Webster had a rivalry going, it appeared. "You'd give us a sheltered place to paint?" I asked.

"Got an empty new barn, painted with that same white that I bought too much of," he said.

After a brief conference inside the wagon, I climbed out and struck a deal. We would give a show the next evening. If we stayed out of sight, Mink would never know where we were. He'd think us vanished.

We set up camp in the barn, away from prying eyes. We found the paint already there, along with brushes. The boys commenced a wild romp in the hay that lined stalls at the back of the building, despite the thick, sweet afternoon air. I threatened them with murder if they kicked up chaff anywhere near the wagon when we began our work.

Minnie clambered from the wagon and ran to me crying. "My dolly, my dolly. Can't find my dolly."

I enlisted Bertha's aid, but we could find the corn doll nowhere.

"It must have fallen out on our journey," I said. "Never mind. I'll make you a new one."

"Don't want a new one," Minnie wailed.

I left Bertha to comfort her.

Apollo helped me bring the rigid Tauseret out of the wagon. Even if she seemed lifeless, paint fumes couldn't be good for her. She felt warmer and softer by the time we laid her in a brand-new empty water trough in front of the stalls.

The boys gathered around her, chattering. As I left, Moses poked her with a stick. I glared at him, and he whipped his hand behind his back.

"Mind yourself," I said. "That's a real person, not a parcel."

"And I know magic curses," rasped a sinister, cracked voice, and the boys scattered, screaming. A husky chuckle came from the trough.

"Are you all right in there?" I asked, bending over her.

Tauseret's eyes sparkled with happiness at the sight of me. Her skin softened as I watched, her face filled in around delicious cheekbones, and her plump lips curved. "Touch me," she said.

Her words sent my blood surging.

She laughed again, softer and with more affection. "I take my strength from your hand and the ring. The more you touch me, the more I come alive."

I yearned to touch her but feared if someone saw, they would sense my desire and be disgusted. Even I found it hard to admit what I felt about someone referred to recently as the "beef jerky lady," but despite her sallow flesh, I kept on seeing glimpses of the beautiful dancer of my dreams, and my whole being reached out to her.

Out of the corner of my eye, I noticed Mr. Bopp in one of the stalls, curled up like a pill bug, feigning sleep. He drowned in deep gloom, I knew. Apollo was already rounding the children up for a rehearsal. His facial hair bristled in a frown as they danced around him and refused to be hushed. Miss Lightfoot and Mr. Ginger talked by the wagon.

I reached over and brushed Tauseret's lips with my fingers. She sighed, and the rise and fall of her chest quite distracted me. I stroked her cheek, and she closed her eyes. I touched the one hand that lay free of her wrappings, and it grew less leathery. My heart beat faster. My hand caressed her shoulder, and warmth rose through the cloth. What had been bony became soft and round. With a tearing purr the ancient linen ripped apart at the juncture of her armpits as her chest filled out. My hand slowly followed my eyes, and my mouth dried. She did not complain or try to stop me. How could she? She was bound. This both appalled and excited me. I snatched my hand away.

Her eyes opened and her mouth pouted. "Don't stop."

"I must," I said. The words came out as a squeak. "There's work to be done." How could this seem right and not right all at the same time?

"Don't neglect me," she begged. "Come touch me often, that I might become a real woman again."

"You have no need to worry about that," I promised before I left her side. I felt sure I could manage to get over my embarrassment with practice.

"Are you well?" asked Miss Lightfoot as I passed. "You look quite flushed."

"Just a mite warm in here," I said, tugging at my collar.

Mr. Ginger and I set up as painters, with Moses as our assistant. I encouraged Apollo to continue with the other children. I couldn't begin to think of how I'd wash paint out of his tawny pelt, and I knew he would splash it all over himself if I allowed him to help.

I put my ring in a pocket to keep it safe from paint, but after a while I slipped it on again and went to see Tauseret. I couldn't keep away. Her existence was too amazing. She greeted me with open eyes and a smile. I marveled at the way she changed even more as I touched her.

"Lillie's taking a nap," Tauseret told me, "at the temple of love."

Mrs. Delaney's bawdy house, I interpreted. "How can you know?"

"She touched the ring, did she not?" said Tauseret. "I was able to control her then, and that gives me a path back to her."

Tauseret seemed so sure of herself.

"I asked her to send help, but she laughed at me," Tauseret said.

"You were just a silly dream to her," I answered, allowing myself to accept Tauseret at her word.

"Perhaps, but I told her where to find money for a journey. That bully lost his purse behind the butter jars when you hit him."

I chuckled. That would serve him right if it was true.

"The tiny woman at your home recognized me, however. I met her early this morning. Ah, that woman has powers."

"Miss Dibble!" I exclaimed. "She touched the ring when she told my fortune."

"Your colonel is looking for you," said Tauseret. "Miss Dibble will send him a message by wires." She looked puzzled by this.

The colonel might be on his way? My spirits soared. "He must have guessed I'd try that circus," I told Tauseret. I wanted this to be true so much that I pushed all doubts aside. "He probably looked up their schedule and went after them. I expect he keeps in touch with home, though. He has a business to run." My words caught in my throat, and I hung my head. What a nuisance I had been. What a fool. I could add expensive telegraph messages to my debt, perhaps even telephone calls. "Well, thanks for helping," I mumbled, and then realized I didn't sound thankful at all. I glanced up and smiled awkwardly at her, in case she thought I didn't appreciate her efforts.

"Is she awake?" Moses asked when I came back, and I nodded.

"Watch that can," Mr. Ginger told him, and gave me an odd look.

Moses tugged my sleeve. "Can I go talk to her too?"

I glanced over at the water trough. The children and Apollo were gathered around it, all reaching in. Perhaps they thought their touches helped too. I hoped she was amused.

"Go," I said. "But be back soon, and tell them to leave her be if she asks."

"You act as if their game were real," said Mr. Ginger.

I smiled. He would find out for himself soon.

On my third visit I was dismayed to find Miss Lightfoot perched on a bale of hay next to the trough, a basket of sewing at her feet. I had hoped to have Tauseret to myself.

"I have lived among marvels for a fair number of years now, but I have never come across anything quite as strange," said Miss Lightfoot. "She is filling out like a soaked bean."

Tauseret's eyes were closed, but a smile lingered on her lips. I touched those lips, and her eyes opened.

"Good heavens!" exclaimed Miss Lightfoot.

"This is Ruby Lightfoot," I said. "It's all right to speak to her."

Tauseret stared past me. "Ah, the woman touched by Sobek, the crocodile," she said in her whispery voice.

Miss Lightfoot pressed her hands to her mouth to cover her astonishment.

"Yes, Minnie's story was true," I said.

Miss Lightfoot lowered her hands. She leaned over the trough, and her look of consternation transmuted to one of wonder.

"I believe Miss Lightfoot would enjoy making your acquaintance," I told Tauseret.

"I have not the strength yet to speak much when Abel is not here," said Tauseret, "but I would be glad of company. Would you tell me about yourself and the world I am to live in?"

"Why, you darling, I would be delighted," answered the alligator woman.

"Is Miss Lightfoot talking to herself?" asked Mr. Ginger, frowning with concern. He had been glancing in her direction with more and more agitation. "I thought she was playing with the children at first, but she's talking into that trough even when they aren't around."

"Why don't you go and ask?" I said, unable to hide a grin.

He protested at first, but it didn't take much to convince him. As I'd guessed, he welcomed any excuse to talk with her. I watched with amusement as he made his way over. I couldn't wait for his exclamation of surprise.

Mr. Ginger was addressing Miss Lightfoot, his hands clasped behind his back, when he abruptly stopped. He glanced around, a puzzled expression on his face, and then looked into the trough.

He crumpled to the ground.

MISS LIGHTFOOT WAFTED SMELLING salts under Mr. Ginger's nose while I checked him over for broken bones. The children clustered around us.

"Is he dead?"

"Is it the fits?"

"Dang, did you see him drop like a girl?"

The little twin attached to his forehead sneezed, then Mr. Ginger groaned and opened his eyes. "Oh, my."

"Now, now, children," said Miss Lightfoot. "Even the best of us will succumb to shock, and Mr. Ginger truly is the best of us." She stroked his cheek with a lacy handkerchief, and Mr. Ginger closed his eyes again, but now he had a smile upon his face.

"Are you all right?" I asked Tauseret. It may have been a blow to her pride to make a grown man faint.

She grinned. "Ah, it has been a while since men swooned at the sight of my beauty, but I think I shall enjoy it once more."

I grinned back. I was seeing more and more of her sense of humor, and I liked it.

"I'll leave you in Miss Lightfoot's care until you are well enough to paint again," I said to Mr. Ginger, and hurried the children off. I felt sure Miss Lightfoot could introduce him to Tauseret successfully.

Moses and I made good progress with the paint and had only one interruption, when a trio of Webster children tumbled through the barn door squealing in fear, Willie behind them cheering.

"They was peeking through the door crack," said Willie. "I climbed out a window and scart them."

The youngest Webster—about five I'd guess—blinked in astonishment at piebald Willie, her thumb poised halfway to her mouth. The middle child craned his neck, eager to see what he could see in the barn, and the oldest, maybe ten years old, glared at me. "We came to see how many to make supper for," she said, tossing her curls.

Mr. Ginger and Miss Lightfoot had retreated into the shadows. I didn't know where the others hid. "Thank you very much," I said. "That would be four adults, one big lad, and four children."

Bertha's voice echoed from the loft, "I'm a big girl."

The younger Webster started, and the middle Webster searched the rafters for the owner of the voice. "Thank you," the eldest said stiffly. She grabbed the sleeves of her siblings and hurried them out. On the way she poked out her tongue at Willie.

"She likes you," Moses crowed, and Willie punched his arm.

At suppertime Mrs. Webster and a sturdy kitchen girl brought several large baskets of fried chicken and biscuits with all the fixings. They knocked on the barn door, and I sent all the children, except for Moses, to hide in the hay. We didn't want to spoil the surprises of the show. Mr. Ginger stayed in a stall while Miss Lightfoot and I greeted the ladies.

"I declare. Fried chicken," said Miss Lightfoot. "How kind."

The farm women smiled politely and tried not to stare.

"Plenty of milk, too," said Mrs. Webster, nodding at the jugs. "We sell cream to the Osceola Creamery—send it up by flatcar from the train station. They make a fair bundle when they sell it on as butter to New York."

"Is there any place near here called Toms Junction?" I couldn't help but ask about the place in Minnie's prediction. If it was real, it could be our doom or our deliverance. Mink had to be following us. How close was he? I prayed that we were well hidden.

Mrs. Webster shook her head. "Toms Junction? No, can't say as there is. There's a Tompson's Dairy down the road, though." She sniffed in distaste. "Word has it they paid off the railroad so the milk stop would be nearer their barns."

That must be the same Tompson of the harvest hoedown, whom Mr. Webster wished to outshine, I guessed. I tsked and shook my head in sympathy, and Mrs. Webster beamed at me.

After the farm women left, we set up for dinner on various bales, buckets, and stools next to the water trough. Tauseret had become quite flexible, so I helped her to sit upright. She felt as if she was warm and soft beneath the crackling bandages she wore, and I felt a pang of anticipation. I looked forward to seeing her garbed in more-attractive clothing. I hoped she would consider her body sound enough soon.

You would think having a mummy to dinner the most natural thing in the world, to judge from the children, who ate like little savages. Only Mr. Bopp refused to eat. He had a quick look at Tauseret, muttered something that sounded like "Bugger me," then went back to his nest in the straw, after Mr. Ginger had helped him with some necessaries.

"How did you get to be a mummy lady?" Bertha asked, which had the other children clamoring for a story.

Tauseret told a shortened version of her tale as we ate.

"I lived as a happy, pampered only child, protected by spells and amulets, and given the finest of linens and perfumes to wear," she began. "I loved poetry, music, and dancing, so when I was in the first flower of my womanhood, my parents encouraged me to enter the service of the goddess Hathor. I was beautiful. When I danced for the goddess at festivals, all eyes followed me."

Thank goodness she didn't go into detail about our past connection except to say we fell in love and angered her husband. This was still enough to make Apollo roar with laughter. I didn't know why he should find that funny.

"How romantic," said Miss Lightfoot, her eyes full of dreams.

"More than one has waited forever for the person he loves," said Mr. Ginger to Miss Lightfoot.

"But I do believe this lady has the record," she replied. I sensed she had missed his point, or avoided it.

"Sounds like humbug to me," said Apollo. "She's just practicing her act."

Tauseret didn't seem bothered by his assessment. "I think I could take some sustenance," she said. Her eyes followed my hand to my mouth.

"Oh, give Lady T. some chicken," said Minnie.

"Let me, let me," volunteered several of the children.

I would have to take her word that she could eat. I held a tender piece of chicken to her lips. All eyes were upon her. Her teeth were now small and white but appeared a little worn. I wondered if the desert sand had gotten in her food and ground them down. She took the chicken in her mouth, grazing my fingers with her teeth as she did. I could see from her eyes this was deliberate, and the tingle of that gentle abrasion shot from my fingers to distant parts. Tauseret took a few more morsels this way and a sup of milk from a tin cup. She licked her lips with a pink, wet tongue, and I forgot there were others there.

"I'm taking the young ones to bed," said Apollo. "Or are you too busy with that girl to care?"

"Oh." I looked at the others, feeling foolish. Mr. Ginger and Miss Lightfoot glanced at each other and smiled. I hoped they weren't laughing at me. The children slumped against one another like tired puppies.

"That's a good idea, Apollo," I said.

He rolled his eyes.

Minnie tugged at my sleeve. "The bone man's coming," she whispered.

I stroked her curls. "Don't worry, Minnie. We'll keep ahead of him." I hoped I was right.

Apollo hustled Minnie and Willie up to the hayloft to settle down for the night. Bertha and Moses went along to help, they said, but I could see they were exhausted. No one returned.

Tauseret lay down and closed her eyes.

"Are you well?" I asked.

"Tired," she answered faintly.

For a while I talked with Miss Lightfoot and Mr. Ginger on how we would present a show, but I glanced repeatedly at Tauseret.

"Do you think she'll be all right?" I whispered. "That's the first food she's eaten in centuries."

Miss Lightfoot patted my hand. "If she's lasted this long, I doubt a few scraps of chicken will hurt her."

"She's a miracle," said Mr. Ginger. "I'm not sure miracles get sick."

Soon Mr. Ginger's eyes grew as droopy as those of his twin, and he excused himself to one of the stalls. That left Miss Lightfoot, applying cream to her cracked arms.

I fetched my jacket from the baggage piled near the wagon, and pulled out the documents in my inner pocket. I handed them to the alligator woman.

"What are these, sugar pie?" she asked.

"The legal papers for the children," I replied. "See who is named guardian." I opened the first document and pointed to her name.

Her eyes widened. "Land sakes!"

"Did you not know?" I asked.

She shook her head. "Honey love, my parents were too embarrassed to send me to school. I can't read nor write. I can barely sign my name, and it was Mr. Ginger who taught me that."

"What did Mink tell you when you signed the papers?" I asked.

"He said I was the witness. 'Shut up and sign where I point,' he told me. Usually a lawyer came, but I rarely saw any parents. I expect many of the documents are forged."

"Why make you guardian?"

"I don't know that I can speak for that devious little man," Miss Lightfoot replied. "But he doesn't always go by the name Lazarus Mink. Perhaps he used mine because he believed he could always produce me as his dupe." She looked away from me. I wondered if she was hiding tears.

"I suppose it may have reassured parents that a lady would be responsible for their child," I said.

"I'm not sure people who sell their children need reassurance," she answered.

I remembered her situation and fell silent.

"I'll excuse myself now," she said, and took one of the two lanterns and left for the stall that she'd named her boudoir.

How relieved I was that Miss Lightfoot was innocent of all collusion. I had no doubt now that we were all united in our quest for safety. Everything had to turn out right. All I had to do was get everyone back to my home.

I leaned against the trough in the pool of lantern light, too exhausted to move. Out in the darkness were the snores of the sleepers and the rustle of mice in the hay; beyond those sounds were miles and miles of unknown. Home still seemed a long ways away.

"The clown is drunk."

I started. Tauseret was awake. "What clown?"

"The clown I made throw you off the train," she said. "The one who opened to me when he clutched your ring amidst the shirt at your throat."

"Um, is this helpful?" I asked.

"We shall see," Tauseret answered. "He's telling everyone about a dream he keeps having. A 'dusky strumpet' tells him over and over to rescue Abel at tomsjunction in the state that is Iowa. He thinks it's because he feels guilty about what he did to you, but he's too stupid and mean of heart to feel guilt."

I was sure the clown's carrying on like all possessed wouldn't do me a bit of good, but I didn't say so, I just put my face in my hands.

"Ankhtifi?"

I turned to her.

"Unbind my arms," she said. Her voice trembled, but she tilted her chin up and tried to look proud. *Well,* I thought. *If she is ready, then so must I be. There are no experts here.* However, a horrid idea slipped through my mind—what if I removed the bandages, and her arm came off in my hand? I gulped.

Her arms were wrapped separately from her body. They stretched down her torso and were crossed and tied at the wrists below her waist. She wiggled the fingers that poked through the bandages. They were no longer clawlike, but long and elegant; the nails that had been yellow were still ragged but were now colored peach. This gave me faith. I tugged at the torn linen at her armpit and tried to unwind it, but her arm pressed too close to her chest. For a moment I was stymied, but then I pulled a serrated knife from one of the picnic hampers and used it to cut the old linen all the way down to her wrists, and I peeled the fabric away. Her limbs were plump and firm, and I exhaled in relief.

"All is well," Tauseret said. Was it me she reassured or herself?

I set to unwrapping her fingers, but my hands trembled, for if I slipped, I might touch her in a personal place—a place I imagined to be no longer arid as the desert, but as hot and moist as the Nile Delta. I bit my lip. I fumbled. Sweat beaded on my brow. When I pulled the tube of fabric from the final finger, she took my hand with a strength I didn't expect and pressed it close to what I had carefully avoided. I flooded with warmth.

"Free my wrists," she whispered, and let me go.

I sawed at the bonds in a slipshod hurry and tried not to think of the tightness in my loins.

She raised her arms and examined them. She turned them this way and that, bent them at the elbow, flexed her fingers, opened and closed her hands. "I never thought I would do that again," she said. She held her arms out to me, and I pulled her to a sitting position. Her skin was soft.

She loosened the wrappings around her neck, then ripped the remnants of linen back from her skull like an offending cap and tossed them aside. Dark hair, matted and dusty, fell past her shoulders. She shook it around her, creating a cloud of particles in the air. She sneezed and laughed. "I had a shaven head when they wrapped me," she said. "How odd." She tugged at her locks and grimaced. "I may shave it off again."

"Wait," I said, and retrieved my brush. I sat behind her on the edge of the trough and smoothed the tangles from her hair. Her tresses were thick, with a slight wave, and under the dust had a sheen that defied reason. She leaned her head back and made a throaty sound like a purr. I knew that movement, I knew that sound, and my body responded so fiercely that I had to bite back a moan. I bent and kissed her by her ear, and she uttered something guttural and encouraging in a language I didn't know.

The kiss left grit on my lips, and this brought me some sort of sanity. I wasn't sure what I made love to, nor what the consequences were. I stood.

"Won't you help me with my legs?" she asked.

"It doesn't seem right," I said.

"Why?" she asked. "You are my lover."

"I don't remember that," I answered, half lying.

"Then, it's time to give you new memories," she answered, and smiled sweet enough to melt any man's resolve. That face! I had seen that face before I ever met this woman in the flesh. She truly was the woman of my dreams.

She braced herself on the sides of the trough and raised her lower limbs with newfound strength. I cut the fabric above her knees and wound the linens that bound her legs together down toward her feet. Sometimes the material frayed and came apart, and I had to pick at the ends to get it started again. There were many layers, and soon the bottom of the trough was littered with ancient yellow cloth, like an untidy nest. I peeled the last layer away to the tops of her thighs with growing wonder.

I had seen many showgirls in my young life, and most had had sturdy and shapely limbs, but I don't think I had ever seen legs as perfect as hers. She raised them one at a time and bent them at the knee. She stretched them and curled her toes. I wanted to kiss and worship them and damn the dust. I choked and realized my mouth hung open. I snapped it shut and hoped she hadn't seen.

She hadn't. She was too intent on worrying the wrappings at her chest. Perhaps they squeezed her now she had filled out. She freed an end and passed the shreds around her, hand to hand.

"What are you doing?" I gasped.

"Finishing," she said as if I were foolish.

I wanted to tell her to stop, I thought I should run and find her a sheet, I knew I should turn my head away, but I stood there too hypnotized to move.

And she kept on unwinding.

And unwinding.

Until the last thin band of gauze that covered her breasts slid down the tawny stem of her like the skin of an asp to reveal the most perfect, ripe fruit.

She cupped her breasts happily in her hands.

I was lost, wanting the taste of them. I went to her as her slave and knelt at her side, and she wound her arms about my neck. I lifted her out of the trough and onto my lap. Her fingers tangled in my hair, and she drew me to her and captured my lips with hers. My tongue explored and found no resistance, and I took her mouth as mine. She tasted of exotic nectars and smelled of spices. I wanted to dissolve and be a part of her.

"Rid me of the rest of these rags," she breathed against my lips.

I heard pounding. For a moment I thought that sound was my heart, but then the source became clear. Someone was beating on the door.

I pulled away, confused, shaking, guilty—found out in my sin.

"Open up in the name of the law," demanded a stern voice.

PAY HIM NO MIND," GRUMBLED Tauseret. She reached for me, but I held back. A whimper came from the hayloft. I felt like whimpering too. Did Mink stand outside with the sheriff?

Miss Lightfoot appeared beside me. Without batting an eye, she helped Tauseret off my lap to a seat on the side of the trough. She took a garment from her shoulder and laid it in Tauseret's arms. "Honey pie, I do believe you are in need of this."

My cheeks flamed.

Tauseret exhaled audibly and rolled her eyes. She held up the offered chemise to examine it. Sleeveless, shapeless, and white, it did not appear the garment of her dreams.

"Open the door, Abel," Miss Lightfoot said. "We must deal with this inconvenience." I could tell from the fear in her eyes she expected Mink to be outside, but she pressed her lips firmly together and helped pull the shift down over Tauseret's head.

I tugged the barn door open, my innards in shock at my rapid change of emotions. An annoyed man, a silver star on the lapel of his tightly buttoned blue jacket, with nightshirt cuffs apparent under the sleeves, walked inside. Mr. Webster, with a lantern, entered behind him, accompanied by his wife, clad in a voluminous wrapper, her children clustered around her. Mr. Webster shot me a look that accused me of betrayal, and I felt ashamed and injured.

I looked beyond our visitors but saw neither Mink nor any of his henchmen. This had to be his doing, however. Had he bribed this lawman to be his dupe? A sense of doom suffused me.

A row of scared faces now peered down from the hayloft—some little, some big, one hairy. Mr. Bopp had either not heard the ruckus or ignored it.

Mr. Ginger joined us. He appeared rather odd in his underdrawers and a hastily donned hat. "What is your business here, Officer?" he asked.

Tauseret favored the sheriff with a radiant smile from her perch on the trough. The sheriff smiled back, then examined his boots, cleared his throat, and took on an official glower once more. "There's a feller at my office claims you stole his wagon and a valuable exhibit, and abducted children in his care."

"Would that be a Dr. Mink?" Mr. Ginger asked.

"That would be the feller," agreed the sheriff. He looked like he had smelled something bad when he said it, and my hopes returned.

"Dr. Mink owed us salary, Officer, and refused to pay," I explained. "We decided that we had better seek our fortunes elsewhere. A wagon hardly covered what he owed us."

The sheriff nodded as if he could well see our case. I could tell he didn't like Mink at all. "But there's a matter of a . . ." He paused, as if what he had to say was too unbelievable. "An Egyptian mummy," he concluded.

Mr. Ginger glanced at Tauseret, now a stunning little beauty in a long white chemise. "Search the whole place, if you like," he said. "You will find no dried-out ancient lady here."

"Go ahead, Eli," said Mr. Webster. "Might as well."

The sheriff poked in corners, turned over hay, and examined the inside of the wagon. At one point he let out a yelp that sounded most undignified. A familiar growl followed his cry, and I knew he'd found Mr. Bopp.

My heart thumped when he approached the water trough. What if he found the wrappings? The sheriff might overlook the wagon, but if we proved to have taken something else, the situation might not go well for us. Tauseret chose that moment to slide backward into the trough and recline. She yawned like a cat and patted her mouth with her fingers most prettily.

"Sorry to disturb your night's rest, young lady," the sheriff said, and turned away, looking flustered.

"Well, I see no sign of antiquities here," said the sheriff, "but what about the children?" He looked up. "Mink says you kidnapped them."

"I beg to differ," countered Miss Lightfoot, and swept to where I had laid the legal papers. "I think you will find that I, Ruby Lightfoot, late of Poeville, South Carolina, am the legal guardian of these dear children and am sworn to protect them from evil men such as Dr. Mink." She handed the papers to the sheriff with a flourish.

"Well, well," said the sheriff. "I will suggest, then, that Dr. Mink pull foot before I arrest him for wasting the law's time."

"I'm very, very sorry," I professed to Mr. Webster when the sheriff was gone. "We didn't mean to put you to this inconvenience."

"Now you know why we are leaving this business," added Miss Lightfoot. "We want no more truck with vermin like Dr. Mink."

Mrs. Webster shivered. "He must be a bad egg, that one," she said. "Bearing false witness. Kidnapping children. As savage as a meat ax, indeed. Come on, chickadees, let these good people go back to their rest. My, my, you poor dears." She hustled her children off, and I didn't know whom she considered the "poor dears," them or us.

"Did Mink say how he found us?" I asked Mr. Webster.

"Heard one of the neighbors who was at the tavern up in town boast about the show," said Mr. Webster. "Went straight to the sheriff. Banged on his door until he got out of bed." Mr. Webster shook his head and left.

"They're all gone," Willie called down from where he perched like a squirrel on the ledge of an air vent.

"Did you see Billy Sweet or Bonfiglio out there?" I asked. Mink may have stayed at the sheriff's office, but it would be like him to set a tail on the lawman.

"No, just the sheriff and the Websters."

"Maybe they split up to search for us," said Mr. Ginger.

"Maybe they are guarding what is left of Mink's show," said Miss Lightfoot.

Wherever they were, I had a horrible feeling that they would be here soon. Mink had tried bluffing with the law and it hadn't worked, but he wouldn't give up easily. We hadn't seen the last of him.

I'd had enough for that night, however. I now wanted nothing but sleep.

Miss Lightfoot must have seen the exhaustion on my face. "You take the far stall, Abel," she said. "I'll keep this lady company."

I might have been put out if I'd had an ounce of energy, but Tauseret acted unperturbed. "Take your rest," she said. "You will need it."

I wasn't quite sure what she meant, but I was quite content to drift off to sleep in the scratchy hay, imagining.

In the morning Tauseret greeted me warmly as I woke. "Welcome to the day, my love. It waits for you."

She leaned over me, her dark hair tumbling around her lovely face, her full breasts threatening to escape the neckline of her cotton chemise. I blinked and wiped the grit from the corners of my eyes.

"We must touch often," she whispered, and tumbled down beside me, enfolding me in her arms. "I am afraid if we don't, I will shrivel again."

"You needn't worry," I said, trying not to breathe in her face. "I will endeavor to touch you as much as possible, I promise—after I have washed." What would the others think if we were found in this embrace in broad daylight? I extricated myself from her arms and sat up. "How go the messages to our rescuers?" I added to distract her.

"I haven't been able to enter Lillie's dreams," said Tauseret. She leaned back on her elbows and watched me brush the hay from my clothes, a slight frown on her beautiful features. "I don't think she sleeps."

"Perhaps you put her off sleep," I said.

"Or she is traveling," Tauseret answered, looking triumphant.

I chuckled. How wonderful it must be to be so sure of oneself.

"Well, I hope Mr. Northstar came back before she left and she told him where I went."

Tauseret raised her eyebrows in question.

"That is Willie's father," I told her. "Remember, Mink stole Willie, too. We sure could use Mr. Northstar's help."

Tauseret spat out a puff of air. "Then, I will try harder. The clown still hears me and raves to the world about it," she added, and grinned.

It wasn't a mean-spirited clown or a lady of the night I counted on, however. It was the colonel. Could he find us before we came to Toms Junction, wherever that was, or would Mink and his bullyboys corner us first? I bit my lip. Did I set my hopes on pure fantasy?

The new day started with the application of another coat on the wagon. Tauseret wanted to paint, but I assured her that she would help more if she told the children stories to amuse them. They were restless and fragile and needed distraction. She was bound to have a store of new tales, and Apollo must be plumb out of them. Tauseret sniffed at this suggestion, but Miss Lightfoot came to the rescue with her sewing kit and a shirtwaist she proclaimed would "do a treat for our new friend." Tauseret, entranced by the calico, was lured away, and the children had to settle for one of Apollo's games.

"Come to me often," she ordered.

I suspected she was accustomed to obedience. No wonder that husband of hers had annoyed her. It was the nicest sort of order, however, I thought, and she deserved attention after all those years alone.

"I don't think Dr. Mink will waltz into this farm in broad daylight," said Mr. Ginger. "But maybe we should keep a watch just in case."

He was right. I didn't know what tricks might be up the skeleton man's sleeve. I sent Bertha to watch through the loft ventilation slats.

Moses and Willie scrounged up poles from a shed, and I helped lay them across the rafters. We tied rope through the eyelets in two canvas tarps we found in the loft, and hung them from the poles to make curtains. They wouldn't swing open, but the performers could hide behind them and come out front for their acts.

"They have no pictures of you on them," said Tauseret to the assembled company. "In my dream walks I saw cloth with effigies."

"We had to leave them behind," said Mr. Ginger.

This distressed her. "But how will your *ka* be preserved after death?"

"No one is dying," said Miss Lightfoot. She sounded a little shrill.

Mr. Ginger patted Miss Lightfoot's shoulder. "There, there, that's not what she means," he said. "I can paint more," he told Tauseret.

I hugged Tauseret to reassure her, and did so frequently all morning.

There was chicken again for luncheon, this time cold, accompanied by big, crusty loaves of farm bread and fresh churned butter. I called Bertha down to eat. Tauseret once more partook of the meal, sitting so close to me I felt electric shocks each time our thighs touched. The curious children watched each bite she took. "Careful she don't spring a leak," cried Moses when she swigged some milk, and even Tauseret laughed.

In between bites she endeavored to answer all the questions the adults had for her. Miss Lightfoot was delightfully scandalized by what Egyptian ladies didn't wear, and Mr. Ginger was excited by the idea of Egyptian poetry and confused by their religion. I had to agree with him.

"Was there people like us, back in them days?" asked Mr. Bopp.

"Even among the gods," she answered.

"People with alligator skin?" asked Miss Lightfoot.

"Sobek the crocodile," said Tauseret.

"I'm a froggie god," Moses crowed, and popped his eyes.

"Me, me, I'm a bear goddess!" cried Bertha, jumping up to do a little dance that had the other children almost crying with laughter.

"Perhaps not frogs and bears," said Tauseret gently. "But there is a dwarf god called 'Bes.'" She looked kindly at Mr. Bopp. "I thought it odd that one among us should share that name and shape. Perhaps she walked on Earth awhile and has gone back to the stars and lives there yet."

Mr. Bopp looked away and didn't answer, but he didn't curse, either, so perhaps he accepted her compassion. I loved her for it.

"About the show," said Apollo impatiently. "You have to be our talker, Abel, since you don't have anything interesting about you."

Apollo had brought lack of tact to a high art.

"So I shall," I answered, laughing. "And we'd better begin setting up."

The afternoon became a blur of activity as we rehearsed our acts. Willie and Moses took turns in the loft lookout post, and I noticed I wasn't the only one who nervously glanced at the barn doors too often. I wished we could forget the show and leave as soon as possible, but we had promised a performance, and we would be good to our word.

Tauseret seemed quite happy to fetch and carry, and everywhere she went, at least one child trailed behind her. I was preoccupied with the creation of my patter, and I didn't touch her as often as I had promised, although I did notice she wore her new calico unbuttoned a little farther than was necessary and undulated as she walked. "Look at this needle," she exclaimed as I passed where she was helping Miss Lightfoot with costumes. "Isn't it cunning? I never saw one as fine. What is this metal?"

"Wait until she sees a sewing machine," said Miss Lightfoot.

"Abel!" Apollo ran over. "Can you be the first act?"

"Finally, appreciation," I said.

"Knife-throwing is not too original," Apollo continued, "but maybe they haven't seen much of that in these parts."

"Oh, thank you," I replied.

"You'll need a lovely assistant," said Miss Lightfoot.

"Me," said Tauseret.

"You may not want to," I said. I didn't want to frighten her.

"Show me what to do," she demanded.

I posed her in front of a wall, arms wide, while the children called encouragement and advice. She was a tiny thing, I realized, less than five feet tall. Her attitude made me think of her as being much taller. "You stand there," I explained, "and I shall throw knives to outline you." Since she had been bossy, I couldn't resist a little teasing. "Don't worry, I don't often miss." I pulled out one of my knives with as much flourish as I could muster, then pretended to almost drop it.

I expected her to squeal and protest like any girl, but she remained motionless except for a slight proud tilt of her chin. "Certainly," she said. "I knew you had the warrior in you still." I felt quite pleased at her words, although I didn't know why I should.

I threw three knives, and the children cheered each one. She didn't flinch. Perhaps she was scared, but I suspected she would never show fear, not if the devil took her. My heart filled with pride, and a fond and silly smile spread over my face. "Can you make her a costume?" I asked Miss Lightfoot. "A knife thrower's assistant should show her shapely legs."

In the late afternoon Mr. Webster appeared with a wagon full of benches he'd borrowed from the schoolhouse. Mr. Ginger and I unloaded them, and the children arranged them in front of the curtains. I asked Mr. Webster if he had some soft lumber that I could knock into a simple target. While he went off to check, I decided to see if Mr. Bopp felt up to participating.

"Well, I don't feels too good," said the human caterpillar, "but I s'pose I could do some of me embroidery to get the show over and us on our way."

Embroidery? This I had to see.

The evening came faster than expected. No sooner had we lit assorted lamps around the walls and along the front of our improvised performance area than our audience arrived. The attendees included the farm help as well as the landowners. I thought that generous of the Websters. I wondered if the Webster hospitality had gone so far as to invite their rivals of Tompson's Dairy. Soon every bench was full with adults and children in their simple summer finery.

"My, I wish I owned Sears and Roebuck," said Miss Lightfoot when she peeked through the curtains.

I don't think I was ever so happy to see an audience. Surely we were safe from Mink with all those eyes upon us. We only had to get through the night now and leave before dawn with our newly disguised conveyance.

I wore my best suit, but the weather was too warm for a jacket, and I abandoned that. I would have to put my knives on soon anyway, and I couldn't do that over a coat. I looked around for my assistant. I hadn't seen Tauseret for a while. Perhaps she wanted to surprise me with her costume.

"The nasty man's outside," said Minnie out of nowhere. I started, lost my balance, and walked through the curtains before I meant to. The audience applauded and there was no turning back, despite the racing of my heart.

"Ladies and gentlemen," I began, and my voice squeaked. I took a deep breath. "Welcome to the most amazing show you will ever witness in all your born days."

I TRIED TO CONCENTRATE ON THE show and not on Minnie's words—after all, she was a little girl who might not be able to tell the difference between visions and fears. So I promised the audience miracles, I offered them marvels, I whetted their appetite with hints of what was to come, and after that I introduced the greatest wonder they would ever see and didn't even tell them that's what it was.

"My assistant, please."

Tauseret stepped through the curtains, carrying my knives in their leather bandolier. A soft gasp of appreciation came from the men, and I may have gasped too. Her face was enough— made up with kohl and ruby lips, it reminded me of a defiant flower—but she also wore a costume that sealed the fate of any man who glanced at her. The blue-and-gold bodice showed off her tiny waist to perfection, and she sported bloomers that didn't hide an inch more of her white tights than they had to. Miss Lightfoot had magically provided shoes with buckles and high heels that enhanced her magnificent legs even more, if that was possible.

Tauseret approached with a dancer's grace and draped the bandolier over my shoulder, her hand lingering on mine. From afar she had looked stunning, but up close I was distressed to see fine lines around her eyes and the skin of her hands leathery again.

"Are you all right?" I whispered as I tightened the buckle of the bandolier.

She nodded. "But you must not neglect me," she whispered back.

I let my fingers skim along her arm like a promise as she stepped away.

I showed one of my knives to the audience. "A simple knife. A tool."

With a flourish Tauseret pulled off the cloth that draped my target.

"And a place to hone my craft."

I warmed up with simple target work, creating an X pattern on the wood. The audience applauded politely, and Tauseret retrieved the knives.

"But a knife can be deadly in the wrong hands," I proclaimed. "Will the beautiful lady trust my skill?"

Tauseret nodded and stepped in front of the target. The audience murmured. She spread her arms and legs into a delicious X, an echo of the pattern I had drawn with steel. I wanted to miss her with my knives, but I did want to pin her there. I tried to wipe that desire from my head before I embarrassed myself in public.

The audience gasped as I outlined her with sharp blades while she stood motionless, smiling and serene, her eyes on me the entire time. I vowed that I would never betray her trust. The last knife I placed snug between her legs. The crowd cheered.

After we bowed to the audience, I escorted Tauseret through the curtains, my hand lightly on her elbow to lead her out.

"I must lie down," she whispered.

"Did I frighten you?" I asked.

"No," she reassured me, touching my face. "But I am weak. I cannot expect to be the woman I was for too long. I shall change to my shift and rest."

I couldn't follow; I had to introduce Apollo.

The children in the audience loved the dog boy. Some of them set to barking and had to be hushed. Apollo growled back at them, and the girls screamed with delight. I told an outrageous tale about him that featured his great hunting abilities and his preference for raw meat. "But his greatest skill is his singing," I said to obvious disbelief.

The disbelief faded when Apollo sang the popular song "Come Home, Father" in his angelic voice. The words—those of a child who begs her drunken father to return from the saloon to the bedside of his dying son—caused more than one lady to wipe her eyes. After his song Apollo took my place and became the master of his own little troupe.

Moses made the ladies squeal when he popped his eyes. One young woman in the second row obliged him admirably by swooning not twice, but three times. Her beau almost dropped her the last time, he laughed so hard.

I wanted to check on Tauseret, but Minnie had a tantrum

when I tried to leave the stage area. She said something bad would happen to me "at the stone bath." I tried in vain to persuade her I was safe, for what could happen with all those people present? The skin of my back crawled, however, and I inspected the shadows.

In the background Willie sang minstrel ditties onstage. His father would probably find lyrics like "Possum fo' yo' breakfast" less than dignified, but the audience loved the boy, and I could tell he was enjoying himself too. In fact, there was an especial exuberance to all the children. They were performing because they wanted to, not because they had to, and they liked it.

I promised Minnie I would stay while she performed her act. My presence calmed her, and she achieved great success with her fortunes, even if she told one farmer there were crawly things in his corn. "You'll have lots of lovely, fat babies," she told the delighted young lady who had swooned. "And one ugly one," she added, to howls of laughter from the audience. When she came off the stage to thunderous applause, she ran right by me and into Miss Lightfoot's arms, as if she had never a care for me. Who could fathom small children?

Bertha announced she would recite a poem. I was surprised she knew one, but when I observed Mr. Ginger in the wings with an open volume, I knew him as the teacher. It made me apprehensive when she began "Requiescat," by Oscar Wilde, considering the gentleman's reputation, but near the end I realized that Mr. Ginger had merely tried to give words to Mr. Bopp's grief.

"Coffin-board, heavy stone,
      Lie on her breast;
   I vex my heart alone,
      She is at rest.

> Peace, Peace; she cannot hear
> Lyre or sonnet;
> All my life's buried here,
> Heap earth upon it."

I heard a strangled cry of pain.

Mr. Bopp undulated past me and stuck his head through the curtains. "I've got a poem too. 'There once was a girl from Nantucket—'" I grabbed him by the waist and pulled him behind the curtain again. There were tears on his face, and my harsh words died in my throat. I patted his back.

"That's over the line," I said gently. "Bess would thrash you for that."

Nervous laughter and anxious whispers came from the audience. "Can you go on with your embroidery now?" I asked.

"I reckon so," said Mr. Bopp, somewhat chastened.

"Excuse my presumption, honey pie," Miss Lightfoot said, and dabbed at his face with a handkerchief.

Minnie arrived with the embroidery frame. "Don't forget," she whispered at me fiercely. She glanced at the wall as if looking through to terrors outside, and I felt a chill.

While I introduced the act, Minnie displayed the blank white cloth for the audience's perusal. I couldn't believe how calm she was. Was I a fool to let her rattle me so?

Mr. Bopp's appearance instigated gasps from the audience. While I told the tragic story of his birth to an indigent mother and his years in the poorhouse, where he supported himself by sewing, Mr. Bopp withdrew a needle with his teeth from the package Minnie offered, stuck it into the cloth stretched on the frame she gripped, and proceeded to thread it with his lips, using a wire needle threader and bright red embroidery silk. He then sewed. Sometimes he darted his head to the other side of the frame to pull the needle through, sometimes he wove it in and out of the cloth from one side by clever use of his lips and teeth. He stopped only to change to green silk, and together we embroidered as I continued the tale of his entry into show business. What a perfect act, I decided. He couldn't speak with a needle in his mouth.

Mr. Bopp grunted and snapped the thread with his teeth. Minnie presented to the audience a beautifully aligned row of chain-stitched flowers. The crowd burst into applause, as did I. I could tell by the surprised looks of the others that he had never embroidered in a show for Dr. Mink, but I'd wager Bess had known he had it in him. She had seen the worth of that man. I ached again for his loss.

Miss Lightfoot took center stage to tell of her expectant mother, who was frightened by an alligator, and of her subsequent birth. She displayed the scales on her arms and chest in her sleeveless, low-cut dress and raised her full skirts to her knees to show her scaly calves in such a dignified manner no one would dare call her indiscreet. I had never seen her quite so animated.

"However, this alligator woman has breeding of another scaly nature," she said. "For I must confess that the study of music has been one of my loves." There were appreciative chuckles.

Mr. Ginger stepped from the curtains, oboe in hand, in smart evening attire, marred only by the strange cap he wore.

I had planned to visit Tauseret during the song, but I decided to walk the perimeter of the barn instead. I would feel better if I was sure that no one besides the neighbors was watching us this night.

Miss Lightfoot sang "A Bird in a Gilded Cage" to Mr. Ginger's accompaniment, and I couldn't help but think it ironic that she, too, had been a captive on display. That made the song all the more poignant.

I checked in the stalls and then skirted the wall. What would I do if I did find Mink or one of his men? I slid a blade from my bandolier and prayed I needn't find out. Finally, I stood behind the audience. I peered outside through a crack between the barn doors. The night was starlit and calm. A cat crossed a beam of moonlight, paused a second to stare at me, then moved on. I exhaled. Had I let a little girl's imagination spook me?

"Perhaps you think I have one accompanist," Miss Lightfoot said at the end of her song. "But I assure you, I have two."

I turned to watch.

Mr. Ginger whipped off his cap. The audience inhaled as if one. At least four ladies toppled into the arms of escorts and family.

Mr. Ginger raised his oboe to the tremulous lips of his submerged twin, and into the silence emerged one squeak and then a second.

"I'm afraid my brother isn't as musical as I," said Mr. Ginger.

The strained hush continued. I held my breath. Had we appalled them? Was this more than they could bear?

"And he ain't near as pretty as you neither," called Mr. Bopp.

Someone chuckled, then another, and the response grew to a roar.

"That's some pumpkins," called an old-timer.

"Yeah, a jack-o'-lantern," called another to more laughter.

"Brave fellow," a lady insisted, and rose to her feet to applaud. Others followed. I took this as a signal to hurry behind the stage and urge the whole troupe out for their bows.

"That sure beat the county fair," a towheaded boy said as people left the barn, and Mr. Webster beamed.

The Websters threw a party after the show, with plenty of cider. We were invited to join, and even Mr. Bopp agreed, mostly due to the cider.

"I should see if Tauseret is well," I said.

"She's sleeping in the water trough," said Bertha.

"Let her sleep," said Miss Lightfoot. "She is quite unused to the exercise she's had today."

"Carry me," insisted Minnie. "I'll cry if you don't."

I gave in and went with them to the party. Mink's men wouldn't know Tauseret was connected with us, and I felt safer among a crowd.

There were paper lanterns on the porch and streamers hung from the trees. Miss Lightfoot expressed delight. "Why, I haven't attended a garden party in years," she exclaimed as she crossed the lawn on Mr. Ginger's arm.

"Stay in the light and away from the bushes," I told the children. I ordered Apollo to keep a close eye on them. The Webster offspring took it upon themselves to be possessive and solicitous, since our children were their claim to local fame, and soon a healthy game of fox and chickens ensued, with all participating amicably.

Miss Lightfoot and Mr. Ginger chatted with curious guests, while Mrs. Webster congratulated me on a fine show and plied me with homemade muffins.

Maybe Apollo considered himself too old for the games, for later I saw him at the side of Mr. Bopp, who sat enthroned on a lawn chair. This couldn't be a combination ripe for decorum, but the farmhands who gathered around them were laughing heartily. I wouldn't doubt Apollo was getting an education.

Two girls paid much attention to me, and their eyes continually darted to the knives I wore. I thought this might put their escorts' noses out of joint, except they were too interested in the whereabouts of my pretty assistant. She slept, I told them, and explained that she had felt peaked. The young men were disappointed. I understood. I would much rather be in her company. I resolved to leave the party early, but every time I tried, I was trapped in another conversation.

Eventually the guests were called away by thoughts of early morning chores. Our troupe bade our farewells alongside the Websters, and Miss Lightfoot glowed with the thrill of inclusion. Mr. Ginger encircled her arm with his, and I could tell that constituted his thrill. I wished to encircle Tauseret. I had neglected her indeed.

As soon as we reached the barn, the children scattered to the loft. "Toss down those curtain poles before you go to sleep," I called, and they obliged me.

Cider and good company had comforted my fears. Mink wasn't going to show. He was a coward. He'd cut his losses and run.

Mr. Ginger kissed Miss Lightfoot good night on the back of her hand. *Hurry to sleep,* I urged silently. I dared not rush to the water trough, for I didn't want to remind Miss Lightfoot of her self-appointed duties as a chaperone. I didn't want a chaperone, not one bit. Slowly I pulled the curtains from the poles and carefully folded them. I took as much time as I could.

At last we were alone.

Moonlight fell from the louvered air vent over the great barn doors. I walked along a silver path to the trough. My heart beat in my throat, and a sweet ache awoke in me—only to turn into bitter disappointment.

I found her stiff and still, as if she had never become a beautiful girl, as if that had all been a dream, like the other dreams I'd had since I'd been given the ring. I laid my hand on her brow, but not even an eyelash flickered. I stroked her cheek, her arms, her legs, willing the flesh to warm; yet nothing happened. What if she never woke up again? The thought was unbearable. Panic battered my heart with dark wings. I clutched her hand and bowed my head over her and prayed she would awake.

"How lovely to find you alone," said an icy, hushed voice.

MY HEAD WHIPPED UP SO HARD my neck cracked.

A slim figure with lank hair stood outlined in the moonlight.

I rose to my feet in terror. "What do you want here, Ceecee?"

"Everything." Ceecee giggled. Silver light shimmered on his open razor. "Everything but you, that is. You, my dear, must go." His eyes glowed black and feverish in his pale face.

The trough lay between us, but that offered no protection. After praying so hard for Tauseret to move, I now prayed she wouldn't, so she'd be safe. I glanced around. Could I reach the ladder to the loft? How fast was Ceecee? Would it help if I yelled, or would that simply put the others in danger?

"You're a troublemaker, Dandy," Ceecee whispered as he

drew closer, razor poised in spider fingers. "But I think they'll fall in line once they see you dead."

"I didn't think you'd find us so fast," I said, stepping carefully backward.

"Don't let your brats drop toys on the right road when you've made tracks on the wrong one," he answered, pushing his lank hair back with his free hand.

Minnie's doll. That's where it went.

Sweat tickled my neck. I wanted to scratch, but would Ceecee think I was reaching for one of the knives I still wore?

My heart beat faster and my mouth dried. Maybe I *should* reach for a knife. They were sharp enough—but was I quick enough, and did I dare use my throwing knives on a person? I shuddered at the thought of my knives sinking into flesh.

"Where's Mink?" I asked, playing for time. My right fingers twitched slightly as I calculated the placement of the nearest knife.

Ceecee giggled again. "Toasting my success in an Osceola tavern. Waiting for my return with the prodigal prodigies."

"I won't let you take them." Could I really stop this crazy man? I narrowed my eyes so he wouldn't see the fear in them.

"Who made you protector of the freaks?" Spit flew from Ceecee's mouth. "Do you feel handsome surrounded by nature's rejects?"

I flamed with righteous indignation at his words. My friendship wasn't shallow.

He took another step forward, and I wondered if I could pull and throw a knife before he reached me. All I had to do was wound him enough to shock him, and then perhaps I could knock him out and tie him up.

What if the knife stuck in its sheath? I took another step

back. What if he got to me before I could throw? Would I have to fight him, knife in hand? How much damage would he do to me with that razor? Lightning fear fizzed through me.

His eyes narrowed and a thin, cruel smile stretched his lips. "I'm going to make a mess of your face," he said, as if answering my thoughts. "You won't reach your grave pretty."

"Don't touch him!" Tauseret reared up between us, sunken-cheeked and cadaver-like.

Ceecee cringed from the corpse that hissed at him, and horror twisted his face as her dry skin took on flesh. Then he snarled and lunged at her.

My heart lurched and my hands flew to my bandolier. Tauseret ducked. My first knife sliced the dark. I don't know where it went. My second, a silver streak, sank into the wall of a stall. I yanked more knives in a panic as he came at me, waving his razor and grinning—casual and sure. One knife tore his sleeve and spun to the ground. Another sliced into the hay behind him. I was going to die. I grabbed for more blades. *Stop being a fool,* I chided myself. *You have the skill. Concentrate.* I had to make the next knife count, or he would kill me.

The knife left my fingers.

Ceecee dropped his razor and clutched at his throat. Blood spurted between his fingers, and his eyes bulged as red foam escaped his lips. He went down, gurgling and twitching as his heels beat a tattoo on the ground, a blade stuck in his neck. It had sliced the artery.

My gorge rose. I'd only wanted to wound him and slow him up.

He gave one last convulsion and lay motionless, his mouth agape. Cold struck me to my core, but I couldn't look away. I opened and closed my mouth as if I, too, were gasping my last.

Tauseret climbed from the trough, clothed in beauty once more. Her white chemise draped her like the garb of a Fury. She put her cold hands on my cheeks and forced me to look at her. Her eyes were wise with the ways of death and betrayal. "We must leave here," she said calmly. "The bone man has other minions."

I clutched her to me and choked back a sob. She was right. We should take the chance and flee before Mink realized his plan had gone awry. "You saved me," I whispered harshly into her neck.

"You saved yourself," she answered gently. "You took the chance I offered you. Go. Wake the others. I will deal with this."

Tauseret pulled the knife from Ceecee's neck. She gave it a vicious twist as she did. "To be sure," she said, and wiped the knife on a handful of hay.

I turned and left hastily before I vomited.

"Apollo, rouse the children," I yelled up the ladder to the loft. "Ceecee's been here, we've got to leave!" I ran to shake the adults awake, thankful to leave the corpse behind me.

The children scrambled down the ladder, crying questions all at once.

"I've killed him. I've killed Ceecee," I blurted out to Mr. Ginger as he threw his cover off. I heard Miss Lightfoot's scream from the other stall. My words had reached her. Mr. Bopp cursed. They all followed me to the trough, where Tauseret handed me the knives she had retrieved and cleaned. I took them numbly and resheathed them.

The children gathered around the body, whispering with excitement.

"You did that?" Apollo asked, eyes wide.

I was too distraught to answer.

"He did indeed," said Tauseret.

"Dead suits him real good," Moses said, and kicked the corpse for good measure.

Willie raised his eyes to the roof—whether he prayed or thanked, I couldn't tell.

I could hardly bear to look at Ceecee myself. I still shook from my abominable act.

Tauseret moved close to me. "You acted with the hand of Ma'at," she whispered. "Justice makes you tremble with the awe of her presence." How good of her to try to comfort me.

Minnie wiped at her nose with her fist and bent over Ceecee's face. "No more buzzing," she said. "All empty."

Bertha put a crooked arm around Minnie. "Good and empty," she said.

I was appalled at how calm and satisfied they were, but I blamed life. No amount of love and care could return their innocence. "We have to get out of here," I said. I looked in desperation at Mr. Ginger.

"Pay mind to Abel, children," said Mr. Ginger. He glanced at Ceecee and crossed himself. "Bring the horses in, Moses. We have to hitch them up." He shooed Moses off. "Children, gather our belongings."

"You did Bess proud," said Mr. Bopp, rising up by my knee. "No one will blame you, lad. I only wish it was me what did the world the favor."

I didn't answer but prepared to take to the road.

"We can't leave Ceecee here," I said to Mr. Ginger as we finally guided the horses and wagon outside. "We can't do such a disservice to our host, and we don't want the sheriff after us. We have to take the body with us."

"I'm not having a dead man sit next to me, especially that one," said Miss Lightfoot in alarm.

"Hang him under the wagon," said Mr. Bopp. "There's hooks down there for carrying goods."

"Now they can carry bads," said Apollo, looking pleased with himself.

The flesh of my back rippled with revulsion as I dragged Ceecee's corpse under the wagon. The touch of his skin was like the cold belly of a snake, and when his hair flopped across my hand, I thought of spiders and snatched my fingers away. Apollo crawled under after me. The body flopped impossibly as we tried to tie it up with rope so it wouldn't drag. I didn't like wrestling with a dead man.

Finally we had the body secured, and we crawled back out.

"What will we do with him?" asked Willie, his brow furrowed.

"We'll bury him later," I said. "Somewhere else."

"Soon, I hope," said Apollo as he brushed himself down, "else we'll start a fly circus."

Tauseret sat beside me on the driver's bench. I thanked the Lord for the moon and clicked the horses into motion.

We took the road toward Des Moines. With luck we would find a route that bypassed Osceola and Dr. Mink.

"Abel! Abel!" Miss Lightfoot knocked on the window slats behind me. "Minnie said a big man is coming. Do you think it signifies?"

"Is she upset?" I asked, exchanging glances with Tauseret.

"No. She seems quite cheerful," said Miss Lightfoot.

"Then, do not fear," answered Tauseret.

We rumbled across a wooden bridge over a small stream. We weren't too far down the road when another rumble sounded. I clicked the horses up a pace, and my sweaty hands clutched the reins tighter. "Can you see out the back?" I demanded over my shoulder. "I think someone's following."

Muffled bumps and complaints greeted my ears.

"It looks like a huge suet pudding driving a cart," called Bertha.

"Heavens! That's Earle," said Mr. Ginger. "And he's driving like the devil."

"Let's hope the devil isn't with him," I answered, for if Earle followed, was Mink not far behind?

I slapped the horses' rumps with the reins but to no avail; the horses were challenged past endurance, and as we slowed, the torrent of cries from inside told me that Earle gained.

Tauseret leaned out preposterously far, with a hand through the boards of the seat to steady her. "He's almost on us," she cried.

"Sit down," I ordered, grabbing at her futilely and almost losing the horses.

"He's pointing and gesturing our way something fierce," Moses said through the tiny window behind my head.

"He's waving and yelling for us to stop," yelled Bertha.

"Ouch!" protested Moses. "Gosh darn it, Apollo! That's my ribs."

"He says Mink's ahead," came Apollo's frantic warning loudly in my ear.

"Stop, Abel! Stop!" cried Miss Lightfoot.

Mink ahead of us? I couldn't take the chance. "Whoa!" I brought us to a halt on the grassy verge.

Earle pulled over behind us, and I jumped down to go to him. "What's this about Mink?" I insisted as the others scrambled out of the wagon.

Earle panted as if he'd been running, not the horses. "Hey, there!" he said to Tauseret. "You cleaned up right good."

"What about Mink?" I pressed.

"Hold up." He patted his brow with a handkerchief that had started life as a tablecloth.

"Tell us first if Mink is near, then you can take your time," I said.

"He's up the road a pace, waiting for me," said Earle. "Far enough still. I left him there a whiles ago to come down here."

We had stopped in time, it seemed. I trembled anyway. Tauseret must have sensed this, for she pressed herself against my back and slid her arms around my waist. It was a comfort.

"Were you running from Ceecee?" Earle asked.

"You know about that varmint?" Mr. Bopp said, and snapped his teeth.

Earle winced. "Yeah, he was supposed to kidnap Abel and signal me with a lantern so's I could get Mink and his hired help to round you all back up while you was scart and confused."

"Earle!" gasped Miss Lightfoot.

"I wasn't gonna do it!" he proclaimed. "Once Ceecee was out of there with Abel, I was gonna go in and warn you. Sorry, Abel," he said to me. "Best I could do. Not much a fat man can manage."

Tauseret let me go so she could stride up to Earle and reach up to grab a handful of his dungarees at the knee. "You didn't know that Ceecee would slay him instead?" she asked ferociously.

Earle's mouth fell open. "Where's Ceecee?" he whispered.

"Hanging dead from the undercarriage like a side of beef," said Moses, relishing the revelation.

Earle's gulp sent shock waves down his ample form.

Bertha laughed shrilly. A cloud crossed the moon and left us in shadows. The other children joined in the laughter, disembodied voices in the dark, like spiteful elemental spirits. I shivered.

"That's okay," I said to Earle. "You weren't to know what Ceecee had in mind." The moon showed its face again. "Who's this hired help you mention? Does he have more men now?"

"We was up in Osceola this morning," said Earle, eyeing the underbelly of our wagon. "And I was outside a tavern by the square 'cause they don't build doors for folk my size. The doctor was inside rounding up thugs for the price of a few drinks. The sort of feller who drinks in the morning is a rough character, and he was recruiting an army of 'em. Telling them tales of how he was robbed. Promising them ample *re*-wards. He loaded them in some wagons with a barrel of ale, and we came down this way with a plan."

"We should go back," said Miss Lightfoot. Her voice shook.

"And know Mink is breathing down our backs?" I answered. "He's not going to wait long when Earle doesn't show."

"A railroad line crosses the road ahead," said Earle. "Mink is across the tracks. Hid in a hollow off the road. There's a lane on this side of the tracks that follows the railroad west. We could sneak on up there and be on the lane before he noticed."

"I don't like our chances," said Mr. Bopp, and Mr. Ginger nodded agreement.

"The bone man will get us," cried Willie. He held on to Bertha.

"We should sweep them from our path like the cowardly scum they are," proclaimed Tauseret, waving her fist.

"With what exactly?" I asked. Her opinion of my military skills was obviously not based on this century's incarnation.

"Can't we cut across the fields?" asked Miss Lightfoot.

Earle pouted like a giant baby. "I couldn't be coming with you across no fields," he said. "My cart would stick for sure."

"He's right," I said, "and so would our wagon." I groped for an idea of what to do. Any idea. I felt helpless.

A whistle sounded in the distance.

"The morning train," guessed Moses.

"That train's gonna come between us and Mink," said Earle in a rush of excitement. "It'll cross the road slow."

Tauseret gazed at me expectantly. With a jolt I noticed that they were all looking at me that way. When had I become a leader? I couldn't let them down. "Come on," I said. "Let's find that path."

We scrambled into the wagon and set off, Earle in the lead. Tauseret sat up front with me and sang a low song. Perhaps it was a prayer. I didn't hear a sound from the children inside.

The train whistled again, closer now, warning us it approached the crossing. The tracks were ahead. Earle's shadowy arm waved to the left, and he turned his cart off the road.

The rumble of huge metal wheels shook the earth.

I heard a shout. Up the road, on the other side of the tracks, a stick figure gestured toward us. Like phantoms, men emerged from the bushes. They pushed a covered wagon out of the weeds, then a paneled wagon, and clambered aboard.

"That's Mink!" I cried. Maybe it had been Earle's size or the outline of our stolen wagon, but he had recognized us.

The train grew louder. It neared the crossing and slowed to mind the road. I prayed it didn't slow enough to let Mink cross the tracks to our side.

I turned our wagon to follow Earle onto the dark path.

The train screamed. Tauseret grabbed my arm, and her nails dug into me. The Eater of Souls, I remembered, and knew her gods haunted her.

I heard curses and screams of dismay from behind me. "They made it," yelled Mr. Bopp. "The bastards beat the train."

"Mink is on our tail," I screamed to Earle.

Earle whipped his horses up and took off.

How could we outpace those men? I could only hope they were as overloaded as we were. I slapped my reins, and the horses picked up their feet a tiny bit faster.

The narrow path was rutted and rocky, and the wagon near shook to pieces; my bones clanged with the jolts. Moans and muffled shrieks came from inside. Ahead, Earle's cart joggled and bounced. A few times it even left the ground, though how it could with Earle aboard, I could not tell.

The train let out a series of staccato shrieks, to warn us away from the tracks.

Earle stuck out his arm, and the giant square of his table-cloth handkerchief flapped in the breeze. He was signaling the train to make it stop. Perhaps he thought they'd save us from Mink and his minions.

The train huffed and puffed level with us.

My wagon couldn't take much more.

Earle charged ahead, waving his banner furiously.

The engine passed me, snorting and growling.

Had Mink and his men caught up? "Dump what you can on the road!" I cried. "Make them crash."

The train closed in on Earle. It didn't slow down.

My wagon bucked and bounced as who knows what went flying out the back.

Earle swerved in to wave his banner in the dragon's face.

The engineer set off a short then a long blast—"Look out."

Earle's cart burst apart like a matchstick toy. Fat man and mattress went in opposite directions, and the panicked horses, their traces broken and flying, fled up the track, dragging a few spars of wood behind.

Had an axle caught? Had the wind from the engine wheels set his balance astray? Maybe his cart had merely given up the ghost. But oh, my God! He had to be the fattest hero that ever lived, for the train screeched to a halt, wheezing like a consumptive dinosaur.

I wrestled my team still and leapt to the ground. "That's a damn stupid way to get into the *Police Gazette,*" I yelled, and felt unwelcome tears on my face as I ran to Earle's prostrate mound of a body.

Tauseret caught up with me while I patted Earle's cheeks and tried to find some sign of life. "The enemy approaches," she cried.

EARLE LAY ACROSS THE PATH, HIS eyes closed, an impassable hillock. No wagon could get around him and down the lane. Shards of his cart lay across the track in front of the train; his horses had disappeared from sight.

"We must stand and fight," said Tauseret.

We had no choice. I quaked inside. Where was Toms Junction? Had Tauseret's calls for help all just been fantasy?

My passengers abandoned our wagon and ran to us. Apollo led the way. Mr. Ginger held Miss Lightfoot's arm tight, and he almost dragged her. His steps were fast and firm, for his slouched hat covered the face of his twin and his vision was sure. Moses and Willie carried Mr. Bopp in a blanket sling between them, huffing and puffing with the load. The other children followed. Moses lost his grip, and they dropped Mr. Bopp near my feet, eliciting a curse from the limbless man. Moses stuck his hands in his armpits and made faces.

"Abel, Mink's coming!" cried Apollo needlessly.

An engineer leaned out of the locomotive. "Is that fat feller crazy? Who's going to move this trash?"

Jeers and catcalls rang from the enemy wagons, and then the trap of debris we'd dumped behind us must have claimed the villains, for their calls turned to oaths and cries of distress, and horses screamed. I felt a surge of triumph as I heard a crash.

"You gotta help us," called Moses to the engineer. His eyes popped without calculation this time.

The engineer glanced back down the line nervously. "Hey, you," he called to me. "Move some of that crap off the tracks. I've got a schedule to keep."

Mink's shrill voice split the night as he angrily rallied his scattered troops.

Tauseret grabbed a spar of wood from Earle's smashed cart and brandished it like a club. "There's one less for your metal road," she cried. Mr. Ginger and Apollo followed her lead.

Moses hauled Willie onto his shoulders, and Willie beat at a carriage window. "Let us in! Let us in!" he called. Bertha and Minnie screamed up at the passengers too, and pale faces peered out in confusion, curiosity, and annoyance. No one opened a door, and my hopes of victory dissolved.

The engineer and his mate jumped down from the locomotive to clear the tracks, cursing loudly. They wouldn't help us. I had to stall Mink while my friends got away.

"Take the children across the field," I called to Miss Lightfoot. "You too, Tauseret. Get out of here, everyone!"

"Never!" proclaimed Tauseret.

"I'm not leavin'," said Mr. Bopp.

"What about you, Abel?" Miss Lightfoot cried.

The sky brightened in the east, but the predawn light was still murky. Mink's angry curses told me I had a few minutes yet while he reorganized his thugs. "I have a plan," I answered.

"I'm helping," said Apollo, to my dismay.

"No!" I said.

Miss Lightfoot and Mr. Ginger dashed around to gather up the children, and then they all thrust through the hedge to the field beyond.

Tauseret shouldered her spar of wood and stood her ground. I cursed and took off back toward our wagon, with Apollo sprinting beside me. I waved him off frantically, but he wouldn't heed.

"What are you going to do?" asked the dog boy, grabbing my arm as soon as I came to a halt. There were dark tear tracks in the fur of his face, and I knew he was very frightened. But damn him, couldn't he do what he was told?

Approaching yells told me Mink's men were on the move again.

"Don't follow me. Get out of here," I ordered, but I knew that stubborn look.

Mr. Ginger ran up behind the dog boy. He hadn't gone with Miss Lightfoot after all. He clutched a buggy whip in his hand. Tauseret arrived close behind him. I almost choked on my fear for her.

I dived under our wagon. There wasn't time to argue. At least I could try to give the children and Miss Lightfoot time to hide.

"Hey, you said you had a plan," called Apollo.

"I do," I cried, and pulled a knife from my bandolier.

Heaven knew if it would work. I freed the remains of Ceecee and hauled him erect with an arm around his chest. I leaned the slight man against me as if he stood slumped and defeated, yet alive. His jacket was stiff with blood, and my skin crawled, but I dragged him away from our wagon, and the others backed up with me.

A dozen ruffians, rogues, and tramps charged around the side of our wagon, Mink protected in their middle. Among the men were Billy Sweet and Bonfiglio, a dirty bandage around his head.

I raised the knife to the throat of the corpse. "Hold your horses if you want your cat's-paw alive," I called. I hoped to God it remained dark enough that they wouldn't see he was dead already.

"Whoa, boys," squeaked Mink, raising his skull-topped cane. "We got some negotiating to do." The rabble halted and glanced at one another out of the corners of slit eyes like weasels straining on frayed tethers. Mink glared at me. "What do you want, Dandy?"

"Send those men back to town," I said, "or it's the worse for Ceecee." Surely someone from the train would intervene now and we'd be saved. I'd worry about explaining Ceecee later.

An evil smile slid across the skeleton showman's face. "Well, do your worst, knife boy. Slit his throat in front of God and everybody. Yiss, do."

My mouth fell open before I could help myself, and he cackled.

Bonfiglio sneered, but some of the riffraff seemed as disturbed as I. Mink would sacrifice his pawns without blinking. What made me think I could bargain? At least I may have bought some time for the children and Miss Lightfoot, but what of us?

The engineer gave two long blasts on the train whistle to tell the brakeman to release the brakes. The sound startled me and I tottered a few steps back. My movement caused Ceecee's head to loll, which bared his throat and, with it, the blackened hole that my knife had made.

"He's already dead," cried Billy Sweet. "The varmint done murdered him."

My stomach lurched and I choked back vomit. I was found out.

The band of roughs and tramps surged forward as I futilely waved my knife at them and clutched the corpse to me like a shield.

"Find the children," ordered Mink.

They had no need to look, for the children and Miss Lightfoot swarmed back through the hedge, wielding sticks and branches, and whooping war cries. My heart sank. They'd given away their chance of escape.

"Go back!" I screamed in frustration. "Please, go back!"

But what a troupe they were—a lumbering bear girl, a piebald boy, a tiny balloon-headed child with barely a twig to save her, and a frog boy who popped his eyes to scare the enemy. They resembled a band of militant elves and fairies in the misty dawn, and I couldn't help but be proud of them. The thugs hesitated, perhaps at the sight of such odd children, or maybe they thought that someone on board the train would care.

On that count they were wrong. With a whoosh of steam and a squeal of wheels, the train inched forward. We were abandoned on the side of the tracks like refuse.

"Grab them!" Mink commanded. "Get those brats to the wagons."

Finally the villains moved.

Bonfiglio came at me with a meaty fist raised. I broke into a sweat. My arm ached from holding the cadaver; the hand that held my weapon was cramped. Could I use a knife on another man? I remembered the sick thud of blade into flesh, and I shuddered. I could stand the waxy, cold touch of the corpse no more. I flung Ceecee at Bonfiglio, and the big man yelped, cast the corpse aside, and thrashed his arms in the air. I thought I had scared him, until I heard growls. Mr. Bopp had his teeth sunk into the man's leg, his iron jaws locked. Bonfiglio staggered away from me, trying to kick Mr. Bopp off.

I caught a glimpse of Mr. Ginger, who looked panicked as he fought off two men with slashes of his buggy whip. Then he snatched off his hat, and the second Mr. Ginger took his assailants by surprise. While they stood there dumbfounded, Miss Lightfoot sneaked up behind them and swung a hefty branch into their heads with a quick one-two. The nearer of them fell, stunned, the other ducked and ran away. As more men took their place, Miss Lightfoot and Mr. Ginger stood back-to-back like warriors of old, jabbing and slashing to keep the enemy at bay.

As I moved to help them, I saw Tauseret follow Miss Lightfoot's lead and give Bonfiglio a few whacks to the brow with the spar from Earle's wagon. Mr. Bopp curled himself around the man's ankles, and Bonfiglio tumbled to the ground like Jack's giant. Tauseret bared her teeth in a most terrifying grin, which made me thankful she loved me. Bonfiglio clambered to his feet and stumbled away. Perhaps he hoped to dislodge the caterpillar man, but Mr. Bopp bumped behind him, fully attached to his victim's calf by the strength of his jaws—until Bonfiglio pitched headfirst into a drainage ditch in the hedges. Then Mr. Bopp let go and tumbled free, laughing.

I ran to Tauseret and grabbed her hand. "Jump on one of the

couplings between the carriages," I ordered. "Ride the train out of here."

"Never!" she proclaimed. "I will never leave you, now I have found you again."

I felt helpless to protect her. "Please, go."

"And leave children to fight alone?" she argued.

The children ran figure eights with five or six ruffians behind them. Bertha with her queer gait raced as fast on all fours as any man upright. The children lashed at the men's knees with sticks when they came close, and the men ran into one another with increasing frequency. Apollo joined the fray with his length of wood, barking and growling like a dog of war as he thrust with his spar; Moses found some barbwire for a whip. The men uttered oaths most unsuitable for children's ears, and the children hurled back invectives twice as bad.

A big fellow cut Minnie off from the others like a wolf cuts a lamb from the flock. Tauseret cried out and ran to help.

Two men came my way before I could follow, and I pulled out a knife with my left hand to match the one in my right. They dodged my jabbing blades and smirked. The big fellow swooped up Minnie with a whoop of triumph and headed back to the wagons. Apollo used his spar like a battering ram into the big fellow's back, and the man dropped Minnie. Moses caught her and gave the fellow a kick in the shins for good measure. Tauseret smacked him across his chest with her pole.

The train crawled by. The passenger cars had passed, and the freight cars followed.

My attackers rushed me. I slashed with my knives. They weren't designed for fighting, but the tips were sharp, and I scored a hit on the smaller man and drew blood. He squealed. They both leaped back and eyed me.

"Finish them off, you lily-livered cowards," Mink called from the roof of his wagon. "A bonus to the first to throw a brat in my coach."

Tauseret tripped, and a fleshy man flung himself on her while two cronies cheered him on. She wrestled like a she-cat. Oh, my God, he meant to defile her! I had to stop him. I flung my knives at the men I faced but missed with both, and I cursed my stupid haste. The men ran at me. I felt a fist to my jaw, and then I gazed up from the ground and the world spun. I thought I dreamed what I saw next.

A camel and rider jumped over me.

I fought for consciousness and sat up woozily in time to see another camel and rider leap from an open freight-car door as the train chugged by. I shook my head and blinked in disbelief. My attackers fled. The fleshy man let go of Tauseret and crossed himself. The two thugs with him ran. The camel pursued. Tauseret scurried away on her hands and feet.

A horse landed clumsily just beyond me, hooves scattering pebbles and sod. An older man was in the saddle, whirling a cavalry saber in circles so fast it sang. Behind him sat a dwarf.

"Colonel! Archie!" I cried as I struggled to my feet.

They set off toward the tramps that beset the children.

A filthy man, too full of gin and false courage to run, assailed me. I landed several blows with newfound strength, my hopes elated, but he seemed immune and I lost steam. Then a pungent stench of manure and hay enveloped me, and I was knocked askew by a long, hairy leg with a knobby knee. I gasped as someone yanked the drunk from above. "Tallyho!" the man on the camel cried, and hung the drunk from a tree by his suspenders. He gave me a smart salute. "I don't know who those fellows on the horse are, but I don't mind the help." It was Frank, the younger Arabian brother from Marvel Brothers Circus. I was too amazed to answer. Beyond him the taillights of the train retreated up the track.

Tauseret confronted me and wrapped her arms around my neck. "They have come," she cried, and threw her head back in a wild, glad laugh that made my heart sing.

Mink still screamed invectives from the roof of his wagon, but he was losing control of his men once more. Most were running off. Archie had slid from the colonel's horse and joined the cheering children. He wasn't much taller than they. The colonel chased a fellow along the path in the direction the train had gone. The fellow scrambled through the bushes to get around Earle just as a cart arrived. My heart lurched. Was it friend or foe?

A dark-skinned man jumped from the cart and came at the fleeing villain, swinging his fists like a gentleman.

"Poppa!" Willie called. "I knew you'd come." Mr. Northstar knocked the villain unconscious and ran to embrace his son.

A red-haired girl stood in the cart waving a broom in triumph. "Lillie!" I yelled with joy. Bless her wanton heart. She had heard Tauseret's call all the way off at Mrs. Delaney's house of ill repute and brought Mr. Northstar with her. He must have come back like he said.

The thug scrambled to his feet and ran around the cart, while Lillie whacked at him with her broom. The colonel jumped his horse over the fat man and followed the fleeing varmint up the lane. He could have run the man down, but he ran him off instead.

Two remaining thugs fled in the other direction. Eddie, the older Arabian brother, pursued them on camelback past their wagon, topsy-turvy on the path. The wagon horses plunged and snorted at the sight of the camel but couldn't escape their tangled harness. The men swarmed up the side of Mink's paneled wagon to join Mink on the roof. Mink screamed something at them, and they flung themselves from the roof at Eddie, carrying him off his leggy beast. I ran to Eddie's rescue and jerked one of the thugs away by the scruff. Eddie limped and had a gash in his cheek but swung gamely at the other.

With the horse rider gone and one camel rider unseated, some of the ruffians must have found their nerve. Half a dozen, led by Billy Sweet, poured back onto the path. I took one on, and as I pummeled my foe, I saw Tauseret climbing a tree. The bastard I fought kicked me in the shin. I kneed him in the groin and watched him fall, shrieking.

Above the chaos rose a hideous ululation. Tauseret launched herself from the tree and onto the back of Eddie's loose camel. She snatched the reins but didn't know what to do with them. Her tugs drove the beast wild. It ran into the knot of villains around the children and Mr. Northstar, spitting and nipping viciously, and scattered them, then it crashed through the hedges and into the field. Frank whipped his camel after her.

I wanted to chase her too. What if she fell? What if she broke her neck? But I had children to protect. Or did I?

Moses and Bertha each now clutched an end of the length of barbwire, padded with handholds torn from someone's clothes. They ran at the legs of Billy Sweet and wrapped him like a maypole. He fell to the ground and bloodied his hands as he pulled at his bonds. The children pelted the men with rocks. Mr. Northstar laid out those who came through the barrage with his fists, and Archie crunched kneecaps and punched stomachs. All around tramps ducked, covered their heads, protected their groins, and hopped on one foot.

We were winning! Against all odds we were winning.

"Don't move, or I'll blast your head off," said Mink from behind me. Cold metal pressed into my cheek. My blood froze. When had he left his perch?

"Tell them to give up the fight," the skeleton man demanded.

They wouldn't abandon me to my fate like he had Ceecee. They would do as I said and be defeated. I refused to speak.

Mink jabbed me with the gun barrel. "Do it, boy. They value your hide, and you do too."

He was right. I valued my hide, and how could I help them if I was dead?

"Stop, everyone," I cried. "Mr. Northstar, Archie, everyone, hold your blows. Stop, or he'll shoot me."

Moses noticed and yelled to Apollo, who pointed my way and caused the others to look. Action ceased.

An eerie stillness fell over us, and for a moment we posed like a circus tableau—a battle from history, frozen in the silver light that precedes the sun.

Some of Mink's men were long gone—this task had presented too much work for the lazy vagrants. A few lay on the ground, out cold or broken in some way. The drunk still hung helpless from a tree. Bonfiglio hadn't moved since he'd fallen; maybe he'd broken his neck. The remains of Ceecee lay heels over rump like a dropped puppet. The tramps still standing peered around with shifty, anxious eyes. Billy Sweet moaned on the ground. "Fer Christ's sake, someone untie me."

"You children," Mink shrilled. "Get yourselves to my wagon, or I'll kill this bedchamber sneak."

Moses put his arm around Bertha. Mr. Northstar reached for his son.

"You lot"—Mink pointed at his men with his free hand—

"back my wagon up to the road. Unhitch the horses and push if you have to. Get moving!" The barrel of the gun shook with his rage. I prayed the trigger wasn't sensitive.

A scream sounded closer and closer, across the fields. Was this my death? Tauseret, atop the camel, leaped the bushes. Her hair flew, her eyes blazed, and she kept her seat like a desert chief as the camel hurtled over Earle. She was magnificent. "Release him," she cried. She thundered toward us, using a stick to whip the beast she had mastered. Friend and enemy alike dived out of her path.

My Lord. She wouldn't recognize a pistol. He'd kill her.

I had but a second while Mink was distracted. I slid out a knife and plunged it under my arm. A squeak and a whoosh of air came from Mink before he fell into me and slid to the ground. His pistol thudded at my feet.

Tauseret reached me and flung herself off the camel and into my arms. "You are safe," she proclaimed. "He faints at my rage. This time I saved you."

I held her tight. "Three times," I said. "Once from Ceecee, once from Mink, and once from loneliness. You have more than balanced the past."

Cries rang through the morning as camel and horse galloped back down the lane. A crowd of farmers bearing pitchforks and scythes followed behind.

All tramps and rogues who could run did so.

The mound on the path stirred. "What? Huh? Darn if my head don't hurt," groaned Earle.

The sun rose.

MOST OF THE BRIGANDS ESCAPED, except for those felled by injuries. When he arrived, the sheriff said the scene reminded him of the Spanish War. He ordered us all to the milk stop down the track, where he would sort out what had happened. The milk stop was a new little train station, Archie Crum told me. The farmers had been waiting there to load the morning's shipment when the colonel galloped up and enlisted their aid.

Tauseret and I helped round up the horses. Two farmers loaded Mink's wagon with the afflicted, including Mink. They almost left Mink for the undertaker at first, since he looked nearly as much like a corpse as Ceecee, but Mr. Ginger set them straight. I shivered as they carried him by. Amazingly, not one of my friends had sustained a wound except Earle.

We set the villains' covered wagon to rights, and I rehitched the horses, but we had to remove the canopy to get Earle aboard. He clutched his head and moaned, blessedly alive. I drove our own paneled wagon, Tauseret on the seat beside me, looking proud and fierce.

"And who *is* this young lady?" the colonel asked.

"Would you like the unbelievable truth or a digestible tale?" I asked.

"The one that makes the best story, of course," he said.

"Then, you'll have to wait until we have more time," I told him.

A doctor had been sent for and arrived at the station in his buggy soon after us. "You'd better hope that wound on the skeleton man ain't mortal," said the sheriff to me, "else I'll have to do my duty." A shock of fear shot through me. Did he mean arrest me for murder? I had acted in self-defense, surely.

Apollo and the children clustered around the camels at the side of the little redbrick station building where Earle was parked, and pestered the Arabian brothers with questions. The rest of us huddled in small groups on the dusty platform of the train station, exchanging few words and many glances, as the sheriff called us each aside to be interviewed. Tauseret clung to my hand, and I hated to think what she might do if the sheriff tried to take me away.

Only our recent host, Mr. Webster, was in a good mood. He pointed to a newly painted sign above the train station. "They changed his name," he chortled with delight. "Tompson paid off the railway so's they'd stop nearest his farm, and they shortened the station name anyway."

I gulped. The sign read TOMS JUNCTION, just like the one Minnie had seen.

"I sent the truth to your friends, did I not?" said Tauseret. She looked so satisfied that I imagined her licking cream from her lips. I grinned. I wanted to lick those lips too.

At last, a bespectacled head rounded the heavy station door. "He'll live," the doctor called.

The crowd of show folk and locals sent up a cheer—not for his sake, but for mine, I realized as Mr. Webster and his fellow farmers pumped my hand in sturdy congratulations. Their support flustered and warmed me. Then Tauseret kissed me most inappropriately, and they cheered again, which flustered me more.

One would think a knife thrust to the chest of such a slight fellow would have caused him mortal harm, but Mink's prominent ribs had deflected the blow from any vital organ, and he lay sorely hurt but alive, the doctor reassured us before he went off to check on Earle.

Whether Mink would be charged with anything beyond causing a public nuisance, I didn't know. Mr. Northstar said he would be happy to return for a trial and see if the Iowa kidnapping laws covered little colored boys, and Miss Lightfoot offered the forged papers to the sheriff gladly. Tauseret wanted to accuse him of theft, but I pointed out most folk would find it hard to believe if she presented herself as both the item stolen and the witness.

Before he left with a wagonload of prisoners, the sheriff declared that since no one had seen Ceecee's demise, he must assume that one of the fled vagrants was the culprit. With elation I realized that the sheriff did not have much interest in pursuing the matter. Shame followed. I had killed a man, and no matter how he deserved it, I shouldn't celebrate, but thank the Lord for his mercy.

"What now?" I asked as Mr. Webster hurried off the remaining locals with promises of a hearty breakfast.

"We go home," said the colonel.

I wrapped my arm around Tauseret's waist and looked about me for the others, suddenly afraid to lose them.

Mr. Ginger, hat on head, held Miss Lightfoot's hands as they talked quietly. The excitement must have agreed with her, for she glowed as much as a scaled woman could. Bertha and Minnie sat at their feet in the dirt of the platform. Not far from them, Moses and Willie leaned over the platform edge and poked at something with a stick.

Farther away, Mr. Bopp leaned against Apollo's legs like an ugly dog and laughed as Archie Crum told a joke no doubt unsuitable for a boy Apollo's age.

Lillie sat with Earle on his roomy new wagon. He sported a lopsided bandage on his head and a sling on his arm. Lillie turned the pink pages of a *Police Gazette* salvaged from the wreckage of his old cart, while he read aloud, and she made appropriate noises of shock, disgust, and approval.

"Your friends can join us if they wish," said Colonel Kingston, amusement in his voice. "Eddie and Frank have already said they'll come." He gestured to the nearby lot where the Arabian brothers tended to their camels and the assorted horses.

Mr. Northstar rounded the corner of the brick station house, Willie's small hand in his.

"Mr. Northstar," called the colonel. "I'd like to offer you a job."

Mr. Northstar gathered Willie in close as he approached. "He's not a performer, sir."

"You, sir, not your son," replied the colonel. "You are a lawyer, are you not? Do you know contracts?"

"My specialty," answered Mr. Northstar, looking confused.

"A business has need of contract lawyering," said the colonel.

My mother would be proud that her lectures about the colonel's casual business practices had borne fruit at last.

"You won't find it easy having a colored lawyer," said Mr. Northstar.

"Look around you, Mr. Northstar," said the colonel with a sweep of his arm. "Do you think that any one of us has found life easy?"

Miss Lightfoot and Mr. Ginger came over as if drawn by his gesture.

Mr. Northstar hesitated and then smiled. "I have not found reason of late to trust showmen," he said, "but you have helped me rescue my son. I do believe I will accept your offer of a job."

"What about you, ma'am, and you, Mr. Ginger?" asked the Colonel.

Miss Lightfoot looked at Mr. Ginger, and Mr. Ginger cleared his throat. "Dear Ruby, as long as you use the name Mrs. Ginger, I'm sure I shall not mind you performing a song or two."

Miss Lightfoot nodded, a smile of sublime relief on her face.

"Oh, well done!" I cried, and grasped Mr. Ginger's hand to congratulate him on his engagement.

"But I'm afraid I do not care to tread the boards again as the two-headed man," Mr. Ginger announced.

"No one has to exhibit himself in my show, if that is not his wish," the colonel said. "There are plenty of jobs available. I'm sure you have other skills."

"He paints lovely pictures," cried Bertha.

"And he plays a squeaky pipe," growled Mr. Bopp from somewhere near my knees. He and Apollo had joined us.

"It's an oboe," Miss Lightfoot corrected.

"You should have snakes," said Apollo to Miss Lightfoot. He bent and wiped Mr. Bopp's nose with a tattered cloth. "The Alligator Lady and Her Reptile Friends."

"My goodness me, sugar plum pudding," she said, fanning herself. Nevertheless, I could see her interest.

"I've got the timetables, Colonel," Archie proclaimed as he strode up on short, bandy legs.

Before long, I was sitting on a train to Maryland, surrounded by the companions of my adventure—well, except for Earle, who had to stay in a freight car with the camels, owing to his large size. We made one of the dining cars our clubhouse and squeezed around two tables on either side of the aisle. The children were quiet, among strange grown-ups as they were, but they seemed to enjoy all the tales to be told. Minnie sat on Miss Lightfoot's lap and sucked her thumb, Willie held on to his father's hand contentedly, but Bertha and Moses hung over the partition from the table behind, and every time they acted up and kicked the backs of our seats, Archie Crum patted them kindly on their cheeks and fed them penny candy to settle them down. He had been like that with me when I was a child, I realized, and I wondered why I had ever thought him mean before I left my home. I obviously hadn't been thinking straight.

"I guessed you'd joined that circus," said Colonel Kingston, "but by the time I caught up with Marvel Brothers Circus, you were nowhere to be found. The brothers Marvel were none too helpful, except to say you jumped from the train to avoid responsibility for harboring an incorrigible fugitive stowaway who subsequently escaped, and no, they didn't know where. Apollo, you cost me the price of a trick ball, a soiled costume, and several bushels of fruit," said Colonel Kingston.

"Those varmints," objected Apollo. "I didn't eat that much!"

"But those elephants you fed did," returned the colonel.

I expected more arguments from Apollo when I told our side of events at the circus, but he grew unnaturally silent as we neared home. I worried about the boy. I missed his high spirits.

My audience gasped when I told of how I was thrown off the train.

"Sorry we didn't speak up for you, Abel," said Eddie, looking sheepish.

"We didn't want to lose our jobs," explained Frank. "Then we decided we hated our jobs if keeping them made us act like blighters."

"Then that clown took to drink and told everyone the dream he'd been having," said Eddie. "A dark lady kept telling him to rescue Abel at Toms Junction in Iowa."

Lillie's hands flew to her cheeks. "That was my dream too."

The colonel raised his eyebrows. "That was in Miss Dibble's telegraph to me."

"We couldn't find Toms Junction on a map of Iowa," Frank explained, "but there's new stations popping up every day. So we took the train east and started asking."

"Granny read tea leaves," said Eddie. "She taught us not to ignore dreams."

"What a sight we made, I'm sure," said Frank. "Changing trains with our camels loaded with luggage."

"I telephoned an agent I know who plans routes for his acts," said the colonel. "He has all the latest information on the railroads."

"I know men who worked on this railroad," said Mr. Northstar. "When Lillie told me her dream, I made some inquiries."

"Thank goodness that fat man blocked the track," said Frank, "else we might not have had time to saddle up."

"When I ran for my horse, I didn't expect to find two men climbing on camels," said the colonel.

"I didn't believe the dream, really," Mr. Northstar said, shaking his head. "But I was desperate."

"I didn't believe we'd end up with a whole passel of children," said Archie.

"Just gots to bite 'em," growled Mr. Bopp. "That shows 'em."

Bertha laughed. "You don't bite us."

"Ought to," he said, and closed his eyes and pretended to nap.

The wonderful thing about the show folk I grew up with was they took a person's story at face value, even if the tale was unlikely. If that's what you wanted to be, fine. It's how you acted in the now that counted, not what you may have done and been in the past, and there's a lot to be said for believing in your own tale to make your act come alive. That was why I didn't hesitate to tell Tauseret's tale, and my heart swelled with pride and love as I did so.

I tried to skim over the embarrassing parts, however, but Tauseret, unlike Apollo, did not keep her mouth shut, and her many interruptions made this impossible.

"Oh, I knew he was a ladies' man at heart," Archie said, and slapped as many backs and shoulders as he could reach. "He takes after me." He winked at Lillie, who boldly took inventory of him as if she intended to test his word.

Only Mr. Northstar challenged Tauseret.

"I thought Egyptians were white folk," he said, inspecting her tawny complexion.

Tauseret cocked her head. "I don't believe I've ever seen a white person," she said, to some amusement. "I have heard that in the far north there is eternal snow. Perhaps these white people you talk of live there to disguise themselves."

"Your parents will be a little surprised by Tauseret," said the colonel into the dumbfounded silence.

"I will make them a wonderful daughter," Tauseret said, and wound her arms around my neck.

Yes, what would my parents feel about this voluptuous and possessive young woman? I wrapped my arms around Tauseret's waist and kissed her cheek. "My parents are very understanding," I said.

Apollo exploded to his feet. "My father isn't!" he cried. His fur rose in a nimbus of static electricity. "I can't go home, Colonel. He'll beat me dead."

I winced and groaned. What a thoughtless fool I'd been, absorbed in my own concerns. That was why he'd been quiet.

Apollo tried to storm off, but he couldn't squeeze between Mr. Northstar and the table. Colonel Kingston grabbed his arm. "Your father's gone, Apollo. I made him go."

Apollo stopped struggling. "Gone?" His hair settled like spider silk. I think I was as relieved as the dog boy to hear this news.

"I will not have women and children mistreated in my establishment," explained the colonel. "He had been warned several times. When you ran away, that was the final straw."

"My mother and sister?" Apollo asked hesitantly.

"Chose to stay under my protection," finished the colonel.

Apollo beamed with joy. "Can I still be in charge of the children?" he asked, bouncing with excitement. "We've figured out some marvelous acts. You'll be proud of me, honest, and I've got some great ideas for Mr. Bopp. . . ."

"Ouch, my foot," squeaked Mr. Northstar.

"Oops! Sorry." Apollo wriggled by him and tumbled into the aisle.

"We'll see," said Colonel Kingston, "but we must set some ground rules."

"Yay!" cried Apollo. He tugged at Moses' sleeve. "Come on, you laggards. We need to practice." He raced down the car, ready to lord it over the children once more, and the children dutifully stirred to follow him.

When we reached home, I wouldn't see as much of Apollo as I used to, now he had younger companions. This made me sadder than I would have believed. Phoebe would be more distant also, now she was affianced. I should be happy for that, but part of me hoped that Phoebe would be jealous of Tauseret. That didn't make me a very good person, but I smiled anyway. I thought I had the better deal—an exotic companion with tales of distant days and places was superior to an ordinary hairy man from Baltimore.

I was going home—that sank in at last, and to my surprise my heart sank also with the thought. I had planned to be a wage earner when I returned, an independent man.

"You look unhappy, Abel," said Lillie.

"Everything has gone wrong, and now I'm going back to where I started and I haven't accomplished anything except murder." I couldn't believe that had spilled out of me.

"You defended yourself," said Mr. Ginger.

"Any man would have done so," added Frank.

Miss Lightfoot patted my hand. "He's worried that he hasn't found his fortune," she said.

I remembered how Miss Dibble had told my fortune when I was trying to sneak from home unnoticed. "You will fall in love with an older foreign lady," she had said. I stared at Tauseret in shock. Stars above. Damned if she wasn't right.

"You've certainly brought fortune to others, honey love," said Miss Lightfoot. "Where would Mr. Ginger and I be without you? You stood up to Mink when we were afraid to. We found strength in you."

"Willie might not have had his father again if not for you," said Lillie.

"You can depend on Abel," said Colonel Kingston. "That's his finest quality. He takes responsibility. And look at these marvelous acts you have found me, boy. I do believe you have saved Faeryland from bankruptcy. Bully for you, Abel."

I couldn't help but grin. All I had wanted was to be carefree, but everywhere I'd gone, I'd had to take charge of something or someone. Apparently I couldn't be irresponsible even if I tried, but I had certainly found adventure because of it and I may have found my fortune after all. Maybe being dependable wasn't as boring as I had believed.

"I always thought you had management qualities, lad," said Colonel Kingston. "We'll have to develop that." He ruffled my hair and made me feel like a boy again—safe. "A show's not a show without a good manager."

I had management qualities? I had left home because I felt I didn't belong, and now I learned I had had a needed talent all along. I had found my fortune indeed. It was right where I'd left it.

I looked around and saw love on the faces of my friends.

Yet Mr. Bopp's eyes were focused far away. He had lost his love. No skill of mine could change what had happened. Life wasn't that simple.

I stood with Tauseret under an August moon on the road in front of a Maryland train station, the air as lush and moist as a jungle evening. Laughter rang far off as the camels and baggage were unloaded, but here we were surrounded by the tiny chatter of the night.

"Abel, I don't have anyone but you," said Tauseret, and for the first time I understood that under her bravado lurked fear.

I put my arm around her. "Everyone will love you," I said, "and what an act we make. I can see it now—you as my target on a spinning wheel in your mummy form, and as the wheel spins and my knives outline you, you change into the beautiful girl you really are. It will be a sensation!"

"I'm afraid all this happiness will be taken away again," she said. "That I will never be mistress of my own fate."

I took the ring from my finger and pressed it into her hand. "This is all that controls you," I said, "and now it is yours. Once, in another life, you gave it to me to bind us. It brought us back together across the centuries, and now I give it back. You can be bound to me or not, as you choose."

Tauseret touched my cheek. "In that there is no choice," she said, and kissed me. "And who's to say that the ring by itself has any power? Perhaps it needs to be worn by you."

We stood silent with our own thoughts for a while.

"Will I age now, do you think?" Tauseret asked after a long sigh. "Will I grow old with you?"

"We don't know anything, do we?" I answered. "We must just live our lives and find out."

She pressed the ring back into my hand. "I will trust you with my new life."

I cannot describe how I cherished her in that moment. "I suppose I am an oddity after all," I said, "to have the love of a beautiful woman three thousand years old. How many can say that?"

"Hey, Abel! I'm riding a camel home."

Apollo sat atop a camel led by Eddie Bridgeport, and the children ran at the creature's heels.

"He's a natural," said Eddie.

"Me next," cried Moses. "I'm the oldest next to him."

"No, you're not. I am," said Bertha.

"But you're a girl," Moses countered, and popped his eyes at her.

"Minnie's next, and she rides with me," said Apollo, settling the matter.

Frank led the other camel around the station. The colonel followed on horseback; Earle drove a cart borrowed from the stationmaster, with Lillie, Mr. Bopp, and Archie Crum aboard. Mr. Ginger and Miss Lightfoot brought up the rear, hand in hand.

"I'll run the show one day, you know," I told Tauseret, and I took her arm. We fell in with the others for the journey down the road to Faeryland.

If any children peeked out their windows on that summer night, they might have seen the strangest parade—all of us oddities, all of us going home.

AUTHOR'S NOTE

I have always been fascinated by human oddities, so some of the research for this novel was done long before I decided to write on the topic. To add to that knowledge, I dug around in libraries, bookstores, and the Internet, and found way more information than I could ever use in one book. EBay, especially, was an invaluable source of old photographs, known as *cartes de visite*, which performers sold to make some extra income. I have some on my mantelpiece and I tell people they are my relatives.

The people in my story are imaginary, but their physical differences are inspired by those of people who really lived, and many characters are composites of people I came across in photographs and accounts. One of my original inspirations was Tod Browning's classic movie *Freaks*, which came out in 1932 and which I first encountered as a college student. One of the reasons I loved the movie so much when I was a teenager was that it treated with respect the people considered freaks by the "normal" world. There were many times I felt like an outsider myself, so I identified with the human oddities in the film. In the 1960s the media called the type of people I hung out with "hippies." Less-than-kind people called us "freaks," but we took on that title of Freak and wore it proudly. I use that title for this book in the same spirit and also to pay tribute to Tod Browning, who endured much criticism and censorship for his attempt to show that even those who look much different still have the same feelings we all do.

Mr. Bopp's appearance is based on a real-life performer in the movie *Freaks*, Prince Randian, who performed as the Human Torso for forty-five years starting in the late 1800s. Abel's father is patterned on Johnny Eck, the Half Boy also featured in *Freaks*, already a sideshow star in his own right before the making of the movie. The sawing-the-man-in-half performance in chapter one is adapted from a vaudeville act that Johnny Eck performed onstage with his twin brother. I hope he wouldn't have minded me borrowing it.

I borrowed some other acts too. The ammonia trick Billy Sweet uses to lure the mouse is revealed in *Carnival* by Arthur Lewis. The bicycle act Abel's parents are said to perform may have been similar to that presented in 1897 by the legless man Eli Bowen, and his partner, the armless Charlie B. Tripp. Moses the Frog Boy's trick of popping his eyes out and scaring the ladies in the audience was really part of the act of Pop-eyed Perry, a much more recent performer, as documented in *Freaks: We Who Are Not As Others* by Daniel P. Mannix. The ball and tower act in chapter eight is based on one created by a performer named LaRoche in the nineteenth century, described in

Learned Pigs & Fireproof Women by Ricky Jay. From the same source, I learned about Joseph Pujol, known as Le Pétomane—the fartomaniac—who performed in Paris in the 1890s. This gave me the idea for the act Earle Johnson thinks up for himself. What Abel says is true; it had been done on the stage in France.

I tried to incorporate accurate details of nineteenth-century life in the shows and out. There were many midget villages in America from the nineteenth century through the 1930s, so Faeryland's Pixie Village could have existed; and there were genuine tales told of circus elephant ghosts by the train tracks. The songs I use in this book are authentic songs of the time.

I didn't expect to learn old songs when I began this book, I didn't know I'd be printing out glossaries of circus slang, and I didn't know I would fall in love with my characters as much as I did. I may have started reading about unusual people out of curiosity, but what I brought away was respect—respect for people who fought the odds and created lives for themselves. They made the best of what they had, earned a living, loved, married, had children, and left a legacy when they could—just like anyone. We are all different—and how boring life would be if we were all the same—but some of those differences may be more obvious than others, and present greater challenges. Yet one thing unites us—we are all human.

Annette Curtis Klause was born in Bristol, England, and moved to the United States when she was a teenager. As a child she spouted such fanciful ideas that her peers thought she was an oddity. Having an imagination turned out to be valuable—she grew up to become a storyteller. Annette currently lives in the Maryland suburbs with her husband and six cats. Three are from SiameseRescue.org, but none are actually Siamese twins—although one is the fastest cat on three legs and another likes to balance on top of the scratching post like a circus cat. Annette still works full-time as a children's librarian. Bouncing around like a giant bunny during preschool storytime is just another way of being paid to be odd, she says.